OUTSIDER

Stephen Tobias

BOOK PUBLISHERS NETWORK

Book Publishers Network
P.O. Box 2256
Bothell • WA • 98041
PH • 425-483-3040
www.bookpublishersnetwork.com

10 9 8 7 6 5 4 3 2 1

Printed in the United States of America

LCCN 2013948897
ISBN 978-1-940598-02-4

Front cover illustration by Ken Ballard, Melted Mind Design
Cover designer: Laura Zugzda
Editor: Julie Scandora
Typographer: Leigh Faulkner

CONTENTS

Chapter One 3
Chapter Two 8
Chapter Three 18
Chapter Four 34
Chapter Five 43
Chapter Six 50
Chapter Seven 60
Chapter Eight 64
Chapter Nine 71
Chapter Ten 79
Chapter Eleven 88
Chapter Twelve 94
Chapter Thirteen 99
Chapter Fourteen 106
Chapter Fifteen 117
Chapter Sixteen 122
Chapter Seventeen 129
Chapter Eighteen 135
Chapter Nineteen 139
Chapter Twenty 147
Chapter Twenty-One 150

Chapter Twenty-Two 157
Chapter Twenty-Three 160
Chapter Twenty-Four 170
Chapter Twenty-Five 179
Chapter Twenty-Six 192
Chapter Twenty-Seven 203
Chapter Twenty-Eight 211
Chapter Twenty-Nine 220
Chapter Thirty 229
Chapter Thirty-One 234
Chapter Thirty-Two 246
Chapter Thirty-Three 249
Chapter Thirty-Four 253
Chapter Thirty-Five 261
Chapter Thirty-Six 265

PART ONE

CHAPTER ONE

By the time Sotheby's called, begging me to come to Zurich, I'd reached equilibrium, a neutral point where days might elapse without my giving more than a passing thought to Herman Viereck. Not that I'd expunged him by any stretch. He'd dominated every aspect of my life for so many years that part of him will always be with me, like a surgical scar, a slightly aching reminder of traumatic events best left undisturbed. But still, before they called, my life had changed enough where I had pretty much corralled Herman into a mental space that contained an "after" as well as "before."

As the man who had "discovered" the little guy, I'll have my name linked with Herman's forever. I'm the *éminence grise* of Chicago's outsider art scene. Even after all these years, I still get invited to the institute's symposia and seminars. There's always a stack of mail from people whose lives had been touched by Viereck's art. A large envelope and e-mails get forwarded to me from the Institute for Intuitive Art at least once a month. A lot of it I don't bother answering anymore. By now, there isn't a theory or opinion about Viereck's work that I haven't heard hashed to death: the tortured genius, the filthy pervert, the victim of institutional cruelty and bureaucratic neglect, psycho, idiot savant, rip-off artist, take your pick. It's enough to make me want to type F.U. and hit "reply all."

Of course Sotheby's didn't care what I felt about the poor bastard one way or the other. They'd scheduled a major auction of American outsiders and art brut from the best collections, assembling all the heavies, from Adolph Wölfli's religiously obsessed mandalas to the root sculptures by Bessie Harvey. They had a collection of quilts from Gee's Bend and the numbing "Horror Vacui" of Scottie Wilson's pencil work, but it's the poster boy for outsider art, my Viereck, that they've chosen for the catalogue's cover. Now a few weeks from the auction, some embarrassing questions had been raised about their Viereck being a clever knock-off, and they were relying on my expertise to help them sort it out.

My first inclination was to tell them no. First-class plane ticket, deluxe hotel accommodations, an obscenely generous consultant's fee—it was obvious what they were up to. They wanted a hired gun to give them a free pass, an easy A. I taught photography and industrial design at the Chicago Institute of Fine Arts for thirty years, and of course, I'm familiar with the landscape of Western Art, but ordinarily, I'm not the person you would pick to fly halfway round the world to vett a suspect Caravaggio or to do a thumbs up on a small Corot.

I would never be called into court as an expert witness. No anxious family would nail its financial future on my passing judgment on their inherited painting; the one alleged to be a Goya. It was only the specific work in question that made my opinion worth Sotheby's extravagant investment in my comfort. If their piece was authentic then, undoubtedly, I owned it over twenty-five years ago.

The painting in question is not a painting in the truest sense, but a six-foot-long fold-out, done with an unusual combination of cheap paintbox watercolors and collage using incorporated images, assembled from magazines, Sears catalogs, and comic books, and then glued to the underlying "canvas." The supporting medium itself is actually cheap sketchpad paper carefully glued edge to edge, giving the work the unintended quality of an early Japanese scroll.

This work, if authentic, was created by a borderline lunatic named Herman Viereck, a reclusive hospital janitor and laundry folder who was a tenant of mine in an apartment building I once owned on Chicago's Near North Side. When I first let his pieces go, I felt guilty asking a thousand dollars for them. Now, Sotheby's estimate is five hundred times that, and the excited voice on the phone assured me, "It could go a lot higher."

In the end, curiosity got the better of me. Who would try to duplicate Herman's iconic style, and could it be done well enough to fool me? Like a lot of iconic artists, Herman had a deceptive simplicity about his work. Stand in the Pollack gallery at MOMA; I guarantee you'll hear someone say, "What's the big deal? Give me a can of paint, and I'll knock one out." Mondrian, de Kooning, a lot of Warhol—just give me a ruler and an opaque projector and stand back. I mean it's true; as a draftsman, Herman was an untaught dauber who had to crib his figures from a Sears catalogue, but there was a lot to his overall style, his manipulation and use of color, the childish bravado of the energy in his pieces that would be hard for someone to consciously duplicate.

There was also the voice on the other end of the phone. What American male, even an old coot like myself, can resist the seductive lilt of a young woman with an English accent? "All of us here at Sotheby's are positively enthralled with the piece you wrote about Viereck for *Aesthetica* a few years back. I'd love to talk to you about it …"

I tried sounding non-committal and unenthusiastic, but I agreed all the same. The tickets came by FedEx the next morning. I wondered if she'd stuffed them in the mail before she'd picked up the phone.

Unfortunately, I discounted the effect taking the trip would have on me. As the time of departure got closer, I slipped into a state of preflight anxiety that struck me as doubly disturbing because it was so out of character. Travel always came second nature to me. I'd spent so many years as a freelance vagabond—my camera case always stuffed with film, my battered Nikon, loaded and ready, sleeping bag rolled, and knapsack packed at the ready in the hall closet—just waiting for *LIFE* or *Nat Geo* to give me the call. I'd gone to some pretty hot places and shot some pretty Gd awful shit. Now the thought of negotiating an unknown city, sleeping in a strange bed, or finding a bathroom in time filled me with disproportionate dread. What I can I say? I, Nathan Learner, have become an old man.

My wife, Makiko helped me pack. Of course I asked if she wanted to come along. After all, it had been her idea to show Herman's work to the world, and she knew as much about the origins of his work as anyone. If it had been up to me, Viereck's famous trunk might have ended up in our basement with the rest of life's detritus, but Makiko turned me down. I think the thought of seeing his work going for so much money was too much for her to take.

So I take the taxi to O'Hare alone, dressed in a sports jacket and a tie instead of my usual work shirt and 501s, an attempt to look age appropriate—something Makiko learned from a TV show she liked to watch. The ensemble is a mixed blessing. Walking across the vast space of the international departures terminal, respectably dressed with a first-class boarding pass and a wad of Swiss francs in my pockets, I feel the victim of an overly elaborate and misguided practical joke.

I come through the outer door, and the vast horizontal expanse of the airline terminal spreads out before me. It reminds me of one of Viereck's mini-murals—a low horizoned space teeming with multi-hued battalions of amped-up travelers, locked in rag-tag parade formation, a Glandelinian war storm of marching men.

By the time various attractive but vaguely disinterested Swiss Air staff guide me onto the plane, Herman's world, a world I thought I'd exiled to a place distant from my own, begins to replay itself in my head. Sitting in first class, I watch the back of the plane fill up with tourists and college students. How old would Miriam be now if she were alive? Could she be magically sitting in the back of the plane? Miriam; my ex, Tamar; Herman; and all the rest of them, our lives and stories entwined.

They shut the doors, and the plane begins to undulate slowly away from the gate, a huge beast not yet in its element. I look at my watch; only six hours to Zurich; lines on a half-forgotten globe, the great circle route. Surely they'll serve us dinner, some movie, a formulaic romantic comedy I would never ordinarily pay to see; the crossword puzzle I saved from Sunday, but it doesn't help. The plane turns onto the tarmac, and I get a glimpse of the old Sears tower on the distant skyline. So much has changed since it was the tallest building in the world, and little of it for the better, if you ask an old man.

The stewardess comes down the aisle; she pays special attention to my seat belt. Does it really look as if I've never been on a plane before? The pilot powers up the engines, and the plane strains against the brakes, anxious to be off. I'm a passenger who pays attention to takeoffs and landings, no matter how many times I've been aloft. I believe that the uniqueness of flight should not be taken for granted. Yet even as the plane imperceptibly leaves the ground and the rooftops and baseball fields of Chicago drop away below me, I can't enjoy the uniqueness of the perspective. The trip to Zurich has called me back to the beginning of my story and the end of Herman's.

CHAPTER TWO

In the winter of 1982, after a year of watching him struggle up and down the stairs, I convinced Herman to move to the Little Sisters of the Poor. "Only until you're feeling a little stronger," I lied as Makiko and I helped load him into the cabulance.

"I'll come by in a few days to see how you're getting along," I had reassured him as the attendant slammed the door. All I got in return was the cloudy-eyed stare of a soon-to-be euthanized dog.

After the cab pulled away, I felt nothing but relief. The guilt came later, but it took till spring before I got up the courage to go see him. Why did I put it off? What do you think—a charity home for indigents? Picture the smells, the sounds. As a photographer who'd made his bones chronicling the lives of the wretched, I had experienced enough institutional squalor to last me a lifetime. After all the photo-essays I'd done of vagrants and street people, I had no problem conjuring up a photomontage of life at the Little Sisters.

I saw the residents in black and white, lined up in a narrow hallway, slumped in a progression of cast-off wheelchairs, their leatherette backs cracked and peeling. The tires totter along with chunks of rubber gouged out of the rims, the bent, grease-starved axles groan as bored attendants shuttle them down to the dining hall.

The windows are glassine with grease and congealed dust, and the faces—slack jawed, unshaven, eyes fixed vacantly on an unchanging horizon six feet away. The half-fecal smell of death surrounds them, more a promise than a threat; a rush hour going nowhere. Did I really need to inflict this morbid experience upon myself just for the sake of an ex-tenant?

Sitting in my own living room and looking across the street at the vacant windows of Herman Viereck's apartment, I imagined the inmates' sunken eyes following me as I sneaked past them, headed down that hallway toward some sort of dayroom. I'd be sure to find Herman in there, staring blankly out a dirt-streaked window that opened on a claustrophobic airshaft.

He'd be surrounded by the usual cast of nursing-home stereotypes: the obligate crazy woman in a shapeless housedress singing monosyllables, the long-term schizophrenic with drug-induced tardive dyskinesia, the quadriplegic in his motorized chair, controlled by blowing into a soda straw. Here'd be two toothless geezers playing an endless checkers game on a drool-spotted board and a fat ward attendant with a Southern accent, dressed in dirty whites. He'd be doling out cigarettes while subtly threatening physical violence.

To cap it off, to add to the cheap, sophomoric irony, the whole snake pit would be watched over by the benevolent gaze of Jesus the Christ himself. He'd be everywhere, a crucifix over each narrow bed and his picture, cheaply framed, hanging on the far wall of the dayroom. His hand raised in benediction, his face bathed in the glow of the divine light, magically emanating from the canvas itself.

Don't be fooled by the radiation of that inner light. It's an easier technique than it looks, a trick everyone learns in art school. Use lots of titanium white. It makes the canvas glow with an inner divine radiance. With a big-enough tube of the stuff, you too could fake a Rembrandt, or at least a Thomas Kincaid—but could you do a Viereck?

So I kept putting it off. In the end, though, guilt overcame my nursing-home-e-o phobia. I didn't think he had anyone else, and even at the lowball rate I'd charged him, it still added up to a lot of money.

After thirty years of collecting his rent and listening to him ramble on about the weather, I owed him at least a visit.

Speaking of money, I did have some final business we needed to clear up. All his belongings were still in the apartment. Once it became obvious that he wasn't coming back, we couldn't afford to leave his place vacant.

Gentrification had reached our neighborhood. Rents were going up, and Makiko wanted to bring in her green-cardless crew of Mexican wonder boys, slap up some sheetrock, redo the floors—and quadruple the rent.

"What should we do with all his stuff?" I'd asked. She'd looked at me as if it were beneath consideration.

"I don't care. Call one of the 'I haul trash' guys and have him take it to the dump. Believe me, there's nothing up there worth saving. The place is a pigsty."

When you read about Herman Viereck in the coffee-table books or that seminal article about him in *Art Forum*, it sounds as if he'd lived in a hovel, but now that his stuff has been safely catalogued, photographed, and reinstalled in its new home at the Chicago Institute for Intuitive Art, you can tell that underneath the stacks of cardboard boxes, piles of magazines, and the other effluvia of Herman's obsessive collections, I'd provided him a nice, well-lit, and spacious studio apartment.

When we finally ripped up the layers of linoleum, the floors were the original quarter-sawn, tight-grain oak. His three large windows looked out on Webster Avenue and provided northern exposure; a perfect atelier, but ever since Herman moved on, the turnover has been high. As Makiko says, the place has its ghosts. Now that I've pretty much quit the real estate biz, Makiko's son is planning to gut the building and condo it out. Maybe that will finally convince Viereck's band of spirits to move on, but I doubt it.

Am I sounding more like a real estate agent and less like an artist? Well, we tend to become that which we once only pretended to be. My rep is as a serious photographer and art critic, but buying and selling Chicago real estate has been a bigger part of my life than I would care to admit. I suppose I could get cute with words and explain how there is no fundamental difference between the two—how all man's creations, whether a nice brick bungalow or Haida war canoe, carry their own esthetic—but underneath, you'd know my moral compass would still be struggling to find true north.

My career as upscale slumlord started out nobly enough. In the sixties, my first wife, Tamar, and I didn't want to be part of the white flight from Chicago. So instead of buying some hippy-dippy acre or two out in Roxbury and raising goats, we opted to stick it out in town. We bought the fourplex Makiko and I still live in. To give the block stability—not to mention it being too good of a deal to pass up—we bought the apartment building across the street. Herman came with the building: 821 Webster Avenue.

Initially, all we said we wanted was a decent, safe place for our daughter, Miriam, to grow up, but you don't get into real estate unless you have some kind of passion for the concreteness of four walls. As it turned out I loved buying and selling property. I enjoyed fixing places up and seeing them realize their potential. Our faux Weather Underground friends put us down, called us capitalist pigs. But it didn't stop them from coming and asking our advice once they decided to take the plunge.

One building led to another. And though I never intended to become rich at it, real estate has given me a certain amount of what I like to call artistic freedom, the independence to follow my own bliss, to pay attention to that elusive distant drummer. It's also been a good excuse not to pick up a camera. But more about that later.

It's the usual story about being at the right place at the right time. In the sixties, these small inner city apartments and solid red-brick bungalows were going for a song. By the time I shipped Herman off to the Sisters, Makiko and I owned six rentals, plus two that were still in Tamar's and my names. I saw myself as a more-or-less humane landlord. At least I should get credit for living in one of my own buildings.

Lincoln Park is one of those funky neighborhoods caught between downtown and the opulence of the north shore. With the park and DePaul University nearby, the neighborhood has always felt more like a college town than part of Chicago proper. Today, with a Starbucks on every corner and a little baby boomlet of privileged brats, I hardly recognize my old neighborhood.

Every village has its idiot—and Herman Viereck belonged to us. Minimal as his needs were, as his landlords, it fell on our little family to keep an eye on him. He came across as a strange little creep, but I admired him from the get-go.

People like to describe him as this angry hermit, muttering to himself as he patrolled the streets, rummaging through trash cans, frightening little children, and rambling on obsessively about the weather, but he had a fey side to him that always caught me unawares. It's why I never got around to raising his rent.

One December, a few weeks before Christmas, and a few, years before Miriam got sick and our world fell apart, he showed up at our door.

Tamar opened up and he's standing there, five foot two at the most, dressed in an old army surplus trench coat that drags the floor. He always favored a bristly military haircut and a clipped mustache. I couldn't help it—with his Germanic name, he always reminded me of Hitler, the way Chaplin played him in *The Great Dictator*. Risible, but with an air of deranged menace.

"Can we help you, Herman?" Tamar asks.

Herman says without any pleasantries as to the season, "I think you and Mr. Nathan should give me a Christmas present."

"What kind of present?" I ask him.

"I think you should give me a week off on my rent."

It took me so aback that I said okay before I could even think about it.

He handed me thirty dollars. I had him down for forty a month. Ten bucks a week. It's hard to imagine.

Well, in January he showed up with thirty again.

"Ten dollars off for New Year's," he told me.

I'm lucky he didn't try to double-jack us for Lincoln and Washington's birthdays, not to mention St. Valentine's Day.

That was Herman for you. You'd think he could barely dress and feed himself, yet he talked me down to thirty a month. At the time, it seemed so out of character I laughed it off. But it took me years before I managed to coax his rent back to the original forty. By then, everyone else in the building paid three times that.

So yes, Herman and me, we had history. He would not go gentle into that good night on my account. Every time I looked across the street at the blank windows of his old apartment, I could feel his reproachful, angry eyes staring at me as the attendants lifted him into that cabulance. To make it as easy as possible on myself, I waited for a freakishly warm day in early spring, one of those days where your winter dead skin rejoices just to feel the brush of the air against it.

"Nothing can bring me down today," I thought as I drove out along the shore. The lake loomed horizonless, the sky as blue as the water. On the side streets, overarching cherry blossoms made a bower over my rusted-out Volvo.

I counted the house numbers as I drove out along the shore. As they went up, the houses got grander, and the lawns got bigger. It felt like the wrong end of town for an indigent's nursing home, but back then, the Catholic Church still owned half of Chicago. Even so, when I finally pulled into the circular driveway, the size and weight of the building came as a shock.

The Little Sisters of the Poor had once been built for a half-forgotten nineteenth-century meatpacker or railroad tycoon. Three stories: field-stone for the first two with exposed Tudor-style timbering for the top and attic. The gabled windows of the servants' quarters punctuated the steep slate roof. Condo it out today; you could get six nice units in there easy. At eight hundred grand a pop? You do the math.

I parked in a visitor's slot and went inside. The walls were freshly painted, and the place shined like a rectory. Even the air smelt fresh, not hammered into submission by some cloying industrial cleanser but natural, ebullient with cherry blossoms and a faint tang of freshwater mist coming off the lake. There wasn't a busted wheelchair in sight.

I wandered around till I found a nursing station on the second-floor landing. A pretty nurse in archaic starched whites sat at the desk, and she greeted me as if I were someone special. Nobody seemed to know Herman's whereabouts, but they didn't seem worried about it.

"Check outside," she told me. "He likes to sit in the sun."

Sure enough, I found Herman sitting on a stone bench next to a weathered marble fountain, some Italianate trophy brought back to

Chicago from a *fin-de-siècle* collecting orgy. Columns of cherubs frolicked with budlike open mouths that once formed small spouts. Its creator had chiseled "*Il Inocentis*" on the plinth—"the innocents."

I hardly recognized ol' Herman in his new outfit. He wore a brown suit, recycled from Saint Vincent DePaul and two sizes over. They'd found him a button-down, white shirt and had knotted a skinny black tie tight around his neck. The last pair of shoes I'd seen him in had had one of the soles bound to the uppers with duct tape. Now he sported black wingtips with white patent leather inserts that clashed sweetly with the suit. He reminded me of a ten-year-old kid, waiting to go to his grandmother's funeral.

Despite the odd get-up, he looked better. That last year I'd spent watching him try to make it on his own had been grim. He'd gotten too gimpy to traverse the stairs, and I think he'd been slowly starving to death. For as long as I'd known him, he'd taken all his meals at the Starlight Diner over on Melrose Avenue. I think they'd comped his ticket. He had this air about him that made people want to do something nice for him, no matter how rundown or off-putting he appeared. People never felt they were giving him a handout. It was more as if he deserved to be helped. I guess that's the way Buddhists feel about their begging priests.

Don't get the impression that Herman lived on the bum. He'd worked as a janitor at St. Joseph's Hospital for most of his life. He paid into Social Security like the rest of us, and he deserved his check. Still, with his glasses held together by friction tape and his oversized greatcoat, you could imagine him as penniless. I don't think he'd cooked a meal in his life, not even to nuke a Swanson's. By the time he went into the Sisters, he must have been down to eighty-five, ninety pounds.

In addition to giving him the nearly new second-hand suit, they'd shaved his stash and let his hair grow out a little. He'd put weight back on. But even from across the courtyard, I could tell by the way he slumped inward that the fight had gone out of him.

I found out later that some shrink had come by and put Herman on medication, probably Thorazine or some forerunner of Prozac. My own experiences with depression being what they are, I'm not too big a fan of chemistry, but whatever they'd put him on helped, at least superficially. All those years I'd known him on the street, he'd been rabbity and uncommunicative. The most I ever got out of him were diatribes about the weather and how our local meteorologists had predicted it all wrong. Now as I walked up to him, he smiled and did a half-wave. He seemed relaxed, avuncular.

I've often wondered what would have happened if some doc had gotten to him fifty years earlier and doped him up on a happy pill. Would he have still turned out all those thousands of single-spaced legal pages, possibly the longest work of fiction ever written? Would he have made all those fabulously disturbing illustrations? Would he have been happier with his demons and obsessions tied down by Lilliputian bands of neurochemical restraints?

In essence, that's the Viereck dilemma. It's why he's eaten up the last thirty years of my life and why anyone who gets bitten by the Viereck bug can't let him alone. No matter what people say about the importance of his art, of his pioneering technique of using collage to wed popular images with his own aesthetic, it's the mythos of Viereck the crazy hermit that makes people so passionate about his work. It's "Crazy" Herman we want to know about, the mad haunter of trash cans, the inventor of his own planet, and god of his own perverse universe.

Much as we try to emerge from the smothering cloud of nineteenth century romanticism, no matter how many market-savvy MFAs our art schools turn out, armed with not only a paintbrush but also a business plan, we want our artists to be *mad*. We need them to be different from the rest of us, to be disconnected from the mundane realities of earning a living, raising children, and remembering to get their teeth cleaned.

We take comfort in knowing how bad at life they are. Otherwise, where is the dividing line between our own narcissistic mediocrity and their genius? If it's not their unique misery that leads them to create their masterpieces, then what is it that holds us back? Why can't we be like them? Those gloriously dysfunctional rock stars fascinate us. The Gauguins, the Van Goghs, the Lautrecs, the Pollacks and the Modiglianis—they're all outsiders!

We want to sleep well. We want to grow old in leisure, dither in our gardens, and take up some hobby that involves a lot of wood shavings.

We take comfort in knowing that these crazy artists are out there, stand-ing guard against the forces of bourgeois complacency and now and then howling at the moon.

This jazzed-up cyber-millennium has made things worse. No one makes the distinction anymore between the artist as a person and his creations. Making art is only half the battle. Buyers want your back story. They want the sordid details, which are invariably available. There are too many cameras, too many biographers, too many critics, too many ex-wives, and too many people like me digging up the past.

Now, everybody gets to be on TV. Everybody gets to talk to Charlie Rose. Nobody is happy just owning the art. They want to collect you as well. If Herman's work had been found abandoned on the street, the output of some nameless soul lost in his own limbo, would he have generated the same excitement? Would I still be on this plane to Zurich?

∗∗∗

"Hey Herman," I said, approaching his bench. He looked up, blinking in the sunlight. They'd gotten him new glasses that distorted his face. In the past, he had never let anyone sit down next to him, but when I did, he made no attempt to avoid our sleeves touching.

"Hey, Mr. Nathan, how you doin', pally?"

I told him I felt fine. Asking after my wellbeing constituted a new social skill for him.

"You enjoying the weather?" I asked. No point trying to get around it. Any interaction with him always devolved into his talking about the weather. I thought I might as well jump the gun. Herman nodded. He allowed as that it was a rare day, but the obsessive passion he 'd once brought to the subject felt forced. He didn't care anymore. Another medication effect, I wondered.

"So, how are you liking it here?"

He nodded. "They treat me swell, not like some places I could tell you about. The sisters is awfully good to me."

"So you think you'll be staying on, then?" I coaxed him gently. He nodded. "Where else do I got to go?"

I asked him about the apartment and how I needed to think about renting it out. "What do you want me to do with all your stuff?"

He smiled. An air of mystery glinted in his watery eyes. "It's all stuff I got out of the trash. I guess it should go back to where it came from." And then he reached out and took my sleeve. "Anything you find up there that you want to keep—it's yours," he told me.

As they say, I should have gotten it in writing.

CHAPTER THREE

Ever since Chas. Addams drew the first one for the *New Yorker*, the scene has become a cartoon icon. The archeologist, wearing a pith helmet and holding a flashlight, is shown entering an undisturbed Egyptian tomb, only to find some anachronistic relic mired in cobwebs: a Volkswagen, a Barbie doll, Judge Crater—you can insert your favorite gag line.

The seminal discovery, the one that inspired the cartoon and enraptured an entire lost generation, occurred in 1922. Henry Carter, a grave robber of the new, enlightened school, unearthed the tomb of the boy Pharaoh, Tutankhamen, in the Valley of the Kings. Everybody else in the Pharaonic dynasty had been accounted for. One by one, their tombs had been found, each looted and desecrated. But Tut's was still out there. Carter held a slim hope that no one before him had found it and that its treasures might still be intact. By 1922, despite taking time out for the First World War, Carter had been punching dry holes in the Sahara for fourteen years. All he'd gotten for his trouble and expense were a handful of carved scarabs and some broken pottery.

Back in England, his financial backer, Lord Carnarvon, had had about enough. Despite his vast financial resources, he'd grown tired of seeding the Egyptian desert with ten-pound notes. Only Carter's unflagging optimism had convinced him to grubstake the expedition one more season.

In keeping with the dramatic overtones of the tale, Carter's permit from the French department of antiquities had only days left before it expired. His crew hadn't been paid, and the weather had grown foul. He'd been only days away from packing it in when he literally stumbled upon a rubble-filled staircase descending into the desert floor. Apparently, laborers from prior excavations had used the stairwell as an easy place to dump excess rock, and it had been covered over for years.

It took Carter's crew a week to clean away the debris that packed the stairwell, but finally he reached the bottom. There he confronted a bricked-over wall that appeared never to have been breached. A few cartouches carved into the rock told him he'd found the tomb of the boy king. In a show of fierce loyalty and superhuman restraint, Carter stopped digging, posted armed guards at the top of the stairs, cabled his boss, and told him to get his ass down there ASAP.

Two interminable weeks later, with Lord Carnarvon and the lord's daughter standing behind him, Carter broke through the outer wall of the tomb. A rush of stale tomb air escaped, and Carter thrust in a candle. His light obliterated three thousand years of darkness. Carter stuck in his head, not daring to draw breath. It took a moment for his eyes to adjust.

Behind him, Carnarvon could not contain himself.

"What do you see?" he asked.

Carter, his voice a dusty hush in the capsulated air replied— "Wondrous things."

Needless to say, to the general delight of the world at large (and Universal Studios in particular), things went downhill from there. A mere month later, Carnarvon was dead from a septic mosquito bite, adding impetus to the deeply Christian fascination with the sin of grave desecration and fueling the titillating myth of "The Mummy's Curse."

Carter, of course, fell prey to something much deadlier: the curse of finding what you're looking for.

The rest of Carter's life played out as pathetic anticlimax. It took him years to systematically photograph the tomb's contents, box everything up, and ship it to the national museum in Cairo, but he never did much with the treasure after that. He never published any monographs, never became a respected professor of Egyptian antiquities. Instead, he went on a lot of tours, lecturing in town halls and movie theaters around the globe, titillating audiences with necrophilalical pornography.

There were some minor but reputation-ruining scandals about him pilfering some pieces and selling them to wealthy collectors. He lived to see Egyptian motifs become the official decorative face of the jazz age and influence the architecture of movie palaces from London to Shanghai, but that was it. He never synthesized any of Tut's artifacts into more than what they seemed to any casual observer—the gaudy lost art of an earlier gilded and equally decadent age.

As Tut's tomb had been for Carter, Herman Viereck's treasure had been under my nose for thirty years. His wasn't exactly the tomb of the boy king, and hidden treasure was the last thing on my mind the day I went up there to clean it out. Still, there are similarities. I too had my moment when I opened the still air of an undiscovered tomb and first gazed upon "wondrous things."

Carter came to the Valley of the Kings supported by platoons of turbaned laborers armed with picks and shovels. He'd even brought along a few judicious cases of dynamite to help with the heavy lifting. I came alone with a broom, a mop, and a Costco-sized box of Hefty bags.

"Are you sure there's *nothing* in there that you want me to save?" I'd asked Herman that afternoon in the garden behind the Sisters. I should have known he had an ulterior motive when he gave me that sideways, Borstal-boy look of his and said, "You see anything in there you want, pally, it's yours." So I told him okay and left him sitting in the sun.

But once again, I put things off. I found the idea of hauling away the mountains of trash that Makiko assured me were up there too daunting. But more than that, emptying out the apartment filled me with a melancholy that I couldn't describe—not even to myself.

I have this cheap sentimental attachment to tangible remnants of other people's lives. It makes it hard for me to throw things away. I reflexively hold onto other people's diplomas, marriage certificates, children's scrapbooks, and anything from any war fought before my time. It's not the best obsession for a landlord who's constantly cleaning out apartments.

At one time, Tamar and I dealt casually in antiques, a natural out-growth of our real estate interests. We were looking at lots of property, and to get an early peek at what might be coming on the market, we'd follow up on the classified ads for estate sales.

Friday mornings (if I didn't have a class) or Saturdays, we'd often end up standing in line in a freezing drizzle, waiting to be let into some old geezer's house to paw through the detritus of his life. It became a minor obsession, like any other faux hunter-gatherer activity city folk engage in, like ice fishing or mushroom hunting. The joy of the hunt far outweighed the value of the prize. But apart from the greed-driven satisfaction of stumbling across some overlooked treasure we could resell for fifty times what we paid, little else in the activity buoyed the spirit.

The sales became predictable. After going in and out of a hundred houses, a pattern of possessions emerged. I could walk through the front door and write the owner's biography in a glance. Most people end up owning more or less the same things: an almost-complete set of second-rate postwar Japanese china, an overabundance of Christmas decorations, a cheap exercise bike from Sears (used as a towel rack), too many shoes, an assortment of baseball caps, an Avon bottle or two, wedding presents from fifty years ago (chafing dishes, waffle irons, never used then, never used now).

Oh sure, here and there would be the oddball heirloom or the detri-tus of an eccentric with an unusual acquisitorial bent, someone with a penchant for collecting pine cones or smudge pots. Groupings of sad-irons or eggbeaters are fairly common. After a while, I lost interest. The profit margins were too small, the rare finds all too rare. I came back from these expeditions feeling irritable and depressed.

The personal stuff that families left behind began to bother me. Down in the basement or in the back of a closet, I'd come across a box of old photos, certificates, diplomas, honorable discharges, medals for valor, even Purple Hearts—the whole assorted flotsam and jetsam of a lifetime, left to be pawed through by strangers.

Is that all there is to a life? Didn't anyone in the family want these mute testaments to the years spent on this mortal coil? Didn't they know how special and precious each and every one of us is?

I'd find myself alone in a basement, peering at the remainders of a lifetime, looking for what? Did I hope to find some universal connection that would link me, the perpetual outsider, with the warp and weft of America? Who were these people I saw in these brittle snapshots? The men, dressed in ill-fitting suits and ties, posed in front of some now vintage Ford, looking slightly imbecilic and malevolent, like a gang of depression-era bank robbers. I half expected them to be brandishing machine guns.

There were babies in bassinets, boys in Scout uniforms, girls in cheap formals— the whole parade of family, Gd and country, now headed for the dump. No wonder Tut's family desperately tried to hide him. At the end, it didn't matter. Carter pried open the tomb, and the remnants of the boy king's life became just another tag sale with swarms of strangers pawing through his underwear.

Pictures, pictures—I taught photography at the Chicago Institute of Fine Arts for years. Basically, there are two types of photographers: the shy and the bold. There are those quiet types who stand back from their subjects. These guys are happy capturing the moon over the Half Dome at Yosemite, water trickling in the desert, or a close-up of a caterpillar munching a leaf. Then there are guys like me, the street brawlers, social realists. We're not afraid to take our camera and stick it in a cop's face the moment after he's beat the crap out of a college kid.

Well, that's not true. We are afraid; but we do it anyway.

In the sixties, my stuff appeared in *LIFE*, *Newsweek*. You couldn't open a rag without getting an eyeful. All those shots of cops working over the crowd during 1968 Democratic Convention? I took the best of those.

But I've never been big on taking photos of my own family. I've been afraid they'd end up in a shoebox stuffed in the back of a closet. I have almost nothing of Miriam from that last year. I don't think you can preserve what's real and important in those moments.

Much as I love the process, there comes a time when you have to put the camera down. You have to force yourself to step into the picture.

With all these memories and bad experiences cluttering up my interior landscape, it's no wonder I put off going up to Herman's apartment. Even without my own emotional baggage, the sheer physical dimensions of the job were enough to make me procrastinate. We'd had obsessive hoarders in our buildings once or twice before. It's a more common mental illness than you'd think. I imagined trash mountains piled to the ceiling. It might require a backhoe to get the job done.

I was forty-five at the time, not feeling old exactly, but already noticing that things I used to do without thinking now required a certain amount of mental preparation and visualization, like a gymnast running through her floor routine before a meet. It took a slight gut-check before I plunged up two flights of stairs with, oh, let's say, an eight-by-ten Oushak rug over one shoulder—a gut-check and a handful of Advil.

Makiko had been inside his apartment last, just before he'd moved out.

"It's a rat's nest in there," she had told me when she got back.

"Anything good?" I'd asked—the inveterate junk hound.

"I don't know," she said. "Something told me I better not look to the right or the left. It's so crowded that there's only this narrow path down the center of the room."

I thought again about taking her advice and hiring a couple of guys to come in and take it down to the bare walls. It's what any sane property manager would have done. But something held me back. There had been some subliminal communication between Herman and myself that had been going on for years.

"Anything you see up there that you want, it's yours," he'd said. Something told me I had better take him at his word. So, one Saturday, feeling like a pilgrim on a divine mission, I retrieved my ring of master keys from the junk drawer and crossed the Rubicon.

"Wondrous things," indeed.

It took a good, shoulders-into-it shove just to get the door open far enough to peer around it. A stack of newspapers a yard high had toppled over and wedged themselves behind the door, an overture to the trash opera yet to come. Opera? It played the whole goddamn *Ring Cycle*.

In country antique stores, there's often a back room filled with old *LIFE* magazines and *National Geographics* (don't waste your time; you'll never find a cover with Marylyn Monroe or JFK). There's a unique smell that the cheap newsprint gives off after it's been fermenting for half a century: a combination of mold and decaying printer's ink. For some reason, it's not unpleasant, like going into a potting shed or an old barn. It's the smell of history, an olfactory record of the passage of time. When I got Herman's door open enough to peer in, that same smell hit me.

Unlike Carter, my first brush with the immortal power of a lost civilization took a while to make itself known. Carter had stuck his candle through the outer wall of the tomb and "everywhere saw the glint of gold." My first glance at Herman's floor-to-ceiling clutter gave no clue to what treasures lay within. On first impression, the place looked like the garbage dump I'd pictured in my mind's eye.

At that crucial point, with my feet still in the hallway, I had two choices, two avenues of approach. The smartest thing would have been to not frighten myself by looking at the enormity of the task. Like a recovering alcoholic, I should have taken it one day at a time. I should have started with that first pile of newspapers and shoved them into a virgin Hefty bag and then worked my way mindlessly in, pile by pile.

The second choice, the thinking man's choice? Treat myself to an overview. I stood on the shore of this inland sea of garbage and tried to appreciate the scope and grandeur of what lay ahead: the apartment, basically a one-room studio with a long, spacious area and a closet-sized kitchen at the far end. Even with years of dust covering the three large windows that looked north on Webster Avenue, light streamed in.

There were so many boxes crammed into the space that the wall away from the windows couldn't be reached, even with my outstretched hand. To my right, the space under the windows, he'd furnished with a long table, actually three old kitchen tables. The middle one jutted a quarter of an inch higher than the others, and Herman had seamed the tops together with strips of his favorite material, duct tape.

At the center of this table, long enough to seat the Last Supper, he'd placed an old office chair that jutted out into the narrow defile that ran the length of the room. The chair once had had a cane bottom, long since fenestrated, the strands of the busted seat hanging like a neglected basketball net. He'd replaced the seat with an irregular chunk of Masonite, covered with a patchwork pillow that looked as if it had been stitched from the sleeves he'd torn off his flannel shirts.

Apart from the chair, no other place in the room acknowledged human habitation. Not even a bed. I walked over to the center table and eased myself into his chair. As soon as I sat down, I felt right at home. I peered down at the tabletop, its surface scarified with a thousand knife cuts. And there in front of me, as obvious as a telltale blood splatter at a crime scene, I saw a few drops of paint.

I flicked at them with a fingernail, but the color had soaked into the wood. Discovering the paint put things in context. The room rearranged itself before my eyes. Where before there had been chaos and insanity, now I saw order and purpose. I sat at the center of an artist's studio, the workplace of a kindred spirit.

In front of me, at what would have been Herman's eye level, he'd put up a small shelf loaded with stacks of irregular pieces of cardboard. I pulled them down. They were silhouettes of doll-like figures, their arms and legs pinned on with paper fasteners like primitive marionettes. Damn strange.

I stood up and continued prowling up and down the narrow space in the center of the room. The paint speck affected my thoughts. It became a prism through which the room's contents spread themselves out in a haunting spectrum. A faint little humming started in my head, a sub-conscious realization that I'd only scratched the surface of something deep and mysterious.

Still ostensibly looking for a piece of certifiable trash to throw away, I needed something to start the process. Where were the empty bottles and cans, the dirty clothes, and the nonfunctioning electrical appliances? Wasn't there at least a broken toaster I could stuff into the black hole of my garbage bag? Nothing looked disposable. For all the superficial clutter, everything in the room hinted at some as-yet not-understood subtext: some higher purpose, some deeper significance.

Oh, things had dumpster potential, but even objects that had no value singly grew in importance by the fact that Herman had amassed hundreds of them. I opened a carton at random and found it filled with small glass bottles. Great, I thought, here's a no-brainer. Out they go. When I picked them up, they were all identical: triangular Pepto-Bismol bottles, arranged neatly, to make the maximum use of the box's space. Their isosceles sides allowed for what physicists call "tight packing." It gave the mass a crystalline, molecular structure.

Each bottle had been carefully rinsed, and its label soaked off. Then Herman had reapplied a small gummed label, inked with his neat but childlike hand, a hand with which I soon became all-too familiar.

This archeologist had found another archeologist. Each label recorded a date and a location: "Webster and Vine, Aug, 11/1962, 81 degrees, modest precip." "Lancaster and Cherry, Sept. 2/2/1974, 47 degrees, sunny, high cumulus," "DePaul and Haslet, March, 23/1967/ 51 degrees, no rain despite predictions."

I should have stopped there. Herman obviously had his own lunatic agenda, and I should have put up my hands and backed slowly away from the box as if I'd heard it ticking, but I didn't. I had too much respect for the artistry. As an industrial designer, I knew more than most about the power of endlessly repeated shapes.

The Pepto-Bismol bottle is a perfect design. See how it fits the hand. The flat sides allow each joint of the finger to lock around a softly angular edge. No matter how puke-sick, gin-soaked, and shaking you may be, that bottle of Pepto isn't going to slip and hit the floor.

I put a few of the bottles down on the tabletop, and they caught the low-angled afternoon light. On the far wall, little prismatic rainbows danced where the bottles split the shaft. I couldn't help it; I kept pulling bottles out of the carton and arranging them on Herman's workspace. The spectra on the far wall began to overlap in complex patterns: Roy G Biv, Vib G. Yor.

When I had about twenty, a thought came to me. These were all bottles he'd obviously rescued from the trash, each labeled as to when and where he'd found them. Did they constitute some kind of secret language? Could they be a code, or a treasure map, a Turing machine made up of Pepto-Bismol bottles?

"Bennington and Avenue D, 4 January 67, 28 degrees, overcast."

I'd seen him pawing through the trashcans in our neighborhood for years. I'd always thought he collected deposit bottles, but this had its own deeper level of arcana. Herman had developed a system for transcending four-dimensional space-time, and weather constituted his fifth dimension.

I had a faux eureka moment. Before I could dissuade myself, I dashed back across the street to our apartment. I could hear Makiko practicing in the back room. When she heard me slamming kitchen drawers, she came out to investigate.

"I need some duct tape and a city map," I told her.

I had the artist's "man with a vision" look. Viereck's bottles were going to lead me to Nirvana. Even as I ran back to his apartment with the tape, an out-of-date *Thomas Guide*, and a magic marker, part of me knew I'd set myself on a fool's mission.

In the hallway outside Herman's door, I laid out the streets and avenues of our neighborhood with tape and labeled them with the magic marker. Then I started placing the bottles on the grid according to where he had found them.

Immediately I realized the limitations of my model. The map fixed the bottles' locations in relation to each other but not their temporal relationship. On the grid, decades of collecting became compressed into two dimensions. I needed a third axis for time. Maybe strings tied to the ceiling with little loops to hook the bottles on—and I wasn't even thinking yet about the weather conditions he'd noted. How would I plot those?

I would need a computer program with spreadsheets, overlays, and 3-D graphics. I'd need Fourier analysis, quadratic equations, and Poisson's distributions—too much. I cursed the crazy old bastard. I cursed myself, but I kept at it, arranging his Pepto bottles on the grid till I had a small glass city. There did seem to be one corner of our neighborhood that had an exceptionally high incidence of dyspepsia, but outside of that? *Nada.*

Makiko finally showed up and snapped me out of it. As soon as she came up the stairs, I felt embarrassed, like Richard Dreyfus's character in *Close Encounters*, when he sculpts the Devil's Tower out of mashed potatoes.

"Look, he must have collected a thousand of them," I told her, trying to get her into the flow.

"I just hope he didn't drink them all himself," she said.

I showed her the little paper labels with the dates and locations. She looked down at the grid work on the worn linoleum.

"The only people this could be of any possible interest to are Pepto-Bismol's marketing department," she told me. "Do you think they sell more Pepto in the summer or the winter?"

"They must mean something," I insisted. "The oldest one I found goes back thirty years. What was he thinking?"

"I don't know. What does anyone think about when they try to create order out of chaos? He's a sick, crazy little man, Nate. He's just attempting to gain control of his environment. He has OCD; anyone could tell that in fifteen seconds. Don't get caught up in someone else's meshugaas," she told me. "You have enough problems of your own."

Sure, a psychiatric diagnosis, the first of umpteen theories I would eventually collect. Still, for now, Makiko had broken the spell. Whatever secrets the bottles contained remained known only to Herman. It took me a half-hour to repack them and rip my tape map off the floor. By then, my vision swam with the breastwork formations signaling an incipient migraine, and my back throbbed. I retreated back across the street to our apartment, not one Hefty bag closer to cleaning out his place than when I'd started.

With that as a prelude, it took me all week to summon up the strength to go back for seconds. Hercules had the Augean stables; I had Herman Viereck's apartment.

We were locked in a contest of wills. Whose concept of order would prevail, mine with my garbage bags—or the retired janitor's with his Pepto bottles?

The bottles provided only an appetizer for the meal yet to come. On my next foray, this is what I found: fifty-seven balls of string, varying in size from Mercury, five inches in diameter, to Jupiter, a thirty-two pound gargantuan hairball of multicolored twine. Some of the scraps were as short as three inches. He'd diligently granny-knotted them together.

If he'd wound them into one big ball, Herman might have had a shot at Guinness. But like everything else he did, Herman had his own agenda about the string. I had to admit, the fifty-seven balls taken together had their own perverse aesthetic appeal. I could see them displayed in a stark white space, like the work of some postwar German minimalist or beads of a giant's broken rosary.

Speaking of Gd, there were thirty-eight dime-store statues of the Virgin Mary, all cheaply made of plastic, chalk, or ceramic. As best I could tell, they spanned five decades of mass-production technique. Five of them were stamped "Made in Occupied Japan," somewhat rare nowadays. Still, they'd only fetch about ten bucks max, and this was way before eBay.

He'd collected individual serving syrup packets—undoubtedly scrounged from the Stardust Diner. The ones at the bottom of the box showed signs of granulation and ossification. At least he hadn't labeled them.

I found a carton full of plastic ReaLemon containers. These had a special significance to me. I'm the one who designed the ubiquitous little plastic lemon for the Mott Corporation. Outside of Herman, it's my most iconic contribution to society.

I wonder if he knew they were my design when he fished them out of the trash. A subtle salute from one artist to another?

He'd saved everything, so I saved everything. I quickly abandoned any plan for an early purging of the apartment's contents. A total of 3,832 items were removed from King Tut's tomb. There were his hair combs, beaded sandals, and little candleholders shaped in the form of whimsical little ankhs that wouldn't have looked out of place in some upscale mall outlet, Restoration Hardware, or Anthropologie. Carter had them all numbered, catalogued, and photographed *in situ* from at least two different angles. The larger pieces he had packed in bandages and plaster for their seventy-five mile trip to Cairo.

What self-control he must have had not to rampage through the place, ripping the lids off boxes, shoving aside the mounds of canoe paddles, chariots' parts, footstools, and chamber pots—a five-thousand-year-old

garage sale full of crap—just to get to the gold. How did he force himself
to wait for almost two years before opening the sarcophagus itself?

My discovery that the apartment contained something more than
the obsessive accretions of a semi-autistic savant didn't take nearly that
long. A few visits after I found the Pepto bottles, I reached what must
have been Herman's bed. He'd hidden it behind a barricade of boxes
and buried it under stacks of old magazines. It must have been years
since he'd last been able to sleep in it. If he ever slept at all. Nonetheless,
it had been crisply made. The sheets were yellowed and decomposing,
but they were tight across the thin mattress, a wool army blanket turned
down a regulation four inches. I didn't try to bounce a dime on it, but
I bet I could have. All very military, very institutional, made the way
they would teach you to do it at some place like a hospital, or a military
academy … or an orphanage.

Under the bed, I found a battered metal steamer trunk, the lid caved
in and covered with dust. Obviously, he hadn't opened it in years. Its
hasp had been jimmied open by a prior grave robber, maybe before
Herman rescued it from the street. Years of estate sales had inured me
to the lure of locked trunks. They were almost always a disappointment.

Nonetheless, I hauled it out and plunked it down on the center of his
table. It must have weighed fifty pounds. When I flipped the lid back,
the contents expanded upwards like a released spring. Inside were stacks
of various bound and loose papers.

Afraid it would decompose in my hands, I lifted out what appeared
to be a hand-bound volume resting at the top of the stack. It was twice
as thick as the Chicago Yellow Pages, each page an oblong of legal-sized
typing paper. He'd done the covers in blue cardboard. A frayed red ribbon
held the mass tentatively together. I read the hand-printed block letters:

IN THE REALMS OF THE UNREAL:
THE STORY OF THE VIVIAN GIRLS
IN WHAT IS KNOWN AS THE REALMS OF THE UNREAL,
OF THE GLANDECO-ANGILINIAN WAR STORM
CAUSED BY THE CHILD SLAVE REBELLION.

I gazed down at the manuscript that would forever change my life, and this, only the first volume of Herman's *chef-d'oeuvre*, possibly the longest single work of fiction ever written! Let Guinness put that in their records. Forget the bottles, the balls of string—15,847 pages! Yes, that's thousands. Single-spaced, typed out on an old dinosaur model Underwood (I found that, too). Later I found a box with his used ribbons—287 of them. If only he'd saved their tin containers. They're collectible.

Eventually, I also found a second copy, this one hand-written. There was also an eight-thousand-page diary and his autobiography of sorts, filled with observations and comments about Chicago's weather over the last thirty years, all written on cheap notebook paper, now brittle and starting to fracture like lake ice in spring thaw.

Pencil stubs? Three hundred and twelve Ticonderogas, none over an inch long, no bite marks, their erasers untouched. Herman never erased. He didn't agonize over word choice or changes in sentence structure. He never suffered writer's block or floundered for the right word. He never threw out shoeboxes of undeveloped negatives. Everything else in his life had been filled with endless compromise, but in this room, his vision flowed from his head intact. He'd created his own universe.

But the written word made up only the lesser half. The *Realms* was embellished by Herman with hundreds of full-color illustrations. He'd designed the paintings as foldouts to accompany the text.

The longest spanned eight feet. It was made from eighteen-by-eleven sheets of sketchpad paper, carefully glued edge on edge and accordion pleated to fit within the confines of the text. I've described them in detail too many times. At this point, let me just say that they were a fantastic mixture of schoolboy graffiti and the most sophisticated use of color and collage that I'd seen in a long time.

It was way too much to take in all at once. I flipped through the pages, reading random paragraphs here and there. But it made for rough going. He'd done it all single-spaced, and his old Underwood had been slightly out of register causing the *r*'s to jump. In the lengthening shadows thrown by my own building from across the street, the words started running together, and I could feel the flicker of another impending migraine.

Herman's literary style didn't lend itself to casual reading. It was not as idiosyncratic as his illustrations. It had more of the obsessive feel one got from talking to him in person. From what I could gather, after several protracted attempts to read some of the text, the story seemed true to the general outline of the book's title. He'd written a long historiographic account of an imaginary conflict taking place on some unnamed, gigantic planet that had flora and fauna roughly similar to our own.

The action, easily gleaned from looking at the episodes he'd chosen to illustrate, centered around seven little girls, all apparently sisters inexplicably named "The Vivian Girls." Though the book ran, as I said, in excess of fifteen thousand pages, they never seemed to emerge as separate characters. Snow White's dwarves were Shakespearian in complexity compared to Herman's "Vivs."

He depicted these little girls in perilous situations and in various stages of undress. On some pages, they were pursued by solders in fanciful uniforms; on others severe weather, especially tornados, threatened to whirl the poor little girls right off the page. There were occasional bucolic scenes, but for the most part, the illustrations were perverted fantasies about the torture and wholesale murder of Viereck's slave children.

Despite the gruesomeness of his subject, Viereck's paintings were done with the bright cheerfulness of a children's book. This unnerving disconnect between subject and affect was made even stranger by his incorporation of commercial images scissored out of catalogues and magazines. Whether this wedding of the hellishly profane to the cutesy optimism of a Disney cartoon was conscious on his part, I couldn't tell. I still can't.

After an hour of amazed examination, I closed the book, stuffed everything back into the trunk, and stashed it back under the bed. I sat down in Herman's chair and heard myself give out an involuntary groan.

"If you see anything in there you want, it's yours."

Could he really have forgotten what he'd hidden under his bed? Fifteen thousand pages? That amounted to the equivalent of about forty-five novels. Who knew when he'd started the project? How long had it taken to finish—if he had finished? Did he really mean for me to have it? And if so, what did he want me to do with it? Find him a publisher?

Perhaps he hoped I'd throw it out before anyone else got to it. Was the trunk itself just another crazy quasi-hallucination, like the labels on the Pepto bottles? Would it crumble into prismatic fragments the moment I tried to analyze what I'd found?

I got up and took one more cruise around the room. As it grew dark, the walls closed in. In this grayed-out light, I could feel my normally sound aesthetic instincts desert me. I could picture Makiko looking at the pictures and laughing, pointing out they were nothing more than demented graffiti spawned by a tortured but limited imagination. I thought about grabbing a volume or three of the *Realms* and lugging them across the street, but some premonition told me they shouldn't be removed, that once I got them out of this enchanted castle they would turn to dust. When I left, though, I made a special effort to make sure I double-locked Herman's door.

CHAPTER FOUR

Wives. When you need them the most, they're never around. I barged into our apartment, about to burst with my discovery, but she wasn't there. On Thursdays, she taught a few advanced students at the Metro League. It pissed me off. I felt like a kid with an A on his report card and no one to show it to.

Grumpy, but still buzzing with that strange energy only rabid collectors and gold prospectors can appreciate, I pulled a beer out of the fridge and began to put things in perspective. In other words, I tried to talk myself out of what my eyes had just seen.

It didn't pay to get carried away. There were lots of queer old guys out there with strange obsessions. I might even be one myself. It didn't mean that what I'd just found in Herman's apartment meant anything significant. Prodigious? Well certainly that, but did it really mean anything to the rest of us? In other words—was it art?

Picking garage sales, you always hoped to find things that were more valuable than the seller knew. The problem, of course, was that this time I didn't know, either. Trash or treasure, art or scribble?

Examples of the extent of arcane knowledge a picker needs? Take the Fuller Brush Company. They made Bakelite letter openers as give-away premiums. The handle was molded in the shape of a well-dressed salesman with his case. As you can imagine, even today there are thousands of them floating around. They came in several colors. But finding a yellow one is almost impossible. Naturally, any serious advertising or Fuller Brush collector has to have a yellow. If you can snatch one up for a buck, you're in fat city.

Sunkist made glass lemon squeezers that you could get as a mail-away premium. Half the kitchens on the North Side have one in the basement. But try to find a black one. If you do, it can make your car payment for the month.

How many times had I stumbled across something that hinted at being rare and wonderful, and yet I hadn't been completely sure? Either I couldn't remember where I'd seen the item before, or I didn't trust my own aesthetic sense. Had I made a find or an enthusiastic mistake?

Sitting in my kitchen, surrounded by odds and ends of my own eclectic acquisitions—the Bauer mixing bowls, the Russell Wright water jug, the black plastic, rhinestone-encrusted Felix the Cat wall clock (whose eyes moved back and forth as its tail swung in the opposite direction)—I tried to discount Herman's strange drawings. Maybe, I told myself, to compensate for the Pepto Bismol fiasco, I'd overreached, saw things that weren't there? I needed Makiko's levelheaded actuarial cynicism to help put my discovery into context.

***

While we're waiting for Makiko to get back, let me tell you a little about my wife. At the time we moved Herman into the Little Sisters, we'd only been married two years. It was the second go-around for each of us, hardly a statistic worth mentioning anymore. Two years, that's time enough for my previous fifteen with Tamar to be swathed in memory's selective gauzy haze out of which isolated episodes loomed, like rocks in a Marsden Hartley seascape.

I had lots of reasons for wanting to lose Tamar in the mist, and by the time I stumbled upon the *Realms of the Unreal*, Makiko had become my whole world. They say that when we remarry, we make the same mistakes. All that changes is the superficial packaging, and sometimes not even that. The same attractions and repulsions that got us into the first mess are hardwired. It's the chief counter-argument to getting a divorce. You might as well deal with what you already have.

With me, I don't know if that's the case. They both have the same pragmatic toughness, the same veiled suggestion of the streetwise urchin about them, but Makiko and Tamar are so different physically that it's easy to think, as my friends have pointed out, that I'd run far away from the one when I married the other.

But there's more to being the Venus of Willendorf than all-encompassing breasts. In her own way, boyish Makiko is more of a nurturing figure than Tamar had been—or at least had ever been to me.

I'd been on my own for over a year when our paths crossed. It had been two years since the beginning of the end—the day we'd lost Miriam. By then, I'd gone through my post-divorce mania where I tried to screw anything that crossed my path. I felt ready for what we self-flatteringly call a "serious relationship."

I'd seen forty in my rearview. Makiko was thirty-five. Before we met, I thought myself too old for the visceral illness and toxic affliction called being "in love." But the week after she sat down in my booth at the diner, I found myself driving by her house to see if the lights were on. Love at first sight. We met in a snowstorm. It's what film people like to call a "cute meet."

The snow, a product of a fast moving "lake effect" front, arrived officially unexpected by Viereck's denigrated "experts." When I'd left my house that morning, the weathermen were predicting only scattered flurries, the type of thing that any self-respecting Chicagoan would shrug off. I didn't even grab a pair of galoshes.

By 10 A.M., though, peering out my office window, I watched as the day got grimmer and grayer. The first flakes fluttered down around noon. By two, the cars on the street began to look like Hostess Sno Balls. I thought I could make it home before the streets socked in.

I owned a pre-GM Saab at the time, supposedly a good car in snow, at least for its day. I started out bravely, but by the time I got to the far end of Webster Avenue, my tires were spinning, and the car drifted perilously close to disaster. Instead of waiting for the inevitable, I nosed the car into a semi-legal parking spot and trudged on down the street toward my empty apartment. Snow filled my pants legs and found its way inside my collar.

By the time I passed Herman's old haunt, the Stardust Diner on Fenworth, I needed a cup of coffee. Nowadays, more or less finally at peace with myself, the thought of being snowbound sounds positively delicious: a time to read, watch old movies, and stoke up on carbohydrates. But back then, alone, lonely, and stuck in purgatorial grief, the idea of having to spend a few days isolated in my apartment, marooned with my thoughts, terrified me. In other words, I wasn't in any rush to get home.

The Stardust was one of those throwback beaneries that even now don't seem all that incongruous in this city of broad shoulders. The façade glistened in the near white-out, broad bands of late-deco polished aluminum, the name "Stardust" spelled out in Jetsons' calligraphy. Inside, atomic-age motifs poked through the worn Formica countertops. A massive milkshake machine that could handle six orders at once dominated the back counter. Meatloaf on Tuesdays, ham steaks Thursday, clam chowder Fridays—get the picture?

I came in and stamped the snow off my feet. A few guys at the counter looked up. Just another pilgrim seeking shelter. No one there looked as if he'd be leaving any time soon. They still had plenty of their famous chowder. The steam rising from the bowl felt good against my raw skin. I sat in a booth looking out at the swirling snow. I had nothing to go home to, and the Stardust had a comforting hum that reminded me that I wasn't the last man on earth. As long as the place felt warm and the coffee hot, I'd be content to sit there all night long. I'd rescued an old copy of the *Partisan Review* from the back seat of my car. What more could I ask for? Safe and secure, I peered out the window, enjoying the ferocity of the snow speeding sideways inches from my face.

That's when I saw her in the phone booth at the far end of the Stardust's parking lot. Through the storm, I could make out her yelling into the phone. Finally she slammed the receiver down and pulled in the folding door. She looked like a teenage runaway, underdressed for the weather in a short leather jacket that didn't button all the way, her feet clad in an old pair of useless Keds hightops.

What is it about a person that communicates from a hundred feet and through a blizzard that she's the one? I don't know, but as soon as I saw her, I got up, started pounding on the glass, and windmilling my arms. She looked up and saw me, and I beckoned her in. She didn't even pause to consider, just trudged across the lot and came in, looking around expectantly and blinking in the bright fluorescent lights. I waved her over to my booth.

I don't think of myself as particularly intimidating, but I'm a big guy, right on the edge of getting my clothes at the Big and Tall stores. I hope I radiate a friendly bear image; though on those very rare occasions when I get angry, I'm always shocked by how quickly people back down. But if my bulk intimidated her, she didn't show it.

I didn't realize she was Asian till she sat down across from me.

"Where do they get these operators?" She started in right away. "You'd think every nickel you shove in the slot went straight into her pocket."

"Who were you trying to call?" I asked.

"I just wanted to find out if they'd canceled our concert. It's been on the schedule for months. Schönberg."

"I wouldn't think you'd get too much of a crowd," I said, but I recognized the tunnel vision of the artist. Did she even realize the weather had frozen Chicago in its tracks?

"I tried to explain to this idiot that I was stuck in a phone booth in a snowstorm, but she said she couldn't reverse the charges for a local call."

"I've got plenty of change."

"Screw it," she said. "I'm sure you're right. Nobody's going to go out on a night like this to hear some string quartet perform a coda in mixolydian scale. Anyway, I'd be a fool to bring out my cello on a night like this."

I nodded, only half listening. Something lurked under her stereotypical Asian baby-doll features, an inner balance. She had a single-mindedness about her passions but was pragmatic about things she couldn't control. At the same time, she looked all of twelve years old.

"You're shivering," I said, feeling like an idiot for not noticing sooner. I took off my sensible Midwestern Burberry and draped it over her shoulders. If she had looked young before, the huge coat made her look a Fellini waif.

"Morons," she went on. "The whole system is built on a foundation of morons. Can't anybody here think for herself, take a little initiative?"

"Hey," I reminded her, "you're talking about the phone company."

"I know, but just once you'd like to see somebody break out of their incipient fascism. Why is it that most people are happier when someone is telling them what to do?"

"Oven stuffers, my dad used to call them."

"What?"

"You know ... nothing. Some people are just herd animals; they follow whoever is in front of them."

She shrugged. I could have kicked myself for the Holocaust reference, but I couldn't tell for sure if she'd missed it.

"You look like you could use something hot to drink," I said. "They have some clam chowder left."

"Ma Bell took my last fucking dime."

How could you take this much attitude coming out of such a frail body seriously? I didn't care. I'd fallen in love with her already.

In reality, and for the long haul, a lot can be said about the similarities between the role Jewish and Japanese women play in their respective societies. Both cultures labor underneath a superficial veneer of male superiority, but in reality they're matriarchal. Well, in the end, what culture isn't? Look at the Muslims with their women dressed like chess pawns waddling along in those burkas. But when daddy gets home, I bet he gets an earful about what's what. Aren't we all the same, rabbis and salary men, wandering home late and expecting a hot dinner on the table?

So are they similar, these two wives of mine? If nothing else, Tamar and Makiko both possess a certain hard-nosed eye for the bottom line. I'm sure if I had still been married to Tamar when I "discovered" Herman Viereck, she would have figured out how to market him with the same hyperbolic zeal that Makiko quickly showed.

I suspect that's not the part that you want to know about, their checkbook-balancing abilities. You want to know what went on once I got them to take off their pants. Once Makiko and I started going out together, half of my friends hinted at it, finding subtle ways to ask me what she was like in bed. And not just the men.

Is it true what they say about Asian women? My friends wanted to know. And what is it that they say exactly? Is it the child-woman thing? Does it hint at the latent pedophilia in all of us? Though they look like innocent girls and butter wouldn't melt in their mouths ... well, who hasn't seen some of those Japanese woodblocks, or a Xeroxed page from the Kama Sutra in somebody's dorm room? Once the lights go out? Yeah, baby.

Well, there are all sorts of "yeah, baby." So who knows?

I can say this. If Makiko has the look of an exotic child, Tamar is the kind of woman men describe by their bra size. So which is the one I wanted all along?

Tamar and I met at NYU. The first time I saw her, all the way on the other side of the cafeteria, I could feel my stomach tie itself into a knot. She had on jeans and a black sweater. Every guy in the room had been staring at her and pretending he wasn't.

She majored in dance. Modern of course. After all, you could have fit two standard ballet rats inside her. That day she was sitting next to the woman who modeled for my life-drawing class, so I had an excuse for going over to say hello. The fact that I'd been studying her friend's anatomy for weeks added to the already sex-charged undertone. I tried to act uninterested, but I couldn't keep my eyes off her. She'd been dating a Nigerian exchange student at the time. New York in the late fifties. You could almost get away with it.

For weeks after that, I managed to show up whenever I thought she'd be around. She treated me like a fool but always with just this little hint of accessibility. I forced myself to keep my eyes above the horizon line. Tamar left the door open a tiny crack, and I gradually levered my way in.

The reality of it? We were made for each other. Not in any cosmic, finding-your-soul-mate but in the usual nuts-and-bolts, socioeconomic sense. We both came from the same radical immigrant Jewish background. We shared the same values, the same *weltanschauung*. I suspect that's what finally did us in.

Tamar always resented the fact that we were both Jewish. It never fit with her self-image as the rebel and free thinker. It pissed her off that her family actually liked me. She resented that her dad and I could talk for hours or play chess without turning the game into a pissing contest. Where was the rebellion? Where was the drama in trading Tamar Leavenson for Tamar Learner? No point even in making an issue of keeping her maiden name.

In the end, she made me pay for making her life so safe. We both paid.

At the time, I didn't care. I couldn't keep my hands off her. Of course, she'd grown used to it. Men had been reacting to her that way all her life—the dentist, a school teacher, some creep on the bus, the inappropriate comments, the accidental gropings, who knew what else. No wonder things turned out the way they did for her. She put up with me, though. I couldn't keep my hands off her.

I came to resent it eventually, her Molly Bloom-ness, her yeastiness, the warm-dough sensation and odor of her. She was my earth mother, the moon goddess. But when it came down to protecting our daughter, she proved as helpless as the rest of us.

Our marriage counselor thought our postmortem sexual disconnect constituted a natural reaction to losing Miriam. He told us he'd be surprised if we were still sleeping together at this point. He kept telling us over and over that Miriam's illness wasn't our fault, as if he could convince us by sheer repetition. He seemed to be waiting for it to hit us like some sort of epiphany.

I tried to agree with him. Of course it wasn't our fault, but she'd died on our watch, hadn't she?

If Miriam hadn't gotten sick, would we still be together? Not for our daughter's sake—Gd knows she had already outgrown us both by her tenth birthday. Still … being a family moors you, makes you appreciate the simple security of having a home, a place to come to at the end of the day where you can put aside the burden of being creative, sensitive, and wise. A place where you can drink milk out of the carton and scratch your ass. It's hard to give that up.

What did I see in Tamar? I mean, really? That's always the part that's harder to describe. Everything I say about our relationship makes sense, but none of it resonates. I could tell you she had a great rolling chuckle of a laugh. That she didn't suffer fools gladly, except for me. That she would coax a spider onto a piece of paper and carry it out of the house but scream death threats at the screen when Nixon rambled incoherently though his State of the Union address. Well, I guess a picture emerges.

Makiko has a boyish figure and a boyish personality, too, in a lot of ways. Forget any residual fantasies about Geisha submissiveness. Makiko always knows what she wants. I suppose, like all sixties acid trippers, I yearned for a certain Zen-like Kung Fu serenity, but I didn't want to do all the hard work. I thought it would be easier to screw my way to quasi-enlightenment. You may say I'm a dreamer—but I'm not the only one.

Makiko is skinny. Her shoulders are slender. She has small breasts and a flat ass that gets lost in a pair of jeans. I don't know what it is about her that drives me crazy, and it's not just me. I can't go anywhere with her that some guy doesn't start hitting on her.

Is that all we men want, to make it with some prepubescent wood nymph? Where's the biological imperative in that? Why do we want to waste our genes on someone who looks too young even to have her period? So this is what bothered me while I sat there drinking beer and waiting for her to come home. How come my Makiko looked a lot like the little girls in Viereck's paintings?

CHAPTER FIVE

It had gone past seven by the time she wandered in. By then, I'd finished off the better part of a six-pack. It was enough to make me a little lazy about trudging back to Herman's apartment but still revved up enough to run on about what I'd found in his trunk. I described the work in such a disjointed way that it didn't really help my cause. I could tell that Makiko, the Pepto-Bismol treasure map episode fresh in her mind, couldn't be easily seduced. She half-paid polite attention while she made us some BLTs (haute cuisine for us in the middle of the week). I couldn't keep my mouth shut about the pictures, and when mayonnaise started to dribble down the side of my chin, Makiko called my bluff.

"Okay, let's go have a look," she said.

It had begun to drizzle, and the fine mist produced hallucinogenic Van Gogh halos around the streetlights. Crossing Webster Avenue, I felt we should be carrying torches, like the townspeople who flush out Frankenstein's monster. Inside Herman's building, the hallway glowered, dingy and underlit, like any other semi-slum where bulbs burned out and weren't replaced. I looked at our property with a critical, building-inspector's eye and felt ashamed. Makiko felt the same way.

"We ought to put in some brighter overheads," she said as our shadows hip-hopped menacingly up the stairwell.

Herman's apartment proved no better. The retrofitted gas chandelier could only support fifteen-watt bulbs. The only spot with steady light was over the center of his work table. Herman had installed a swing-arm work lamp he'd salvaged from the trash. Some of its springs had broken loose, and he'd jury-rigged the arms into place with—what else? Duct tape.

I sat Makiko down in his chair, pulled out the trunk, and started serving her the manuscript, soup to nuts, as it were. By the salad course, she had seen enough.

Makiko pushed herself back and shook her head slowly. "That sneaky little bastard," she said. "I bet he never slept. How do you suppose he did them? These little girls look as if they were drawn by Disney animators. They're fantastic. There's also something definitely Japanese about this stuff. They have the feel of Meiji-period woodblocks."

Over time, that aspect of his work has become more and more significant. Herman seems to have presaged our love affair with Japanese manga and anime. His work surfs on a ragged edge between comic book and fine art. The subject matter, too, appeals to some distorted Far Eastern sensibility, though you'd have a hard time getting anyone to admit it.

"Herman never said anything to you about this stuff being here?" she asked me.

I shook my head.

"He couldn't possibly have forgotten. It must have taken him half a lifetime."

Makiko refolded an eight-foot scroll back along its accordion pleats. Already, the primitive binding showed signs of coming apart, as if Herman's work had never meant to see the light of day.

"What do you think we should do with them?" I asked her. "I can't bring them over to the nursing home. They'd crucify him if they saw what he'd been up to."

"You know—technically they're ours," she reminded me. "They're pretty much abandoned property. And anyway, he said you could have them."

"What's that supposed to mean?"

"We ought to show them to someone. They might have some value." She turned to me, and I saw dollar signs rolling across her pupils, as if she were a character in a Warner Bros. cartoon.

In truth, her mercenary approach didn't bother me that much. As artists, the idea of making money selling our creations didn't seem strange at all. It's well within *our* realm of the real.

"This whole outsider art thing is starting to catch on," she reminded me. "There're dealers now traveling all over the South looking for stuff like this. Your Herman might be a major find."

"You think it's really any good?" I asked her.

"Good? I'm not sure in what context that word applies," she told me. "But they're something."

For a few months, we kept my discovery to ourselves. But art, like murder, will out. Herman had kept his work a secret for thirty years, but once I got hold of his novel and the illustrations, it was only a matter of time before I had to share them with the world.

To this day, I'm pretty sure that's what Herman wanted. The *Realms of the Unreal* might have been his own gyroscopic centering vision, but Herman must have known he had a strange and terrible talent, and he wanted the world to know about it. Why else would he have sent me over to clean out his apartment?

Till the very end, I couldn't bring myself to haul his trunk out of there. In the back of my mind, I knew that Herman's apartment with its clutter and his oddball collections were as much a part of his art as the scrolls and paintings. His rooms were a conceptualization, a performance piece. Everything in them contributed to the mystery and power of his creations.

I went back to see him right away. I had to tell him that his work had been found. I wanted him to know that I saw him in a new light, though I guess if I were him, it would have pissed me off. Before I'd discovered his trove, he'd been just some crazy janitor, the town idiot. Now, because of his creative efforts, I'd elevated him to my equal. Is that the worth of a man—a stack of photos and a plastic lemon juice container?

Since my first visit, he'd gone downhill. They had him propped up in bed, remnants of breakfast staining the front of his pajamas. He dozed off while I told him about how I'd found the *Realms*, and I had to prod him awake.

"Gosh, Herman, I never knew you were such an artist. Your stuff is wonderful."

He frowned and shrugged his shoulders as if I'd pointed out a fact so widely accepted that I didn't need to bring it up.

"Yeah," he said. "I know."

"Any idea what you want me to do with all of it?"

Herman looked out the window and didn't say anything for a few seconds.

"It hasn't rained since Thursday," he said finally. Then, while I sat there, he drifted off again. His breathing turned harsh and wheezy, his lips turning a raw-liver blue. I could tell the old man had one foot planted on heaven's front lawn. One way or another, soon his life's work would belong to me.

I felt like a man who has discovered a gold mine but fears bringing his nuggets back to Fairbanks till he can nail down the claim. Abandoned property or not, I didn't feel that Herman's work belonged to me. I hadn't started thinking of his work in monetary terms, at least not out loud, but I knew they were valuable.

Any successful artist thinks about things in ways any accountant would understand. Terms like "cash flow," "assets and liability," "variable vs. fixed costs," "net gross residuals" flowed off my tongue as easily as talking about composition, f-stops, and exposure times. Not that my photography produced much income anymore. By the time I'd stumbled on Herman's treasure trove, I hadn't picked up a camera since our daughter's death.

We weren't starving by any means. I'd wrangled tenure at CIFA. As my creative energies waned, my real estate interests took up more of my time. I'd developed a developer's way of looking at things, always calculating and totaling things up as I went along. Stopped at a street light, I would look at a building, wonder at the cost, and consider the potential of the neighborhood. How many units could it be converted into?

So, given my current frame of mind (and I'm certainly not proud of this), I began to wonder if Herman's work might have market value. At the time, our cash flow had hit a small speed bump. Nothing disastrous, just the overextension that buyers and sellers get into from time to time. A property we'd sold hadn't cleared as we'd expected, and we were stuck making double payments. I don't remember the details, but it worried me enough to ruin a night's sleep.

As I lay awake, mentally listing my liquid assets, the *Realms of the Unreal* popped into my head. Not that I would—and then the thought came unbidden, as enlightened self-interest often does—at least not while Herman was alive, I told myself. Then I started wondering how much time he had left.

Could I make him famous?

My inner imp conjured up a tableau. I imagined Herman as a guest on the *Tonight Show*. Here he comes from behind the curtain, cringing in the Klieg lights and the unexpected, tentative applause. Leonine Leno bounds across the stage, towering over him, and pumps his hand. The makeup people have put him back in his usual costume: homeless war veteran.

Herman would take old flannel shirts and rip the sleeves out at the shoulders. It made him look like some geriatric gangbanger. Just give him a pack of Marlboros rolled up in the sleeve of his undershirt. Add some baggy pants, his brogans with a bandage of duct tape holding on the sole, and you'd have the gestalt. That's the way they'd trick him out for Leno. They'd need him to look the part.

Herman waves shyly at the crowd who's trying to sound enthusiastic. They think he must be some kind of comedian. The starlet *du jour*, with her nipples Scotch-taped to the inside of her half-open blouse, gets up from the hot seat and tries to give him an air-kiss before she moves down a slot. Herman mutters and pulls his head away. It gives Jay a chance to start in.

"So Herman, how you doin', buddy?"

"I'm great, Jay. It's great to be here. Man, I've never been out to LA before. This place is like Disneyland. It's going 24/7."

"Yeah, Disneyland. I guess that's a place you know a lot about. Those pictures of yours—WOW! All I can say is, 'What were you thinking?' The critics say your work has a unique style that pays homage to the world of animation while expressing your own twisted vision of a private planet in chaos. Let me tell you, I've seen your stuff over at Zemeckis's house. He's an enormous fan of yours, by the way, and it looks like … gosh, I don't even know if we can show the people what it looks like! This ain't HBO."

Leno turns aside and asks if they can put up of a few of Herman's pictures. They pop up behind the desk and flash by in silence. Even the defanged, dumbed-down pieces they've selected are right on the edge for late-night TV. The audience doesn't know how to react. Up in the balcony there are a few scattered boos that haven't been cued.

Who'd had the big idea to let this guy on, Leno wonders. Where do these clowns in the production department think they work? Effing PBS? They cut back to the set, and Leno forces himself to continue.

"All I can say is—*whoo boy*. It's like Walt's doin' acid. Magic 'shrooms— he must be spinnin'. You're lucky they haven't sued your ass off. Any-who—having a major retrospective at the Los Angeles Museum of Contemporary Art. That's pretty hot stuff for a guy who grew up in the Illinois Home for Feeble-Minded Children. I understand that Spielberg and Zemeckis have a bidding war going for the rights for your life story. Why do you think people are so affected by your work?"

"I don't know. I never really intended for anyone to see it but me." Herman looks around for an escape or for someone to bite. For a long moment, he is unable to go on. He's never had to explain or defend himself before.

"You have some pretty interesting weather out here," he says at last. "These Pacific highs you get, they're not at all like the lake effect in Chicago. Those brush fires, they're pretty interesting too. Like Glandelinian war storms."

Herman looks down in his lap, but the hands that typed fifteen thousand pages of his single-spaced novel are finally still. Normally unflappable, Leno looks ill at ease. Somebody's head is gonna roll for this. Desperate, he looks up: twenty-two seconds till they go to commercial.

Finally, he says, "I mean … boy, oh boy. Look, Herms, I'm just gonna come right out and ask you. What is it with the extra equipment you drew on all those naked little girls?"

CHAPTER SIX

The morning after my *Tonight Show* fantasy, I knew I had to show the paintings to some disinterested third party. But whom? The normal yardsticks used by Chicago's stodgy art critics couldn't be trusted to do Herman justice. In the Midwest during the seventies, outsider art was still considered, well, outsider. This wasn't New York or LA. I felt sure one of our local scribes would go out of his way to burst my bubble. I had been part of the Chicago art scene long enough to have made a few enemies, and there were people out there who wouldn't mind seeing me made a fifteen-minute fool.

On the other hand, I had friends and colleagues who respected my judgment far *too* much. Anything I dragged in front of them would get a free pass. After all, I'd become, if not famous, at least locally known, the classic biggish fish in a not so smallish pond. Between the ReaLemon bottle and my photos of the Chicago riots, I was an icon. Anyone could describe me from across a room: "See that big burly guy with the beard? He teaches design at CIFA. He designed that cute little ReaLemon bottle." I could have shown them a freeze-dried dog turd, and they would have mounted it on a pedestal.

Of course, the real reason why I couldn't show Herman's work to anyone who knew my own was a lot more devious. Even though we worked in completely different media with a different aesthetic agenda,

I couldn't escape the nagging realization that, by whatever yardstick you wanted to use, this untaught quasi lunatic exceeded my meager talents. After more or less phoning it in since Miriam's death, I couldn't face being known primarily as the man who had discovered Herman Viereck.

No, I wasn't going to show his stuff to anyone in Chicago's incestuous art world. If I felt the need to take Herman out for a test drive, I wanted somebody fresh behind the wheel, a new set of eyes. But did it make sense to pick my analyst?

In retrospect it seems so transparently pathologic that I can't understand how I tricked myself into doing it. It seems foolish now. But at the time, the more I thought about it, the more Adrian Holm seemed like an ideal choice.

He came from Glasgow originally, and how he'd ended up in Dallas, Texas, for twenty-five years remained something of a mystery. His reasons for relocating to Chicago remained similarly murky as well, but his diplomas and licenses looked real enough.

Holm had picked up a Texas twang, and when combined with his Scottish drawl, he sounded adorable; playing his dual accents like a DJ with twin turntables, ramping up one or damping down the other to suit the situation.

The way I'd become his patient proved typical of the messy way I've lived my life. No friend recommended him. He wasn't on a preferred list of HMO providers, and he wasn't somebody's brother-in-law. I didn't even pick him at random out of the phone book. My meeting him fit the pattern for the Chicago arts scene back then when it was a lot smaller club. People didn't just collect your work; they collected the artist as well. I met Adrian when he bought a few of my photographs at the Chicago Arts Fair.

He came back at the end of the show to pick up his prints, and I happened to be in the booth. He introduced himself, and we had a few drinks.

I was flattered. He told me how much he admired my work—the deep psychological insights I captured through the lens. He admired the courage it took to confront my subjects, one-on-one in real time.

They were mostly bums and street people who were too shell-shocked to protest when I shoved Mr. Pentax in their faces.

He took pictures too, he shyly admitted.

After that, he came to our open houses and student exhibits at the institute. He bought another picture or two, and I gave him the "good guy" rate. Eventually he dragged out his portfolio and asked me if I'd take a look.

I've noticed that a lot of doctors are technically good with the camera, but they tend to shy away from anything that tackles the human condition. In fact, it's rare to find a human being in any of their pictures. They like to shoot branches dripping icicles, shadows against a brick wall, or seascapes clouded in mist. I used to think they avoided photographing people because they had seen too much human suffering and were trying to get away from it. Now, after seeing a phalanx of white coats during Miriam's illness, I wonder if they allow themselves to feel anything in the first place.

He'd done a lot of high contrast shots of foreboding landscapes—gnarled trees, rock formations, abandoned barns. His work showed technical skill, but was derivative. Frankly, the whole Ansel Adams thing gets on my nerves. He had a feel for composition. But then, once a picture has been blown up, cropped, matted, and placed in a nice frame, almost anyone can take a nice photograph.

I told him I thought he had promise. He traded me for one, and I hung it up in my office. That's what friends are for.

I'd started seeing him professionally after Miriam. Then, after a brief hiatus, I went back during the divorce. At the time, none of my friends dared to confront me about my sullen moodiness, my increasing social withdrawal, punctuated by sarcastic and hurtful lashings out.

No concerned committee of colleagues came to me and told me that I'd become too harsh on my students, that I'd made young women cry, and that some were afraid to take my classes. At least I hadn't taken to sleeping with them.

That came later.

Nobody I knew had the guts to sit me down and say, "Nate, you need help dealing with this."

Actually, given the circumstances, I thought I was dealing with "this" just fine. Maybe too fine?

I started seeing Holm because I didn't feel that my feelings were "griefy" enough. I felt dead and blocked. I needed to suffer more. Somehow I'd cheated the grief process, and I knew I'd have to pay for it later—only at some usurious cosmic interest rate.

The problem I had in dealing with Miriam's death mirrored what haunted my later work. I'd had an innate instinct for capturing the right millisecond of an expression, the irony beyond the grief, the sadness behind the joy, the faint whiff of repressed rage, some intangible quality that made my photographs stand out, and now I'd lost it. My photos lacked sufficient emotional depth. I might be good at fooling people, but I felt something was lacking, somewhere my heart wouldn't let my fingers go.

It wasn't the technical stuff, the lighting or the framing. It wasn't the craft. The mechanics of photography have always come easily for me. I'm a naturally gifted draftsman. I've got good color sense and a flair for composition.

As a child, the ability to draw impresses the grownups and your classmates. By age ten, I could freehand a wicked three-quarter view of a P-51 Mustang. I could do Elmer Fudd or Bugs Bunny and a spot-on caricature of our fifth grade teacher with buck teeth like General Tojo. Before long, teachers and my family began predicting great things for me.

I never strayed from the path. Even switching to photography became a calculated move. By the time I started art school in the fifties, representational art had slipped out of fashion. No one cared about drawing anymore. Of course I could have gone abstract like everyone else, but that came easy too. Moving blocks of pigment around felt like cheating.

The line lost its magic for me. I reached a point where I stopped growing. Instead of completely abandoning art, I switched to industrial design and photography, a path that produced a plastic bottle of lemon juice and photo spreads in *LIFE*.

That should have been enough, and it was until Herman came along. Herman couldn't draw much more than a few stick figures and a Brazilian dragon in profile, but he had the passion, the juice, that I had lost. Herman had duende, the great poet Garcia Lorca's creative fire. My father had gone to hear him lecture about duende when he'd come to New York in the thirties. Dad talked about it as if he'd had an audience with the pope. Growing up, Garcia Lorca was a god in our house.

But deunde remained hard for me to come by. When it came to my struggles over grieving my daughter's death, I saw my frozen emotions as another manifestation of my failure as an artist: just another uptight, emotionally crippled male who didn't know how to cry.

Maybe I didn't know how good I had it.

Naturally, once I started sitting on Holm's couch, our relationship changed. He might say it evolved. I'm not so sure. It wasn't that I traded him my photographs for analysis, but essentially it became the same thing.

It was a bad idea, all in all. I don't think he could help resenting my abilities, even as I sat there and denigrated them. It colored our "therapeutic" relationship. No matter how touchy-feely things were back then, no matter how much Holm liked to talk about the archetype of the wounded healer, no matter how he liked to describe the psychoanalytic process as the meeting of two souls, of souls grown deep, someone had to take charge of our sessions. Someone had to steer the ship, and I never knew who manned the helm.

Of course, I see now that all his talk about "soul-blending" constituted a folie à deux he perpetuated—and I lapped up like a dog. He made me believe we were working on my problems as friends. But underneath his sheep's clothing (English tweed with leather elbow patches, black-ribbed turtleneck), he was the same uptight, over-controlling bastard they all are. How could he help it? I found out his father had been a Presbyterian minister in some Glasgow suburb. The apple doesn't fall ...

I saw him, off and on, for about a year. It was like going to see my chiropractor. I felt better while Holm worked on me, but the next day, the pain returned, and I'd have to go back. After months of coaching, he finally got me to break down in his office and cry. We both looked on it as a major therapeutic breakthrough.

It's true, I didn't cry for that whole first year and, outside of the one sob-fest in Holm's office, not much after that. The ache of losing Miriam became familiar too quickly, too much a part of my every day. After a while, I couldn't dredge up the immediacy of her death, no matter how much I longed for an old-fashioned show of grief.

There were charitable explanations to explain my lack of outward grieving, the usual things people say to explain a seeming lack of emotion in the grief stricken. Friends said I was in denial or stuffing or being strong for Tamar. It's all BS.

The naked truth is that after two years of living with Miriam's leukemia, a monster that had taken over everything in our lives replacing our daughter so I couldn't see a little girl—just medicine bottles, tubes, and an assortment of once strange and meaningless numbers that had come to rule our lives. Having "Leuk" out of our house felt like an immense relief. Along with Miriam's death came a feeling of release, a feeling that wracked me with so much guilt that I couldn't separate the two emotions— mourning her death and my feeling of liberation.

After two years of helplessly witnessing her inevitable decline, following the grim stock market of her rising and falling white cell counts, staying up all night treating her fevers, making frantic phone calls to her doctor who was never available, trying to explain things to some grumpy "on call" guy over the phone, the red-light-running trips to the emergency room … all that was gone! How could I admit that part of me felt nothing but relief?

She'd disappeared, and I could go to work and not jump every time the phone rang. I could go to bed and not lie there semi-paralyzed listening to the sound of her retching from the chemo. "It's okay, Dad. Go back to sleep. I'll be fine."

You had to be grateful to anyone who could help you make some crude sense of these conflicting emotions of grief and relief. For all his faults, I needed Adrian Holm.

So when the time came to introduce Herman Viereck to the world, I chose my erstwhile therapist to play Lord Carnarvon to my Henry Carter. By picking him, I knew I'd selected the one person I knew who would "get" Viereck, the one person who I could rely on to be genuinely blown away.

I couldn't afford rejection. Herman's work almost felt as if it were my own. So I stacked the deck. I packed the house. I put a ringer in the lineup.

***

"Nate! I haven't heard from you in months. *Que pasa, amigo?*" Adrian roared into the phone.

"I've got something I want to show you," I told him. "I think you're a guy who'd appreciate it."

I kept him in the dark about the details. I enjoyed this bit of showmanship. I'd worked with enough marketing gurus and advertising execs over the years. A little well-placed hype never hurt anyone's chances. I told him to meet me at the institute, and we drove over to Webster in my old Saab. He looked at Herman's building with faux disgust.

"Geez, Nate. When are you going to fix this place up? The whole neighborhood is in transition," he lectured me as I led him up the rickety stairs. "Why don't you condo this place out?"

Just what I needed: real estate advice from my shrink. Well, everybody thought he was Donald Trump back then. We stopped at Herman's door, and I fumbled with the keys. I'd cleared away enough trash by then so that I could get the door open. I let him in ahead of me. He paused and gave the room a once-over.

I'd staged the room for him, lining up a bunch of the Pepto-Bismol bottles and dusting off Viereck's collection of dime-store Virgin Marys. At the center of the co-joined tables, in front of Herman's battered desk chair, I'd plunked down the blivit bomb—all fifteen thousand pages of the *Realms of the Unreal*.

"Wow," he said after looking around for a few moments.

"Your diagnosis, Doctor?"

"How long was this guy up here?" he asked

"Over thirty years. He came with the building."

"OCD," he said, "obsessive-compulsive disorder, classic packrat behavior. I bet the guy never threw away anything in his life."

I hung back as he walked down the narrow defile. I wanted to give him a taste of the thrill of discovery. He picked up one of the Pepto bottles and read Viereck's collecting information. He stared back at me, and his eyebrows went up a notch.

"There's some weird powerful energy in this room," he said, and then his hand brushed across the manuscript. He studied the title for a few seconds and then flipped it open at random and then began to read out loud.

> "All at once the sky clouded over and ear-splitting claps of terrible thunder shook the ground. At the same time, there were fearsome jolts of the most powerful lightning, seven million volts of pure electric energy, hotter than the surface of the sun, that lit everything up as bright as day.
>
> "The Seven Vivian Sisters ran and ran through the forest. They jumped over fallen trees and crawled through ditches filled with the foulest water. Flashes of lightning lit the ground all around them. Overhead, there were terrible exploding noises and the cracking of enormous tree limbs as the lightning hit the tops of the trees. Soon the poor running girls were covered in bits of bark and leaves. Their little dresses were plastered against their skin, which was all puckered with goose bumps from the fearsome cold rain.
>
> "Behind them, as sheets and sheets of rain soaked them to the bone, the Glandelinian EXTERMINATION SQUAD was rapidly gaining on them. The Glandelinian solders had long Royal Enfield rifles with gleamingly sharp bayonets that could rip through any armor and certainly pierce the tender flesh of the little girls so that gushes of blood would pour out of their mouths and stomachs and onto the rain-soaked ground."

He flipped a hundred pages or so and resumed reading. To my ear, it didn't sound as if anything had changed. The Vivian Sisters were still running for their lives. His voice faded after a few lines. He closed the book, as if he were Pandora shutting the box. He turned and gave me a quizzical look.

"Is it all like this?" he asked.

"As far as I can tell. It would be near impossible to read the whole thing. It's over fifteen thousand pages, single-spaced."

He shook his head in awe. Viereck had broken Holm's façade. Then he noticed the colored paper sticking out at regular intervals and opened the book to one of Herman's illustrations.

Vivid as some of his prose is, Herman never would have made it on his literary gifts. In all the years I've been around his stuff, I've never gotten through more than a few hundred pages all told. There are a lot of people who have been more committed to the project than I. Adrian, for one, claims he's read both the typed and handwritten versions of the book, looking for things Herman changed. But it's the pictures that are Herman's compelling icons. He unfolded the first one, and I could see his jaw drop. If I'd had any doubts about Herman's universal appeal, they were gone in that instant.

"Unbelievable, fantastic, seminal, archetypical."

The superlatives dripped from Holm's mouth like a badly leaking faucet. After about five minutes, he shook his head as if he'd chugalugged a half-quart of vodka and it had caught up with him.

Naturally, I told him the story. Only then, when I tried to put things into a coherent sequence, I realized how many details of Herman's life I knew nothing about.

"There's a lot of psychopathology here," Holm said. He'd unfolded one of the longer pieces and began tracing over the hermaphroditic figures with an idle fingertip.

"Obviously, a very sexually confused background, with a lot of ambivalent and repressed feelings toward the opposite sex."

He pointed at a figure in the foreground, a naked ten-year-old girl with angelic features. She looked as if Herman had cribbed her from a Sunday supplement or a Sears catalogue. The only disturbing feature— once you got past the added-on penis and testicles—was an elaborate pair of ram's horns that sprouted from her hair like transmuted pigtails.

"What do you make of that?" he asked me.

Obviously, I didn't know. I thought to tell him that I'd ask Herman about them the next time I saw him, but something stopped me. I realized that I hadn't yet told Adrian that Herman was still alive, and now some instinct made me hold back. In these last few minutes, his whole attitude had changed. An hour ago, he had acted as if he'd done me an indulgent favor by coming up to the apartment. Now, I had the uneasy feeling that he approached the work as if he'd made the discovery.

"I don't know. Maybe they're not supposed to be quite human," I told him. "Did you see his library? He read a lot of science fiction, all the heavyweights—Heinlein, Asimov. I'm surprised at how well read he was."

Holm nodded, the way people do when they're not listening. He didn't want to hear anybody's theories but his own. "Do you think I could take some of this back to my flat for a few days?" he asked me.

I shook my head politely no, but the look in my eyes said, "No fucking way." Then aloud, I added, "I don't think so, Adrian. I want to keep everything in the apartment."

"You know, there's a lot of interest in the art of the insane, especially in Europe. I'd like to spend some time going through this material. It might make an interesting monograph."

"Would you really call this guy insane?" I asked him.

Holm flipped through the pages of the *Realms* till he found something he liked.

> "*The Glandelinian troopers had sixteen-inch-long bayonets affixed to their rifles, made out of the hardest steel. They chased the group of little slave children down into a ravine where only the faintest light had worked its way through to the forest floor. Then the lieutenant of the platoon ordered his men to stab the little girls, which they did over and over, hundreds of times till the forest floor was like a swamp of human blood …*"

Holm closed the book and gave me the look of a prosecuting attorney who had just handed the jury a gun tagged "Exhibit A."

"The case bears further study," he said.

I couldn't argue with him there.

CHAPTER SEVEN

I've been living with Herman's stuff now for over twenty years, and the shock has worn off. Part of the unnerving experience of looking at his paintings is how benign and pastoral all his horrific scenes are. It's the faces he cribbed from the popular media. No matter what is happening on the page, his little girls seem to float serenely above the action, as free from perversion as the moppet in the Coppertone ad with the dog pulling her swimsuit off her ass.

After a while, if you have his work hanging in your hallway (I can't really imagine putting one up in a living room), you begin to feel nostalgic about it; like a remembered illustration out of a favorite book you had as a child, perhaps something from Maurice Sendak or Beatrice Potter. It pays, every now and then, to step back and look at his work as if seeing it for the first time, just to appreciate the true nature of Herman's demons.

Take the choking motif for instance. He drew hundreds of little girls graphically being choked to death, their eyes bulging, their mouths open, tongues lolling. Some of the early ones, done before he developed his technique of collage and appropriating commercial images, are unbelievably crude, a schoolboy's graffiti. In these early drawings, he makes the same mistakes all my less talented students make. He has problems with the three-quarter view, problems with the shape of the head and the placement of the eyes. All his self-drawn characters are low-browed; missing half their skulls, and look like microcephalic Neanderthals.

"How many times do I have to say it? The head is an *egg*, people." The eyes are in the *middle* of the face, not up near the top. Why does it take so long to get it right? Even Van Gogh, if you look at his early work, has these truncated heads seemingly missing half their skulls. He wasn't a natural either, but he learned.

The difference is that Viereck couldn't be bothered with the long process of learning to draw. Van Gogh was an artist's artist: the interplay of color and light mattered to him. Perspective mattered to him, especially when he broke the rules. Right up to his tortured end, he stayed acutely conscious of everything he did on the canvas.

Herman? He just wanted to tell his story. He wasn't concerned with improving his talents or abilities, only with the final product. He needed to get the Vivian Girls out of the confines of his skull and onto the page. He'd cut any corner, use any trick he could think of—the images out of Sears catalogues he Xeroxed at the local Rexall store, the soldiers he cut out of comic books, the tanks and guns he pasted in and colored when he needed a background for a battle scene. It was so Hollywood of him, so like Disney or Lucas, any of them: if you can't do it yourself, hire it done.

Herman had a specific idea of how he wanted his work to look. He needed to impart a certain slick commercial quality to his little girls. For all his Germanic foreignness, for all his seeming isolation from the mainstream, the *Realms* isn't a gothic, sci-fi fairytale. His Vivian Girls come right out of America's heartland, and when he couldn't get the figures looking quite right by himself, he appropriated them.

He stole from people like me: talented hacks, people who took the test on the back of a matchbook ("Can you draw this?") and passed with flying colors. He took our schlock and turned it into fine art.

In Viereck's work the saccharine commercial images of American popular culture breathed new life. Pawing through the trash in his over-sized trench coat, he seemed removed from our world and our culture. Yet in everything he did, he stayed connected. In his own weird way, he had his finger on the pulse. That's part of what people find irresistible about him.

***

I met him at the movies once, a re-release of *Snow White and the Seven Dwarfs*. What else? I'd brought my daughter and her friend, Charlotte. We were at the candy counter stocking up for the second half of the double feature. There he stood ahead of us, buying a box of Milk Duds. I hoped he wouldn't notice us, but Miriam called out to him.

"Hey, Mr. Viereck! I didn't know you liked cartoons."

How did he react to the sight of my children, a man whose daily sound track screamed with the torture and death of a thousand vestal virgins? Had he ever heard a real child's musical laugh? Suddenly, there they were in front of him, two giggly ten-year-olds, irrepressible and full of life. It made me smile foolishly just to be with them. All those years, Miriam lived across the street from him. I now know that she lived as part of his fantasies, but back then I didn't have a clue as to what went on inside his tortured head.

He turned away from the counter, his eyes shifting to avoid looking at us. For a second, I thought he'd run out the theater, but he forced himself to walk toward us at the end of the candy line and say hello.

"Hi, Herman, are you enjoying the movie?" I asked him. He looked at me with that sidelong look of his. "Enjoying" must have been a foreign word to him.

"It's useful," he said. "Those Disney guys have a lot of good ideas, but they don't work on their skies enough. They use the same clouds over and over. It's like they don't understand the weather. They don't appreciate how complex it is."

I should have known then that there was more afoot than Herman killing an afternoon. Herman didn't waste his time sitting in the dark, listening to dwarfs sing "Hi ho, hi ho." It was he who was off to work. He went to the movies to scope out the competition, looking for clues, trying to find an edge.

Take his long, panoramic scrolls; it's easy to appreciate them as frames in a movie. I understand now just how much he absorbed and reprocessed from any culture or age that he thought he could use: Chinese scroll paintings, Japanese woodblocks, early newsreels, animation cels, even the Cro-Magnon cave paintings of Lascaux. It's one of his work's most enigmatic properties—how dialed in to the human aesthetic he could be, and how he perverted it to his own ends.

Miriam and Charlotte were studying him without the slightest trace of apprehension. He wasn't much taller than they, and I could see they were both trying not to crack up laughing at the comical little guy. He glanced at them for a second, and I thought I saw one of his feet start to tap uncontrollably against the floral carpet of the old Roxy Theater.

"Hello, little girls," he said, and held out his box of Milk Duds, "Do you want some candy?"

"Thank you Herman, but we're going to get some popcorn. They've eaten enough junk already." He didn't look disappointed as he turned to go back into the theater.

"Be careful going home. They said it wasn't going to rain, but it feels like there should be a big front moving in. The weather men, they're all a bunch of clowns."

CHAPTER EIGHT

O nce I showed Herman's art to Adrian, everything changed. The fact that Herman had kept his work secret made his conundrum mine by proxy.

It's a Zen *koan*. If a painting exists, but no one but the painter has ever seen it, is it art? Is it the act of creation or the sharing of that creation that makes something art? What were the *Realms of the Unreal* if they went unobserved? It constituted my own version of the uncertainty principle. What is the interaction between the work and the observer? Didn't the act of my looking at Viereck's work change it—just as much as it had changed me?

I'm a teacher. It's my job to discover talent, nurture it, and make it grow. The more I thought about it, the more obvious it became. He'd wanted me to find the *Realms* because he knew I would be able to show it to the world.

All of which makes the fact that, within a month of letting Holm into Viereck's apartment, I sold off the first of Herman's paintings no less difficult to justify. I like to think it wasn't avarice, but if someone else thought the paintings were worth money, that would reaffirm my own judgment of Herman's talent. But then, people are always coming up with complex explanations about why they do things that line their pockets.

I could blame it on Makiko. She blabbed about the books and the paintings to her friends. Not that we'd formally agreed to keep the *Realms* a secret. I just thought we had some kind of mutual understanding about them.

"I told Jeff about the paintings," she told me one night after she came back from a rehearsal. "He and Linda want to see them,"

Jeff played viola in her quartet. Of the four of them, he owned the Amati and bankrolled their never quite break-even recordings. He'd inherited an obscene amount of money from some stolid Midwestern family enterprise, carbon blacking or chrome plating, I can't remember which. By the time he befriended us, he'd outgrown his love of Porsches and racing six meters on Lake Michigan and had developed a weakness for anything Baroque.

I'd been up to his pied-à-terre a bunch of times. He had a Rubens. True, it had been de-accessioned from the Victoria and Albert Museum, and it had a slight water stain, but still. He had it hanging over their couch with Queen Victoria's cartouche in the right-hand corner.

Once, he and his wife had gone with us to an exhibit at the Chicago Museum of Art, a major retrospective, Thomas Hart Benton, I think. Just being in the museum made Jeff antsy. He kept glaring at the labels under the paintings and making a clicking sound with his tongue.

"There're no bloody price tags," he said, finally.

Jeff thought Makiko was the cat's pajamas, but he copped a condescending attitude toward my work.

"It's just not my medium," he apologized, after I'd reluctantly pulled out a few photos. Well maybe it wasn't, but that's the kind of comment you can't help resenting.

His wife, Linda? She played along. They had no children.

"Who would want to bring anyone into the world to be exposed to this madness?" she'd told me, before she learned about Miriam. When the four of us were together, we usually drank a lot—it helped, up to a point.

Given Jeff and Linda's Eurocentric world view, I couldn't think of anyone less likely to be impressed by Herman Viereck's primitive draftsmanship and kitschy appropriation of popular culture (not to mention the nascent kiddy porn). But I was wrong.

"When I told him about what you'd found, Jeff got real excited. He really liked the story about you mapping out the Pepto bottles." She chuckled. "Nathan and the Pepto-Bismol treasure map" had become family folklore.

"I thought Jeff wouldn't even look at anything newer than Ingres," I said.

"Yeah, I know, but he's fascinated by the art of the insane. He thinks all crazy people are incipient geniuses."

"Herman's not insane," I almost barked at her. I didn't know why it had become important to me to keep making this distinction between slightly mad and full-blown bat-shit crazy, but I had my tipping point with the old man.

Makiko knew by now not to argue. Herman had stayed up all night talking to himself, loud nasty arguments with Gd where he took both roles—Herman's, a squeaky falsetto; Gd's, a sarcastic bass. That was enough for her to spell c-r-a-z-y. Well, my grandmother had a one-on-one relationship with Gd too. Couldn't Makiko cut the guy some slack?

"They're coming to dinner on Friday. I thought after we could go over there and you could show them around."

I grumbled about it, but secretly I looked forward to it. After the big reaction from Holm, I was interested in seeing what other people thought. I knew that the *Realms of the Unreal* was the kind of thing that would annoy a guy like Jeff to no end. I wanted to hear him try to tear Herman's work to pieces.

They brought a nice California Cab and a dry Spanish sherry for after. Makiko amped dinner up with a few genuine Nisei family recipes. We drank the Cab and started in on saki.

By dessert, the four of us were feeling mellow. With only a little pleading on Jeff's part, we kept hold of our glasses and traipsed across the street. I had this image of a group of upper-class Victorians on their way to a séance.

In keeping with the mood, Herman's apartment at night loomed suitably ghostly. There hadn't been this many people in the room at one time in fifty years. On narrow shelves over the windows, Herman's collection of Madonnas and crucifixes gazed malevolently down on us. Jeff got into the spirit.

"Jeezus, will you look at this place. This guy must have had some kind of serious obsessive disorder. Remember those two brothers in New York, famous gynecologists? When they died, there was so much crap no one could walk into the place."

"I don't think it's quite the same thing. Herman wasn't a hoarder. I think he saw all this as raw material." Linda walked down to the far end and started reading the book titles on Herman's shelves. He was far better read than he ever let on, and that was before I found his extensive Civil War library tucked in a box against the far wall.

I stalled around for a while and let Jeff go on about "the vibe" coming off the place. I got the feeling that he might have read up about art brut before coming to dinner, just so he'd have something clever to say. Finally, to shut him up, I reached under the bed and pulled out the cheap tin trunk that held the heart of Viereck's darkness. I laid the *Realms of the Unreal* down on the center of the long table, and the thud of its dead weight shut him up.

"There it is," I said. "A little light reading."

Linda came back from the bookcase, and I stepped aside so that she could share the shock of seeing it for the first time. I felt an odd sense of proprietorship. I had to remind myself that they weren't looking at my own creations.

The two of them were a paradigm of everyone who has ever seen Herman's work. It either grabs you or it leaves you cold. Partly it's gender. Herman's paintings are glorified examples of the "war pictures" boys used to draw under their desks at school: armies and tanks shooting down planes, bullet tracers everywhere. Maybe now, what with Gameboys and Xbox, all that's obsolete. I don't know.

The average length of time a visitor to the Louvre spends in front of the *Mona Lisa* is twenty-seven seconds. Rembrandt's *Aristotle Contemplating a Bust of Homer* at the Met comes in at nineteen, if anyone even bothers anymore. Jackson Pollack? Some people do his whole room at MOMA in less than twenty seconds. So when Jeff took five minutes to absorb all the details in one of Viereck's large battle scenes, it impressed me.

He said all the right things. "I'd like to see these in better light. These colors are amazing. How did he get that much variation out of a box of Woolworth's paint?" And so forth, and so on. Then he looked at me and said, "Do you think he'd be interested in letting any of these go?"

"What do you mean?" I asked him.

"I'd like to buy this one," he said. "I'd do five hundred on it."

I'd like to say that I looked at him as if he were daft and uttered words of protest, but I thought he'd made a lowball offer, even for a first sale. "Oh, come on, Jeff. I can't do that. These things are his private life. I shouldn't even be showing them to you."

"If they're so private, how come he told you they were up here?"

"He didn't tell me about the art. I just came up here to clean out the place."

"It's your apartment, isn't it? He vacated the premises."

"What he told Nate was that if he saw anything up here he wanted, he could have it," Makiko added. I wondered if they'd put their heads together before he came to dinner.

"It wouldn't be right, Jeff. I can't let them go on a technicality."

"Well, ask him then. See if he would be willing to sell off a few pieces."

"I told you, Herman's in a nursing home."

"Yeah, well he's not in a coma, is he? I'm sure he could use a little extra money."

Linda tried to smooth things over. "Aw, c'mon, Jeff. You don't really want one of these. Christ, they're practically kiddy porn. You could probably be arrested for hanging one. Personally, I've had enough of this for one night. This place is starting to creep me out."

"It's not pornography," Jeff said. "I think this guy was making a real statement about our society's attitudes toward children."

"That's because we don't have any," she said. Makiko gave me a look of hapless exasperation. Jeff and Linda had tuned us out and were heading off on a private tangent. The whole thing began sounding a little too George and Martha-ish for me.

"Yeah, naked prepubescent girls with added male genitalia, being disemboweled," Linda went on. "That really gets to the heart of the problems facing Western society."

"No, it's not that," Jeff said. I could tell the work had really moved him. "There's a subtext here; I can't put my finger on it. The way he incorporates all these saccharine images, takes these cultural icons, and stands them on their heads."

In those days, early on in the Viereck saga, I hadn't yet heard every conceivable theory hashed and rehashed by every critic, shrink, and arts-and-entertainment beat writer in Chicago. I hadn't yet become a sounding board for anyone who wanted to try out their pet idea on what Herman's work meant in the "Jungian framework of our Judeo-Christian collective unconscious" or whether he was a neo-romantic or simply a naïf—no, a romantic romantic.

In other words, I still actually wanted to hear what Jeff thought. Linda, on the other hand, was more like the Supreme Court. Maybe she couldn't define obscenity, but she knew it when she saw it.

"You're not hanging that thing in my living room," she told him, but I wasn't so sure she would win this argument. She hadn't ostensibly married Jeff for anything as crass as his money, but he had it, and she didn't. It colored their relationship in ways that were obvious to everyone but Linda.

"I can't sell it, Jeff," I told him, trying to derail their argument. "It just doesn't feel right."

"Well, it wouldn't hurt to ask him if he wants to let one go. You'd be surprised how people feel once you start waving money at them."

I could see what was happening. The moment I'd told him the painting wasn't for sale, he had to have it.

***

Later that night, lying anesthetized in post-coital semi-coma, with one bearlike arm hooked around Makiko's narrow waist, and marveling as always at the amount of sheer animal heat radiating from her tiny body, I missed the fact that her mind still churned away. Sex always did that to her.

"We can't leave it vacant forever," she said into the darkness.

"Leave what?"

"Viereck's apartment. It's been months since he moved out. We should clean it out and redo the floors before the new term starts in September. We could get $940 a month for it, easy."

"Gee Makiko, you know how I feel. I think people will be talking about Herman for years to come. I don't want to be known as the guy who threw part of art history into the trash."

"Then sell Jeff the painting," she said. "We're not the Ford Foundation. We can't subsidize Viereck's work. If we're not going to rent the apartment, we'll need some way to make up that income. Anyway, once Jeff gets going on something like this, he won't give me a moment's rest till he has it, so why not go ahead and tell him you need a thousand for it. He won't be mad. Money means nothing to him."

"But what about Herman? These are his private paintings. You can't just unload his stuff like that."

"Oh bullshit," she said. "He'll be tickled pink. Tell Jeff a thousand. Take seven hundred for the two months' rent and give Herman the rest.

By then, she'd destroyed *my* moment of conjugal bliss. I lay there in the dark, my mind unwillingly rumbling back to life. She moved my arm.

"It's too heavy," she murmured.

I formulated a few more reasons why, from a karmic standpoint, selling Jeff an original Herman Viereck seemed like a dangerous thing to do. I also wondered how she'd managed to raise Herman's rent *in absentia* by two hundred dollars a month. But by the time I got up the nerve to ask her, she was snoring away.

CHAPTER NINE

Now that I've told you how I became Viereck's agent, let's talk about Herman's lifelong weather obsession. For all the years I knew him, it constituted our main topic of conversation. It got so I'd cross the street a block away to avoid hearing him haranguing me about the foibles and inaccuracies of our local predictionologists. Once I saw his work, the way he presented the skies and the weather, it put his obsession in a whole new light.

Studying his work, you can't ignore the detail and care he put into his skies. The endless permutations of grays and blacks that he coaxed out of his dime-store paintbox, the storm clouds that often lower the horizon to only inches from the bottom of the page, and the driving rains that pursue his little girls like plagues of arrows—these images appear over and over. But of all natural phenomena, it's his depiction of tornados that are the iconic feature of his work.

He illustrated them in Technicolor or grim blacks and grays. He described them ad nauseam in his ponderous, cliché-ridden schoolboy prose. Twisters everywhere, his funnel clouds are Gd's finger, plowing a fearful message across the flat Midwestern landscape.

When I first showed the *Realms* to Adrian Holm, he picked up on the tornados right away.

"Look at those skies," he told me, as if I couldn't see them for myself. "Such torment. They're telling us something about his inner conflicts. They're a metaphor for his repressed sexuality. Look at the way the funnel clouds furrow the earth, like downward pointing phalluses raping the ground we walk on. He's a man at war with himself, with his own repressed urges."

I still can't decide if Holm just isn't very original or if he's simply hooked his wagon to a dying star. Back then, there were still a lot of Freudians rattling around, trying to squeeze everything through the same sex-drenched sieve. Maybe Holm overdid it, but there's no denying that tornados do play a central role in Herman's cosmology, and I'm sure there's a large grain of truth in Holm's heavy-handed analysis. It's true that sometimes a cigar is just a cigar, but Herman isn't the first writer to use the weather as metaphor. It's as old as Homer's wine-dark sea.

Eventually, I did my own evaluation of Viereck's leitmotif, taking a more mundane approach than Adrian's psychic autopsy. After I learned more details about Herman's early life, I called the Clinton County Illinois Historical Society and asked them if there had been any tornado activity the summer Herman told me he'd been there.

Sure enough, a terrible twister had flattened the town of Muscatine in 1915. A bronze plaque and memorial where the schoolhouse once stood holds the names of the thirty-seven children who were inside the day it scattered the building—and them—to the winds.

Eyewitness accounts describe an enormous funnel coming out of the southwest and churning through the center of town, a sentient being bent on divine retribution. The twister ripped the roofs off the church and the courthouse and then barreled on till it hit the elementary school.

If Herman had, as he confessed to me, walked away from the Illinois Home for Feeble-Minded Children and headed for Chicago on foot, it could have put him there the afternoon the twister hit. The experience of seeing the destruction of the schoolhouse, coupled with his inner torment over the loss of his own mother and the adoption of his sister, might have made witnessing the tornado a life-altering event, enough to affect his creative output for the next fifty years.

This tornado was so malevolent that, even in an area known as Illinois's Tornado Alley, this one deserved its own name: Corkscrew Annie. There are no photographs, except of the aftermath, but in an issue of the local gazette, a sketch of the twister shows an exaggerated spiral as if she'd attempted literally to drill herself into the earth.

You see traces of the corkscrew motif scattered through Herman's work. It's in the spearheads of the Glandelinian army, the twisted goat horns coming out of some of his little girl's heads, and the curlicue tails of his enormous dragons.

***

"Were you in Muscatine the day it happened? Did you actually see it?" I asked Herman. It was one of his better days, and he sat on his bench again, warming himself in the sun. I'd begun to get used to seeing him in his suit and tie. I think, secretly, he liked his new outfit.

He looked like some odd little retired intellectual, a humble man of letters, an elderly Becket or Joyce or Genet. He gave me that screwed-up little look of his, his "I'm not as crazy as you all think I am" look. "It was August twenty-ninth," he began. "I was walking down this dirt road. They were all dirt those days, pally. A few wagons passed. People axed me if I wanted a ride, but I just kept on walking."

I'm old enough now that I can relate to his mindset on that fateful afternoon. When we're young, time organizes into past, present, and future. We're sure about where we've been because there's not that much past to remember. As for the future, it's filled with boundless possibilities.

Now I know that time moves in strange, non-linear ways. The past appears as a murky pond with life's events scattered half-seen along the bottom. Events that happened eons ago remain vivid, while whole years, decades even, shoot past in a half-forgotten, disordered jumble. Just when did you take that trip to Italy? Your grandmother's funeral? The year you were rear-ended on the onramp and had to go to physical therapy for six weeks? When Herman starts to tell me about the day he encountered the tornado, neither of us has trouble imagining that it happened yesterday.

So … I see him escaping. The Illinois Home for Feeble-Minded Children has a five-story brick tower, standing in a cornfield like a distant gothic cathedral. As he walks, it recedes into the Oz-like distance. His mother has died in childbirth, his newborn sister given up for adoption, and his father, old and infirm, consigns him to an orphanage. At the orphanage, he earns the nickname "Crazy" and is so disruptive that he's sent to the school of last resort. Now at seventeen, stunted by years of poor nutrition, he looks like a child walking the dusty back roads of rural Illinois.

It is late summer, and dust billows off the sun-scorched cornfields and settles evenly on everything. Herman has planned his departure for weeks. Now it's time to make his move. He decides to leave after breakfast. Maybe he slips a few purloined sandwiches into his pockets. He walks out the dormitory on his way to do his chores at the school's model farm. Instead of turning right to enter the barn, he turns left, hops the gate, and disappears down the road. No one stops him as he walks away from the shambling brick buildings that have been home for the last ten years.

Perhaps two underpaid farm boys, drafted as orderlies, stand outside the main entrance, smoking and shirking, when Herman walks right by them. They look at the little figure with studied disinterest.

"Should we go and tell Mr. Monroe?" one asks.

"Naw, it's only that little kraut, Viereck. He's harmless. Somebody'll bring him back in a day or two."

So Herman is allowed to wander, a small self-contained tornado, his own funnel cloud coiled tight as a clock spring inside his chest, a little tornado of anger and willfulness but no competition for what Gd plans to put down in front of him.

I imagine Herman's feet rubbing in his ill-fitting, state-issued brogans. The blisters the shoes caused when he first put them on have callused over. Now with the endless miles, new blisters develop underneath the yellow, thickened skin on the soles of his feet. Blister upon blister, like growth rings on a tree.

Herman walks north, headed for the anonymity of Chicago, city of his birth but one he has never seen. In the late summer stillness, Herman falls into a hypnotic trance. He has road fever. At the next clump of trees, at the next fork in the road, he thinks he'll pull up and rest in the shade, but when the clump of trees arrives, tired as he is, his feet refuse to stop.

Maybe a knapsack, a blanket roll, a battered saucepan, and a clinking tin cup drum a martial cadence as he marches along. He's a deserter from a battle-shattered army. Nobody pays him mind. The roads are filled with hobos. What's one more set of aimless tramping feet?

Young and seemingly helpless as he appears, Herman's not a figure who inspires acts of kindness. More likely, people pay him off to keep moving. He chops a little wood, sweeps out a store, slops hogs. Here's a nickel or a dime, but please get on down the road. So Herman does. Why not? A loaf of bread and a half-pound of bologna cost a nickel. He could walk all the way to California for five bucks.

Herman doesn't rest in the shade. He doesn't stop at a farmhouse to ask for a drink of water. He walks. Is the clash of warring armies already roaring in his head? Have the battle lines between the Christian North and the Glandelinian South already been drawn? When he looks out at the cornfields, does he see them trampled and running red? Bull Run, Antietam, Shiloh—images cobbled from an illustrated book in the home's sparse library—the battles mean more to Herman than the details of his own truncated life.

At the top of a rise, he looks across a shallow valley and sees the town of Muscatine, tucked into a bend of a gently meandering river. At first, all he can see of the town is the spire of the church and a grain elevator peeking up above massive oaks, but the sky has turned ominous. The road turns down into the valley. But as he nears the outskirts of the town, Herman feels a high-pitched wailing deep in his skull. His ears pop. He feels the tornado at the back of his throat, a palpable force warping the air he inhales.

"It's the drop in barometric pressure that does it," he tells me with the confidence of a meteorologist.

I have no reason to disbelieve him. He looks out across the town and he sees Her.

Herman is still bathed in sunlight, but in the distance, the sky has turned coal-dust gray. At the center of his vision, the darkness reaches down to touch the earth. This is *his* tornado, as it will appear over and over, no matter how many times he tries to exorcize it with words or pictures. He sees Corkscrew Annie, and she has the town dead in her sights.

In a flash of short-term clairvoyance, Herman sees all the future he will ever need. He knows the tornado will not change course. He knows the finger of Gd will not refrain from writing its fearful message across the neatly ruled paper of Muscatine's linear streets. He does not foresee any salvation of the innocent. They won't be able to escape by running away, the way Herman has run from his red-brick asylum.

Herman, having already escaped, feels invincible. He does not turn and flee this oncoming death spiral. Instead, he starts to run toward it. As Herman runs through the town's scant outskirts, the houses are still bathed in sunlight, but ahead of him the sky reconfigures itself into overlapping cutouts of black and gray construction paper: a collage of impending death. He knows he will be too late. He knows he is rushing headlong into his own vengeful meeting with the finger that has toyed with him for seventeen years.

Lanceless, Herman enters the list for his joust with Gd. The finger of Gd versus one stunted adolescent. Why does Herman think it's a contest of equals?

Halfway down Main Street, the storm's outer wall meets him. It's the first volley of musket fire as he continues his one-man Pickett's charge. Now he's inside the cloud, dark as a solar eclipse, roaring yet strangely quiet at the same time. Inside Herman's head, there's the clash of the armies that will wage war for the rest of his life.

The town is built out of small frame houses. Gladiolas and dahlias bloom along their picket fences, the flowers' heavy heads quivering in the growing vortex. Herman runs through the empty streets. On porches and in driveways, a few people stand immobilized, caught in a frozen tableau, paralyzed by fear, like mice before a snake, the corkscrew snake of Gd. Herman runs past them as if they are cardboard cutouts, pasted onto the street.

The roar of the vortex wants to suck the brains out of his head. It's like being inside one of the new vacuum cleaners they've let him use at the home. But under the roar is a softer counter-melody, a new theme in the symphony of destruction, the sound of nails pulling free, tree limbs snapping, siding and shingles zippering off house frames, then the frames themselves deconstructing like a film run backwards.

This cloud of tornado shrapnel tears at him as he approaches the schoolhouse, bricks, tree limbs, splintered two-by-fours moving sideways at two hundred miles an hour. Yet like the charmed flag carrier in a frontal assault, he escapes unscathed. Nothing bigger than an oak leaf whips across his face. Gd's finger spares him. Gd needs someone to bear witness, someone to return to tell the tale. He needs an Ishmael to ride the bobbing coffin after the *Pequod* sinks, "*and I alone am escaped to tell thee.*"

Against all probability, Viereck reaches the door of the schoolhouse and grabs the knob, but the pressure inside is so great that he can't get it open. Then the school's roof comes off, and then the door implodes, sucking him through.

The first thing he sees is a row of little girls. Sets of eyes (are there seven?), dumb and wide with horror, stare at him. The one closest to him reaches out, and he grabs her hand just as the walls of the building fly apart all around them.

He has her hand, but as he watches, the little girl levitates into the air, and he is holding onto her as if she has become an unruly balloon. For a split second, their eyes meet, and then she is gone. Gd plucks her out of his hand, his little sister snatched from him again.

Corkscrew Annie moves on.

Herman Viereck stands in the doorframe of the now nonexistent schoolhouse. The roaring recedes down the street behind him, already diminishing. Why not? It has what it came for. Herman looks in disbelief at his empty hand. The battle is over. Her battered body will be found the next day in the fork of a tree two miles away.

Herman sits in the courtyard of the Little Sisters of the Poor and tells me this, just as he has written it and drawn it a thousand times. Is this therapy? Has finally telling a fellow human face-to-face made a difference? This bitter little bastard, this casualty of his own private war? He never even got the Purple Heart.

"Jeezus, Herman. It sounds awful."

"Yes," he says, "but it turned out worse for Him."

***

Later when I try to tell Adrian about Herman's tornado experience, instead of psychoanalytic mumbo-jumbo, or even plain human empathy, I get the skeptical meteorologist.

"Tornados don't work like that," he tells me flatly. "It's not bloody likely it ever really happened."

CHAPTER TEN

For the record, Makiko is the one who cut the first painting out of the book and sold it to Jeff. We've been taking heat for it ever since, but frankly, who would know about Viereck's work if we hadn't busted it up? At the time, I didn't know what to make of her taking this initiative. She put a different spin on our relationship. Before that, I'd made all the financial decisions.

Technically, when Makiko and I married, she became co-owner of my real estate empire. She had just as much right to make decisions about the *Realms of the Unreal* as I did. But there's a lot of difference between legal rights and the boundaries in a marriage. Makiko selling Herman's painting constituted a giant step in her taking Tamar's place.

Not that that was all of it. I couldn't help but feel that she'd made an aesthetic judgment for the both of us as well. Once we let the first painting go, I'd never be able to look at Herman's work in quite the same way.

"You know the way Jeff is when he wants something," she said, trying to make light of it. "There wouldn't have been a moment's peace, and we've got to get the Beethoven quartets ready in a month. I haven't played them since Julliard. I told him $1,250, hoping to scare him off. The bastard just pulled out his checkbook. I had him make it out to you," she added, by way of an apology, but it just made me feel doubly culpable.

I took out Herman's share of the money in twenties. It seemed more tangible than writing him a check. I felt like my uncle handing out Chanukah gelt. We never get over our love of cash. There's this apocryphal story of Dali signing lithographs while his agent handed him a C-note each time he scrawled his name.

I got there after lunch, but I found him still in bed. He'd dozed off, sitting half upright, his head sagging at an odd, uncomfortable angle. Food stains trickled down the front of his shirt, and he smelled a little like a wet diaper that's fallen down behind the dresser and sat there for a few days.

They hadn't shaved him in a while, and tufts of white hair stuck out of both ears. His untrimmed eyebrows reminded me of incipient satanic horns. Looking at him, I had this intrusive thought that if Hitler had lived to be an old man, this is how he would have looked.

An epistle or bible lay open, face down on his lap. Even in sleep, his breath came in weak and uneven gasps. He awoke quickly enough, though, when I tugged on his sleeve.

"Hey, Mr. Nathan, how you doin'?"

"Hi, Herman, how are you feeling?"

"I'm doin' good. The sisters here are so good to me. I don't deserve it."

"Sure you do. All those years you put in at the hospital cleaning up after everybody else. All the times you went to mass. It's the least the church can do for you."

The old man snorted. I saw a little flash of his old curmudgeonly self. "I've been an irascible old bastard. I don't deserve nothin'," he said and gave me his sideways smile.

"Yeah, well—I've got something for you. I don't want you to be mad at me. It wasn't really my idea. I just couldn't see throwing all your stuff away, Herman. It's kind of like a museum up there."

Then I pulled the wad of twenties out of my shirt pocket and gave them to him.

"What's all this?"

"I sold one of your paintings. Now you're a real artist."

I didn't know what to expect. I'd doubted all along that the sale would produce a happy outcome, but Viereck didn't look the least surprised. Then he smiled.

"Which one," he asked?

There were only about a zillion of them. "I don't know; one of the big ones with those great skies you do."

"Not the Tornado at Gobbler's Knob? I think that's the best."

"No, I don't think it's that one. It had the Vivian sisters in it, I know that."

"What did you get for it?"

"Makiko sold it to one of her friends. I took some out for the rent. I'm keeping the apartment for you, for when you come back."

It seemed like a white enough lie. After all, in the long run, I was doing it for him, creating a memorial, a shrine to his singular obsession.

"Yeah, right," he said, but he didn't believe it any more than I did.

Herman looked again at the money. He made no attempt to count it but held it up, and I saw him brush the bills against his cheek.

"This guy who bought it, he's not some kinda whack job, is he?"

"No, he's a serious art collector. He owns a Rubens."

"A Rubens, eh? Now that guy could draw." He paused and looked at the money one last time. "Ain't that sumtin." I could see a tear forming in his rheumy eye.

"You're not mad at me, are you?"

"What you get for it?"

"A thousand dollars."

"A grand?"

"I told you. You have a lot of talent."

He looked at me and shrugged his shoulders. What could I say? There *is* a point in life when things happen too late. People say "Better late than never." It's true only up to a point.

"What do you want me to do with the money?" I asked him.

"Keep it for me. I've been thinking about buying a headstone. A man shouldn't just disappear. There should be something."

"There is, Herman, more than most. You've got your work. It makes *The Lord of the Rings* look like a nursery rhyme."

"The *Realms of the Unreal*," he said with a self-mocking tone. "What nonsense. It's too late. It's all too late."

***

But it wasn't too late for the rest of us. Between Adrian Holm with his links to the psychiatric community and selling the first piece to Jeff and Linda, word spread that eccentric ol' Prof. Learner had dug up something rare and wonderful. Friends and friends of friends started calling, asking if they could come up and see Herman's apartment. Everyone wanted to be part of the action, like Victorians taking the grand tour of Egypt. The trip wasn't complete till you spent the night in the Great Pyramid of Khufu.

It seemed like once a week I'd go over there with a small group in tow. I began to feel like a tour guide with a set spiel … "And this is where he must have sat. See how he wore out the seat? And these are his collection of Madonnas and the mysterious Pepto bottles. What can they possibly mean? Well, if you can't figure them out, what do you make of this?" Eventually the books and the paintings would come out, with their odd transgender mysteries and tantalizing cultural associations.

Over the next few months we sold off more of his work. Like the buffalo herds when the white man first got there, the supply seemed endless. I tried to steer people away from his bigger scroll-like pieces. I pointed out that most were painted on both sides and would be difficult to display, but friends of ours snapped up some of the single sheets at a few hundred dollars apiece. I didn't even try to keep track. Now, even his small portrait pieces go for ten or fifteen grand.

When selling art, you try to get the best price you can up front. There aren't royalties or residuals in the visual arts. Once a work leaves your studio, it's just another commodity—and you don't own it. The price can triple, but you'll never see another dime.

Nobody knows this better than the gallery owners. They may be able to sell your work two or three times, but they don't owe you anything after the first sale. If you're cagey, or moderately successful, you might be able to get a little vigorish on some of the turnover, but don't try to get a bank loan on it.

Gallery owners are a bit crooked. You have to be if you want to make a buck. Fraud is built into the system. Where did a painting come from? Who owned it, what repairs has it had—and is it real? How real? There are so many questions—and lies of omission are the easiest ones to tell.

Occasionally, you'll find a dealer who's honest, usually because she doesn't have to sell art for a living. The wife of dot-com millionaires, a trust-fund baby, or even the odd semi-legitimate Hungarian baroness. They have money coming in from somewhere else. Running a gallery is their hobby. They're easier to do business with, but their galleries tend not to last. For some reason that I can't quite understand, it takes a lot of work to keep one of these places open, even though every time I walk into one, everybody is sitting around, slurping double-tall lattes and chatting on the phone.

The cagiest owners were once artists themselves, before they wised up and saw that the fifteen minutes of glory they got from having a show every two years didn't go too far at the grocery store. For the last twenty years, I'd been fortunate enough to be represented by a gallery like that: Dave Crandall, Fine Art & Photography.

You can find his work in old copies of *Lens and Camera*. He wasn't bad. After I had my first photos in *LIFE*, he called me and offered me a month of wall space. He'd just opened his gallery and was hungry to build up a clientele. He convinced me to lowball everything, and we sold the show out. We've been together ever since.

By the time he called me, I'd been avoiding him for months. I hadn't mounted an exhibit in two years. We'd had an informal agreement to have a showing of my photographs every fall, and I knew he wanted me to set a date. Of course, I didn't have the courage to tell him that I hadn't shot a roll since Miriam died.

The last really new things of mine he'd mounted had been taken during her final relapse. I thought they were trite. A lot of stark hospital interiors, portraits of staff and patients, some smiling bravely at the camera, others looking as if they'd just received a personal message from Jesus that everything was gonna work out okay. They were only a little better than standard fundraising material.

To my demanding eye, the pictures seemed maudlin, lacking subtext, and devoid of any universal power. I hated the show and told myself I'd give all the money to the Leukemia Society, but I never got around to it. We'd titled the exhibit, "White Blood Count." Dave sold every last damn picture.

Since then, everything I'd given him had come out of a file cabinet. Over the years, I'd amassed thousands of prints and negatives, which I cannibalized to keep him in inventory. Either the Chicago critics hadn't caught on, or they were being kind to me because of my reputation. Even with my most recent effort, an essentially themeless hodgepodge of recycled liberal muckraking, the least favorable of my reviewers only commented on my lack of cohesive vision and felt that I'd lost my focus (ha ha). The kindest called the show "eclectic."

Every hero has to have his secret. Mine? Creative paralysis. It started, paradoxically, with too many ideas. Not too few. After Miriam's death, I fell into a semi-manic state of persistent insomnia where night and day became abstract concepts. Lying awake in semi-darkness near my now-frigid wife, ideas for staggeringly powerful photo essays flooded my mind like an old Kodak carrousel on an automatic timer; click, click, click. Every idea flashed by, each one better than the last.

I planned to fly to the Gulf of Mexico and document the conflict between Vietnamese and Cajun shrimpers. I envisioned a parade of techies in the Silicon Valley, posed like Grant Wood's *American Gothic*, in front of their homes with all their toys out on the lawn. I wanted to do an essay on graffiti artists on the South Side, or maybe indigenous Amazon natives wearing "Guns and Roses" T-shirts while listening to their Walkmans and selling Avon products. The list was endless.

When the problem is not a dearth of ideas but trying to decide which to tackle first, you end up doing none of them. Nothing I thought of seemed worth the special effort it would take to elevate that one project above the rest.

Underneath it all, I felt that anything I did would be sacrilege to Miriam's memory, a tacit admission that I'd gotten over her. I couldn't mourn her loss, but I couldn't move on, either. After a while, the thought of breaking the cycle of this *paralysis artisitica* became too taxing, and I settled into a funk of non-production, a funk so taboo, so counter to the myth of myself, that I kept it from everybody. Even Makiko didn't know I hadn't shot a picture in almost six years.

So when I picked up the phone in my office and heard Crandall's irresistibly ingratiating voice (halfway between a real estate agent's and a long-lost college roommate calling you unannounced from the airport), I winced.

"I owe you money," he told me right away, a ploy guaranteed to hypnotize any respectable artist into a rosy glow of suggestibility. I knew then that I was in deep yogurt.

"That's great," I said, but my voice had harmonics of trepidation.

"I've finally sold you out. You'll never guess who just bought your last two hippie portraits for their new house in Vail."

"John Denver?" Dave didn't act like I'd made a joke.

"You're close. Look, Nate, I need more material. I can't keep recycling you forever. There's a demand for your old stuff, but to capitalize on it, I need to show people that you're still working, that you're still a creative force."

"Cut the flattery, Dave," I told him. "I'm immune, remember?" But he was on a roll.

"You'll never guess who loves your work." He gave me the name of some A-list actress, known for her cultural pretensions. If he'd been trying to impress me, he had. "So what are you working on now? I think we should follow up on this. I've got connections with The Discriminating Eye in LA. They'd love to put you in for October or November. It's the primo spot, just before the Christmas group shows."

My first impulse was to do a quick mental inventory of what I had left in my collection. Among the thousands of negatives, contact sheets, and undeveloped rolls of film, I could surely find enough stuff for another twenty-odd finished photos, but in my heart I knew that in terms of anything I would be proud to put my name on I'd reached the end. To mount a show made up of these second-rate and already self-rejected images would be a sure sign that my career had hit its final wall. My mind raced. I paused for a long ten seconds. Then, out of desperation, I fed him Herman.

"I don't know, Dave. It's kind of short notice. I really haven't been doing all that much lately." I let my voice go a little flat. I felt awful. How long could I use unrequited grief as an excuse? I knew Crandall wouldn't mention Miriam out loud, but I also knew what he thought: six years is a long time to play the grief-stricken parent. And I knew he had the argument, the argument only one other person had had the guts to use.

"Do you think Miriam would want you to waste the rest of your life because of her?" Tamar had asked just before she walked out our door.

"Anyway, I'm glad you called," I told Dave. "I've got this artist I think you should look at. It's outsider art, but very sophisticated in its own way. It's got a tremendous edge."

"Not that old coot that lived in your building?"

"How do you know about him?"

"Makiko's viola-playing friend, you know, Trust-fund Boy from the Acme Tool & Die Company. He stopped by the other day, crabbing about how you'd Jewed him on the price of this amazing watercolor—but how he'd have the last laugh someday."

"Well, he's probably right," I said. "This guy in my building was some kind of effing genius. Don't you have that second space over on Halsted? I think this guy is right for you."

"You're not trying to duck on this LA thing?"

"I'll give it some serious thought," I said. "Just come up to this guy's apartment and take a look, okay?"

Crandall paused. I heard a long silence, but I could sense the expression on his face. "I'm too old for this, Nathan. I don't have the energy to discover a new artist."

"But this is unique stuff. You've never seen anything like it."

"I know," he told me. "That's the problem with it."

PART TWO

CHAPTER ELEVEN

In retrospect, I can see why it took me thirty years to figure out what Herman was up to. There is nothing like the tunnel vision we create from our preconceived notions to blind us to the obvious. Once I'd diagnosed him as an essentially harmless lunatic, I ignored all the obvious clues. I discounted all the little messages he kept sending me. I declined all his subtle invitations to peer into the world he'd been creating, page by tortured page.

I might have been blind to his intentions, but it took Herman no time at all to figure out what I represented. I think he knew from the start that I could be his conduit to a different world, a world, it turns out, he knew more about than I ever imagined.

Tamar and I fostered an aura of artistic creativity in Herman's building. Without consciously trying, we engineered a delicate balance between people we counted on to pay the rent and those we kept out of respect for their artistic endeavors. Over the years, we had scores of art students from the institute and even some Second City people. Gilda Radner once rented a room from us. We had bi-racial couples no one else would rent to. Even the odd drug addict sneaked by for a month or two—but Herman remained our one constant.

Don't let me idealize too much: our building never approached being anything like an artist's commune. Tamar and I were a little too old for the sixties. We had grown up admiring beatniks. We never quite got our hearts around the Peter Max, faux psychedelia, love-and-peace thing. The anti-intellectual spirit of the sixties grated on our Bohemian sensibilities.

We'd grown up wanting to be like Sartre and Camus. We wanted to smoke Gauloises and talk long into the night, engaging in passionate arguments about everything, not get lost in some haze of dope smoke where whatever anyone said was "right on." We wanted friction, discourse. But instead of the sickness unto death, we got a dipshit Maharishi, spouting the same lame platitudes you could find in an issue of *Reader's Digest*.

Despite all the artists who cycled through Herman's building, we never had a building-wide open house or sponsored a group show. But there *was* a certain feeling about the place, an assumption that people there were allowed to hear their own distant drummer.

For Herman, living on Webster Avenue in the sixties must have been a two-edged sword. The neighborhood had a high tolerance for weirdness. People here recognized the importance of the holy fool. Less bohemian tenants wouldn't have put up with his dirtbag scruffiness, but a more involved group, when they heard Herman's arguing with Gd and the devil in the middle of the night (Herman playing all three characters in a radio play being broadcast on station WHELL) would have called in the bad-acid-trip flying squad from our local free clinic.

His clothes passed the point where casual dress becomes costume, past where costume moves to the unkempt, and unkempt moves to repulsive. Yet he kept a military style to his dress, part of his war fever. People have drawn the inevitable conclusion, that the entire *Realms of the Unreal* is an allegory of the American Civil War. He certainly peppered it with enough villainous generals named Beauregard or Claremont.

I later found out he'd been drafted. It's hard to imagine them dredging him off the bottom of the barrel. I think after a week or two, they sent him home. Still, something in that short military experience stuck with him, what with that long trench coat dragging along the sidewalk. In winter, he'd wear a hunter's cap with faux-fur earflaps. It made him look as if he'd held the line in the battle for Stalingrad.

So what do you do for a guy like this? He seemed so terribly alone, yet something cried out for attention to be paid, something that demanded recognition that every life has its value, that all of us deserve to be mourned, celebrated, and remembered. All of us need help to rage against the dying of the light.

***

Miriam, naturally, came up with the idea to throw him the birthday party. Blame it on the Museum of Modern Art. We'd been to New York to visit Tamar's family and had made our annual pilgrimage. Miriam fell in love with Henri Rousseau's *The Sleeping Gypsy*. That's the one with the sleeping man in the multicolored coat and the dream (?) lion suspended above him. When we told her the story of Rousseau's life, the ding-bat Customs inspector who began to paint at sixty, and the birthday party Picasso threw for him, she burst into tears. So who else but Herman Viereck could fill the bill for our own full-tilt surreal birthday boogey?

A few weeks after we got back from New York, Tamar and I were sitting on our stoop in early July. I looked across the street at Herman's apartment building, idly wondering at the karmic significance of collecting rent, when Herman came out and crossed the street toward us.

I'd long sensed that Tamar frightened him, but he couldn't help being drawn to her, like all the motherless children she picked up along the way. In the *Realms's* 15,487 pages and 315 illustrations, there is not a single adult woman. There are thousands of slave-children, muster lists containing the dreamed-up names of entire regiments. He drew goat-horned demigodlets, benevolent dragons, and butterfly-winged fairies, but not one fertile, wide-hipped, full-breasted woman. Not a witch, not a wicked stepmother, not a princess or a queen, not even a nun, not even a saint.

Herman's eyes stayed focused on the ground. Without looking, he crossed the street and approached the Venus of Lincoln Park. She favored Peruvian peasant blouses with wide necks closed loosely with a thin piece of red yarn. She looked as if she could open the top and give sustenance to the world. He stopped, regretting his decision. I could see his eyes darting, looking for an escape.

"Hi, Herman," Tamar said. "Hot enough for you?"

Leave it to Tamar: she'd pushed his one social button.

"This isn't what I'd call hot," he said, a slight professorial lilt taking over his voice. "It's only eighty-seven along the shore, ninety-two out at O'Hare, once you lose the lake effect. You have to get down to Champagne or Urbana before you get some real heat. It's not like it's going to be in August or on Mercury or Venus: 1,700 degrees centigrade."

"I didn't know you knew so much about astrology," she said.

He corrected her. I tried not to smile. "That's astronomy. The other isn't science." Herman looked down at his feet. He knew he should have stuck with the weather. As far as I could tell, they hadn't really made eye contact, but Herman wasn't staring at her chest either. It didn't leave him with many other options.

"Hi, Mr. Nathan," he said finally, looking at me with his sly, sideways glance. He always called me that, a habit, perhaps, left over from his days at the asylum. Last names would be too formal for children, first names too familiar. Children might forget their place.

Of course, at that time, I didn't know anything about his miserable past. There were no visible signs from what he'd endured. I'd grown up in a Jewish neighborhood in Philadelphia. Our barber and our dentist both had camp numbers tattooed on their forearms. I could study the irregular scrawl of ink while they worked on my teeth and hair. (Needless to say, the dentist wasn't too concerned about administering anesthesia.) They hadn't tattooed numbers at the Illinois Home for Feeble-Minded Children.

"Did you ever live downstate?" I asked him. At that time he denied it.

"No, I was born in Sao Paolo."

"Brazil?"

Herman nodded.

"Really?" Tamar said.

It sounded odd enough that I believed him. I still almost do.

"My father got hired to be the tailor to the president of Brazil. He brought him over."

"Over?"

"Yes, from Freiberg. We're a bunch of Krauts."

"Ah," Tamar said, though I knew anything German made her angry and then defensive about being angry. "*Sprechen sie Deutsche*?"

"No," Viereck said. "After my mother died, we didn't speak it."

I began to feel a slight buzz, I imagine, as a detective does when his suspect is about to break down and confess. Somehow Tamar had him hypnotized. *Just don't make any sudden moves*, I thought.

"When did she die, Herman?"

"I was three years old. She got blood poisoning right after my sister got born. They had to give her up for adoption."

"Oh, that's so sad. You poor man."

"Yes," he said, "I've had a hard life. God has had it in for me." He looked longingly down the street, searching for an escape route.

What were Tamar's feelings about Gd? I mean the standard issue "Santa Claus for grownups," flowing white robe, everyday, *New Yorker*-cartoon kind of Gd? Tamar's parents had been in The Party: they hung a framed picture of Trotsky in their living room. Pretty much your classic atheistic Jews. But Tamar had her own laissez-faire attitude toward Him. She was pretty much a moon goddess herself, so she always looked upon Gd as if they were a partnership. He had the day; she took care of the night.

At least this is how she felt before Miriam got leukemia and our world flipped on its ear. I don't know what she thinks about Him now. We never discussed it during Miriam's illness, and now it's a little late.

"So, Herman, when's your birthday?" she asked.

Viereck stopped for a moment. He had to think, as if the day had slipped far away from him. "August 14, 1924. It's the tenth anniversary of the war starting."

"Which war was that?" she asked.

"World War One. If only the French had studied the Civil War, it never would have happened like it did. You have to keep the battle lines fluid. Once they dug that first trench, they were all doomed."

He paused and looked up at the sky, unimpressed by his own history lesson, while I had to think hard about what I knew about WWI—a few scattered images of solders going over the top, flimsy biplanes spiraling into the ground in flames.

"Never can tell," he said. "It might rain later. July is the sixth rainiest month of the year. I better go."

"But Tamar wouldn't let him. "August fourteenth, that's only a couple of weeks. Hey Herman—how would you like to have a birthday party?"

Tamar had this screwball impulsivity that could get us into trouble. I sat perched one step above her and looked right into Herman's watery eyes. I could see how uncomfortable he felt, but his discomfort mirrored my own. I put myself in his place, wondering how a guy like this would deal with being the center of even the casual, ritualistic attention of being sung "Happy B-Day" to. I felt sure he'd freak at the suggestion and run down the street. Instead, he looked down at his feet.

"I've never had one," he said.

"Never?"

Tamar turned and looked at me. Our eyes had a whole discussion about it in half a second. I tried to warn her off, but she had the fixed glow of someone wrapped up in the aura of doing a good deed.

"Well, let's have one. Is there anyone you'd like to invite?"

"My friend Larry."

He had plenty of surprises that afternoon. It showed how little I knew about him. Herman having a friend seemed unlikely. But there you have it.

"What day is the fourteenth?' she asked me, as if I had a Mayan solar wheel rotating in my head. I started with "thirty days hath September" and started on my fingers counting ahead by sevens, but I got lost right away.

It's on a Friday, three weeks from now," Viereck said, before I could open my mouth.

CHAPTER TWELVE

When we told Miriam about our plans to throw Herman a party, she got pretty excited. It had little to do with the party itself. By age ten, Miriam understood the emptiness of organized gaiety. The phony goodwill of Christmas, Humboldt Avenue on the Fourth of July lined with bunting and balloons for the kiddy parade, Valentine hearts glued to paper doilies and handed out in class: somehow, it all made her melancholy.

Her father's daughter. What can I say?

It wasn't the balloons or the cake or the ice cream that appealed to her. Throwing Herman a party constituted a mitzvah, an act of generosity done behind Gd's back with no expectation of heavenly reward or earthly recognition. A deed done from that most underrated of human emotions, compassion. Miriam put herself in lonely Herman's shoes with more than empathy.

Compassion? How did we get so fixated on love while paying compassion so little attention? If only those Old Testament crazies and early Christians could have talked a little bit less about Gd's love and showed a little more simple human compassion, how different things might have turned out for the world. For Herman.

"Oh Nate," Miriam said when I ran the idea by her, "what a sweet idea."

I don't remember when my daughter started calling me by my first name. But I know where she got the idea: from her maternal grandfather, the old Marxist renegade and erstwhile "kibbutznick." He hated anything that smacked of authority, even fatherhood.

"Who should we invite?" she asked.

"I don't know."

That's what worried me about the party. The pitifully short guest list would demonstrate how bereft of friends and human contact Herman was.

"I guess some of the people in the building. We'll ask his friends."

"I don't think he has any. Remember that time we saw him at the movies? He'd gone all by himself."

"A lot of people go to the movies alone," I tried to reassure her, but her face had clouded over.

"Maybe this isn't such a good idea," she said thoughtfully.

"No, you'll see. It doesn't have to be a lot of people."

I didn't want to tell her that I shared her sadness about Herman. Miriam caught my expression and frowned. A ten-year-old shouldn't worry about this existential conundrum of the human condition, but Miriam did. She needed to sample everything, even the angst, the being, and nothingness that grip us all. She knew we are alone, that at some level even those we love the most are forever strangers to us and we to them, that across the loving looks and shared jokes and experiences remains a final barrier that cannot be crossed. And if that is the case, then surely there is that same final barrier that keeps us from truly knowing ourselves.

My Miriam looked over the edge of the chasm between her and the people she thought she knew and found it deep and wide. This discovery resonates with teenagers. They already feel that no one understands them, that they are being raised and educated by talking puppets—aliens and pod people. It's like *The Invasion of the Body Snatchers*. Everyone around them is either an android or a vegetable. They feel that they are the only people on earth who are truly alive. No wonder when they fall in love for the first time it is such a cataclysmic event.

I don't know how Miriam knew all this, an outwardly spoiled only child, showered with love on all sides by three generations—but she did.

I suppose I'm to blame. People worry too much about exposing children to sex. It's infinity they should be protecting them from.

So, existentially speaking, was Herman Viereck more alone than the rest of us? At least now, I know that he had his own fantastic world, and he had his Gd, even if they were always at war. It's more than I ever had.

"Hey, I know," Miriam said, and then she gave me a sideways look.

It was a look that said, "I know you're going to say no because what I'm proposing calls for a lot of work, confusion, and chaos, and you grownups walk around feeling that you can't possibly accommodate one more thing in your lives unless forced into it by the vagaries of circumstance, and never voluntarily would you take on something like this. Even so, by the time I'm done with you, I know you will cave and say yes—so why don't we skip all the preliminary skirmishing and just get it done right away?" That look.

"Why don't we get him a dog?" she said.

I looked at her, and for a second, my face must have lost control because her expression wavered. Could this be one of those times when the "look" would fail, that the terrible, heartbreaking "this hurts me more than it hurts you," parental, final, unappealable "no" would prevail?

Immediately I saw it all, the ensuing disaster of such misguided generosity. Herman seemed barely capable of taking care of himself. How could he handle a dog?

It wasn't that I had a "no pets allowed" policy. There'd been packs of dogs and prides of cats in and out of the building, plus a few ferrets and an iguana. All the floors were shot. A puddle or two wouldn't make a whole lot of difference.

But what if he started barking all night long? What would it do while Herman worked at the hospital or when he went on his long solitary rambles? What if Herman just flat-out didn't want a dog? How could anybody not want a dog? A person might say it was impractical, that it was too much work or too much this or too much that, but who, in their heart of hearts, didn't want a dog?

"How do you know he even wants one?" I asked

"He told me."

"He told you? When did you talk to Mr. Viereck? When did you even ask him about a dog?"

"Up in his apartment. We discussed it. You should see his place, Nate. He has all kinds of cool stuff. I think he's some kind of artist."

I remember the conversation now, but at the time I stopped listening after she told me about visiting Herman.

"You were up there by yourself?"

"Yeah, it was no big deal. I went over to Loraine McBee's, and his door was open. He invited me in."

Loraine lived on the fourth floor of Herman's building, housebound on long-term disability. Miriam hung out there after school and played cribbage with her a few afternoons a week. But Miriam going into Herman's apartment upset me more than I could explain to her. A father's instinct. In any discussion I've had about Herman, the word "harmless" always comes up. What more proof did you need?

"I don't want you going over there by yourself." I tried to keep my voice calm and noncommittal. Best not to show her how upset I felt. Precocious Miriam thought she was old enough to make her own decisions about things. I felt that "walking on eggshells" angst of the parent of an adolescent. Anything I said might backfire, produce the opposite of what I wanted.

"Oh, come on, Nate. He's really an interesting guy. He knows a lot of amazing stuff."

"He does? Like what?" Despite myself, my curiosity about Viereck's inner life conflicted with my desire to protect her.

"He's like this *total* expert on the Civil War. He knows the names of all the generals, even some of the soldiers, what the weather was like at Gettysburg."

"I thought you said history was boring."

"Not the way he tells it. You almost feel like he was *actually* there, that he saw the thing with his own eyes."

"Maybe so, but I don't want you up there alone. You understand?" She gave me a condescending look. I guess I deserved it. I'd never quite gotten the hang of the parent thing. The basic dictatorial element of the relationship never sat well with me.

"He's a creepy guy, Miriam. I'm afraid he might try to do something, you know. He didn't try to … he didn't touch you anywhere or anything?"

"Daaad!" She gave me a little dismissive snort.

They're all so *faux* street-smart. It's all that stuff they get in school about not getting into strange cars and not taking candy. They think they've got it under control, and it gives them a false sense of security.

Of course there's this ironic lunacy about the whole thing. At the time I sat there worrying about Herman's grubby hands, she'd already developed bruises on her shins and had started to look a little pale.

"You're overreacting," she told me. "He would never hurt anyone. He loves children. You know he grew up in an orphanage and then this awful place for feeble-minded boys. One time, he tried to adopt a little girl himself. Did you know that?"

"No."

"The state turned him down." She said "the state" the way her grandfather did—the ultimate totalitarian horror. "That's why we should get him a dog. Everybody needs something they can love."

Check, double-check, and mate.

"I don't know Miriam," I started, but all my arguments seemed cruel. Instinctively, I knew it wasn't right. For all the wild inventiveness of his imagination that would show itself later, he had a glaring lack of sentimentality. To love a dog, you have to be able to project something onto the poor beast that, for all its willingness to jump up and lick your face, it doesn't have. You have to create for your dog a "soulishness," childlike to be sure, but a soul nonetheless. So much of the relationship between man and dog has to come from the man. I didn't think Herman had that in him.

Even before I opened my mouth, I could tell I'd made Miriam furious with me—or worse than furious: deeply disappointed. This had been my chance to step outside myself, to graduate to a higher plane than mere fatherhood, and I'd blown it badly. What could I do? The only thing any of us can do in these circumstances.

"Let me discuss it with your mother," I told her.

CHAPTER THIRTEEN

The day of the party, I got up early. I'd been up and down all night anyway, and when I gave up trying to go back to sleep, the sky had turned milky with the coming dawn. Awake in bed, lying there in the reflected streetlight, the birthday's potential pitfalls were depressing. I tried my usual defenses.

"What's the worst that could happen?" I asked myself. But I couldn't help it: my trepidation about the party loomed in excess of what I briefly considered to be the worst possible outcome.

My worst fear, as I've said, was that no one would show up. Herman, having risked so much in agreeing to participate in one of life's hollow charades, would be rejected, ridiculed for his efforts to become part of the normal ebb and flow of society, and this failure, and its crushing repercussions to his already fragile psyche, would become my responsibility.

If my daughter had had any such doubts, and the imagination to play through the scenario of the four of us sitting in the living room, surrounded by way too much food, and trying hard to sing "Hoppy Birdie two Jews" all by ourselves, she'd kept them to herself.

When I finally gave up and got out of bed, I found her in the kitchen, eating a bowl of Cap'n Crunch and catching up on Michael Jordan's exploits in the *Trib*. Later, she got to meet him when he came to the children's hospital, but by then she had stopped being impressed with the capabilities of the human body. She knew how prone it was to failure—even his.

"Well, today's the big day," I announced. My voice felt forced.

"Don't worry. It's going to be fine," she told me. "M.J. scored a triple-double against the Jazz. We're gonna kick their ass in the play-offs."

I dumped beans into the Braun, and the grinding brought Tamar out of the bedroom. She had on a kimono over a Chicago Bulls T-shirt. We were all major fans. It was a good look for her.

Who had we invited? The three of us and Mrs. McBee, who, in retrospect, must have known Herman better than any of us. They had a running half-battle, half-friendship. Also, she was the only other practicing Catholic in the building. They went to the same church, St. Bart's over on Densmore.

Then there was Ron, my protégé. Every professor goes through one or two in his career—a teaching assistant who never quite manages to get his thesis finished and hangs around, getting extension after extension. Back then, the Chicago Institute of Fine Arts was so informally run, I wasn't sure Ron was even enrolled. I just kept renewing his request for studio space, and he made himself useful.

He knew how to strike the perfect tone. Ron admired my work, but he possessed a critical eye. He always had something perceptive to say that made it seem like he wasn't kissing my ass. It maintained our shared illusion that he wasn't sucking up to me, the perfect sycophant for a professionally modest man.

For a relationship like this to prosper, the protégé has to be someone acceptable to the professor's family. If it's a woman, she has to definitely not be the professor's type. If it's a guy, he has to be puppy-doggish and trustworthy, not someone that will make anybody nervous when he hangs around the apartment till your wife asks him if he wants to stay for dinner.

He has to be talented, naturally enough, but not so talented to be threatening. The important thing is that he has to end up becoming part of the family, someone willing to help you move a couch out of a fourth-floor apartment, clean up the darkroom, and pick your daughter up from her dance lesson if your wife is running late.

So Ron was a shoo-in for the guest list. Best of all, he'd met Herman a few times. Ron loved to shoot pictures in the neighborhood. Like a lot of photographers, he was inherently shy. The intrusiveness of the camera bothered him. He wanted to capture people unawares. As I've said, photography has its own uncertainty principle. The act of observation always affects the picture.

He'd hide his camera in his jacket or shot pictures through a hole in a briefcase he'd modified with concealed shutter buttons. I kidded him about it. Probably because of my size, I'm one of those rare birds unafraid to take someone's picture.

"Just stick the lens in their face and shoot the goddamn thing," I'd told him a dozen times after he'd shown me a contact sheet of slightly out-of-focus or poorly cropped shots.

That's how he'd met Herman. Ron finally got up the nerve and walked up to him while the old man pawed through the trash. It turns out to be the only decent picture there is of the old man.

Herman could have gone postal on him for taking the shot. I'd seen him go into a sputtering rage once or twice when people on the street got in his face. But he was unusually benign with Ron. Instead of screaming at him for invading his privacy, he'd asked Ron what he wanted the picture for. Ron told him he was doing a study of the people who lived in the neighborhood. He thought Herman would make "an interesting subject."

Herman didn't care about the aesthetics of Ron's project. Instead he began to ask him a lot of pointed technical questions about photography: what type of lens he used, what were shutter speeds, f-stops, how difficult was it to do blowups or shrink images. It's hard to think of it now, but before Photoshop, it took a ton of equipment to turn out a decent photo. It's clear, now, Herman wanted to pick Ron's brain to see if photography could help him with the *Realms.*

Ultimately, he must have decided that photography didn't work for him. In all his multiple collages and continued use of expanded or contracted popular images, there are no actual photographs. But after that first encounter, he always had time to stop and chat with Ron about the weather.

In addition to the mysterious "Larry," Herman had invited Father Moscou from St. Barts. I didn't know at the time how much the Church meant to him or the secret life he'd carved out for himself on the planet he'd created out of sketch paper and old Sears catalogues, but the idea of his being on first-name basis with a priest made me oddly uneasy.

What kind of person would Herman be able to call his "best" friend? Another weather-obsessed savant? Perhaps someone he met pawing through the trash or another regular over at the Stardust? In my current frame of mind, it might have been anyone: a troll living in a cardboard box under a bridge or Saul Bellow. Either seemed equally plausible. I said, yeah-sure-fine, the more the merrier.

Ron knew about the dog. The only one they kept out of the loop was me. I don't know why they took such pains to keep me in the dark. Despite my initial show of disapproval, I couldn't possibly have said no to the three of them. My persona as the lovable bear, besotted by his love for wife and daughter, was too well established as family mythology.

I think they didn't tell me because they were afraid that my voice of reason would reinforce their own misgivings. I'm sure Tamar realized the dog wasn't a good idea, but once she'd said yes, she couldn't pull out. The unexamined pureness of mitzvah seduced them all.

It's classic TV sitcom stuff. Here's this little nebbish of an old man, hiding his loneliness behind a gruff, nasty exterior. Inside, everyone knows he must have a heart of gold. How to get him to come out of his shell and embrace the loving world that surrounds him?

Let's get him a cute little dog, a lovable mischievous companion, a trickster figure to chew on his socks and beg scraps from his table. Ol' King Herman needs a court jester. The dog will melt his heart. Herman will learn to smile, and good things will happen. Look what it did for the ratings on *Frazier*!

Naturally, to complete their imagined cycle of redemption, one castoff saving the life of another, Tamar and Miriam rescued a mongrel from the pound. To hide the deed from me, they'd kept the dog over at Miriam's best friend Charlotte's house.

Charlotte had met Herman that time we'd run into him at the movies. She and her mom said they would come. That made two little girls at Herman's birthday party, two little Vivian Girls, though of course we didn't know anything about that at the time. Tamar, Miriam, and I sat around, trying to stretch breakfast out as long as we could, but even after four cups of coffee, too much time and too little to do remained before the afternoon's festivities. By nine o'clock, we got going on the decorations. This party was going to be our full-blown re-creation of Herman's unfulfilled childhood dream.

We'd gone over to Woolworth's and bought everything they had in stock: balloons, crepe paper, and "Happy Birthday!" spelled out in multicolored cardboard letters. These we hung in the archway between the kitchen and the living room. We framed the arch in a necklace of opalescent red and white balloons and stretched paper streamers from the light fixture to all the corners. As usual, it made me melancholy to look at them.

Miriam stood on the kitchen table, holding the string of letters between her teeth and fumbling with the Scotch tape. She reached out with both hands and tried to reach the far wall. I could see her center of gravity starting to extend irrevocably over the table's edge. I told her to be careful and ran around and grabbed her upper thighs in both of my hands. The next day, she would have purple bruises where I held her, the result of her dropping platelet count. I would be accused of being "too rough."

"You think he'll come?" she asked me, giving voice to my deepest fear.

"Do you want me to go over and remind him?"

"No," she said, "we'd better not seem like we're pressuring him." She finished tacking up the letters and stood back on the tabletop. "It's too low," she said.

"It's fine," I told her.

"No, it's not. The other side is higher."

"Really, it looks okay." I held out my arms to help her down, but she wouldn't come.

"That's your problem, Nate. You don't pay enough attention to detail."

"Who told you that?"

"Noo-body."

"Then what do you mean?"

"Oh, you know," she said. "Your shots always look a little unfinished, maybe off center." Our relationship might have been atypical for father and daughter, but she was treading on pretty sacred ground.

"Did Ron say that about me?"

She shook her head. "Just forget it, okay? You're right; it looks fine."

She went to the far side of the table and jumped down on her own and went over to the front windows. I watched her go into the living room and tried to discount what had just happened. Even though I forced myself to ignore it, the first shot had been fired in what, had she lived, would have proven to be a long and costly war.

"He's up there," she announced.

Tamar came out of the back bedroom. She'd changed into a dress with a jacket top, the outfit she wore to parent-teacher conferences. For a second, I thought to draw her in, try to make her take sides, but decided against it.

"I'd better go get the cake," I said.

The birthday cake. The focal point for our festivities. Homemade or store-bought? I'd thought it over for a long time. Homemade usually tastes better, and there's all that effort involved. The implied love that goes into the cake's creation, the messes of bowls that you have to wash, the indecision when you stick in a matchstick to test for doneness. Should I take it out now or give it another five minutes? Then there's the heart-stopping second when you flip the baking pan and hope the damn thing will come out in one piece.

If you get this far, there's frosting and decorations, always guaranteed to be an aesthetic disaster. Crumbs will get into the icing. The top will tilt slightly. You will run out of room and the "AY" of BIRTHDAY will end up scrunched together. The best you can realistically hope for is a homey look of amateur goodness, a folk-art approximation of a decorated cake.

Face it. It takes a certain amount of sophistication to appreciate a homemade cake. You have to have experienced the cloyingly sweet vapidity of the supermarket standard and then reject it. I wasn't sure Herman would get all that. He might think a homemade cake a backward insult, an unwillingness to give the event its due. So after some discussion, we decided on store-bought. I'd even ordered it ahead of time, a first for me.

I drove over to Mrs. Frisbee's Bakery on Huntington Avenue to pick it up. The cost was a shocking $22.50. While I was out, ever-faithful Ron showed up with the dog. They'd waited till the last minute, but as soon as I came up the stairs, I heard it barking. Tamar was in the kitchen when I came in. She gave me the "keep your mouth shut or you'll never get laid again" look.

Ron had the dog in a little carrying case, all neat and tidy. He'd put it down on the kitchen floor. When I walked in, the animal started rattling the wires. It sounded more like a giant rat than anything canine. Ron managed not to look me in the face as he sprung the door. It was a full-grown dog, some sort of terrier mix, not a puppy, thank Gd. As he sniffed around the unfamiliar kitchen, I couldn't get over the impression that we'd imported an oversized rodent, a species native to the Amazonian rain forest.

As a child, we never had pets. Owning a dog felt too American, too evocative of a Norman Rockwellish middle-class sensibility that my communard parents couldn't embrace. There was a frivolity about pet ownership that their immigrant backgrounds wouldn't allow them to enjoy. Having an animal around called for faith in the future. Also, stability and space. Food and love were too rare and expensive to squander on an animal.

The dog peed. It happened too fast to try to pick him up. The puddle didn't look that bad, like spilled tea. Tamar jumped on it with a wad of paper towels, as if she moved real fast I wouldn't notice. But she used three times as many as if it had been anything else besides urine.

CHAPTER FOURTEEN

By 1:15, Miriam had taken up a permanent observation post at the window so she saw Larry walking down our street.

"I bet that's him," she yelled. Tamar went over to look, and for the second time that day, I was left behind as they stared out the window. Even from the back, they were so unmistakably mother and daughter, each in her own way a part of me and yet so distinctly removed from anything I had contributed to. Even at the time, not knowing all we were soon too lose, an exquisite longing for what-I-didn't-know washed over me.

"He's looking for our address."

Miriam saw him checking our house number from something scrawled on the back of an envelope. Then we heard him on the stairs, his step tentative. As the sound got closer, it felt like the climax of a campfire ghost story, scary but funny at the same time: "*I am the viper: I've come to vipe your vindas.*"

The dog, which had been banished to his crate, began to bark frantically. I don't know why we always assume dogs are good judges of character, but I didn't take it as a good sign. Miriam opened the door before Larry could knock.

It took him off guard, and he stepped back into the hallway. The three of us stood in the door, like the three bears if they'd happened to be home when Goldilocks had shown up. Miriam stood in front, then Tamar, and I playing linebacker.

"Is this the Learner residence?" he asked. His voice sounded quite ordinary, neither bass nor unexpected falsetto. So far so good, I thought. The three of us backed out of the doorway. Larry had to duck his head to get through. He stood in our kitchen, holding his hat, already looking out of place and claustrophobic. He must have been close to six feet four inches, but thin and pretzeled in on himself, chronically afraid to expand to his full height.

I've mentioned already that I'm a big guy, which makes my particular talents unusual. You don't expect big hands to have the dexterity to draw and manipulate the tiny controls on a camera. I'm also surprisingly strong. Not that I make much use of it, except occasionally, say, to help move one of the monster lithograph presses in the print department.

I'm neither a hog-butcher nor a stacker of wheat. The city of broad shoulders would get along fine without me. I'm not what the kids call "ripped." I look more like the blacksmith's slope-shouldered, semi-retarded helper than the barrel-chested, massively armed boyo hammering cherry-red iron under the spreading chestnut tree. I'm the guy who holds up the loaded wagon while the smith replaces the wheel.

What I'm saying by all this is that I could have snapped this Larry in half like a dry-rotted two-by-four before he'd even opened his mouth; that's what I'd felt a strange, strong compulsion to do.

"You must be Herman's friend," Tamar said. "Herman's not here yet, but come in. Can I take your hat?"

Larry looked down at his hands. He'd been slowly rotating the brim. He owned a homburg, out of style, but oddly appropriate. He seemed reluctant to let it leave his possession.

"I apologize if I'm a little early," he said.

Tamar assured him he was fine.

"Maybe you should go over to Herman's apartment and see if he's there?" Miriam said. "I think he might be trying to chicken out."

"Oh no, he'll be here. He's been looking forward to it," Larry told her.

"I think it's great you could come. Have you and Herman been friends for a long time?" Tamar acted as if she needed to keep priming him or he would start to flutter and fly away.

"Oh yeah. We've been palling around for years." He looked down at his hands again. They were large even in proportion to the rest of him.

"How did the two of you meet?" Miriam asked him. "Herman seems very shy."

"We met at St. Bart's. There's not a lot of guys like us that attend church regular. Most single guys just want to tear around and chase skirts."

He smiled, but it looked rictus. His teeth weren't in the best of shape either.

"Me and Herman, we're not like that. There's more to life—I mean more important things."

"Like what?" Miriam asked.

I wanted to tell her to shut up, but she had grabbed on to something and worried at it like the dog in the crate.

"Come on, Mirs. Leave the poor man alone. Let him catch his breath," Tamar told her.

"No, that's okay. I don't mind talking about it," Larry assured us. "You seem like a very grownup young lady. Herman and me, we're very interested in helping children. There are so many unhappy little lives out there, little girls who aren't as lucky as you. I mean to have a mother and father to care about them and take care of them."

"So what do you and Mr. Viereck do, to help children, I mean?" she asked him.

The anironic way Larry talked came right at her emotional eye level. His forthright approach appealed to her preadolescent sensibilities. Her sense of right and wrong was so free from adult ambiguity. She had no use for the knowing wink, the pregnant pause, or the cynical poke in the ribs. Who knows what evil lurks in the heart of man? The Grownups know. To Miriam, the world's problems were transparently remediable. All that mankind needed was the willingness of people to exercise their innate good will to do the right thing.

I wonder what would have become of that sensibility. At what point would she have succumbed to the moral compromises all of us are forced to make? When would she have gone from a wide-eyed romantic, forever ready to wave the bloody shirt, to a cynical, sarcastic teenager, locked in her room with headbanger music pounding into earphones she'd cemented to her head?

Perhaps that transition to quasi-adulthood wouldn't have happened. Would that have been worse? What if she had kept her wild and woolly sense of outrage (like some semi-embalmed singer of sixties protest songs) long after she should have wised up?

I could imagine worse things, too. Perhaps she would have fallen prey to some far-right religious group. She might even have been *born again*. What else but fundamental Christianity would have served the tradition of radical extremism that percolated through the strata of generations of both the Learners and the Leavensons? Communism, Socialism, Buddhism, radical feminism? They were all taken long before she showed up.

In the meanwhile, we her parents soldiered on, wallowing in newsprint, watching the evening news, absorbing the daily morass of words and statistics, trying to explain to her why we didn't give away all our money to the poor or sell everything and go teach school in Africa. We found a thousand different ways to tell her: "*Someday, when you're older, you'll understand that things are much more complicated than they seem.*"

"Come on, Miriam," I repeated, "quit pestering the poor man. Let him catch his breath."

"They're very direct at this age," I explained.

Larry didn't recognize that I was trying to rescue him.

"Herman and I, we've formed this organization," he said, answering her question.

"An organization?"

"Well, it's more like a society really. It's a society to protect children. You don't know how many people there are in a city like Chicago who mistreat and abuse little girls."

Well, what do you say to that? "*Hey, Lar, I mean we all appreciate the sentiment, but you're kinda creeping me out here.*"

Here were two reclusive misfits, dedicating their energies to "helping" children? Had I gone and invited a coven of perverts into my home? Protecting children, indeed. These two probably couldn't pass a background check to get jobs as school crossing guards. I tried to catch Tamar's eye, but I think she avoided me on purpose.

Just in time to save us, the doorbell rang. When I opened, the birthday boy himself and Mrs. McBee stood on the landing. Herman had put on a sports shirt and a tie. Charlotte and her mom came up the stairs behind them. They all crowded into our small kitchen, and I tried to introduce everybody. It was such a dissimilar crew that I was sure I'd forget someone's name—like my wife's—but I made it.

Herman, of all people, saved the day. He seemed genuinely in good spirits. Miriam acted especially glad to see him.

"I knew you'd come," she told him, not that anybody had openly expressed doubt.

I began to relax. If we could get through the business with the dog, the whole thing might be a success.

Without any appreciable coaxing or effort, Miriam took over as hostess. It filled me with a surge of pride and accomplishment. It's the unexpected reward of being a parent, the recognition that without any planning or forethought, or maybe despite all planning and forethought, a unique individual has emerged who has really nothing to do with who you are or what you have tried so hard to impart. My Miriam, completely her own person with her own set of abilities, humors, and insights, was managing better than I ever could.

We overflowed out of the kitchen into our living room. I'd moved in a few extra chairs, but I worried that if everyone sat down it would be too formal. Most of all, now that I'd assembled a quorum, I feared of a sudden lapse into uncomfortable silence.

Larry walked over to our piano, and I watched him as he examined the ubiquitous photographs arranged on it, like any bourgeois household. There was one of Tamar and Miriam in dance outfits from some mother-daughter recital, one of the few family photos I'd taken myself. I'd tried for a stark, ironic Diane Arbus sensibility, but I hadn't succeeded. I was too much in love with my subjects. They were both smiling without a trace of sarcasm or self-awareness. I'd taken it the last year Tamar was still seriously dancing, before she started to put on weight.

I went over to him, and he put the photograph quickly down on the piano again.

"You have a very nice family," he told me.

Herman Viereck and his friend Larry Cerinzki, what a pair they made sitting side-by-side on our couch. The stuff of cartoons and one-reelers—Mutt and Jeff, Tom and Jerry, Ren and Stimpy, Laurel and Hardy, Abbott and Costello, Jerry and Deano. As I've said, Larry loomed over Herman. The two of them barely looked as if they came from the same planet, let alone from the same species. Yet, as is often the case, I got the feeling that my little janitor ran the show. He seemed to have some sort of subtle power over Larry. It was the first time I'd seen Herman interact this way with another person, and some of the same feelings of pride I felt for Miriam spilled over onto him.

I never learned exactly what Larry did for a living. I got the feeling that despite the way he deferred to Herman, he stood a little higher up on the economic food chain. He worked for the city, he told us, in some kind of clerical position in the public works department, something to do with curb easements.

"Larry tells me you and he are part of an organization," Tamar said, after we'd all sat down. I think she was just trying to keep any conversation going, but Herman looked at Larry as if he'd told the FBI they were leaking A-bomb secrets to the Russians.

"It's very small, just the two of us. We want to try and rescue as many children as we can."

"Rescue them, from what?"

"Orphanages. Larry and I want to adopt a little girl."

He said it without any insincerity or sense that he knew it was an absurd idea.

"I grew up in those places, pally. Let me tell ya, it ain't no picnic," Herman told her.

"Have you talked to any of the adoption agencies?" I asked. I felt this need to play the spoiler, to derail this vaguely menacing fantasy. "They might be a little worried about, I mean—the two of you …"

"The two of you" what? Moral degenerates, gropers of prepubescent soft spots, and here I had let them in my house, endangering my daughter and her friends. What if they were casing the place right now?

Miriam—thinks she knows everything, a bleeding heart, just like her parents, it could get her killed.

You know how one's train of thought quickly goes right to the edge, so easy to imagine the worst? *Catholics? A couple of wannabe molesting degenerate priests?*

No. I caught myself. Something in their affect rendered them harmless. They were lost innocents. Not perverse—just ineptly strange.

"Those adoption agencies don't understand how important our work is," Larry told us. "Some poor little girl, ripped away from her mother's arms. Not everyone who takes a child has their best interests at heart. They need someone who can give a child a good Christian upbringing."

"A good Catholic upbringing, to be sure," Mrs. McBee added. Gd, was she in on it too? Were they going to fill my apartment building with bratty, Bible-thumping orphans? I got an Oliver Twistish flash with Larry playing Fagan. My fragile feeling of ease about how the party was turning out started to crumple like a rain-soaked cardboard box.

A Catholic Society to Help Children, here in my building. Here's Herman Viereck, pawing through trashcans and rambling on about the weather, and this other guy with his rogue hands, drooling over photos of my family. Despite my feeling they were probably harmless, I wouldn't trust either of them to take care of a potted plant.

"Raising a child isn't easy," Charlotte's mom said. She'd been giving me nasty looks for the last five minutes.

"Yeah," I added quickly, "it takes a lot of time and patience."

"If you boys want to help, there are a lot of good organizations that could use you, like the Big Brothers and Sisters."

"I know," Herman said. Only now he looked vaguely depressed.

Champagne saved us. I'd thought serving it a risky idea, but Tamar laid in a bottle or two, more for the festive sound of the popping cork than anything else. We'd put out a spread, too. Nothing sophisticated, just cold cuts and a tub of potato salad, but set up festively on the sideboard, sitting on a doily with rose-cut radishes and sprigs of parsley. Tamar had a gift for presentation.

It unsettled me to watch Herman eat. How could he do something so ordinary? I knew he took his meals at the Stardust Diner, but I had a hard time imagining him doing anything as mundane as stuffing his face. Mrs. McBee made him a plate, though, and he dug in. She radiated something maternal in the way she dished it up for him. Maybe there was more going on there than met the eye. I found the thought oddly comforting.

Then he said yes to a glass of champagne. He said he'd never tried it before and, after a healthy swallow, allowed that it tasted pretty good. Tamar refilled his glass. I could tell she was conducting an experiment. I could have sucked the bottle down without it taking my edge off.

Before long, after we cut the cake, Herman got as close to garrulous as I'd ever seen him. When Tamar asked him where he grew up, he told her again about being born in Brazil.

"My father was a tailor," he said. "Generalissimo Getulio Vargas brought him over from Freiburg to be his personal uniform maker. The generalissimo, he knew the importance of a good lookin' uniform. My old man … if it was cloth, he could make it. He did gowns for all Vargas's daughters, but his uniforms, those were his piece-deeresistance. Double rows of braid, epaulets, any kind of collar you wanted, tunics, jackets, the whole nine yards."

In retrospect, his father being a military tailor makes perfect sense. It's where he got inspiration for all the uniformed officers and soldiers he obsessively drew. In his paintings, they often appear as a Busby Berkeley chorus line, each one done in a unique, Gilbert-and-Sullivan, over-the-top style. Flags, medals, and miles of gold braid. The records say Herman was born in Chicago, but I still don't think so. I suspect his father must have faked something so they could make Herman a US citizen.

"I bet you guys were rich," Charlotte said.

"I had a Brazilian nurse," Herman told us. "She taught me all kinds of songs, and there were toys—fantastical creatures, jaguars, dragons."

Miriam and Charlotte perked up. This sounded way better than the usual adult conversation at most of our parties.

"Did you ever see an Amazonian dragon?" he asked them. It was the
first time he'd spoken directly to them. They shook their heads.

"These ain't like the ones in your fairy tales. The Brazilian dragons
do good. Some get to be a hundert and thirty feet long, and they protect
the children of Brazil. They're a lot of children who were slaves in Brazil.
Long after the Civil War here in America, the Brazilians still had slavery.
The children there needed something to protect them."

"What were they called?" Miriam asked him.

"Bragdanolinians."

I remember their whole conversation, the way you do sometimes.
At the time, it seemed so out in left field, a nation of slaveholders, the
uniforms, the benevolent dragons, all so transparent now. Like all true
artists, Herman never strayed from his work. Even sitting in our living
room, the *Realms of the Unreal* stayed with him, a waking dream that
colored everything.

So … Brazil? Metaphor or outright lie? He had another glass of
champagne, and then, after we broke the musical ice by singing "Happy
Birthday," he offered to sing us a song his nurse had taught him, a Portuguese folk song. If he had really been born in Chicago and then shipped
off to an orphanage, where would he have learned something like that?

His voice? Limited in range, but he knew enough about singing not
to push it. Surprisingly, he stayed on pitch.

"He got shot in the chest," Viereck announced, after our little round
of applause.

"Your dad?"

"Nope, the general. My father had just built him this new outfit.
Snow white. Linen with a fine wool weft. Impeccable," he added, as
if the word were ambrosia in his mouth. "He'd just finished adjusting
the cuffs, and Vargas walks out onto the front steps of his palazzo to
show off the suit in the sunshine when this Buick drives up and they
gun him down. Both his bodyguards ducked. They must have been in
on it. Anyways, there were these big red splotches exploding across his
chest—like flowers opening. He was dead before he hit the ground. We
had to leave the very next day. It was what they call a coopdeetay. When
we got to Chicago, everything went downhill."

He stopped and looked at us. He had storyteller's magic. The girls sat in rapt attention, but he looked around, suddenly aware that he was talking to a live audience, not like being up in the middle of the night, pounding away on his indestructible Underwood, like one of those monkeys that was predicted to turn out the complete works of Shakespeare if it kept at it long enough.

He clammed up. The silence I'd dreaded descended. We all felt it. Then Charlotte's mother made some comment about the weather. I hadn't warned her, but you could see Herman almost breathe a gasp of relief, like an exhausted, half-drowned swimmer who finally puts his hand on the ladder leading to the raft.

"You might think this is a hot day for August, but it's only about average. Last year at this time, there were already seven days in August where the temperature got over eighty-five. In 1936, there were twelve consecutive days when it was over ninety-five. Of course, it can be cold in August too. Take 1957, fer instance …"

I could see Charlotte's mom's eyes start to glaze over. At least she didn't have to worry about him molesting her daughter.

Did you forget about the dog, our pound-wise ex-con? All the noise and activity in the living room hadn't gotten his hopes up. He'd gone to sleep in his carrying case, tucked away in our bedroom. I'd started hoping that we could cut the cake, give Herman his other gifts, and get him out the door before anyone remembered the mutt. At this point, I felt I'd rather keep the poor little thing rather than hand him over.

That's when he woke up and started barking. At first he sounded a little angry. Then he let out a plaintive whine that tugged at your heart. I kept my eye on Herman. I could tell the noise bothered him. It didn't take much to get his face to devolve into an angry scowl.

"Is that your dog?" Larry asked.

"No," I said. "Not really."

"Now, Herman, I want you to be totally honest with us," Tamar told him. "I mean, if you have any reservations about this, you tell us. We just thought that it might be a nice present for you."

"Yeah, you know, something to keep you company so you won't be so lonely," Miriam added.

"What makes you think I'm lonely?" Herman said.

"It was my idea," Miriam told him.

He turned to look at her, and I could see his face soften.

"They're a lot of company. He's a real friendly little guy. We rescued him from the pound. They were going to have him put to sleep if nobody claimed him."

As they say in poker, Miriam went "all in."

What could Herman say? "I want to protect orphans but to hell with dogs?"

Ron got up and went into the bedroom. He opened the cage, and the dog came prancing out. I looked at Tamar. We were both thinking the same thing—please don't pee. The dog sniffed at everybody's ankles. Miriam got down on the rug and tried to pick him up, but the dog got suspicious and kept backing away. Finally, Herman bent forward and rapped his knuckles on the floor.

"Hey poochy poochy, com 'ere, poochy." Maybe it was the odor of the trashcans he'd been sifting through, but the dog did the tail wag, went over, and licked his hand. Herman broke into a crooked little smile.

"Whaddaya think, Larry? You think this little guy could join our outfit?"

"Sure thing, Sergeant," Larry said.

CHAPTER FIFTEEN

I know Crandall went up to Herman's apartment just to humor me.
He'd been selling art way too long to think it his mission to discover
new and exciting work. Any gallery owner will tell you that, in the
arts, talent is the cheapest commodity of all. The last thing Dave needed,
he made a point of telling me over and over, was to discover an eighty-
year-old wunderkind.

As I've said, by the time I approached him about Herman's paintings,
we'd known each other twenty years, and he treated our relationship with
an exaggerated honesty. It became a matter of honor to him that every
conversation we had included some rant about how sick he'd gotten of
the constant hype that went with owning a gallery.

"I'm just a shop owner," he'd tell me. His gallery? Just a glorified
7-11, a convenience store for people with too much empty wall space.

"Honey, go get a quart of milk, a jar of mayonnaise—oh, and pick
up something to go over the couch, not too abstract."

He'd grown sick of pretending that every sculpture painfully stitched
out of trade beads or portraits made from painted pistachio shells made
a major contribution to the world's canon. In short, "Fuck the whole
thing and the horse it rode in on."

He took perverse joy in reminding me that the two of us were only
sticking it out because we didn't know how to do anything "useful"

with our lives. Usually, by the time he got to this point, we'd run up a hundred-dollar tab, and he'd begun saying foolish things to our cocktail waitress. He threw down the plastic, though, so I had to agree with him.

None of his clients knew how he felt, however, and the sight of an S-class Benz pulling up in front of the gallery got his entrepreneurial juices flowing. Come crunch time, Dave could do the hand-wave with the best of them. Over the years, we'd made each other tens of thousands.

"I'm such an effing whore," he moaned the day I nagged him again about Herman. We were sitting in his back office slurping a peaty single malt, a gift from some grateful hack.

"No you're not, Dave," I reassured him. "I'm the whore. You're just my broke-down, pathetic, chilly pimp."

"Amen to that, Bosco," he said. I swallowed an inch of Thistle Dew, and he sloshed in three fingers more. My tolerance was legendary. After Miriam died, I'd made a concentrated effort to drink myself into oblivion. Eventually, I'd had to give it up, for the expense, if nothing else. Back when I needed it the most, I couldn't even achieve emotional numbness, let alone amnesia.

"Come on," I said, lifting myself out of his Frank Lloyd Wrong chair. "Humor me. Let's go have a look at this guy. I need someone I can trust to tell me if I'm way off beam here."

"I told you I don't want to put any energy into promoting some schizoid self-taught primitive. I think you're trying to duck me on your own show."

"Don't be a jerk," I told him. His hitting the nail like that made me aggressive. "It won't kill you to take a look."

We left his office and walked out into the gallery proper. He had a different girl manning the front desk every time I came in. This one had a gaggle of silver bracelets on each arm, a stud through her bottom lip, and a band of faux tribal ink around one toned bicep. Nice tits, though.

"I'll be gone for about an hour," he told her. "If Harry Lang calls about the Podemski, stall him."

"What happened to the other one?" I asked him as we got into my car.

"What other one?"

"You know. Andrea."

"Oh her," he said, but I never got an answer.

***

It took fifteen minutes to drive across town. I had the game on, so we didn't have to talk about anything but the usual. The Cubbies had a two-run lead, but we both knew they couldn't hold it. Sure enough, Cincinnati had two on with nobody out by the time we pulled up in front of Herman's building.

Dave looked at the rundown structure, and I could tell he was thinking, "*This better be good.*" I led him up the stairs. The railing was a little loose.

"Christ, who owns this dump?" he asked.

But Dave knew his stuff. Given the stage set that I served up, not to mention the myth of the outsider genius laboring for years in obscurity, I could have shown some art dealers freeze-dried dog shit, and they would have gone gaga. Dave didn't care about hype. All he wanted to see were the drawings.

"Jeezus," he said, when I first opened the door. "Why don't you get someone in here and clean the place out? It smells like my mother's basement after the pipes burst."

He wandered down the narrow defile and quickly homed in on the collection of Madonnas. Then he saw the cutouts and stencils that Herman had thumb-tacked to the walls, the ones he used to trace his Vivian Girls.

"What are these?" he asked.

"It's how he did his figures. He'd find an image in an old newspaper or magazine and take it down to the Rexall where they had a copy machine. He'd have them blow it up or reduce it depending on the size he needed. He'd cut off the arms and legs and pin them with paper fasteners. Then he'd trace them onto the painting. It gives his little girls this kitschy effect that's really unnerving. It's like he's ripped off our everyday cultural icons and discovered some dark secret."

Crandall waved me off. He didn't want to hear my "blah blah Ginger blah blah blah …" about the pornographic underbelly of America's collective unconscious. Instead, he sniffed at the cutouts, making a big show of not being impressed. I decided to skip any more theatrics and pulled the trunk out from under the bed.

"They're in there," I told him. I let him open the box for himself. I won't say that his eyes grew big as saucers. I'll leave that for the movie version. But at least he finally shut up.

Crandall worked fast. He leafed through the stack of loose drawings, quickly sorting them into piles. Looking over his shoulder, I had to admire the accuracy of his eye. He immediately sorted out the best ones. If the subject matter shocked him, he didn't let on. I don't think he paid attention to what the pictures were "about." When he'd made a stack of about ten, he lifted them up onto the table where he could use the daylight. He rolled out a few of the scrolls, pinning the ends down, using Herman's Madonnas for paperweights. I tried not to hover, but I felt nervous. Dave looked at the longest for a few minutes making familiar little sucking noise through his front teeth. The noise I'd hoped to hear.

He'd selected a battle scene, the sky a six-foot de Kooningesque swathe of angry grays and blacks. Below the sky, the seven Vivian Girls, half naked and sporting their little dicks, ran across a field of grotesquely lush, feted tropical blooms (the Amazon jungle thing again). Behind them, an army of pursuing Cossacks, who'd already created a trail of bloody corpses, goose-stepped across the plane. Yet the Vivian Girls managed to maintain a look of serenity and composure, as if they inhabited a parallel universe, removed from the violence.

"Well?" I finally asked him.

"They're interesting," Dave said. It ticked me off.

"Oh come on, Dave. *Interesting*? Don't use the *I* word with me."

"All right, they're *very* interesting. He looked up from the painting, but I could tell it took effort to pull his eyes away. "Do you think this guy had any idea what he was doing?" he asked me. "Did he know how sophisticated these damn things are?"

"Personally, I don't think he had a fucking clue. He just had this movie running over and over in his head, and this was the only way he could get it out. Does it matter?"

"It will to some people. Look, I'm no critic. I just sell the stuff."

"Do you think you could sell this?"

For a moment he looked offended; I'd taken advantage of our friendship. Of course, he had to know all along that was why I'd dragged him up here. He just didn't want to hear it out loud. Dave got up from Herman's chair, took off his reading glasses, and made a show of putting them back in his shirt pocket.

"I don't know. It would take a pretty sophisticated clientele to want one of these things hanging in their living rooms. I'm not sure Chicago is ready for something like this. But if you got a hold of the right people … maybe LA."

He paused and looked right at me.

"Did you really drag me up here to ask if I would give this guy a show?"

"What if I did? I need your help, David. The word is getting out about this stuff. I've got people calling me on the phone wanting to come up and take a look. There's a reporter from the *Chicago Reader* who wants to do a story on this guy. There's a buzz growing, and I don't know how to handle it. You know how art is. The stuff has legs. Drips and drabs of it are walking out of here. I'm collecting this money for Viereck, but I don't know what the hell I'm doing. This could be a major find, and I don't want to blow it."

Crandall made a face, but I knew Herman's work spoke for itself.

"My November just cancelled. She had a nervous breakdown or a baby, I don't remember which. Tell you what. If you can come up with six or seven fresh photos, I'll give this guy the other two walls. Your name should pull people in. We'll call it 'Two Urban Gorillas,' or something."

He looked at the scroll again and whistled under his breath.

"The way to move this stuff is not to price him too cheap," he said.

CHAPTER SIXTEEN

We locked up and headed back to my apartment, switching from his Scotch to my homemade, tumbler-sized Tequila Sunrises. By the time Makiko came in, we were at that tipping point where a sober person can't write you off as drunk but also needs to realize that attempting a coherent conversation is a recipe for disaster.

"Dave's gonna give Herman a show," I told her. "Isn't that great?"

Makiko put down her cello in the other room and came back into the kitchen. She didn't look as if she wanted to play catch-up. Instead, she opened the refrigerator and got out some stuff for a sandwich. She didn't offer to make us any.

"Did you show him the little dicks?" she asked over her shoulder.

"Yeah, aren't they fantastically perverse?" Dave said.

"So what's your theory?"

"My theory?"

"Everybody's got one. My take on it is that poor Herman never saw a naked woman in his life and he didn't know we have vaginas."

"No way," I said. "Look at all the books in his apartment. He was too well read. Plus I think he and Mrs. McBee had something going on."

"Don't take me there," she said. "So what have you and Dave worked out? Are we getting our 60 percent?"

There it was. Why we weren't getting sandwiches. Makiko and I were the Saudis of Herman Viereck's subterranean art reserve, and Dave was Texaco. We hadn't been looking for gushers of art, but it was right under our feet, and she didn't plan on giving it away.

"You're going to take your usual fifty for Herman?" she asked Dave. She'd hopped up on the kitchen counter, swinging her feet and taking bites around the edges of her avocado sandwich.

"You know that's what we all do. It's the going rate. You don't understand the risks we gallery owners take. What am I gonna do, tell my landlord, 'Sorry, my last artist didn't sell; I don't owe you anything'?"

Makiko had heard it before. It insulted her that Dave had trotted out that same tired song and dance.

"You only take forty from Nate," she pointed out.

"That's because we go way back. Anyways, your old man's a bankable commodity. Or at least he used to be. Can't you build a fire under him? I don't think he's shot a roll since Miri …," Dave's voice died.

We weren't that drunk.

"Tell him you'll cut him off if he doesn't shoot me some pictures. I'm tired of hearing him go on about the two of you." (A bald-faced lie, by the way. I'd never said a word to Dave about our sex life.)

She gave Dave an even dirtier look than the one she'd already screwed on her face whenever he came around. They were always at each other's throats, each jealous of my relationship to the other.

"Come on, Dave," she said, "when are you going to ask me if it's true what they say about Asian women?"

"I know what they say about Asian woman. I just want to know what they say about you."

"Stick to your gallery groupies from CIFA. They're more your speed," she told him.

I couldn't tell if Makiko secretly liked this sort of thing. Dave acted pretty much this way with every woman he met. It embarrassed me, but women put up with it. Even Makiko never quite shut the door on him. I don't know if they carried on like this when I wasn't around, or if it was only for my benefit. It's obvious that it drove me a little crazy.

"Hey, you two, knock it off," I said.

It seemed ridiculous to me that here we were arguing about gallery percentages when we still hadn't come to any firm understanding as to what we owned. So far, the rationale that we were using the sale of his work to cover his rent had held up, but Crandall planned to add another zero or two to what we'd been letting people pay to waltz the stuff out the door.

You like to think that you're immune to the stuff, that when the time comes, you tell yourself the money doesn't matter. I still maintain it wasn't greed but the desire to see Herman's work validated that made me price conscious. At this point, there were only two possible things to do with the *Realms*. Sell it or burn it.

As for taking a cut, hadn't I found the work and recognized it for what it was? Other landlords would have chucked it all out. Makiko and I were both thinking the same thing. How much longer before all this became moot? How much time did Herman have?

"We ought to talk to a lawyer," I'd told her. But I'd been saying it for months, and we hadn't followed through. "We could set up some kind of trust fund," I said knowingly. The truth? I had only the dimmest idea of what a trust fund was. I knew that money couldn't help Herman much at this point. What would he do with it, move into a condo with a lake view?

Dave got up and looked at his watch. Herman wasn't his problem. He dealt with Makiko and me as any other owners of a work of art. He'd hype it, exhibit it, sell it, and ship it out the door for 50 percent. Whatever we wanted to do with our share didn't concern him in the least.

***

I waited a few days before I went to see Herman with the news about his having a show. I found him still in bed when I got there at three in the afternoon, the second time in a row he hadn't been up and sitting on his bench. I had to shake him a few times. Once awake, he gazed at me dully for a few seconds before he recognized me.

Driving over, I'd thought about what it would be like for him to come to the opening. But I could feel that wasn't going to happen.

Herman was right. Sometimes things happen too late. I'd planned to have him sign a standard gallery contract, too, but at the end, I didn't bother. The sight of a legal-looking document might upset him, and there was too much in it I'd have to try to explain.

"Did you hear what I said, Herman? Your stuff is going to be in a major gallery. All kinds of people are going to see it. Some of the most art-savvy people in Chicago."

He'd nodded his head, but it didn't seem to make much of an impression. When I told him, his face hardly registered a change.

"Did you see the weather report?" he asked. "It looks like rain. There hasn't been more than three-hundredths of an inch since August nineteenth. Could be we're in for a dry fall. Not like '72, though. Thirty-two straight days with zero precip. Boy, did the weathermen get it wrong that time. They never get it right, all their satellites and computers. Why don't they just learn to look at the sky?"

"Is there any special piece that you'd like us to put in the show?" I asked, trying to get him back on track.

"It's up to you, pally," he told me.

On the way out, I ran into one of the nurses.

"Mr. Viereck doesn't seem to be doing too well," I said, trying the same non-confrontational diplomacy that had sometimes worked with Miriam's nurses when I knew screaming at them wasn't going to get me anywhere and they'd find some way to take it out on my daughter.

"He's got the dwindles," she said.

"Maybe they should take him to see a specialist."

She looked surprised. There weren't too many friends or family at the Sisters who were big on advocating changes.

"Mr. Learner, poor Herman's just old and worn out. We have a wonderful physician's assistant who sees him at least once a month. She's very good with him."

I didn't protest. I'd been through it with my own father. All the CT scans, the pulmonary therapists, the consultants whose bills kept arriving long after he was dead, all the *Sturm und Drang*. In the end, the results were the same.

Still, I felt a little guilty about how quickly I acquiesced to her arguments to "leave the poor old guy alone."

Face it, the myth I'd begun building around the little German janitor proved a lot more compelling than the man himself. His shadowy
presence out here at the Sisters could be holding up his career.

I drove over to the gallery, Herman's unsigned contract still in my
pocket, and told Dave the whole thing was copasetic.

**

Selecting samples of Herman's work turned out to be trickier than
we thought.

To help us go through the pieces without handling them repeatedly,
I decided to make slides. I set up a bank of studio lights over Herman's
work table and started taking archival photos. It wasn't creative, but at
least Herman had managed to get me handling a camera again.

There were over five hundred works of art, some little more than
sketches, some eight feet in length and executed on both sides. I couldn't
get the larger ones into one frame. It took me a lot of time and nitpicking
to get the sections to line up and then to reproduce them onto a single
slide. Eventually, I gave up trying to catalogue everything. Even at a
rate of three an hour, it would have taken me months. To this day, with
his stuff safely moved to the archives of the Institute for Intuitive Art,
I'm not sure anyone has been through all of it. Not even Adrian Holm.

I set up the Kodak carousel on Dave's desk and started throwing
images up on the wall. We settled on the six major pieces quickly, mostly
battle and weather scenes. When we got to the smaller pieces, it got
harder. In many ways, they proved more interesting, if less flamboyant.

He'd done individual portraits of all the Glandelinian and Christian
generals. One or two looked like possible self-portraits, Herman posing
himself as the weatherman hero of his own Homeric saga.

I've mentioned that all his little girls are anonymous and interchange-
able. In all his drawings of the Vivian sisters and in the thousands of
pages they appear in print, nothing marks them as individuals. The Seven
Dwarfs are Shakespearean in complexity next to the Vivs, which was

why his portrait of Annie Proturick jumped out at us when I projected it on the wall.

"Whoa, go back to that one," Dave yelled.

We both stared at the image. The Vivs' were uniformly blond, but Annie's dark hair fell loosely down her back. It was one of only a few works where, if you look closely, you can see erasures and tentative pencil lines under the watercolor. Herman had struggled to get what he wanted. Her clothing, too, wasn't derived from a Victorian fantasy. It had a contemporary feel. Last, he'd drawn a scalloped dark border round the portrait. At the bottom, he'd labeled her in his usual childish hand, "Annie Proturick."

"You know what this looks like?" Dave asked me.

"What?"

"It looks like it's a copy of a photograph. It's the proportions, the central way she's posed, with the scalloped border, too. Like a kid in one of those school photos they rook people into buying, ten wallet-sized, five eight-by-tens. My mom's got a shoebox full of them. Any idea who she is?"

"I bet it's just an image he salvaged from the trash."

"Maybe she's a character in his book? Is she in there?"

"Who knows," I told him. "The most I can get through in one sitting is about five pages. I'll ask Adrian. He's becoming an expert in the realms of the *Realms*. I think he intends to read the whole bloody thing."

"He's not that smarmy sod you were seeing after Miriam and the divorce?"

"Yeah. You know he's written a treatise on the art of the insane. He's an expert on that German guy, Wölfli."

"That's the one with the guy in some Swiss asylum who made sculpture out of chewed bread because they wouldn't give him any art supplies."

"No, I think that's someone else. Doesn't matter. Adrian's been spending nights in Viereck's apartment, reading the book. He claims he's trying to commune with Herman's spirit."

"Just don't let him commune away with any of these paintings," Dave said. "I've got a feeling this show is only the start of something."

He pointed to the slide of Annie Proturick still shimmering on his wall.

"She goes in," he said.

CHAPTER SEVENTEEN

Despite Dave's penchant for cynicism, as the day of the opening approached, he got more and more excited. I kept an eye on the growing number of pieces he'd selected and calculated how much wall space he had left. I kept my mouth shut. Our initial agreement to give me half of the gallery had fallen by the wayside, and I wasn't anxious to pick it up.

So when Dave tacitly quit bugging me about my half, I didn't bring it up. But a week before the opening, he called me.

"At least get me a few pictures of his apartment," he told me. I want to give people a sense of his environment."

"Okay," I told him. It seemed like a cheap way to get out from under our agreement and a concrete assignment that didn't involve living subjects. I could do that.

"Do you have a picture of Viereck?" he asked me.

"What for?"

"I'd like to put it up in the front of the gallery. It'll give people some idea of who this guy is."

Trust Crandall. He realized the commercial value of creating the proper mythology.

"He's a pretty sick guy, Dave. I'm not sure his picture is something you'd want to hang in the gallery."

"Well, maybe something from before. At one time, I thought you'd shot a portrait of every bum and street freak in Chicago."

"He's not a bum," I snapped, but he was just teasing me.

So, to please Dave, I went up to Herman's and shot a few rolls. It felt okay, but it didn't break the logjam of my blocked creativity. I got shots looking down the long axis of his room with his work table on the right and all his boxes and stacks of crap on the left.

When I see these pictures now, they remind me again of the shots Carter took of Tut's antechamber. There are the same piles of the boy king's worldly belongings, his heaps of chairs, stools, bows, arrows, lances, and chariot parts. Everything heaped up, like stuff people put out on the curb, waiting for trash day.

Back in the seventies, gallery openings in Chicago were traditionally the first Tuesday of the month. In November, it put them in competition with Election Day. Quadrennially, for the presidential debacle, they'll postpone them, but this being an off year, Dave didn't think too many potential gallery crawlers would be sitting in front of their TVs watching Daly win by another landslide.

The weather concerned me more. It would be poetic justice for Herman if an early snowstorm wrecked his big moment.

The morning sky loomed gray and nasty. To us native Chicagoans, it smelled like snow. I had the radio on in my office. All morning, the news guys hyped it for all it was worth. Then around lunch, the sun came out, and it got up to fifty. I'm sure Herman, lying in his bed at the Sisters, got joy out of seeing our local weather hawks blow their predictions once again.

Filled with vicarious opening-night jitters, I headed over to the gallery around three. I felt more anxious than if it had been my own show. I'd pushed pretty hard to get this exhibit hung. If it flopped, Dave would let it revert to my responsibility. Sitting in traffic, I visualized again what we had picked out. In my current mood, Herman's work felt infantile. Not so much shocking as pathetic.

Had I let Herman's fan club of fools and fanatics lead me down the garden path? Jeff, Holm, Crandall, even Makiko: were they all under my power? Had the forcefulness of my personality made them abandon their artistic and moral compasses? By the time I walked in the door at Crandall Fine Arts and Photography, I wanted to hide my head in a paper bag.

And there they were, stretched out luxuriously on the gallery's beige walls. Two of his double-sided murals had been sandwiched between Plexiglas and were hung from the ceiling in the center of the room, allowing the viewer to walk around and see them from both sides. The light coming through from the other side added to the feeling that they were animation cels from a cartoon drawn in hell.

It's amazing what hanging a show will do. You could crush Marlboro boxes in frames, and with a few halogen wall-washers and some labels typed in Invicta, it looks like A.R.T. Dave had done his usual masterful job of showmanship and marketing. He always tried to maximize his sales on the first night, and I knew he wasn't above seeding the show by putting a few little green "sold" stickers on some pieces, just to generate a little buyer's hysteria.

"What do you think?" his tattooed assistant asked me. She was putting out plastic glasses and uploading a case of three-dollar-a-bottle Chilean Chardonnay.

"It looks great," I said.

She paused and looked at the stuff on the walls. The shock value of Herman's work must have worn off, but she seemed to be having one of those moments when you look at something familiar as if seeing it for the first time.

"I don't know," she said, her voice taking a professional tone. "I think Dave's taking a risk. November is a good month for us. Maybe he should have gone with something safer."

"You don't think Chicago is ready for this?"

"Prepubescent girls with goat horns and penises, getting stomped and choked to death?"

"Try to look past that," I said, but not unkindly. Even with the hardware and tattoos, I thought Dave had finally picked someone who could, physically, intellectually, and sexually, body-slam him onto the mat.

Dave wasn't there yet. While we were talking, Barbara Hackett, the reviewer for the *Trib*, wandered in with her small entourage.

"Hey, it's Nathan Learner. I might have known you were mixed up in this. I must have gotten fifteen calls from Dave about this show."

I began to realize that Crandall Galleries had called in all its favors to push Herman on the masses. I felt flattered.

I stood back and let her take the tour. One of her guys wore Prada, the other had knee-windows in his Jeans. Maybe they came that way and cost three hundred dollars. What did I know anymore? It took them ten minutes to take everything in. Between the three of them, they engaged in an above-average amount of hand waving, the leaning in for a closer look, the stepping back, the placing of the open palm against the side of the tilted face. Deep thought.

With Dave AWOL, it devolved to me. I stood respectfully back a step or two and tried not to hover. I couldn't help it. My heart beat fast, and I had the feeling that everything I'd eaten in the last two weeks began to solidify in my stomach. Hackett turned and looked at me. "What's the story on this guy again?" she asked.

I gave her the version I'd perfected for those with short attention spans.

"You mean all those years, you didn't know what he was doing up there?"

"Not a clue," I said.

"They're pretty amazing. I mean, let's forget the subject matter for a moment. Just the way he incorporates these images from popular culture, subverts them to fit his own personal vision. It's quite remarkable. And yet it's all so detached somehow. The way these little girls just seem to be floating through all this carnage. It's as if nothing can touch them."

I nodded my head while she went on. The comments about Herman were starting to fall into recognizable categories. Chiefly there were those who confronted Herman's pornographic aspects and incipient perversions straight on and those who pretended they were irrelevant. Barbara played too hip to wonder out loud about the little wangers. I wondered how she'd get around mentioning them when she wrote her review.

"He's still alive, I heard."

I nodded. She didn't have to pry it out of me. I knew she'd start snooping around.

"I'd like to interview him," she said. "Maybe bring one of the regular beat guys with me. It's great human interest."

"That would be pretty hard. He's in a nursing home. He's dying. I don't think you'd get much out of him. All he ever talks about is the weather."

Did I feel protective of Herman, replaying my *Tonight Show* fantasy in my head, or did I just want to keep him for myself? I didn't know, but it seemed wrong having these glad-handers and opportunists trooping out to the Little Sisters. I'd violated him enough already.

"Well, let me know," she said. "This could turn out to be a good local story. This isn't LA or New York. We don't have an endless supply of homegrown weirdoes."

Then the guy in Prada came over, and I got a slightly different version. Everybody got the Disney thing, and they loved it

Disney on acid, Psycho-Walt, Alice in Shudderland, Mickey goes to Hell—over the years, I've amassed quite a collection, but that night it felt new. And I have to admit, I dug it.

I'd planned to go home and change into something more proprietary and professoresque, but the crowd arrived early. By the time the *Trib* people left, one of the reviewers from the *Chicago Reader* wandered in, and I began the same song and dance all over again. The place began to fill up. As I said, Dave had pulled out all the stops. Plus, I think it being Election Day actually helped his turnout. The hollow reality of the lack of any real choice had sunk in, and the electorate, fighting its post-voting depression, wanted an escape onto some higher plain.

I didn't have time to leave and come back. Dave finally trooped in with a woman in tow, but not one of his art school groupies. California tan and fit, with skin stretched surgically tight across her cheekbones. Dave must have driven out to O'Hare to pick her up in person.

She didn't say much to me, but Dave shepherded her around the floor, and they had their heads together, the way people do when they're talking money.

With no Herman on scene, I became the logical stand-in. By eight o'clock, my jaw ached from continuous smiling and spieling. I'd just started taking a new blood-pressure medication. I hadn't eaten, the gallery was warm, and the wine cheap but palatable.

By the time Makiko came in, I'd been holding up the wall for the last half hour. My lips still moved, but I'd given up paying much attention to what came out of my mouth. Every once in a while, my ears would catch a snatch of my spiel. I'd begun to sound as if I'd done the drawings myself.

"Quite a crowd," she said. Another group came up and shook our hands. Between the two of us, we knew everybody. Makiko came out on the court ready to play some ferocious D. I shut my mouth and let her take over. By then it was 8:30, and the place rocked, way more festive than down at election headquarters.

In the back of the gallery, art students were dredging up the last of the wine and cheese. Guys in Birkenstocks, women in sequined sweaters, all talking hyper animatedly. A gaggle of smokers congregated out on the street, and every time the door opened whiffs pleasantly irritated my nose. Then, as if someone had rung a bell, the crowd started to break up. I witnessed a lot of exaggerated hugging, and people promising to call each other.

I managed to disengage myself from the wall, and we walked across the now-empty gallery and double-checked Herman's work one last time. Two of the larger pieces had green "sold" circles on their labels. Dave had knocked them down at $4,500 a pop. Two of the smaller works were sold, as well. He'd already made double his nut for the month.

"Shit," Makiko the truck farmer's daughter said, standing next to me. "That's a lot of strawberries."

CHAPTER EIGHTEEN

A month later, after he'd wrapped the show, I went by the gallery, and Dave cut me the check for our half. As I've explained, it didn't bother him to make it out to me, but seeing him write my name made me uneasy. I'd taken such a proprietary interest in the show, and so many people had come to associate me with Viereck's work that I felt he'd paid me for my own creations, a distinction I didn't want.

The show hadn't completely sold out, but Dave had managed to generate a lot of the right kind of buzz. Now it was just a matter of which name-brand collector would be willing to take the plunge and take Herman national.

As for the general run of gallery lookie-loos, they were delighted with my crazy janitor. Hackett's review in the *Trib* couldn't get past the idea that Herman proved more valuable to Chicago as a human-interest story than as an artist. She'd devoted more than half of her column to describing Herman's background and strange behavior.

A lot of people who didn't frequent galleries came by, people from our neighborhood and coworkers at the hospital who remembered him. The comments in Dave's guest book ranged from "tortured genius" to "filthy pervert."

In all, he sold seven of his works. The two large scrolls (whereabouts of one, unknown at this time) and five of his smaller pieces.

Crandall acted delighted. "At this point in his career," he told me, "volume isn't important. It's placing the work with the right people."

Viereck was eighty-two years old, but Dave went on and on about his career as if he was one of my wunderkinds from CIFA. Art dealers are the only people I know who have proof that there's life after death.

The woman he'd fetched from O'Hare, the one with the electric tan and the Botox brow, turned out to be a way-upscale interior designer and private curator. Dave assured me that all her clients had faces I'd seen on the covers of *People* magazine. I suspect Dave did some kick-back deal on the resale. But he probably would have given the stuff to her if she'd asked for it.

"From leeeeetle acorns, Nathan," he chortled, giving his knuckles a Dickensian crack.

I cashed the check and made one out to Herman, less his rent money. When I drove over, I found Herman out of bed and sitting in the day room. I'd like to imagine that sheets of rain were pummeling the window, but the day proved gray and nondescript, temperature in the midforties, the sky overcast. The way the world is most of the time, blah and average. Herman had the TV on. He was watching *Oprah*, something I don't think he'd ever done before in his life. I had to stand right in front of him before he noticed me.

"Hey, Mr. Nathan, I didn't expect to see you back here so soon."

"I've got something for you."

I handed him the check. He stared at it awhile, trying to make sense of it. Then he nodded slowly, something long anticipated, something he felt sure would finally come.

"Did you ever think you'd be making money from your artwork?" I asked him.

He shrugged. He was an old man. Just sitting still and being were enough. "I guess I didn't do too bad for a moron," he said finally.

"Hey, Herman, you're not a moron. You're anything but."

"You don't know nuthin' about it, pally."

He seemed to be slipping into another persona, using another frame of reference.

"Be'n' a moron ain't so bad. That's what they diaga-nozed me when I got to the home. Moron's kinda high up on the scale. Of course, they made us do all the work. You gotta scrub down the place and help the attendants feed the idjets. The idjets, they're the worst, just lay around in their slop all day or drooling all over themselves. There's 'leptics too, havin' fits all the time. I guess the ims had it the best."

"The ims?"

"Yeah, imbeciles, they weren't trainable so they just got to hang out all day. Nobody made 'em do nuthin'."

A look of incomprehension must have come over my face. Herman shook his head, marveling at my ignorance.

"That's the way they did it in those days, pally. You went in and saw the doctor and he 'zamined you and askt you a few questions and then put you down as either a moron, an imbecile, or an idjet. The idjets were the low end. The 'leptics were a different group all together."

"God, Herman," I said, "it sounds awful. How long were you there?"

"'Bout ten years—they shipped me in from the orphanage when I was seven, said I constituted a disruptive influence."

He got quiet for a few seconds. I couldn't tell if he was thinking about things that had lain dormant for years or whether the home for the feeble-minded had been with him every day of his life.

"So when did they release you?"

"They don't release you from those places. You get to be old enough, they send you up to Mortonville, to the asylum. Lots of the idjets never made it. They carried them out the back."

"But you got out. I mean they must have realized that you weren't … that you didn't belong there."

I realized my own naiveté as the words came out of my mouth. Once you were in one of those places, you could be Einstein, and no one would dare admit they'd made the wrong diagnosis.

"I kept runnin' away," Herman said. "I guess they finally got tired of trying to find me. One day, I just walked off and came up to Chicago. The hospital gave me the job."

"And that was it?"

"Pretty much. That's the story of my life, as they say."

"Of course you had your art—you had the *Realms*."

Herman gave a little snort and a half chuckle. "I finished that a long time ago, pally. It's all over with," he told me.

"No it's not. People are beginning to notice your work. The check is for almost three thousand dollars." Herman picked up the check and looked at it again, but it didn't impress him.

"What do you want me to do with it?" I asked him.

"I don't know. I'm still thinking about that headstone, you know, for after. I'd like something nice. There should be something left about me. You think you could arrange that?"

CHAPTER NINETEEN

Mike O'Malley. Now there's a name for a Chicago cop. When he told it to me, he sounded apologetic, as if some scriptwriter had made it up for him. After all, he had a professor of art on the phone. Men like us couldn't be expected to suffer clichés.

Despite the name, O'Malley didn't sound like a detective. His soft voice had a brogueless and unassumingly Midwestern tone, better suited to a library than for making oneself heard over the chaos of a squad room.

"It is *Doctor* Learner?" he asked. I assured him that Chicago Institute of Fine Arts wasn't hung up on academic titles, but I suppose he'd looked me up in the school directory. Technically he had it right. Somewhere in all the chaos of the sixties, I'd picked up a PhD.

"I just don't want to offend anyone," he assured me. "Around here, we're touchy about rank. I was wondering if you'd have time to answer a few questions."

This is the way it starts, I thought. The Gestapo, the KGB, now Chicago PD. If other kids had been raised to fear some shadowy boogie man under their beds, in our house it was the Gestapo. A few "questions"?

"And vat is the nature of your business here in Berlin, Herr Learner? Vere did you get these papers? They're very cleverly done ..."

Hanging on the phone, I did a flyby of all my sins. Most of them didn't violate the Illinois criminal code. There might be a few things centered around the Democratic National Convention of '68 that I'd assumed the statute of limitations had run out on. That and the odd lid of Columbian gold.

"May I ask what this is in regards to?" It didn't take long to start sounding like I wanted to lawyer up.

"It's nothing about you directly," he assured me. "I need to talk to you about one of your tenants."

Oh great, I thought. We'd had enough casual dope dealers and potential bomb throwers in the building over the years.

"Who?'

"Guy's name is Herman Viereck. Didn't he rent a room from you?"

Herman, of all people? I scrolled through his behavior for any likely scenario. Outside of pawing through trashcans, I came up blank.

"He's been in a nursing home for a few months. What's the problem?"

"It would be easier if we talked face to face," he said. "Could I meet you somewhere?"

"There's a funky espresso bar on Fennimore and Vine. It's near my office. Can't you give me some idea what this is about?"

"I'm with homicide," he said. "There's a picture in the gallery I'd like to talk to you about."

He didn't have to elaborate. By the time I got down to the coffee shop an hour later, subconsciously at least, I'd figured it out.

O'Malley looked even less like a cop in person than he'd sounded over the phone. He was a small, quiet, unassuming man, just like his quarry. Shaking his hand gently, I wondered how he had made it all these years on the mean streets of Chicago.

He looked about ready to retire. His hair had begun to thin. Not a bald spot, just a general wispiness. His eyes, though, were blue, clear, and had that storied Irish twinkle.

He had no problem looking me straight in the face. When he did, I could feel his gaze causing what felt like a pressure sensation against my skin. When I looked away, I could feel that they never wavered from studying me. I felt like I'd sat down in front of a human lie detector.

Even so, I had a hard time imagining him chasing some perp down an alley or putting six in the black at the firing range. He had on a nice, high-end suit from someplace respectable, like Barneys or Nordstrom.

Later, I learned that Chicago detectives make sixty to seventy grand a year, not counting overtime, enough that O'Malley could afford to dress any way he wanted. Me? I had on my usual, the lefty-college-professor, sixties-retro, slightly age-inappropriate jeans and an unironed shirt.

Seeing him, I wished I'd put on a tie.

We fumbled with a little small talk while we waited in line. This was before a Starbucks lurked on every corner, but he seemed to know what to order. He insisted on paying. That started to make me nervous. Was he pulling some kind of elaborate Colombo routine? Later I realized that Peter Falk could have learned a few things from him.

"I saw the Viereck exhibit," he said after we sat down. He blew gently across the top of his doppio cappuccino.

"You did?" I tried not to sound surprised, but outsider art didn't look to be one of his major interests. "Imagine," he said, "all those years, up in that little apartment, churning that stuff out. Where did he get the energy? I get home, it's all I can do to make it to the ten o'clock news without falling asleep on the couch."

"I know," I said. "It's part of the growing mystique about him."

"For someone like you, a fellow artist, it must be quite an experience, getting involved with this."

"It's pretty powerful stuff," I said, doomed to have the Viereck conversation yet again. No way was O'Malley going to be rushed.

"Obsession," he said. "That's the kind of thing that keeps people going. There's a lot of pathology there. As soon as I walked into the gallery, it jumped out at me."

"They're very powerful images, but they seem to resonate with many different kinds of people. We've sold a lot of his work."

"Not the portrait, I hope."

"Which one?"

"The little girl. Annie Proturick."

"I don't remember," I lied. I suspected Dave's LA connection had snapped it up.

O'Malley paused long enough for me to know we were into phase two.

"There's a cold case I've been working off and on for twenty years," he told me. "I got it the first day I made homicide. I've been there my whole career. I never thought there was much point in working anything else. After all, anything else can be replaced except a life, right?"

The little knot of unease I felt about talking to O'Malley expanded into places I didn't want it to go. Against my will, I could hear the Miriam tape starting to cue up in the background.

"You have a point," I said.

"That little girl—Annie Proturick—do you know anything about who she is?"

I shook my head. "I just thought she was a character out of his book."

"Annie Proturick disappeared off the streets of Chicago twenty years ago. She got off her school bus. No one has seen her since. It ran in the papers for weeks. You sure you don't remember? We must have followed up a thousand leads. All dead ends. It's like she'd vanished off the face of the earth. There's been nothing about the case for years, till her picture shows up at your art show."

"I'm sorry," I said. "I don't remember it. So many horrible things happen. It seems like it never ends."

But it wasn't quite true, the part about not remembering. Now that O'Malley had put some context to Annie's name, I dredged up something.

"They kept running her picture. It's the same pose that you had in the one in the show."

"Oh, yes," I said, finally. The same way you pretend to remember someone you might have known in college who turns out to be someone else's brother-in-law. By the time you tell the lie, you've convinced yourself it's true.

"Don't kids disappear all the time? I mean, all those milk cartons?" I asked, after a pause. I felt ready to defend Herman, and O'Malley hadn't even mentioned his name again.

"Yes, but her disappearance captured the public's imagination because of that picture. She had this innocent smile that gets to you. And her mother, too, they were such a happy, normal family. Her mom kept getting on TV, pleading for any information. People's hearts went out to them."

O'Malley took another sip. He'd learned to do it without getting any foam on his upper lip. No way could I make him look bumbling. He waited for me to fill in the blanks, but I played dumb, reluctant to make any connections without him forcing me to go there.

Of course, I knew what he had on his mind—15,487 pages of gloriously illustrated mayhem committed against little girls. It's not as if I hadn't already had the odd paranoid thought, wondering what Herman might have been capable of if he lost control.

"You think there's some connection between her disappearance and Mr. Viereck?" I felt like the number one son in an old Charlie Chan movie, but he'd left me no other place to go.

"I've worked on hundreds of homicides in my career," he told me. "Usually we wrap it up in a few days. Forget all that CSI stuff. Someone usually talks. After a week, though, if we haven't made an arrest, our chances start to drop off exponentially. If you can get away with murder for six months, statistically it becomes the perfect crime. Don't let all those cold-case TV shows fool you. It almost never happens."

"I didn't think it did," I assured him.

"I've got a bunch of unsolved cases, but some things just stay in your mind. I guess I'm a little obsessed, too. When Annie disappeared, I'd just made detective, and I thought I was pretty hot stuff. Anyway, I promised Annie's mom I'd find out who did it. A stupid thing to do, make a promise like that to a woman who's hysterical with grief, but I was new on the job, and it just came out. It's a horrible thing, to lose a child like that, just have her disappear into thin air."

Well, for all his experience talking to people, O'Malley had missed the look on my face. It was partly my fault. When he started in about dead and missing children, I should have warned him off. I could have said something to let him know he was on dangerous ground, but he snuck it in too fast.

There are things you prepare for ahead of time. The anniversaries, the Christmases and the Chanukahs. You know they're coming, and you can do things so you don't have to be alone, say, take a trip to Hawaii or go on a Zen retreat, like an alcoholic in recovery who plans his routes so he doesn't pass any bars or liquor stores.

There are little alleyways of thought that I'd schooled myself not to go down. I try never to wonder how old she would have been on a certain date, what she would have wanted for her birthday, what she would look like, sound like.

I no longer linger in shopping malls. I don't plant myself at the food court, watching gaggles of teenagers strutting by, occasionally thinking that I've seen her face, caught a glimpse of her as a group of girls gets lost in the crowd or disappears into a multiplex and almost plunk down nine bucks just to go in after her, wondering how I could be this primitive and desperate to think that she is actually walking around in a mall.

Would He play that kind of trick on you? Except that after all the things Gd has done or let happen, He could certainly resurrect my dead daughter and have her go see *Finding Nemo* on a Saturday afternoon if He wanted to.

Naturally, I had none of this complex machinery of avoidance and denial running until the moment O'Malley flipped the switch. As usual, when reminded of Miriam, I had conflicting urges. I didn't want to hurt O'Malley's feelings. After all, there was no way he could have known that talking about Annie's disappearance would affect me, but then part of me wanted to rub his face in it. What other small self-serving reward is there? A little mordant self-pity, a little cheap tabloid shock value?

"Why yes, Inspector, I think I can relate to her parent's situation. It just so happens I have some experience in the death of a child."

Of course, it's not the same thing. I have the solace of knowing where Miriam is and how she died. I know that confronting a violent sudden death is harder than dealing with a slow, remorseless disease. There's less anger, less self-remorse, less of the pointless replayings of the "if onlys."

If only I'd met her at the bus. If only I'd let her stay home with a little sore throat. If only …

How many forms does evil take? Is the aberrant strand of DNA that causes a white blood cell to keep dividing any different from the aberrant strand that tells a mind that it is okay to indulge its murderous fantasies? Why should Annie's mother's grief be more terrible than my own?

At first, my desire not to hurt O'Malley won out. I didn't say anything, but against my will, I felt my face screwing itself up into a look of impending tears.

"Hey, is there something wrong?" he asked.

So I told him. It came out flat, a matter of fact. "I'm afraid you've hit a bit of a nerve. I had a daughter about that age. We lost her to leukemia."

To his credit, O'Malley didn't fall all over himself trying to apologize. I began to get a sense of what he meant when he told me the case obsessed him.

He immediately saw my confession about Miriam as an opportunity. "I'm sorry. I guess this must bring up some painful memories."

Of course, what really angered me about O'Malley is that he'd made the fears about Herman that I'd long suppressed tangible. "It's okay," I told him.

"Well, even so. I didn't mean to spoil your day," he said.

Which, it seems to me, is what Mr. O'Malley has spent the better part of his career doing. I shrugged it off, and we both studied the tops of our cups.

"I'm surprised you're interested in the Chicago art scene," I said.

"No, not generally. I don't know much about art. The wife and I went to Europe a few summers back. We went to the Vatican, the Sistine Chapel, the Louvre. The *Mona Lisa*—it's a good painting, but I don't quite get what all the fuss is about. We get over to the museum every now and then when we have guests from out of town. I like that one of the people in the park, what do they call that technique, pointralism?"

"Oh, yeah, the Seurat. It put Chicago on the map."

"O'Malley smiled. "I thought that was the Picasso bull," he said, not to be outdone.

"I can't help wondering how you ended up at Dave Crandall's gallery for Viereck's show."

"Just a coincidence. I was tailing a guy."

"In Dave's gallery? I thought you were with homicide."

O'Malley gave a little shrug, wondering what my point was. It left me trying to deal with the idea that a murder suspect prowled Chicago's art galleries, possibly someone I knew.

"It turned out to be nothing," he tried to reassure me. "But that's how I happened to see the portrait. Why would he have drawn her if she didn't mean something to him? If he wasn't involved in some way? Who would spend the time dreaming up all those ways to kill and torture little girls—unless he wasn't consumed with homicidal impulses?"

"But Herman sees himself as the savior and protector of these little girls. In the book he wrote, he's always coming to their rescue."

"Come on, Dr. Learner. I don't need to lecture you about psychology. You've spent more time looking at his work than anyone. You don't have to be a forensic psychiatrist to know what went on inside his head, the conflict of good and evil. Here's a guy who's at war with himself. It's not much of a stretch to think he may have acted on some of his impulses, that eventually they overwhelmed his defense mechanisms. That eventually, just writing and drawing about them weren't enough."

"Maybe her disappearance caught his imagination like everyone else. Maybe he just felt like doing her portrait."

O'Malley looked me right in the eyes. It made me feel like confessing, even though I hadn't done anything.

"You really think he knows anything?" I asked him.

"It's in the realm of possibility," he said.

"I can't see it," I told him.

But of course he was right.

"Did you say Mr. Viereck is in a nursing home?"

For a few seconds I thought of telling him that Herman had died, but there seemed no point trying to hide anything from O'Malley. I'm sure he already knew Herman's whereabouts. Why did I feel this need to protect him, anyway? If Herman had something to do with Annie's disappearance, I had to know. Of course I didn't know what it would do to Herman's "career"—a career from which I looked to be the chief beneficiary.

"He's at the Little Sisters of the Poor, out on Lake Shore."

"I know the place," he said. "My daughter did charity work out there. When do you think we could go see him?"

CHAPTER TWENTY

The shockwaves of taking Viereck public kept spreading. Days after meeting with O'Malley, my phone rang again. Caught up in Herman's recent success, it took a few moments before I became suspicious of what my caller wanted. I expected everyone to be a fan of his, or at least an interested critic.

"Is this Mr. Learner?" the voice on the phone asked.

"Are you the Mr. Learner who was involved in that art show, the one with that old janitor who did all those pictures with the little girls in 'em?"

I could tell right away it wasn't anyone connected with the Chicago art scene.

"Yes. I helped arrange for Mr. Viereck to have an exhibit." Instinctively I wanted to downplay my involvement. "Who is this?"

I heard a pause.

"I don't quite know how to tell you this—but I think Herman Viereck may be related to me."

Her voice had an affected little-girl quality, hints of a badly done seductive baby-doll drawl, like a theater arts major from Minneapolis trying to do Maggie the Cat. Someone had taught this woman that the best way to survive was to never grow up. There are few women who are harder to deal with once they decide what they want.

"That's impossible," I said, a little too fast; in truth, I knew only the rudiments of Herman's family history. "He doesn't have any relatives," I told her brusquely. "Herman grew up in an orphanage."

"I know that," she told me. "But he had a sister that had to be put up for adoption."

"How do you know that?"

"My mother was adopted, and I think she might be Mr. Viereck's sister. He may be my uncle."

I started to protest. Even before she told me the plans she had for Herman's work, my mind rebelled. Viereck was becoming more than I could handle. Every time I turned around, someone else wanted a piece of him. Holm, Crandall, O'Malley, even Makiko counting up our assets and liabilities—and now this?

Her story sounded so simple that it made sense. I knew Herman had a sister, and after his mother had died in childbirth, his dad couldn't take care of the both of them, so he adopted her out, an event so common at the time that it made hardly a ripple in the fabric of society. And who's to say which child fortune smiled upon? Herman's sister had grown up far away from the Illinois Home for Feeble-Minded Children and the cluttered tomb on Webster Avenue. She'd had some approximation of a normal life. She had gotten married and had children.

Now, possibly, one of them was on the phone.

"I read about him in the paper," she told me, "and when I saw his name, Viereck, it all made sense. You see, I have a brother who, well, he has *adjustment* problems, and my mom did a search to find out about my grandparents. You know, to see if there was anything that my brother Henry could have inherited. Well she found out that our family name was Viereck. I think this guy, I think he has some kind of *adjustment* problem too."

"That's not much of a connection," I told her, lamely.

"Me and my husband, the Reverend Robert Gallagher, we have a fellowship in Pannier, Illinois. Well, we drove up there to Chicago and we went to where you've got those pictures hung. Is it true that they're sellin' 'em for five thousand dollars?"

"That's not a lot for a work of art," I assured her, but I already thought I had it figured out. It was like winning the lottery. Relatives you never knew you had come scurrying out of the woodwork.

But I'd misjudged the whole situation.

"Mr. Learner," she went on, "I'm sure you can tell that I'm a deeply committed Christian woman. My faith in the Bible runs very strong. I've been exposed to the Devil and his temptations many, many times, but never have I seen anything as truly blasphemous as those horrid paintings."

"You're entitled to your opinion," I said. "But a work of art is often far more than just the subject matter." I began to lecture, but then I told myself, "Do not rattle this woman; do not say anything that will make things worse."

"Mr. Learner, I believe that as Herman Viereck's closest living relative, those pictures—if you can call them that—rightfully belong to me."

"You're only saying that because you think they're worth a lot of money," I said spitefully.

"Oh, no," she said, "we're not interested in that. They're the work of the Devil, and we plan to burn every last one of them."

I fell silent at my end. I could hear her hyperventilating, waiting for my answer. But all I could think to do was ask one more question.

"Your mother," I asked, "any chance her name was Vivian?"

CHAPTER TWENTY-ONE

A question for our celebrity-obsessed time: can we separate a work of art from the person who creates it? Do the details of its creation alter our appreciation for the object at hand? Would Van Gogh still generate the interest and excitement he does if he hadn't cut off his ear? If Modigliani hadn't thrown his sculptures into the Seine? If Pollack hadn't hit that tree?

The sordid and the pornographic become marketing tools. Bring on the drunken escapades, the infidelities, and the spousal abuse. If this hunger for biography is true for established artists, it's even more so for outsiders. Their motives are so personal, so obtuse. There's no touchstone. Everything they do is driven by internal vision.

When we look at their work, it's the first thing we want to know. What made them do it? What events in their lives shaped them? We don't want the just the art. We want the entire mythology. We want to find the Viereck that lives in all of us.

***

O'Malley could have gone over to the Sisters by himself, so I felt grateful to him for inviting me along. At first, I thought he'd done it out of courtesy, but after I hung up the phone, I grew suspicious.

Did he want to use me as a stalking horse, letting my presence lull Viereck into a false sense of security, putting him at ease just before the detective sprang the trap? I went anyway. Maybe I thought I could protect Herman from O'Malley's rat-terrier single mindedness. Or maybe I just couldn't resist watching him move in for the kill.

"I'll pick you up," he told me over the phone.

"That'll be great," I said.

Scenes from a hundred cop movies ran through my head. We'd drive over to the Little Sisters in an unmarked dirty brown Crown Vic, the hopped-up police interceptor engine rumbling at stoplights, just waiting to be unleashed.

On the way over, the radio would crackle—a one-nine-seven. *"Officer in need of assistance ... robbery in progress ... hostage situation."* Whatever.

He'd stick that little magnetic blue cop light on the roof, and we'd go tear-assing through the streets of Chicago.

Then he'd ask me, "You know how to use a double-action pump?"

"No problem, ossifer."

Instead, he showed up in a Dodge Dart, containing enough personal touches that I knew he hadn't checked it out of the motor pool. The car was as neat as O'Malley; no crumpled Burger King bags, no used coffee containers rolling around on the floor, just a rosary hanging from the rearview mirror. The car didn't even have a police scanner.

As we dawdled through traffic, I had an unnerving thought that O'Malley might not even be with the department. I tried to remember if he'd showed me his badge when I'd met him for coffee. If he had, I hadn't paid attention. He could have flashed me a piece of tin from Woolworth for all I knew.

After hanging up on Herman's purported niece, I didn't trust nobody.

We stopped for a light on Michigan Avenue. Some kid in a tricked-out Camaro pulled up next to us. He had the bass on his ten-inch Stinger speakers turned up to eleven, and our car started rocking in sympathetic harmony. Rap or hip hop, I'm still not sure there's a difference.

When Miriam had been born, I'd promised myself that I wouldn't let anything in contemporary youth culture piss me off. No matter how weird or offensive it seemed, I'd always remember Elvis and the Beatles and how subversive they were supposed to be.

Now you can't go up an elevator without hearing *Hey Jude*.

But that preceded rap. I couldn't help it. The snarl coming out of the speakers set my teeth on edge. It wasn't the rage. Gd knows there's plenty for youth to be pissed off about; the angry staccato affronted my overly developed class consciousness. Didn't they realize that for all their ersatz gangsta violence, they'd been co-opted, absorbed into the system, betrayed at the deepest possible level? I had this urge to jump out of O'Malley's car, put my fist through the Camaro's rear window, and rip the magnet out of the speaker like an Aztec priest extracting a still-beating sacrificial heart.

O'Malley looked over at me and smiled.

"Doesn't that crap drive you crazy?" I asked him. "How can they listen to that stuff all day?"

"They always figure out some way to get to you," he said. "If there's one thing you won't be able to understand or accept, your kids will figure out what it is and bring it home."

The light turned and the Camaro roared off. I had a brief vision of Miriam thumping a bible, the only thing I wouldn't have been able to accept from her—being born again.

"You must have kids," I said. Up till then I'd imagined him living alone in a small apartment, a confirmed bachelor and obsessed workaholic.

"Six," he said.

Well, of course. No birth control for this little Mick. "They turn out okay?"

"For the most part. I've got one on the force. One's in the navy. The oldest girl is about to take her vows." When he said the last, his normally placid voice became animated.

"Vows?"

"She's going to be a nun. I guess my wife and I must have done something right."

What could you say to that? We rode together through busy traffic with hip-hop music assaulting us from all sides, but it felt as if O'Malley and I weren't even sharing the same century. We were like two characters in a science-fiction novel whose plot hinged on the intersection of parallel universes.

He drove carefully, his seat set far forward, draping his forearms around the steering wheel as if he were guiding the car with his whole upper body.

He slipped as silently through traffic as he did through life. Despite his claimed obsession over finding Annie, he appeared a man uncommonly at peace with himself. I more than admired him. Despite driving like an old lady, he got us halfway across Chicago in cab-driver time.

The parking lot was full. He circled once or twice, and then, almost as if it embarrassed him, we left the car in front of a "no parking" sign on the circular driveway. He pulled a "Chicago P.D. Official Business" card out of the glove box and left it face up on the dash. I felt less like a vigilante.

We walked up the front walk and in under the Virgin. O'Malley made a quick sign of the cross.

Watching O'Malley's reflexive act of blessing brought something home to me that I hadn't considered till now. O'Malley and Viereck were both good, practicing Catholics. It made me more self-conscious about walking into the poorhouse than usual. As we crossed the marble entryway, I was more aware then ever of my healthy belly and my slightly stooped posture. Nathan Learner, a shambling Jewish bear, chained to this wisp of an Irishman. And to see whom? A half-crazy kraut who looked like Hitler would have, if they'd managed to pry him out of his bunker and send him to Spandau.

We found Herman propped up in one of those hospital-type La-Z-Boys. They were no longer bothering to dress him, and he had that nursing-home look—four or five days of stubble, haunted, sunken eyes, food stains on his pajamas. A crusty gumminess of his moving parts.

"Hey, Herman, I brought you a visitor."

He gave us a baleful look, a flash of his old paranoid street-self. For a few seconds, I wasn't sure he recognized me. Then he nodded.

"Hey, Mr. Nathan."

"This is Mr. O'Malley. He saw your show, and he wanted to ask you some questions."

O'Malley didn't correct me about the "mister." I wondered if that consisted of entrapment. There was only one chair in the room, and O'Malley dragged it over.

I hovered behind them, my usual position when it came to Viereck.

"Some weather we're having," O'Malley said. I don't know if he'd done some research on his quarry, or if this was his standard approach, but he got either more or exactly what he'd bargained for.

Viereck's hollow face lit up, and he started in on O'Malley right away with a five-minute discourse on springtime in Chicago. The detective made appropriate noises, but once Herman got going about the weather, nothing could make him stop. O'Malley used the time to scope Herman out.

Finally, he put a hand on Herman's narrow shoulder and gave it a squeeze. Just hard enough to turn off the faucet.

"I bet you were an altar boy," O'Malley said, out of the blue.

Viereck stopped in midsentence. "That's right, yes—at the home," Herman said. "They'd only get a priest to come out once a month."

"Me, too," O'Malley told him. "At Holy Trinity, I was the only kid who wasn't Polish. The other kids made my life holy hell. You're German, aren't you?"

"Yep."

"They must have been hard on you, too."

"It was all hard, pally," Viereck said.

"Some of those priests could be kinda queer, too. You ever have one of them try and pull any kind of funny stuff?"

Viereck's gaze drifted away from O'Malley. For a brief second, I imagined he was looking at me for guidance.

"It was a long time ago," he said softly. "Before the tornado."

"I could see that," O'Malley said. "In your pictures."

"Oh, those. I never got it right. They were never dark enough."

I wanted to stop the detective right there. If O'Malley wanted to snoop around a twenty-five-year-old missing persons case, that was one thing. But I couldn't have him tearing into my personal vision of Herman the artistic savant. I'd always assumed that Herman thought his own work was perfect. I didn't need O'Malley to expose his self-doubt and indecision. I had enough of that for the both of us.

"What about the one you drew of Annie Proturick? I thought that one was pretty good."

You had to admire the way he'd slipped it in. The old man didn't react right away. For a few seconds I thought maybe he had forgotten all about the portrait.

"Why did he do it?" Herman asked.

The hairs on the back of my neck twitched to attention. I stole a look at O'Malley, but his face was as passive as ever.

"Why did who do what?" O'Malley asked.

"God," said, Herman. "He stole her picture from me. It was on my table, where I always kept it, so she could look at me while I worked, and then one day it was gone."

"And you think God took your picture?"

"I was going to help find her, but I never could. All I had was her picture, and God took it away to punish me. He was never happy with what I tried to do for Him. Her picture was all I had, and he took it from me."

"Why would God want to punish you?" O'Malley asked. They weren't speaking in metaphors.

"I told you, he always had it in for me. Ever since I was a kid growing up. I tried everything to get him to give it back. I told Him I would clean the rectory at St. Bart's every day for a year, but he didn't care. Then I promised him seven novenas. It was never enough."

"So you drew her portrait, to replace the picture he took?" the detective suggested to him.

Herman nodded. I breathed a little easier.

"I tried," Herman told us, "but it's not very good. I'm not very good with faces. I like to draw the weather."

"I thought Annie's portrait is one of your best," I said, over O'Malley's shoulder, but I knew how Herman felt. When you've decided that everything you stand for is represented by just one work, it doesn't matter what anybody else thinks.

"So you don't have any idea where Annie is? What might have happened to her?"

Herman hadn't really made eye contact with either of us, but now he stared up at the detective.

"Tornados," he whispered. "When they come for you, there's nothing you can do."

***

We left the Sisters and drove away in silence. Sitting next to him, I tried to get a sense of what O'Malley was thinking.

"Well, I guess that's that," I said finally. I couldn't keep a tone of relief out of my voice. "I told you he was pretty far gone. I think he just fixated on her picture. It became an icon for him."

"Maybe," said O'Malley. "I think I'll wait a few days and go talk to him again. There's something smoking here. I can smell it."

CHAPTER TWENTY-TWO

"I don't think the Hank Williams case applies here," Jeff's lawyer told us. "In that instance, Mr. Williams made specific provisions for assuming responsibility for his child, and subsequent to his tragic and untimely death, those provisions were willfully ignored. I don't think this woman, even if she is biologically Mr. Viereck's niece, has any legal basis to ownership of the art."

The four of us—the lawyer, Makiko and I, plus Jeff, acting as go-between (but also having some considerable vested interest at this point, having bought three more Vierecks) sat huddled at the end of a long ebony table that could easily seat all the partners of Evans, Delong, and Broadbent.

Their offices were in a new high-rise with a sweeping lake view, but the interior designer had gone for a Dickensian, *Jarendyce v. Jarendyce* look. The imported Indonesian mahogany paneling glowed dark and rich. I thought our barrister should have sported a powdered wig.

It had been a long time since I'd been up in a building this high, and staring out of the full-length windows only added to my feelings of disassociated vertigo, not an uncommon way for me to feel when dealing with the law. It felt like my divorce all over again.

Jeff's lawyer looked disarmingly young with a body honed by Bow-flex. He'd developed an affect where you felt he had your undivided attention, no matter where his mind wandered. I kind of liked him in spite of myself.

"So you think there's no way she can legally claim Mr. Viereck's paintings?"

"Not in the state of Illinois. In Colorado, Louisiana, Rhode Island, and Texas, the adopted person's right to inherit from birth parents and birth relatives is retained to some extent. But in Illinois, once a child has been adopted out, he or she loses all rights to inherit from the birth family."

"The case of Hank Williams's daughter is a very special circumstance since the singer recognized his daughter—who, incidentally, wasn't born until after Mr. Williams deceased. In point of fact, his daughter was well into her twenties before she discovered that Hank Williams was her father. Even then, the case went all the way to the Supreme Court before she got the right to receive royalties."

He paused to see if we appreciated that we were getting our money's worth. Actually, Jeff had him on retainer. He was just showing off. I nodded. Did that mean Illinois was less or more enlightened than Rhode Island? I tried to ask him, but he went on talking.

"Then, too, outside of claims made, there is no actual proof that this woman is a blood relative. That would need to be established. At best, she's a niece, so DNA evidence might be challengeable in court. Then, too, after this long, getting her mother's original adoption papers might be difficult."

"So you're telling us that there's no need to be concerned," Makiko said.

"Well, yes. Ultimately, I'd say any claim made by the Gallaghers on the Viereck estate would be extremely weak."

"That's great," Jeff told him. But I could sense that our legal eagle wasn't quite through.

"The problem is that all these shadowy areas create the potential for a long and protracted legal battle. If her attorneys wish to contest the estate, it could put the ownership of Mr. Viereck's work in limbo for years—during which time the sale of said work would be difficult, if not impossible."

"What are you saying?" Jeff asked. I wondered if he already had plans to turn the work over by selling it back to Crandall.

"I'm saying that, given the economic potential that his work represents, it might be expeditious to offer the Gallaghers some sort of preemptive cash settlement."

"Are we talking an estimated percentage of future value?" Jeff asked, but I interrupted him.

"You don't understand, Jeff. It's not money they're after. They're some kind of fundamentalist fanatics. They want to have all Herman's art destroyed. They think it's the work of the Devil."

"They haven't made any direct threats to harm the paintings, have they?" the lawyer asked.

"Not really," I said, but Makiko looked uncomfortable.

"I didn't want to tell you," she said.

"You didn't want to tell me what?"

"I got this letter stuffed in our mailbox. It wasn't postmarked. Apparently, God is giving us one last chance to destroy the paintings before he unleashes his wrath."

"You didn't want to tell me! God, Makiko, you didn't talk to this woman—she's absolutely crazed."

"Yes, I have talked to her. She's called the house a couple of times."

"And you didn't mention it?"

"Well, I knew you'd overreact."

"I'm not overreacting," I shouted at her. "I don't think you understand how dangerous these people can be. They're absolute fascists."

"Perhaps you should give some thought to getting a restraining order." Our lawyer said. He wasn't being paid to listen to our family squabbles.

"Maybe you could write one up," Jeff asked him, but this lawyer didn't do that sort of thing, though he knew someone we could go talk to if we were serious.

Naturally, we let it go till it was too late. Not that any words not written in the bible would have made any difference to this bunch.

CHAPTER TWENTY-THREE

With Dave Crandall plotting his assault on the villas of Hollywood's glitterati, O'Malley breathing down Herman's neck, and the KKK's Junior League threatening to burn a cross in front of my house, I thought I had enough tsuris, but I hadn't counted on Adrian Holm.

"Maybe you should just go ahead and give him the keys," Makiko told me. "It's the third time this week he's rung our doorbell at seven in the morning. I think he just likes to get me out of bed so he can stare down my kimono."

"Holm?"

I looked across at her over the top of the *Trib*. It's not an accusation you want to hear about your erstwhile therapist. We were having our morning coffee before we parted ways for the day. She had on her signature Rolo jeans and a black top, offset with embroidered pink roses. I hadn't gotten further than my boxers.

"I know you think he's a great therapist and that he saved your life, but there's something creepy about the way he relates to women. Believe me, I think he's way too personally involved with Herman's work."

I shrugged. I knew she had a point, but I didn't want to deal with it. Makiko and Crandall flirting and sniping at each other was one thing, but thinking about Holm doing a Peeping Tom routine on my old lady made me feel violated.

Even without visions of him coming on to my wife, Holm's growing obsession with the *Realms* made me antsy. After that first time I'd taken him up to Herman's apartment, he'd called me repeatedly, asking if he could "borrow" the book. I'd managed to think of some polite way to tell him no, but I could tell that my proprietary stubbornness pissed him off.

"Why can't you read it up there?" I asked him.

"Okay, that would be great. I'd like to spend a few nights up there anyway. Absorb some of the atmosphere."

The first few times he came by, I went up with him, but when it looked as if he was settling in to read the whole fifteen thousand pages, and taking notes besides, I got bored and left him to his own devices. It made me uneasy though, having him up there unsupervised.

Weeknights, after Makiko and I yawned our way through Leno's monologue, I'd peek between our curtains and into Herman's windows. I could see Adrian's shadowy form sitting in that beat-up office chair. I'd check again when I got up to go to the bathroom in the middle of the night. It looked as if he hadn't moved.

Then one of my tenants mentioned that she'd heard Holm having conversations with Viereck.

"I don't like it," Makiko said. "I don't trust him with the art. What's he doing up there all night, anyway?"

"I don't know. Something about a monograph he's writing for one of the psych journals."

"You don't think he'd walk off with a painting, do you?"

"Holm?"

"Yes, Holm. You put a dollar sign in front of something, and it starts doing funny things to people. We need to get that stuff out of there."

"You want me to bring it over here? More or less a rhetorical question. We'd been over this a bunch of times already. She made a face of resigned disgust. For all her avant-garde musical endeavors, Makiko had a working-class puritanical streak. Critical acclaim or no, she didn't want Herman's brand of kiddy porn in our apartment.

"What do you want me to do," I asked her, "pat him down every time he leaves?"

"Just talk to him. Find out what the hell he's doing up there all night."

***

"Viereck worked at night," Holm told me a few days later. "I feel closer to him, more in touch with his creative energy. His body may be over at that nursing home, but his soul is still on Webster Avenue."

We sat at a small sidewalk table in front of the Bourgeois Pig, my favorite café. By then, Lincoln Park had espresso on every other block. That or a bodega, signs of the neighborhood's transition. I wondered how my new neighbors with their Land Rovers and thousand-dollar baby strollers would respond if Herman showed up today in his trench coat and started rummaging through the trash in front of the their renovated bungalows.

At a nearby table, a woman with a shaved head breastfed her baby. The kid looked old enough that it might have preferred a Coke. I'd managed to ignore her, but Holm's eyes couldn't stay away. I could tell by the daggers she was staring back at him that she'd gotten the response she'd hoped for.

While his eyes darted furtively around, I waited to ask Adrian point-blank what great insights he had developed about my Herman—and, by unspoken inclusion, the psychopathology of artistic creativity. But it seemed crass and belligerent to quiz him as if he was a grad student defending a thesis.

Though crass and belligerent pretty much summed up how I felt.

"Makiko is getting worried about you," I lied. "You look like crap. Maybe you ought to give this Viereck thing a rest."

"I know," he admitted. He got up, went inside and pumped the drip-pot for a refill. I watched him through the window. He said something to the girl behind the counter. I could tell by her forced smile that it hadn't been quite appropriate. The breast-feeder took the opportunity to give me a withering stare, button up, and leave. I guess Holm had made somebody's day.

"What happened to our Madonna?" he asked when he sat back down again.

I gave him a closer going over. He'd always gone for the rumpled academic look, but now something positively unclean emanated from him. His hair had a greasy, matted quality, and the collar of his dirty shirt rolled against the neck.

"You seeing clients today?" I asked him. He shook his head.

"I'm taking a break from my practice. I want to devote all my energy to the *Realms*. I'm trying to read all of it. He made some interesting changes between the first draft done in pencil and what he typed. Very revealing."

"You're trying to read the whole thing? Both drafts?"

He looked sheepish. "I know, it's probably nuts, but there's something there, Nathaniel. I can't explain it totally, but I think studying Herman Viereck is going to be my signature work. I want to publish the definitive study. It may take me years."

"That's a hell of a commitment."

He nodded. "Do you know anything about the art of the insane?" he asked me.

"Herman's not insane," I told him. Whenever I defended Viereck, it always sounded in my ears like overkill. Maybe I had lower standards of mental health than everyone else.

Holm gave me a condescending look.

"Well, you have to admit that he isn't a paragon of normal adjustment."

"Who the fuck is?"

He ignored me. "Viereck is part of a long tradition of schizophrenia and the visual arts. I think it has a lot to do with the way the occipital cortex processes information." Adrian took a sip of his coffee and made a face. I prepared myself for a lecture.

"The first formal attempt to study artistic expression in the mentally ill goes back to the turn of the century. It was the Germans, surprisingly—I mean when you consider the roots of National Socialism and the untold hundreds of thousands of the retarded and schizophrenics they liquidated. It's where they learned all the techniques they scaled up later to handle their final solution."

Holm's eyes had a fixed stare while he talked to me. He seemed on the ragged edge, suffering from an over-amped imagination and sleep deprivation, what Dostoyevsky called "brain fever."

"Hans Prinzhorn, a German psychiatrist, was the first person to do a systematic study of the art of the insane. He compiled a collection of over five thousand works by 450 artists who were, at one time or another, inmates at asylums all over Europe. You're familiar, of course with Adolph Wölfli."

"He's not that guy Freud wrote about, the Wolf Man?"

Holm made another face. I was trying too hard to impress him.

"No, Freud's Wolf Man was just your garden-variety, sexually repressed neurotic. Adolph Wölfli was truly deranged, but he had this powerful, innate visual sense. Totally self-taught, of course. It's doubtful that he ever set foot inside an art museum. His paintings have balance, a composition of elements that shows true artistic genius. But they're totally pathologic. Of course, all this happened in 1922, just at the time that Picasso and Braque were breaking open the whole hermeneutic universe of European art. Interest in the works of non-Western, so called primitive cultures, was at its peak. The post-impressionists were fascinated with African and Native American art. Naturally, this fascination spread to members of their community who manifested the same primitive technique. People felt that the mentally ill and the primitive artist were both plugged into some different, superior level of reality. You still get a lot of people who feel that way."

"I know that," I told him. "I teach art history, remember?"

"Sorry, but that's why you should know what I'm getting into here. This Adolph Wölfli_character is a pretty amazing story, vis-à-vis our friend Herman. Wölfli was born in some little Swiss farming town in the 1860s. Apparently he lost his mother at an early age and was raised in foster homes. It's doubtful he got any formal education, leave alone any art training. As an adult, he worked as a farmhand and bricklayer, but apparently he had a hard time fitting into the community. He kept getting in fights with his employers. He also had a thing for little girls."

He paused long enough to give me a significant look.

"Eventually they arrested him for molesting the daughter of one of the farmers he worked for. The authorities hospitalized him for a while, and then they let him go. It's amazing how modern the whole story sounds. You'd think we would have learned something in the last hundred years. Anyway, eventually he fucked up again and sexually assaulted a little girl. This time, they put him in an asylum and threw away the key. For the first several years, he continued to be violent and impossible to control. Then one day, an attendant noticed him covering the walls of his cell with illustrations done with a lump of coal he'd picked up somewhere. In an attempt to keep him quiet, somebody handed him a pencil and paper, and he just took off."

"Sounds familiar," I admitted.

"For the next twenty years, as long as they kept him in colored pencils and paper, he was happy. He did these complex, religiously charged drawings. He had *horror vacui*, the fear of leaving an empty spot on the page. His work is filled with fine lines and minute detail. It's typical of the schizoid worldview: they abhor any part of the page left untouched. Think of Pollack. Not that I'm saying he was crazy, but it's the same attempt to control space, the need to bend the edges of the canvas back on itself to create this closed world.

"Wölfli was obsessed with doing these large religious scenes. Most of them contained his alter ego—this stock character, Saint Adolph, who kept trying to save the Christian world from some satanic disaster or another. Just in case the viewer didn't get it, he'd cover the backs of his paintings with long explanations of what they represented. His script has an even, repetitive quality, also typical of the writings of schizophrenics. Some of it is pretty similar to parts of the *Realms*. He actually got quite famous and made a nice living selling his work to tourists. When he died, he left a pile almost two meters high. Some of it made its way into private collections, but most is in the Heidelberg collection. I'm planning to go have a look at it in a few weeks."

"You're going to Germany?

"Sure. You want to come along?"

"I don't think so," I said.

"Makes you think, doesn't it?" Holm said. "You see your Viereck as being totally unique, but he really comes from a long line of sexually repressed, damaged artists. That's the thing about insanity. It doesn't liberate you from your age or your culture. Wölfli drew himself as a saint, Viereck as a weatherman. Wölfli took his inspiration from cathedral windows, Viereck from Walt Disney movies. But underneath, they were both driven by the same dark images."

"You don't need a weatherman to know which way the wind blows," I said.

Holm wasn't amused. That's always a bad sign, losing the ability to make fun of your own obsessions. There seemed to be a lot of that going on all around me. I hoped it wasn't catching.

"Do you think Viereck would be capable of something like that?"

"Like what?"

"You know—harming a child. Or do you think he just played out the scenarios in his head so vividly that he didn't have to act on them?"

"Are you kidding me?" Holm looked animated enough to tip over a coffee cup. "The guy's a textbook case. Abandoned by his mother at an early age when she dies giving birth to a sister, a sister he never sees, but subconsciously both idealizes and resents, blaming her for the death of his mother. Can you imagine the ambivalence this creates? Then his father leaves him in an orphanage where he's exposed to Gd knows what kind of abuse, the massive amount of resentment that builds up. But he's a weak, sickly child. The other kids bully him. They've already nicknamed him Crazy. What other mode of expression does he have?

"I'd say that all his art, the novel set on this fantasy planet, the mural-like scrolls, everything he did, were all attempts on Viereck's part to control the demon, to subvert it, channel it into a creative wellspring. But if Viereck's defenses ever failed him, if his creative abilities became insufficient, I think he'd be capable of just about anything."

I sipped my latte and listened to his theories. They made perfect sense in a Dr. Phil sort of way, but they didn't resonate. Holm's explanations felt empty, hollow, and obvious, as everything psychoanalytic always does to me. I'd expected more from him after all his insights I credited with jump-starting my life. Only now, listening to him ramble on, I wondered what exactly he had done to jolt me out of my melancholia, other than pump me up with a few platitudes.

When it came to Viereck, I wanted more. I wanted some key to an unspeakable mystery. I wanted the touch of the divine. I wanted to see the hand of Gd, not something from the *Jerry Springer Show*: *"Perv artists who molest little girls, and the guys who love them."*

Still, it chilled me to have Holm put my worst fears into such a neat little box. Apparently, he had no qualms about seeing little Herman Viereck as a child rapist. He seemed almost pleased with the idea. It made his work meaningful, gave it a social context outside of the small, insular, and shrinking world of Freudian psychology.

If I'd still trusted Adrian, this would have been the perfect time to tell him about my meeting with O'Malley and the significance of Annie's portrait. It's odd how a tiny seed of doubt, one false facial expression or half-muttered aside, can eat away years of friendship.

Once I quit trusting Holm, everything he said possessed its own malevolent agenda. I kept my mouth shut.

"Of course," Adrian told me, "there's no proof that he did anything untoward. But given the right circumstances, the right set of stimuli, even someone with as rigid a framework as Viereck could break down. Believe me, I've seen it happen."

For a minute, it sounded as if Holm could be speaking from personal experience. Just why had he left Dallas for Chicago, I wondered. He'd eaten a scone, and now he moistened a fingertip and picked up the last few crumbs with the fleshy pad of his forefinger.

"It sounds fascinating," I told him. "You have any idea when you'll be finished?"

He looked shocked all over again. "I told you; it may take years to do Viereck justice. This may be a synchronistic event, placing him and me together like this. There's a wealth of stuff there, Nate; I don't have to tell you that. But it needs to be put into some kind of contextual framework, not broken up. Separately, all his drawings and pictures are just curiosities, but taken as a whole, it's a treasure trove of psychopathology. When I get back from Heidelberg, I want to try to do some sort

of statistical analysis of the words Viereck used, see if I can strip away
what is stereotypical and get closer to the real personality underneath."

"I'm not sure I can give you that much time," I told him. I'd been
trying to think of some way of being diplomatic, but once I started talking I couldn't help sounding like a landlord. "Makiko and I are going
to need to do something with the apartment. I can't afford to keep it
vacant forever."

Holm looked at me as if I'd become Goliath, king of the Philistines.
"I didn't expect to hear something like that from you. Of all people, I
thought you were his friend."

"I wasn't his friend. You know that. Not in any real sense. Herman
wasn't capable of real friendship. Look, there's more to it than just
the apartment. The paintings are starting to generate a lot of interest.
There's a market developing for his work. The whole field of outsider
art is getting hot."

"Oh, now I get it," he said. "I should have seen the hand behind the
throne, your Lady Macbeth. I want to know what gives the two of you
the right? It's not like you own the material."

I put down my cup, trying to figure out how to deal with this sudden
turn of events. I'd always been a little confused about Holm's and my
relationship when it came to money. Somewhere during our sessions
together, he had stopped billing me. I'd been foolish enough to feel flattered, that I was such an interesting case that he didn't want to alter our
friendship by charging me, but I'd never gotten over the feeling that I
owed him, that a favor might come due at some point.

Now, of course, I wondered if friendship meant all that much to
him, not with him inventing a new career for himself. I realized that he
needed to feel persecuted somehow. Studying Viereck and the art of the
insane had to carry with it some psychic price tag of its own, some sense
of personal sacrifice. Holm needed a villain for his personal drama, and
if it not me, he'd dump it all on Makiko.

"We do own the work," I told him. "He left everything in the apartment to us."

I reached an all-time personal low. Back when I was in high school,
I played chess every afternoon with a kid who always managed to beat

me. I never made it easy for him, which only made my agony worse. I kept thinking I had a chance. One day, he made a foolish move, and I forked his rook and bishop with my knight. Normally, we'd let each other take back moves, but this time I wouldn't let him take it back. Our games were never the same after that.

Now with Holm, I felt the same way.

"You're not serious?" he said, "You think ownership of something like this can be left up to chance? You think you've won some sort of lottery?"

Since that day, there have been times when I've looked at Herman's paintings, now so familiar to me that they've lost almost all emotional value, and wished that I'd gone ahead and thrown everything in the apartment out onto the street. But that morning, sitting in the bright sunshine, a beneficiary of the prosperity of my rapidly gentrifying neighborhood, his accusation that I'd won some karmic lottery came as a shock.

"Well, what do you want me to do with them?" I asked him. "Throw them out onto the street?"

"I don't think it's up to you. Viereck's work belongs to the people of Chicago!"

"Yeah, like the Picasso sculpture they want to melt down and replace with Ernie Banks? Come on, Adrian, you can't turn him into some sort of folk hero. The guy's no Grandma Moses."

"Well, I'm not giving him up," Adrian said and got up from the table. He wasn't going to give us a chance to reach a compromise. I tried to put it down to his sleep deprivation, but he'd made me angry, too. He had hit a nerve. I did feel guilty about our part in the exploitation of Herman's legacy.

"His stuff should be in some kind of a museum," Holm said as he stalked off down the street.

CHAPTER TWENTY-FOUR

O'Malley never got his chance to talk to Herman again, but I did. "Is this Mr. Learner?" a woman's voice asked me over the phone. Behind her, the hum of the nursing home gave her identity away: the entropic clatter of a falling tray, a frustrated yowl, the beehive murmur of too many people crammed into too tight a space.

"Nurse Stark?" I said. I'd made a special point of remembering her name, knowing that few people would, and at a time like this, it might give me a slight edge. "What can I do for you?"

"I'm calling about Mr. Viereck. He isn't doing too good. I think maybe you should get out here if you want to see him before ..." Her voice faded. Nurse Stark felt sure she'd said enough, but I missed the cue. I hadn't memorized the script.

"Before what," I asked?

It was after eleven. Makiko and I were doing what people never do in novels— vegging out in front of the TV. Not even something uplifting on PBS. Just some commercial-infested rerun of a network crime show. Ever since meeting O'Malley, I'd developed a newfound interest in police procedurals. I kept tabulating the differences between his mild-mannered professionalism and the hyperkinetic cowboys or burned-out headcases they scripted into the cop shows. I thought a series starring O'Malley would really be something.

When the phone rang, we were watching three plainclothes detectives storm an apartment. We knew the perp had fled. After all, the show still had twenty minutes to run. The cops had their guns drawn, holding them in both hands while they moved with that jerky, point-and-shoot, robotic motion that we expect from TV cops. The quick cuts and the handheld camera work gave the scene the feel of a documentary. Nurse Stark's phone call worked its way into the script.

"Mr. Learner, Herman is *dying*." Her voice had an exasperated tone, like a schoolteacher trying to explain fractions to some dull-normal for the umpteenth time. Makiko got up and clicked off the TV. I tried to keep my voice calm, and held up a finger, enough to reassure her that no one we knew had been in a car wreck.

"Don't you think we should send him to the hospital? I asked her. Nurse Stark sighed over the phone. "It's not really our policy in cases like this," she explained. "We're a hospice-oriented facility."

I could have said something stupid and nasty about the quality of healthcare for the poor, but I held my tongue. I should only be so lucky enough that, at the end, someone will do for me what the Sisters did for Herman.

"I think you might want to come out and see him," she added.

I paused, calculating everything in a selfish instant. Getting dressed, the drive, being up all night, how I'd feel the next day. I'd be blurry eyed and cranky, too old for this nonsense. In short, I practiced denial. But what could I do, lie in bed all night while poor Herman tilted off this mortal coil? Fortunately, even the pretense of making a decision got snatched out of my hands.

"He's asking for you," she added.

I put down the phone. I told Makiko the facts. She didn't try to stop me, but she didn't offer to come along either. She had a stake in Herman's art, but his mortality belonged solely to me. Makiko remained on the couch while I scrounged my coat, wallet and keys.

"It's not fair, them sticking you with this," she said.

"Who else does he have?"

Makiko got up and walked me to the door. I reached down and surrounded her. She felt so insubstantial, like a child in my arms.

"I'll be okay," I told her. "Don't wait up."

***

Places seen only in daylight take on dreamlike familiarity when revisited in the dark. Even the usual traffic-congested drive out to the North Shore took only half the time. I actually hoped for a red light so I could pull myself together.

The Sisters sat monolithically unlit, the parking lot empty. As I walked toward the front door, two giant elms I'd hardly noticed in the daytime swayed in the wind, their shadows dancing on the pavement while branches clicked against each other, communicating in some primordial arboreal language.

They'd locked the front door, and I had to pound on it and wait for Bella Lugosi to open up. A few blocks away, a siren wailed, beautiful music of the children of the night. While I waited, the finality of Herman's death, of the raw, unsubtle nature of dying, washed over me. I'd been expecting him to die for so long that I had quit thinking it would ever happen. But death has its own schedule, its own agenda. It wasn't interested in whether or not we got the chance to say goodbye. He could be breathing his last, I thought, while some night watchman dozed, oblivious to my pounding on the door.

Nurse Stark opened it herself. "Ah, Mr. Learner, good of you to come so quickly."

"I'm not too late?" My voice went up a hopeful half-octave.

"No," Stark said, "he's still with us. You just missed Father Paderewski. He did the last anointing. He's very good about coming when we need him. Mr. Viereck seemed to take great comfort from it. He's breathing a little easier."

I nodded, trying to stay neutral, like an anthropologist in the New Guinea highlands. The "last anointing," "last rites," "extreme unction"— they sounded as strange to me as some ritual form of cannibalism. The blood and the body of Christ? Well, why not? Didn't we all share the same collective unconscious? Only somehow, at this moment, I felt left out, lost in the funhouse.

Nurse Stark held the door, and I stepped into the foyer. When she locked it behind us, the heavy tumblers made a self-satisfied whisper. Was she keeping people out or locking them in?

We went up the main stairs to the second floor. I'd expected that the night would bring a sheltering quiet to the place, but it didn't. Halfway up the stairs, I could tell that the Sisters was just as alive at midnight as at noon.

In half-light, the hallways felt narrower, the vanishing points closer. As I followed Stark, each open doorway laid down its own penumbra over the already darkened floor. Animal noises came from the patients' rooms. Healthy snores, rheumy coughs, curses and muttering.

At the far end of the hall, a voice pled, "Jesus help me. Help me, Jesus. Jesus help me. Why the fuck don't you help me? Help me, GOD DAMN IT!"

I turned to my Beatrice. She gave me a reassuring smile.

"That's Mr. Cotter. He always does that. We have a lot of sundowners."

I nodded again, smilingly determined to accept everything with humble equanimity, but the urge to run gnawed at the base of my spine. What was I doing here? How much did I actually owe this weird little guy? I was just his landlord, for crying out loud. Did I have to be the one to stand there and witness the last tick of his clock, the last uncoiling of the mainspring?

Help, help, somebody call me an ambivalence! Jesus, you're not helping me at all.

Stark wore nurse's whites, down to a starched cap with a red cross embroidered on the front, her straw-colored hair done up in a little bun. She should have been an ancient crone, a relic of another time, not young, her face blandly attractive. Didn't she watch the tube? Nurses wore blue scrub suits now. They talked tough, and they looked as if they could plug your bullet hole with their thumb. They were shock troops, not virginal Florence Nightingales. Was Stark even real?

No, Nurse Stark is a ghost. They're all ghosts. I'm in a haunted nursing home, disjointed and out of time.

"Yes, there was a Nurse Stark who worked here in the fifties—terrible story, a real tragedy."

Stark, of course, those nurses he killed. No wait. that was Speck. Stark—Starkweather, that's the guy who went on the killing spree. Didn't he have a girlfriend they finally let out of jail a few years ago? Or was that a different case? Try to keep your mass murderers straight, Nathan. And what about our little Annie? A secret taken to the grave.

From each doorway, I conjured Lovecraftian sounds, flayed skin scraping over wet flagstones. Each room had a pit in the floor with some hideous, half-human creature chained at the bottom. *Is Stark looking for an empty room to lead me into? Am I going to wake up naked in a cornfield a hundred miles from here? Zombies are coming through the walls. The ghosts of Chicago's paupers circle around me.*

"Here we are," she said, stopping at an open door. A rectangle of yellow light lay on the floor of the hallway like a discarded playing card. I took one last breath of free air and looked anxiously back down the corridor from where we had come, but Stark might as well have been holding a gun to my head.

Inside the room, the unresolved conflict between letting Herman die with dignity and the reflexive drive of the medical staff to keep him alive played itself out. To help him breathe, they'd cranked the head of his bed up as far as it would go. An enormous oxygen tank rested in a wheeled cart, reminding me of the welding rigs in our sculpture department. A plastic mask fit loosely over Herman's face. Plumes of excess misted oxygen puffed out into the room every time he took a discordant breath.

The room had a smell that no amount of disinfectant could hide, as if the chemicals in the deodorizing agents had combined with Herman's decomposition. That smell—a triggered memory of Miriam's last night at Children's Hospital. Looking at the wizened little form sitting bolt upright and gasping for every breath, I thought for a brief second he might as well have had her face.

"I can't fucking do this," I muttered under my breath, but when I turned to flee, Stark stood quietly blocking my retreat.

"Look who's come to see you, Herman," she called cheerfully across the room. She acted as if Herman's situation was completely natural. I took a deep breath. *You can never totally comprehend this,* I told myself. *You can never fully be in this moment. Just do the best you can.*

Herman's pajama top lay open, and I could see his thin, sagging chest heaving mechanically with each seesawing breath. The light in the room emanated from two sources—a harsh fluorescent overhead and a small bedside lamp. The intersection of these lights made for interesting contrasts. With my photographer's eye, I began to frame Herman's deathbed portrait—how it might look shot in ambient light, where the shadows would fall, how the light from below would accent the stubble on his face.

Oh, I knew what I was doing all right, purposely disassociating, putting myself on the other side of the lens, fated to be always on the outside, always framing the shot.

"Hey, Mr. Nathan," Herman gasped from across the room. The sound of his voice forced me to drop my imaginary camera. I took a few steps across the room and stood at the bedside.

"Hi, Herman," I said. "How are you feeling?"

Surely I could have done better than that.

"I'm okay. It won't be long now. The priest was here. He heard my confession."

"I'm glad he came," I said, trying to put myself in Herman's place. How would it feel to be able to get it all off your chest once and for all?

"Are you in any pain?" I asked. "Is there anything I can get you—a glass of water?"

"No, I'm fine." He pulled the oxygen mask away from his face, and it spewed fog into the still air.

"You've been very good to me, Mr. Nathan. All those years, about the rent. I know I cost you a lot of money. And the show, imagine a real artist like you putting my stuff in your gallery like you did. I know they're not very good. It's not the way I pictured it in my mind. When I closed my eyes, all the pictures I saw—they were clearer. I just did the best I could. I can't even draw."

"The drawing doesn't matter," I told him. "Nobody's done what you did. People look at those paintings, and they sense something, something about themselves that they can't even say what it is."

As I talked, Herman looked past me, as if someone with wings floated over my shoulder. Maybe there was. At any rate, I'd lost him with my art babble.

"You're the real artist, Herman, not me. I'm just a hack. I haven't even taken a picture in years."

"It's because of Miriam, ain't it? I'm sorry. You must have loved her very much."

"These things happen," I told him. Talk about not reading the script.

I took the mask out of his limp hand and tried to put it back over his face, but he pushed it feebly away. I couldn't believe he could make this much sense. In these final moments, his whole carefully developed superstructure of benign village idiocy fell away.

"Is there anything you want me to tell her?" he asked me.

"What?"

"Miriam, when I see her in Heaven. Anything?"

"Oh God, Herman."

What the fuck was I supposed to say? *How dare they call me out here in the middle of the night for this deathbed seduction. This horrid little man, this fantasy murderer of millions of children, now feeding me fairy tales? Miriam sitting by a limpid pool on the green grass in some tent-evangelist's idea of heaven?* Hadn't I done enough for Herman? How could he be running a cheap scam like this on me? All his life, he'd spent in his own secret, perverted world, and now he was proposing I give him a message to take to my dead daughter. How did he know he wasn't going straight to hell?

"Tell her that her mother and I both still love her very much and that we miss her every day, but tell her that we've tried to keep going. I wouldn't want her to think that we stopped trying, stopped living … Oh, God damn it."

Was this all it took to achieve that precious thing called closure? Some simple-minded leap of faith into the realms of the unreal?

"I'll tell her," he said.

I noticed Herman breathed easier. An expert in these things would tell you that he had grown too tired to breathe. Poisonous gasses built up in his system, slowing everything down. I, of course, had the false impression that our conversation had had some kind of calming, curative effect.

I pulled a chair up to the bedside. Behind me I heard a slight rustling. Nurse Stark left the room, the doorway unguarded. She knew I wasn't going anywhere. Somewhere I'd read that the worst fear people have about dying is doing it alone. Did Herman feel that way? He'd spent his whole life in a world of his own design, peopled with hosts of his own imagination. What did he need me for? Where were his precious Vivian Girls now?

I reached out and took his hand. I could almost imagine that paint still clung under the fingernails. His hand was as small as a child's, and when he gripped mine, his fingers went only part way round.

"What's it doing out there?" he asked.

"What?"

"They said possible flurries. It's never going to happen. The cloud cover is too low."

"I guess you're the expert on that."

"We better check," he said, pointing to the window with his chin.

"Do you want to look out?"

Herman nodded. I wondered how to arrange it. Should I call Stark or an orderly? Would they have some excuse not to move him? Would it take an hour to assemble the manpower? Superfluous, all of it.

I leaned forward, and tucked my arm under him, steadying his head with my other hand. He couldn't have weighed more than eighty pounds: a child. I stood up, and he came off the bed effortlessly. The oxygen mask pulled free from his face and hit the floor. His body felt cool. He shuddered a little and leaned his head against my chest. Somehow I managed to kick-drag the chair over to the window and sit down with Herman on my lap. I felt the stubble of his beard pricking through the fabric of my shirt.

When, I wondered, had he last been held? Maybe his mythic Portuguese nurse, some part-time grandmother in the orphanage a hundred years ago? The human touch, a kiss, a hug, even a reassuring pat on the shoulder. I thought of Makiko, her thin body pressed against my back as we slept, the sensation of her child's arm around my waist. It didn't matter. It was the touch. The touch.

Outside, black silhouettes of the trees tossed up shadows against the fainter black of the sky. The lights of Chicago bounced off the clouds, deluding me into thinking that dawn was breaking.

"See," Herman said, "high cumulous, no chance of snow at all. They've got it wrong again. They're always getting it wrong."

We sat quietly. Out in the hallway, I heard things quieting down. Even the "Jesus help me" man drifted off. Herman and I were running out of time. I sat there and replayed what I knew of his life, all the questions that I'd wanted to ask him that would remain forever unanswered. Where he had really come from? What had fueled his vision? O'Malley? Christ-Jesus. O'Malley would want to know what we'd talked about during these last moments. Wasn't there some legal thing about statements made on the deathbed—some assumption of truthfulness?

"Herman, tell me something."

"It will be a warm winter. Don't believe what anyone tells you. Watch the jet stream."

"I want to know about Annie, Annie Proturick, the little girl whose picture you drew, the one the detective asked you about."

Against my chest, I felt his body stiffen. I'd become a human lie detector.

"It wasn't me," he said. "You need to talk to Larry about her. That's why he and I don't pal around together no more."

CHAPTER TWENTY-FIVE

It's common for people to tell you, that at moments like this, they lost all track of time. I think it's just literary convention, a little hyperbolic breathing space inserted into the narrative to build tension. You'd go along with it, wouldn't you? If I told you that I didn't know how long I sat there with Herman in my lap, staring out into the dark?

In reality, it wasn't that long. Ten minutes tops.

Shortly after he dropped the bomb about Larry, his breathing once again became irregular and shallow. His eyes lost focus. He let go of his feeble grip. For a moment, he didn't breathe at all. Then his chest heaved, see-sawing up and down, his body refusing to give up.

No way was I going to let him die in my arms. I got up and carried him back to the bed.

"Herman?" I called to him.

His eyes moved slightly to the sound of my voice.

With the same literary license, I could also tell you that I felt at peace with myself, that being with Herman in his last moments had helped calm my own fears of the abyss. But that wasn't true either. All in all, a deathbed vigil isn't much of a life lesson. Standing there, as I watched him breathe his last, I didn't explode with fresh insights. We live. We die. We're all road-kill on Gd's celestial highway—blah, blah, blah.

All I can say is that I hope you have all your ducks in a row way before you get to this point in the journey.

Gd's truth? Up to the very last, I couldn't believe Herman's final moments were upon him. Despite the rites of the last anointing, despite the horrible sounds emanating from his chest (sounds that could only be described as his death rattle), I refused to see it coming.

So when I did hear that final gurgle, I freaked.

No wonder, despite their pressuring us to sign a pathetically inadequate living will, the staff at Children's Hospital had called a Code Blue during Miriam's final moments, rushing us out of her room before we could say goodbye. Her nurses and doctors refused to accept she was finally dying: they'd pulled her through so many times before.

Maybe Nurse Stark had been watching us at the door, but when Herman finally quit breathing and I looked around desperately, she was there, standing beside the bed. She reached out confidently and felt for a pulse at Herman's neck. She put her other hand on my shoulder and pushed me back down into my seat.

Herman gave a slight shudder, his eyes drifted upwards, and despite the harsh light of the overheads, they dilated. If I'd been expecting some twenty-eight-gram ghostly apparition to rise from the body, it happened too fast for me to see.

"He's gone," she said. I waited for her to reach out, close his eyes and draw the sheet up over him, but she just stood there. I looked up into her face. Her lips were moving soundlessly in some prayer of her own design. You could do a lot worse, I thought, than have Nurse Stark be your guide to the underworld. Down the corridor, I could hear the "Jesus help me" man starting up again, but the overall sense of horror and foreboding I'd felt on the way up to Herman's room had vanished.

I suppose, for a more dramatic story, a more cinematic framing of events, dawn should have been breaking. As I said, the city lights reflecting off the clouds tricked me into thinking that it was starting to get light. I inched up the sleeve to glance at my watch. It was only two thirty.

I stood up slowly, my feet inching toward the door. Herman hadn't changed any in the last five minutes. He still looked as if he could wake up and start in on me about the weather.

"There's Herman Viereck, who is beastly dead."

I felt a little twinge of irrepressible glee as these words flashed inside my head. No matter how close we are to the deceased, or how tragic the circumstance, there's that little shudder of relief. The angel of death has been temporarily appeased. Maybe next time he will be for me—but not this time.

"What happens now?" I asked after what seemed like an appropriate pause for self-reflection.

"That's up to you. Mr. Viereck said you'd be making all the arrangements."

An icy tingle superimposed itself over my already chilled interior. Herman had reached out from beyond the grave to reel me in. It was like the time he'd Jewed me on the rent. All that random talk about headstones and memorials, all his feigned disinterest in the money. He'd set me up! What the hell did I know about a Catholic funeral—or any funeral for that matter? Even with Miriam, Tamar had been the one who'd ended up handling everything. I'd pretended to be too grief-struck—but the truth? I just hadn't wanted to deal with it.

"I wish he'd said something to me about it," I told her, trying to keep a very un-rabbi-ish whine out of my voice

"We use Scully-McMann. They're very understanding about these situations. I'm sure you'll find them quite reasonable. I've got one of their cards in the office."

"That's okay," I said. "I'm sure they're in the book."

Time to get out of here. I took one last look at the little janitor. He'd lived such a quiet, interior life. It was hard to realize that he still had so much impact.

"What do you do now?" I asked Stark.

"Oh, I have a lot of charting to do. I hope day shift put him on the list of 'expecteds.' I don't want to have to call the police and the coroner. It upsets the other patients."

"You mean he can just stay here?"

"We've got a few empty rooms right now. Our social worker is on vacation, so we're not getting any placements processed. Once you contact the funeral home, they'll send a car around to pick him up."

I looked down tentatively at Viereck's mortal form. I felt that being dead was an embarrassment, and I wanted to get him under wraps as soon as possible. Stark read the concern in my stare. I might be dense as a post, but she'd developed a liking for me, not the most gifted of students, just earnest and sweet.

"Don't worry, Mr. Learner; he'll be fine. Why don't you go on home?"

She dismissed me. I nodded. I felt an urge to put my arms around her, to give and receive some life-affirming hug, but I didn't dare. Instead, I reached out and patted her on the arm.

"You did great," she told me. "You sure you can find your way out?"

I assured her it wouldn't be a problem—but I didn't look to the right or the left till I felt the front door click shut behind me.

Outside, it had grown cold. A Manitoba wind was blowing in off the lake. As I sat in my car, waiting for the heater to clear a spot on the windshield, the snow flurries that Herman had assured me wouldn't happen wafted down.

Leave it to Gd to have a sense of humor.

At this hour, I could have been back in my warm apartment in fifteen minutes, but I felt too jazzed to crawl into bed. Instead, I drove over to the Denny's on Lincoln Avenue. I called Makiko from a payphone outside their front door.

"How did it go?" she asked.

"Good," I said. "It seemed very natural. An easy death, like my grandfather always told me to wish for."

"Cheerful old bastard, wasn't he?" she said.

I paused, trying to think of what I could say that would convey everything I'd just been through. It wasn't until I opened my mouth and heard myself speak that I realized that I wasn't quite in my right mind. Without realizing it, I was in the middle of some sort of transformative experience.

"I held him in my arms," I told her. "Can you believe that? It's hard to explain, but when he died, I got a sense of all this creative energy suddenly being freed, looking for some place to go, you know, a *metempsychosis*—a transformation of souls."

Makiko chuckled on the other end of the line "You're a *mashug-gener* mensch," she said, and then she paused. "Actually, you're the most wonderful man I know."

I'd never heard her say anything like that before.

"We've really got to talk about his work," I said. "This thing is going to really get out of control now he's gone."

"There's plenty of time for that. Where are you?"

"I'm at the Denny's over on Lincoln. I'm going to get something to eat. You want to join me?"

"What time is it?"

"I don't know, three something. Look, it's okay," I interrupted before she could make some excuse. "I'll just grab a sandwich. I'll be home in an hour."

"Go easy on the fries," she said. "I need you to be around a while."

∗∗∗

At three A.M., Denny's dining room plays host to a sparse collection of whores, meth monsters, and the marginally homeless, all scattered far enough away that they don't have to look at each other. This wasn't a perky, hyper-sanitary Denny's across from some suburban mall. The place felt as if it was barely holding onto its franchise.

My waitress looked me over, trying to fit me in any of the above-mentioned categories. Maybe I'm a lost tourist, miles from the interstate, or a professor at an art school having a late run at a midlife crisis.

What's a burger without fries anyway?

I sat in a booth and looked out at the half-empty dining room. If I squinted, I could get the light to look like Hopper's clichéd painting, *Night Hawks*. I drank Denny's thin robusta, even though I knew it would make me more wired. I told myself that I needed to think, to come to conclusions. I needed to call O'Malley and get him going on Herman's friend, Larry, see if he could track down anyone who knew him, but I couldn't really get myself to believe that I'd solved a crime that had gripped Chicago for weeks.

Instead of getting out a scrap of paper and making some kind of
to-do list, I found myself studying the shadows falling on the faces
of two characters sitting at the counter. After years of shutter-block,
everywhere I looked, I saw potential photographs.

"Tell her that we miss her very much but that we've tried to keep going."

Had I? Tried to keep going? I'd given Herman a lie to take to Miriam.
I'd lied to myself, to Makiko, to Dave, most of all to myself.

Now it was time for things to change.

I felt a power-surge of creative energy, like being in art school again.
Back then, I could spend twenty-four hours in the darkroom, half-stoned
on hypo vapors, mesmerized by the magic developing before my eyes.
Sleep had been the enemy, a thief out to steal my most precious possession: time.

After years of paralysis and self-destructive cynicism, where I thought
that every picture known to man had been shot, reshot, cropped, blown-
up, filtered, and tortured beyond recognition, everywhere I looked,
I saw fresh compositions. The stark shadows thrown by the salt and
pepper shakers on the table in front of me. The line of empty stools at
the counter, receding into the distance. The perspective of the waitress's
face when she leaned over me to take my order. Even the scuff marks
on the linoleum made abstract patterns worth documenting. I wanted
to be taking pictures again. I wanted to shoot it all.

I was ready to stick a lens in anyone's face. If only I'd captured Herman on his deathbed or Nurse Stark or the "Jesus Help Me" man. Each
one was a novel, every face an epic, a self-contained Beowulf, every one
of us a work of supreme splendor. We don't pay enough attention. We
don't recognize the miracle in each of us, but if they could see one of
my pictures, they'd have at least a clue.

My palms itched, and my fingers shook.

It was duende! It had found me at last, leaping from Herman's body
into my own like an alien virus in a sci-fi flick. I didn't know where it
was taking me or what I had to do, but I knew it was going to be great.
Duende filled me with an unfocused lust, a berserker's drive to smash
and pillage. If I didn't have a camera, then I'd take any weapon—a butter
knife or a ballpoint pen.

When you're six feet two inches and weigh 255, it may not be the best mood to be in, especially when I tell you what happened next.

The spirit of the moment temporarily robbed me of hunger, but when the waitress set my plate down, I started eating mechanically. Two booths away, a couple of high school kids were nursing coffees. Off and on, I'd heard snatches of their conversation. What they said wasn't important, but I'd picked up the tone. Right now, they were the only two people on the planet.

I was in a mood where I wanted to get up and say something encouragingly trite about how short life is, how every minute is precious, that they should cradle this time in their hearts because true love might never find them again. But I had the sense to know I would only spoil it. Just as I congratulated myself about having the sense to keep my mouth shut, some guy got up from the other side of the restaurant and approached their table.

He was material for my collection of night-people portraits. He had the hair of a floating corpse, damp and clotted into frayed ropes. His cheeks caved, skin pocked with old acne, and his thin lips folded into colorless slits above his rotting teeth.

He moved across the room with the same hopped up, point-and-shoot, herky-jerky way the TV detectives had in what seemed like days ago. He topped out at maybe 135 pounds, fished out of Lake Michigan, but even so, he vibrated with drugged-out energy, an adrenaline vampire living on stolen neurotransmitters.

"Hey man—you got the time?" he asked.

I could only see the back of the young kid's head, but his shoulder's hunched.

"It's three thirty, dude." He was trying to sound pissed off, but not too pissed off.

"You sure?"

The kid held up his arm.

"That's a nice watch. Where'd a kid like you get a watch like that? You want to sell it?"

I put down my burger and watched the inevitable unfold.

"No, we're not interested," the girl said.

"Hey, did I ask you? Let me see that thing. I got a buddy who'd give you seventy-five dollars for it. He's sitting over there. Let me show it to him."

"Look, man, we're not interested in selling the watch."

The vampire sat down next to the girl, crowding her up against the side of the booth.

"Look," he said. "It's like this. We've got a job to get to in Elmira, and we've run out of gas. Now, if I sell this watch for you, I can get a commission for twenty bucks. You got that much you could lend me?"

"No, we're broke, man."

"Then let me have the fucking watch."

Methamphetamine logic: incontrovertible.

"Look," the girl said. "All we have is coffee money."

I got halfway up out of the booth. "Is there some kind of problem?" I asked.

It's what I hope I would have done no matter how I felt. After all, wasn't I, too, a protector of the innocent? I felt for my wallet, halfway to whipping out a twenty so the guy would buzz off.

Only now, a big part of me hoped that I wouldn't be able to resolve things that peacefully.

"No, we're fine here. I'm just trying to conduct a little bizniss."

"Does this place look like Zales Jewelry Store to you?" I asked

"Hey, look, pops—this don't concern you."

Oh, really? Pops? I stood up and lurched over to their booth. Suddenly streetwise, I looked across the room to see how many guys the vampire had with him. Was I going to be shot in a Denny's trying to break up a two-bit hustle?

Gd, I hoped so.

"What you want to mess with these kids for?"

The long dining room became deathly still. The waitress disappeared into the back. Stuff like this must happen here every night of the week. As I watched, the vampire's friend got up out of his seat and began moving tentatively in our direction. Even from across the room, I could tell his heart wasn't in it. It was time to act fast, before they switched gears.

"Look, you dumb fuck," the vampire said, "don't you fucking fuck with me, fuck wad. This is none of your fucking business."

I leaned over the table, and the vampire half stood up, grabbed a butter knife, and lunged at my face. I jumped back. I thought he might have nicked my cheek, but honestly, I didn't feel a thing. My whole body felt impossibly light, and when I reached out and grabbed his wrist, it was as if I were watching a stranger do it.

By now, if you've paid attention, you know that I'd been suicidal for years. Not a narcissistic, self-indulgent violent suicidality, but a stoic willingness to play a passive role in my own self-destruction.

Bushido, the so-called way of the warrior, though the Italians have a word for it too—the quality of going through life not giving a fuck. At this moment, the possibility that I might be shot by a psychopathic drug addict struck me as no more than an amusing sidebar to my obituary.

For the second time that night, I picked up a human corpse. The vampire wore a filthy nylon windbreaker with the White Sox logo on it (just another reason to want to punch out his lights). The material felt strong enough you could have covered an airplane wing with it. When I grabbed a handful at his throat and lifted, his whole body came out of the booth as if he'd had on a window-washer's harness.

I dragged him out into the aisle and swung him around so that he was between me and his approaching friend.

"Hey, what the fuck are you doing? We're just having a conversation here."

"I don't think they want to talk to you," I said.

"Yeah, well it's as free country. I can talk to anyone I want."

He turned and looked at the girl who cowered, still jammed against the side of the booth. She hadn't decided if my showing up had made things better or worse.

"Why don't you kids take off? I'll get the check," I told them over my shoulder. At the back of the dining area, a chunky Latino cook had come out from the kitchen and wiped his hands on his apron. Everyone else in the place pointedly ignored us, even while silently scoping out where to dive for cover when the shooting started.

"Look man, this is fucked. All I wanna do is borrow a few freakin' bucks for gas."

"Then why don't you ask me for some money, instead of hassling these high-school kids?"

I tightened my grip and lifted my arm a few inches till the vampire stood on his toes. About six feet away sat a glass-fronted case filled with shopworn cream pies. I hefted the guy one more time, reached out with my other hand and took another handful of windbreaker from around his gut. With his feet half off the floor all he could do was flap his arms helplessly. I rocked him back and forth slightly to overcome inertia, like you do when you're trying to get a car out of a snowbank. With a little momentum, I thought I could throw him that far.

Unfolding inside my head, like a stunt in a Three Stooges short, I had a vision of his body flying across the room, the glass breaking, the overfilled pies exploding around him as he slumped to the floor. In the final edit, one last cream pie teeters on the edge of a shelf for a few seconds and then falls, cream side down, on his head. Cut to a close-up of pus-yellow filling streaming down his dazed face.

And then I felt the eye of the emotional hurricane surround me. Everything got calm and peaceful. The waitress had probably dialed 911. The kids in the booth, finally galvanized, scrambled to their feet. I even appreciated the look of resigned terror on the poor bastard I held in my grip. He was a lost, lonely loser, just like the rest of us. Right then, I saw the future as clearly as I saw the past.

"Stop it before you kill the guy," said an interior voice, sounding somewhat like my own. The energy imparted to me from Herman's death wasn't meant to be used this way. I relaxed my grip, and the vampire slumped a little before he stood up on his own.

"I'm sorry," I told him. "I've got a daughter about her age. I don't want to see them hassled." I paused. "You really need gas money?"

The vampire nodded. I kept a hand on his jacket front. I didn't want him backing away far enough to pull out a weapon.

"All I need is ten lousy bucks. Geez, what the fuck's wrong with you? You got some kind of fucking Batman complex?"

I pulled out my wallet and gave him a twenty. He didn't thank me. He looked at his friend, who had frozen halfway across the floor.

"The bitch called 911," the friend said. "Let's get the fuck out of here." And in a second, they were gone.

The waitress came over to where I was now standing quite alone.

"You should get out of here too, mister. They're sending a car over. You don't need that kind of grief from the CPD."

I thanked her. In my mind I had started running headlines: "*Mild-mannered Professor Foils Armed Robbery!*"

But she was right. Who knew how the police were liable to take this? I thanked her and dropped another twenty on the table. Since when could you solve all your problems for forty dollars?

As I pulled out of the lot, a Chicago PD cruiser rolled in. They didn't seem to be in any rush. The waitress was standing in the doorway, and she waved them off.

"We're cool here," she called. But they parked their car, anyway. Probably time for a cup of coffee. I drove home cautiously, checking my rearview mirror constantly for cops or some beat-to-shit Pontiac Grand Am with streaks of Bondo on the doors and a vampire at the wheel. I'd lost my desire for violent confrontations, but my pulse still pounded with creative energy.

By the time I drove the last few blocks, the heater finally began to spew warm air, but I still felt chilled. The only parking spaces were on the wrong side of the street, only good till 7:00 A.M., but I parked there anyway. By seven, I planned to be long gone.

Makiko was in bed, but she came out into the kitchen right away when I started blundering about. Wrapped in my bathrobe, she looked like another lost waif. I reached down to hug her, and she put a finger up to my cheek and pulled it away. There was a tiny streak of blood on it.

"What happened to you?" she asked.

"Nothing." I felt like I was ten years old myself. "I got into a fight," I told her. "This guy was hassling these kids at the Denny's. I don't know what came over me. I almost threw the SOB through a window. It was nuts."

She sat down while I bustled around the kitchen. I'm a nervous eater.

"I thought you had a sandwich?" she asked.

"No, I told you," and I started to explain what had "gone down" at Denny's. Makiko wasn't impressed.

"You're talking way too fast, Nate."

"I know," I said. "This whole thing with him dying, it's put me in this weird space. Look," I told her, "I'm going to take off for a day or two. I want to go down-state and check out the institution they put Herman in. See if they'll let me onto the wards. I want to try to capture the spirit of the place—see what spirits still haunt it."

"You're going to take *pictures*?"

I turned away from the open fridge, a rivulet of milk was dribbling down the side of my chin, and half a slice of olive loaf dangling from my mouth.

"Is that so strange? I'm a photographer."

"It's just that it's been a long time since I've seen you excited about a project. I didn't know you still had this much left in the tank."

"I got plenty," I said.

I could have lifted her up onto the counter and fucked her standing up, but I was in such a fugue state sex wouldn't have made any difference. It wouldn't have switched off the ignition on my runaway engine.

She followed me around the apartment while I got my things together. All the film I had in the house had expired, but there was sure to be a mall with a Kits Camera someplace south of Chicago.

"You're just going to show up there unannounced and hope they let you shoot a bunch of pictures?"

"I guess so. I hadn't thought about it. It's just a bunch of old buildings. What are they going to say?"

"You better shave and change your clothes. You can't go down there looking like a wild man."

Makiko opened the closet, grabbed an overnight bag, and began to pack it for me. It was totally out of character, her taking care of me like that.

PART THREE

CHAPTER TWENTY-SIX

South on I-55, the sky slowly opening with the suffused light of a rain-spattered dawn. Like cliffs marking a dangerous shore, grey buildings loomed out of the fog. In the other direction, I saw the traffic already building, but I was in my own privileged world. I'd forgotten how hard most people worked just for a spot to call home.

Finally, alone in a speeding car, the lunacy of my mission caught up with me. I heard the whirring of my own thoughts guiding me back to reality. It was the Pepto bottles all over again. Even from beyond the grave, Herman had goaded me into another fool's crusade.

"This is fucking nuts," I said out loud.

Only one thing prevented me from turning the car around—anticipating the look of disappointment on Makiko's face when I limped back through the door. All at once, I felt too old and entrenched for cataclysmic change. How could a lifetime of self-doubt and ambivalence be purged by an old man's dying words? I knew this was my last chance, a small opportunity to grow, to keep moving forward. How could I tell Makiko I'd given all that up because I needed a nap?

I'd been awake for over twenty-four hours, something I hadn't done since Miriam's hospital vigils. I'd heard the confession of a dying man. I'd come close to getting stabbed. I'd been gripped by the iron claw of creative passion.

It felt like when I'd dropped acid and reached the point in the trip where the effect of the drug starts to wane and the underpinnings of the ordinary world reappear. I was still not my self, but the way back had become visible, laid out for me like a bird's-eye view of a diorama in the Museum of Nathan's Psyche.

The grandiosity of the task I'd laid out for myself scared me half to death. The poet has his empty page, the painter his blank gessoed canvas, the sculptor his square block of Carrera marble. For the photographer, panic is a zero in the frame counter of the camera, an unexposed roll.

**

I passed the last Chicago exit. The snow flurries Herman failed to predict became an impotent drizzle, so fine that even the slowest delay of my wipers produced streaks on the greasy windshield. I looked down at the speedometer, shocked to see the needle pegged at fifty-five. It felt much faster, but it had been months since I'd ventured out on an open road. The gas gauge read full. My bladder was empty. NPR faded just about the time I passed my first stubble-strewn cornfield. That's all there was to it—the open road and my Gd-given right as an American to get into his car and point it anywhere.

People don't generally know this from the song, but Route 66, the ur-road of the American nomadic dream, starts in Chicago. The original pavement has long since been torn up, but signs and billboards preserve the legacy. Now, without realizing it, I headed toward a rendezvous with the last few original paved miles in, of all places, Lincoln, Illinois.

We hadn't taken many road trips when Miriam was small and never any to the bourgeois destinations on the All-American bucket list. No trips to Dizzy Land, no Grand Canyon. We'd have sooner gone to Florence or Rome.

Alone in the car, I had a vision of myself in a station wagon, cranky kids in back, indulgent wife at my side. She's struggling with an unrefoldable map as we search bravely for old Route 66 markers while the kids whine and ask, "When are we going to get there?" and I struggle to explain to them that, in this case, given the mission, we were on to rediscover the American psyche and reclaim our own, that we were already *there,* existentially speaking, and how someday they would remember this trip fondly as some kind of tribute to the complex character that was their old man.

The raw truth? Given my own Russian immigrant background and the Eurocentric Marxist sensibility of everyone I had grown up with, rediscovering Route 66 meant a helluva lot less to me than finding the location of my great Aunt Sophie's blini stand in Odessa.

So this morning, I made no scenic detours. I roared past the nostalgia, the two-tone Fords and '59 Chevys with fighter-jet fins. I didn't care about diners in the shape of teepees, antique gas pumps, or fifty-foot-high cement prairie dogs. I stayed on the interstate and made it all the way to the Lincoln off-ramp in two hours and fifty-three minutes.

***

Originally called Postville, Lincoln is the county seat of Logan County. It's where Honest Abe got his start as a country lawyer and hack politician. In 1863, in a jingoistic attempt to co-opt some of his presidential magic, a group of local businessmen petitioned Lincoln to let them name the town after him. He reluctantly agreed, actually showing up and baptizing the bronze plaque that bore his name with a spit mouthful of watermelon juice.

Lincoln also turns out to be the home of a teenage Langston Hughes, who wrote his first poem while attending class at the surprisingly integrated Lincoln High School. His teacher thought he showed promise. Later, the existentialist theologian Reinhold Niebuhr taught philosophy at the local university. It's also the birthplace and boyhood home of a pretty good novelist, William Maxwell. Everybody has to come from somewhere.

Packing this much history, plus that small semiprecious stretch of original Route 66 pavement, the local Chamber of Commerce managed to preserve Main Street in its nineteenth-century splendor. Coming in from the interstate, I passed red-brick buildings, ornamented with the same cast-iron columns that you'd find in New York or Chicago. Of course, the hardware stores and millinery shops had been replaced with a children's bookstore, an antique mall, and a restaurant advertising pumpkin soup and onion quiche as their lunch specials.

I drove through this older part of town looking in vain for a camera store. Eventually, I ended up back out on a feeder road that paralleled the interstate and passed a moderate-sized shopping mall. Still no camera store, so, instead, I stopped and picked up some Kodachrome at the Walgreens. They didn't have any black and white. If I felt the need for the harshness of blacks and grays, I'd have to risk the out-of-date stuff in my camera bag.

In the store, I caught my reflection in a mirror. Even with the quick shave Makiko had talked me into, I looked rough in the unforgiving fluorescents. I'd planned to be back in Chicago by late evening, but the drooping eyelids and bagginess under my eyes told me I wasn't going to make it. I'd have to crash somewhere.

I took the film up to the counter. As I fumbled with my wallet, I realized I didn't know where the Lincoln school was. The teenage girl behind the register said she'd never heard of the place.

"It's out on Business Route 55, a few miles past the stoplight," an older woman behind me said. She waved out at the parking lot with one hand. "Just make a left out of the lot. You can't miss it."

Long after Herman made his escape, the Illinois Home for Feeble-Minded Children had updated its name to the Lincoln Development Center. Over the years, it had been in and out of the news. Like every other state-run, underfunded dumping ground, Lincoln had been "wracked by scandal." Accusations of misuse of funds, unexplained deaths, injuries, and an epidemic of sexual abuse and neglect by the poorly trained and unsupervised staff had stacked up over the years.

Eventually, the governor's office announced they were going to close the center. But that had been a while ago, and I couldn't remember the final outcome. There had been protests by parents and social workers. Despite its sordid history, for many of the residents, there was no other viable alternative.

***

I drove out the empty two-lane highway, not knowing what to expect. Somewhere in the back of my mind, I recalled a low-budget horror movie that had been shot at an abandoned mental hospital outside Boston, and I geared up for a similar experience. After a few miles, I passed a crumbling brick wall, overgrown with blackberry vines and leafless sumacs. The wall stood about five feet high and didn't look as if it had been built to keep anyone from escaping.

At the wall's end, the brick heaped itself up to form the frame for a once-impressive entryway. An iron gate had been permanently pushed ajar, and a sign in modern Invicta identified the Development Center. I passed it, screeched to a stop, and backed up.

Once I turned in, the main building, a five-story central tower, flanked by two substantial wings, towered a quarter of a mile away. It was made of the same red brick as the wall, but inlaid with white fieldstone accents. It looked built from an elaborate set of Victorian-era building blocks, the kind only a rich and indulgent relative would buy for his precocious nephew.

The expanse of winter-burned lawn in front of the main building looked semi-mowed. I saw no "no trespassing" signs, but an air of abandonment radiated out into the still winter air.

When I reached the turnaround in front of the building, a Honda Accord and a Chevy Suburban took up two of twenty available parking spaces. There wasn't a Model A or an old Buick Roadmaster in sight.

I pulled into an empty slot. The car stopped abruptly against an unseen parking barrier, hard enough to snap my neck forward with a jolt. My body buzzed from the rhythm of the road. With the engine off, a vast winter stillness rolled off the cornfields and enveloped me. I could have been the last living thing on earth. No birds, no crickets, no droning lawn mowers.

Best not to think too many moves ahead, or surely I would put the car back in gear and head back the way I'd come. I forced myself to grab my camera bag and stepped out onto the frozen gravel. The red-brick tower of the asylum rose majestically in front of me, Lincoln's answer to

Chartres. The tower must have been quite a construction feat in 1873. It still radiated an air of grandiose, nineteenth century, can-do optimism. Such plans they'd had for America. Where had they gone?

I pulled out my battle-scarred Nikon and framed the tower, kneeling on one foot and aiming up to accentuate its height and menacing grandeur. This is how the school must have looked to eight-year-old Herman when they first brought him here. Had he stood in this very spot, flanked between two matrons clutching his little hands in their iron grip as they half-dragged, half-carried him up the marble steps?

I tried not to assign anything more to the picture than what it was, a grounding-location shot, but it was the first creative photograph I'd taken in years. I couldn't disguise that from myself. I got up and advanced the film, looking down as the zero in the frame counter turned over.

"That's one."

Self-consciously, I walked across the frozen gravel. The heavy oak doors were massive enough to deserve a moat in front of them. One side hung open a few inches, as if whoever was inside worried more about not being able to get out than about who might break in.

Goldilocks pushed and found himself looking across a large rotunda, a mini-version of any state capitol building. On the other side of an expanse of glass-smooth marble, a broad staircase led up to a balustraded mezzanine. On ground level, two long hallways radiated to the right and left, going down the two wings I'd seen from the outside.

Crossing the floor, I stepped on a mandala of inlaid stone, the seal of the great state of Illinois, six feet across, a Latin inscription ran around the rim: *"Patronus Innocentium."*

Except for the original marble, the rest of the lobby had fallen victim to a halfhearted attempt at modernization. Along the circular walls, someone had tried to do my work for me. A collection of enlarged archival photographs of the asylum, starting with architectural drawings from 1873, then a bird's-eye view of the school, done at the turn of the century, showing all its outbuildings, had been hung just above eye level. Lincoln once had a model farm, a greenhouse, a steam-generating plant, and a laundry. It looked like one of those utopian communities from the late 1800s.

As I toured the wall, I paused at pictures of the original staff: women with large busts but still unnurturing in starched white nurse's uniforms, men with handlebar mustaches or mutton chops, and now and then, a group photo of some of the residents.

"Miss McMurray and the intermediate class of epileptics 1909."

"Imbeciles." Undated.

A glass display case along one wall displayed a collection of artifacts: a whole shelf of brushes carefully fashioned with graceful wooden handles. Most were of a size and shape that rendered their purpose unrecognizable to the twentieth-century eye.

I couldn't help but be impressed by their clean, modern lines, and the skill and precision of their manufacture. A hand-typed card informed me that brush making had been a skill taught for over twenty-five years by a Mr. Palmer and that the sale of these brushes allowed residents to earn extra income and achieve some level of independence.

In the same case was a pair of leg irons and a leather girdle with buckled loops to restrain the arms.

Whoever had assembled these artifacts had a very high tolerance for irony.

***

"Can I help you?" a voice asked.

I turned, half expecting some apparition in a black dress with thirty buttons up to a high Victorian collar but, instead, saw an athletic looking woman in jeans and a Northwestern University sweatshirt. She was blond in a part of the country where blond is the normal hair color, and she wore it carelessly. She wasn't smiling, exactly, but I didn't feel my presence annoyed her . She had a broad forehead, wide-awake eyes, and a slightly upturned mouth. It gave her a look that said she regarded me as part of some potential cosmic practical joke.

The cars in the parking should have put me on alert, but the possibility that I would have to explain my mission to anyone had bridged itself over in my mind. In the mythical state I had put myself in, I had planned to show up at the asylum and shoot pictures to my heart's content.

Now the whole enterprise appeared threatened by a half-smile.

"Hi," I said. "I didn't think anyone would be here. My name is Nathan Learner. I'm a photographer. I teach photography at the Chicago Institute of Fine Arts. I was hoping someone might let me look around—maybe take a few pictures?"

"You're not *the* Mr. Learner?" she asked. "The one who did the book, *Windy City*?"

I was more surprised than flattered. It had been years since anyone, including myself, had thought about the book. It had been a project between myself and a local Chicago poet, a series of portraits meant to capture our town's broad ethnic and socioeconomic diversity. It came out in paperback in time for Christmas and had done quite well as those things go. But hardly a classic.

"You know the book?'

"Oh yes, it's one of my favorites. My son got it for me for Christmas. They're some very powerful images. My gosh, this is a surprise. How can I help you?"

"I was hoping to look around. I'm thinking about doing a photo essay about the Lincoln school."

She nodded, but a look of slight remorse overtook her. "Oh dear, that would have been a wonderful project. I saw the pictures you did on the children's cancer ward. It felt like you were totally connected with those children and their parents. But I'm afraid … didn't anyone tell you the center is closed?"

"No, I guess I never thought about it. Otherwise, I would have called."

It was such a plausible lie, I almost believed it myself.

The woman descended three-quarters of the way down the stairs. I crossed the lobby, reached up and shook her hand without putting a foot on the worn semicircle of the hollowed-out steps.

"Marjory Russell," she said. "I'm acting director for the development center. We're keeping a skeleton staff. The legislature still hasn't made up its mind, but we're hoping to reopen next year, maybe with some private funding."

"I heard about the place from a friend of mine who was an inmate here back a long time ago. I didn't know what to expect. He just ... well, he just expired. I wanted to sort of do a memorial to him."

Marjory smiled. The home for the feeble-minded was a place that was always colliding with its past. She seemed used to it.

"I'm sorry. We don't like to call them inmates. I'm sure you understand. There were over a thousand residents here at one time. That was before the push toward de-institutionalization. Then, too, epilepsy has become a simple, treatable condition. Not many people are aware that it used to be a death sentence for these kids."

She stopped and seemed to look at me for the first time. She must have given this talk to so many groups of legislators and Illinois State bean counters that it came gushing out of her.

"I'm afraid there's not a whole lot to see right now, I mean, for someone so talented, I mean, so good with capturing people's inner turmoil. I don't know what it is you do. I mean, everyone has the same camera, the same film, but it's like you capture this extra dimension—something in their eyes."

"Do you take pictures, Ms. Russell?" The last thing I'd expected was to run into a fan.

"No, it's too technical for me. I don't have the patience."

"I'm not sure I want to do portrait pieces," I told her. "I'm more interested in seeing if I could capture some of the spirit of the past. You know—the way things get when they've been abandoned, that haunted feeling, as if the people had just been snapped up, spirited away?"

Marjory nodded, and I was overcome with gratitude that I didn't have to try to explain myself any further.

Drug and alcohol counselors have an expression for what was happening. They call it an "IMR" (instant meaningful relationship). My excuse? I was whacked-out and sleep deprived. Poor Marjory was marooned in a sea of cornfields.

"Ah yes, I think I know what you're driving at," she said. "Like those photos of the *Titanic*, all those dinner plates still set out, the suitcases. There are a lot of ghosts here, as well. Does yours have a name?"

"Herman Viereck," I said.

"A relative?"

"No, he was my tenant in a building I owned. It turns out he was a bit of an artist, a painter, and a novelist, too," I added.

"It sounds like he might have been misdiagnosed." It hadn't been Marjory who'd put the leg irons in the display case.

"Possibly," I said.

"You're not doing this for any of the papers, are you? We don't need any more negative publicity."

I assured her my project was completely personal.

"Wait here," she told me. "I'll go get my coat." She went back up the stairs, and I could hear her talking to someone in an office.

She reappeared, coming down the stairs in a massive quilted blue parka, the kind people snowmobile in. She was taller than I first realized, her body lanky like a college basketball player. We walked back across the lobby, and I stopped involuntarily before stepping on the great seal.

"Patronus Innocentium," she read out loud. "Protector of the innocent."

She led me down a hallway, past rows of empty offices. The doors were all heavy oak with frosted glass panels and solid brass doorknobs. I knew an architectural antiques guy who'd have given me one hundred dollars apiece for them.

On the walls near the doors were labels, all done in updated Invicta: "Department of Human Resources," "Aid to Families with Dependent Children," "Environmental Operations." But all the verbiage of modernization hadn't helped. Nothing could jerk the Home for Feeble-Minded out of the past.

Marjory led me through a side door. We entered the Magic Kingdom behind the fairy castle. The overcast had burned off, and the outbuildings struck my eye painfully in the harsh winter sunlight. She wedged a brick against the door so we could get back in and started down cracked cement walks. Shriveled dandelions tenaciously hung on, waiting for spring. The path led us past cottages and outbuildings, their windows shuttered with plywood, their walls half-hidden by blackberry brambles, signs of nature taking back its own.

"Most of these cottages were updated in the fifties," she told me. "But I think B Wing is what you're looking for."

We stopped in front of a red-brick barracks, the walkway up to the front entrance too badly overgrown to pass. Marjory took me round to the back. Here, an old entrance had been replaced with a steel fire door. My guide took out a ring of keys, but she didn't look too hopeful. I prepared to wait while she tried them all, but she found the right one on the first try.

"Imagine that," she said as we pushed the door open.

CHAPTER TWENTY-SEVEN

arjory held the door for me.

First Nurse Stark, now Marjory—a new guide for every ring. Would this, at last, be hell's core? We stood in a little vestibule, designed as a heat barrier. When she pushed open the inner doors, the entire interior confronted us, a hundred feet long, devoid of partitions or walls, both sides fenestrated with tall narrow factory windows.

Shafts of light came in through the side exposed to the sun. Eddies of dust flew up, solidifying the light into slanted shafts, just like the painting of Jesus hanging in the Little Sisters.

Four rows of iron beds occupied most of the floor space, two under the windows and two rows, head-to-head, down the center of the room. Someone had rolled up their thin mattresses, but here and there, rodents had gnawed through the bindings, and the bedding had uncoiled. Tufts of cotton provided cozy nests for field mice. I didn't begrudge them.

A grid of cast-iron radiators, three banks high, lined the far end of the vaulted room, but the end where we'd come in lacked a heat source. Had there been a pecking order of favorites? Which bed had been Herman's? Down here in Siberia?

A leaning tower of enamel bedpans tottered in one corner. In the other, a fortification of twisted wire chairs, the kind you'd find in a

vintage ice cream parlor. Irregular triangles of missing masonry left old
wooden lath exposed. Marjory stood at my side, as proud as a docent
in some small Italian town who had just shown some privileged tourist
a little-known fresco by Tintoretto.

"This what you had in mind?" she asked.

I felt sure that if I'd handed her my camera she could have taken all
the shots I needed.

"God," I said, "how long has it been like this?"

"Since the fifties. Lincoln used to have its own electric and steam-
generating plant. They fired it with cornhusks and cobs from the local
farms. It was ecologically very advanced, but we never got the credit."

I looked at her again. Inside the abandoned dormitory, she was
the only spot of color in the building. She saw me looking at her and
brushed her blond hair back nervously.

"Way before my time," she said, tossing her head slightly. Marjory
put her hands in the pockets of her parka and did a small shiver.

"You must be freezing," I said. It was the same thing I'd told Makiko
the night I met her. Marjory nodded.

"I'm not a native. The winters here can be something awful."

"Why don't you go on back? I won't be long."

She looked grateful to be allowed to leave. Even without the cold,
there was a malevolent energy in the room that could suck the life out
of anyone.

"Be careful," she said. "I'm not sure I trust these floors."

"It's not the floors," I said. "It's the ghosts."

"I can't help you with those." She pulled out her ring of keys and
peeled off the one she'd used to let us in.

"Just lock up when you're done," she said, handing me the key.

After she left, it became both easier and harder. She'd provided the
last buffer between me and what I'd spent the last eight years avoiding.

At least, now that she'd walked out, there were no witnesses. If she'd
stayed, it would have forced me to perform. I'd said I was a photographer. I would have had to start proving it. Without her, all I had goading
me on were the half-baked promises I'd made to Herman's departing

soul. When I finally pulled out the Nikon, I glared at it the way a self-flagellating monk might look at his whip.

The viewfinder has its way of distorting things. To take a decent photograph, to capture the spirit and ambience of the environment, so self-evident when observed with the naked eye, the scene has to be mythologized, made into an icon, and then compressed into the confines of what the lens will hold.

A tourist on safari snaps away at a pride of lions sniffing his Land Rover. The picture comes back looking like a gaggle of house cats sitting on a Tonka truck, everything dwarfed by the enormity of the sky. Once developed, sunlight reflected through an icicle hanging off a faucet is not the fascinating interplay of light and water you'd hoped to capture. It's just a plumbing problem. A stack of enamel bedpans abandoned in the corner of an empty dormitory for idiots is not mute testimony to the mundane nuts and bolts of the caring required for the wounded helpless creature that lives inside all of us. It's just some pots to piss in.

Well, shouldn't I know how to fix that? Hadn't I taught a generation of alternatively ponytailed and now skin-headed young men and their black-lipsticked, tattooed girlfriends how to take a decent picture?

"Don't think," I said out loud. "Just shoot the goddamn picture."

I'd like to say that once I got started it was easy, that time stood still and I became impervious to the cold that turned my thick fingers into the hands of a jerkily controlled marionette, that the spirit of duende that had swept over me at the Denny's so many hours ago reawakened, and that I played the focus ring and camera settings like a violin.

In the movie of my life, they'd film this as musical interlude. It'd be fluid ballet, a montage of crouching and twisting, the background music punctuated by the Nikon's click, click, click. I'd be like Pollack slinging paint, Holliday moaning "I cover the waterfront," Nolan Ryan fanning the side on nine straight heaters, all high and inside.

But it wasn't like that at all. Every shot came from low-grade self-torture.

Even halfway into the second roll, when I realized that it *was* all coming back to me, that it was all good, I still had to force myself to keep going, to keep reaching. But I got it all, the raw rusted springs on the iron beds, the rats' nests in the mattress ticking, the shafts of dusty light stabbing through the broken windows, and the traces of graffiti on the peeling walls: "Bob wuz here," " Alice and Jeremy 4-ever," "Mr. Hemming is a cock sucker."

Frame by frame, I worked myself down the long room till I got to a partitioned area that had been a nurse's station. Inside it, cupboards, thick with a dozen coats of institutional paint, hung, their doors slackly open. A chart rack filled one corner, empty aluminum folders hanging like broken teeth. An enormous bottle of Dilantin, its contents congealed into a crystalline mass, lay open on the counter. An old drug company giveaway pen sat on the desk next to a coffee cup, its contents long evaporated to a crusty black ring. It looked as if whoever had gone away had planned on coming right back.

I got the feeling an inspector from the health department had shown up and given everyone half an hour to clear out. For my purposes, it was hauntingly perfect. I shot up half a roll before I noticed a door at the far end of the little room. I'd missed it because a desk had been pushed in front and a chair had been piled on the desk. From the way they'd been arranged, I got the feeling that someone had purposely tried to obscure the entrance.

Was I destined to play the role of Carter one more time?

Cold as the room was, my fingers had been working perfectly, but now as I went to move the desk, they stiffened. I nearly dropped the heavy swivel office chair on my foot before I shoehorned it out the door and threw it against the row of iron bedsteads. The desk, I merely swung out far enough to pry the door open.

The air inside the little room smelled stale but dust-free. There were no windows, and the only light came in through the doorway. The floor and walls were covered in ceramic tile. No wonder there was so little dust.

Wondrous things?

At the center of the room, under a bank of adjustable lights, I saw an archaic operating table, covered in cracked black leatherette.

In one corner, barely visible, lurked a low steel table, its surface covered with surgical instruments. In the other, an elaborate contraption holding several small fire-extinguisher-sized cylinders sat on horrid little metal wheels, a vintage anesthesia machine.

Believe it or not, I'd seen one before in an antique shop.

The realization hit with creepy certainty. I stood in what had once been, for its time, a state-of-the-art operating room. It looked like a bucket of Lysol and a thick bristled brush could get it back on line in under an hour.

Why was it here? This bustling, barracks-like building provided no place for major surgery. Surely even then, they would have transferred any surgical cases to the local hospital.

The light limed just enough to shoot a few haunted pictures, but the hair on the back of my neck began to stand up, and it was hard to hold my camera steady.

***

I got back to Marjory's office, my head buzzing with questions, questions to which I'd already framed frightening answers. She was the only representative of Lincoln's bureaucracy left, and I couldn't help keep my voice from sounding accusatory as I opened up.

Marjory nodded and settled in for the long haul.

"Let me make you a cup of tea," she said.

Her office, overly spacious by modern standards, had once belonged to one of the home's former directors. At the far end of the room, a wall of single-pane windows let in random currents of winter air. Marjory had moved her desk to the other end, and she kept a space heater going. Before she turned on the kettle, she reached down and unplugged it.

"We're always blowing fuses," she explained.

I came back from staring out the window and sat down in a straight-backed chair across from her desk. She still used an IBM Selectric. Stacks of paper, most with state of Illinois letterhead, fluttered in a draft. Lincoln school might be dead in the flesh, but it still maintained a vigorous virtual existence.

As always, I looked for personal photos. There was only one—Marjory with two adolescents. They were all smiling, but there was something a little off about the boy, a look of surprised confusion and tentativeness.

No man in the picture. No surprise there. I glanced over at her hands. No ring, either.

She had several kinds of tea, everything from chamomile to a smoky Lap Soong. I went for the Earl Grey, idly wondering once again where oil of Bergamot came from.

"So, you found the operating room," she said. She pulled her swivel chair away from the desk and slid forward informally. "I've heard rumors about its existence, but I've never seen it. I try to keep away from there."

"It's fairly elaborate. What kind of surgery would they do in a place like this?"

Marjory looked at me over the rim of her mug. She looked resigned to taking the heat.

"What do you know about the eugenics movement?" she asked.

She didn't have to say anything else. I didn't need anyone to spoon-feed it to me.

"Not much. It's the crackpot pseudo-science that the Nazis used to justify their atrocities."

"Yes, but what people don't want to remember is that Hitler got it from us. The eugenics movement started in the United States. It's part of slavery's legacy, our struggle over race and the fear of miscegenation, the idea of selective breeding, the improvement of the race by weeding out the runts, the malformed, and the mentally defective. All so typical of our misguided expectations that we can manage all our problems with science.

"What's always fascinated me about it was the number of clergymen that were involved. They had no problem with Darwin's theories when it came to sterilizing people they thought were misfits or incorrigible criminals."

***

Makiko tells me that most men feel threatened by an intelligent woman, but I've never felt that way. For me it's always been a turn-on listening to a woman hold forth with passion and enthusiasm, knowing that nothing but a certain brutish masculine energy could make them shut up, energy, naturally, I always felt that I possessed. All I had to do now was maintain eye contact and nod my head.

"Between 1894 and probably into the early fifties," she went on, "the state of Illinois sterilized, and in some cases castrated, close to five hundred people they classed as mental defectives and incorrigible criminals, most without any formal hearings or legal proceedings. Dr. Star Jordan, Lincoln's general director, was president of the American Eugenics Society from 1909 till he went to Stanford University to be its first president. California soon led the nation in sterilizations. So what do you think they used that operating room for?"

Marjory took another sip. I had a vague desire to grab the cup out of her hand and throw her down on the floor. I'd fallen totally in love with her wounded sardonic affect, but so far we hadn't spoken a single personal word to each other. I got the feeling we both didn't dare.

"God, that's terrible," I said.

"Once an institution develops a culture like that, it's very hard for them to stop. It would mean admitting that they were wrong in the first place. They estimate that over sixty thousand sterilizations were performed in America between 1880 and the 1950s. It's still discussed from time to time as a way of dealing with sexual predators. They call it chemical castration."

And who would that be? A sexual predator, the kind of person who might snatch a little girl off the street? I got that little crawling feeling one gets up the back of the spine when you put two and two together. It always seems so obvious after the fact.

Herman had been here when that horrid little room was up and running.

"Tell me something," I said, leaning forward. "Is there some kind of dead-files storage room?"

"You're wondering about your friend, aren't you?"

I nodded. "It would explain a lot about him," I said.

"There's tons of stuff in the basement. I've always thought those old records might be useful, you know, for some kind of research, but maybe we'd be better off burning them."

And the whole place with them, I could tell she was thinking.

"Do you think we could find his chart?"

"I don't know." She looked at me and did the thing with her hair again, brushing it back ineffectually. I looked into her eyes for a second too long.

Were we both thinking the same thing? Could I possibly explain it to Makiko? Never. Could I hide it from her? Doubtful. Was anything going to happen? Unknown.

"This is turning into quite an expedition," she said, putting her coat back on and grabbing a heavy-duty flash light out of the bottom drawer of her desk.

"I like to let the rats know we're coming," she said. I followed her out the door and down the steps into the basement.

CHAPTER TWENTY-EIGHT

Below the frost line, the basement felt warmer than Marjory's office. The air hung still and was faintly tinged with the effluvia of damp earth.

My latest Beatrice walked confidently along in the dark. I imagined hearing the scurrying of tiny feet as she swept the flashlight down the sides of the corridor. At the end of the first short hallway, she groped along the wall for a switch.

Retrofitted fluorescents buzzed and came on in succession—bam, bam, bam. The harsh light flickered at a subliminal frequency, an epileptic's nightmare. Marjory led us past a frosted glass door marked "MEDICAL RECORDS" but didn't stop.

"Those only go back about five years," she explained.

We pushed further into the depths of the basement before stopping at an unmarked door. Once again, tomb-dust filled my nostrils. Marjory flashed the beam of her light, and I saw rows of industrial shelving, piled high with record boxes. She checked the labels on the nearest ones.

"This should be it," she said, and then found the switch. The room had only one fixture, and one eight-footer had burned out, leaving its mate flickering ineffectually.

"When did you say he was here?"

"I don't know. He was in his eighties, and he left here at seventeen.

"His name?"

I spelled it for her, and she searched the rows. Someone had done their job with methodical Midwestern competence, using the same breakpoints as the card catalogue in a Dewey-system library. It took her only a minute to find the right box.

I stood in the doorway and marveled at the work of man. Seventy years, these charts had sat there, millions of pages that would never be read, inanimate, soulless but filled with words, intelligible information just waiting for the right sequence of events, the right connection of synapses to make them communicate.

Marjory pulled the box off the shelf, coughing slightly as the dust flew up around her. We took it out into the hallway where the light was better. There aren't that many last names that start with V—Vandicamp, Vernor, Viereck.

There he was, like tracking down an out-of-print book in a good university library. I pulled out the chart. Not even bothering to get up, I rocked back on my heels and sat down heavily on the floor. How little paper has changed in the last sixty years. I held the same type of folder you could pick up today in any Office Depot.

The child Herman had once been came to life before my eyes. Date of birth, parent's name, mother's maiden name—marked deceased. It was all there, either typed out on an old Underwood with a slight registration problem or else written in various legible hands, back from a time when cursive was a valid form of communication. I could have been reading the prologue to the *Realms of the Unreal.*

> Herman comes to us from the Cicero Home for Orphans and Abandoned Children. He is being evaluated at the request of their director, Dr. James Kessler, who feels that the facility in Lincoln may be more appropriate for this boy who is exhibiting increasingly violent and self-abusive behavior
>
> Several attempts have been made to dissuade young Herman from his habit of self-abuse, but

these have failed. It appears nothing can be done
to break him of this degenerative behavior, which
is slowly turning him from a disturbed boy, yet
of perhaps above-average intelligence, into an
imbecile. In addition, we have become increasingly
concerned with the attention he has been paying to
some of the female inmates who have been entrusted
to his care

In many ways, Herman exhibits normal, or even
above normal, intellectual abilities. He is noted
to be able to read quite fluently and has developed a morbid interest in the Civil War. He has
an obsessive fascination with the details of the
battles. On several occasions, he has been seen
attempting to re-enact specific episodes from the
conflict, enlisting many of the higher-functioning
imbeciles and morons to serve in his battalions.
His attitude, however, when not left to engage in
his own world, remains defiant and unpredictable

Today Herman was observed to be drawing somewhat furtively. When Mr. Kennedy was called in
to persuade the boy to disclose his drawings, he
manifested considerable resistance. When he was
forcefully induced to part with them at no little
physical exertion, they were found to be repre-
sentations of the vilest tortures being committed
against crude but sexually explicit images of young
girls. When confronted about these drawings, Herman
protested that he was merely depicting events that
he had seen occurring here. No amount of physical
persuasion laid on thick by the senior attendant
Mr. Abshelhiem could cause him to retract these
inflammatory and patently untrue statements

It has been observed that as Herman advances in
his pubescence, his deviant and morally reprehen-
sible behavior is only increasing in its intensity
and that his ingrained habit of self-abuse can only
lead him to becoming a greater threat to society
at large. This, coupled with animal cunning and
an aptitude for escape, can only insure that his
violent and sexually aggressive tendencies may
eventually cause havoc here in the peaceful community of Lincoln or where ever he may eventually
find purchase.

Herman Viereck was presented to the surgical
committee today. Members present included Drs.
Young, Chisholm, and Palmer. Also in attendance
were Acting Superintendent Dr. Jordan and Head
Nurse Miss McCoy. Extensive testimony as to the
overall mental competence of young Herman as
well as the likelihood of his ability to continue
propagation of his obviously diseased germ line,
either by voluntary, or more probably forceful
means, was heard. The decision to spare the State
of Illinois further expense and social burden was
unanimous, and Mr. Viereck has been placed on the
schedule for testiculectomy

"Jesus Christ," I said.

The back of the chart contained a primitive operative note. The
surgery had been a success, accomplished with minimal bleeding and
no complications. They'd made no attempt to hide what they had done.
There had been no hearing outside the institution. Nothing had gone
through legal channels. There had been no appeal, no court order.

They'd simply dragged him into that awful operating room, hidden
but doubtlessly known to everyone, and castrated him.

The mysteries surrounding Herman Viereck's life and art fell into place: his pathetic society to protect innocent children, his hapless attempts to adopt a little girl, the male parts he'd sewn back on the Vivian Girls, even his complacency in dealing with his murderous friend Larry, all of it explained by what they had done to him in that awful little room.

I closed the chart and put it down on the box lid. I felt no desire to mythologize or analyze any further. I'd leave that to Holm. I knew all I wanted to know. Marjory came over to where I sat leaning against the wall. She offered me a hand to help me up, but it was clear I'd pull her over. I was pretty sure by now that that's what she wanted me to do.

When she saw the look on my face, though, she slid down the wall and sat across from me. We were like students at a sit-in, our knees almost touching. I folded the chart open and handed it over to her, stabbing blindly at the part she needed to read.

Marjory scanned the pages, nodding her head rapidly as if it were all too familiar.

"You said he was a close friend of yours?"

"Not close enough that he'd tell me something like this."

Marjory didn't waste any time on condolences. I think she'd already figured out there was more to my being here than curiosity or sentiment.

"It's complicated," I said. Then I told her Viereck's story, watching as I always do for the telltale signs of polite inattention and incipient MEGO: the increasing blink rate, the stifled yawn, and the feet making little shuffling movements toward the door. I'd gotten it from an article I'd read in a waiting room once in *Psychology Today*.

But Marjory paid attention. I'd gotten pretty good at spinning out the Viereck saga. I ended the story with the chart she held in her hand, how everything made sense now, how they'd drawn the blueprint for Herman's relentless creative engine here at the school.

All I left out was the disappearance of Annie Proturick. After what I read in these pages, I didn't want her to know that these butchers might have been right after all.

"So you really think this poor guy is a genius?" she asked.

"Genius? I don't know. More like an idiot savant. No, that's not right either. He knew what he was doing every minute. Does it matter? I know more about the man than anyone, and what I know could barely fill an introduction to a coffee table book of his work."

I got into a half-crouch and reached across the hallway. She handed me back Viereck's chart.

"I don't suppose I could make a copy of this?" I asked her. "There's someone I'd like to show it to, a psychoanalyst. He's doing a study of Herman's work. I'm sure it would be helpful to him. He's something of an expert on the art of the insane—not that I'm saying Herman was."

"Go ahead, take it," she said. "There's no legal reason for us to have it. These all should have been thrown out years ago. I don't get too hung up on labels, Mr. Learner. It's a fine line that separates us from your poor Mr. Viereck."

Marjory looked about to start crying, that everything I had gone through in the last twenty-four hours was instinctively known to her. I didn't want to do what I was doing, but I couldn't help myself. I remembered the picture on her desk, the look of puzzled trust and expectation on her son's face.

"Is there anyone in your family who has mental health issues?" I asked.

The minute I said it, I hated the way I'd made it sound, the false clinical language we'd all learned from TV shrinks and high school guidance counselors. You couldn't even listen to a country western song without someone going on about codependency and depression.

Marjory didn't make a face at my choice of words. "My son is learning disabled," she said.

I got up. It had been cold sitting on the tile floor. I heard one of my knees pop, but Marjory didn't notice. She took my offered hand, and I pulled her gently but effortlessly to her feet. It left us only a yard apart. She did the brush-back thing with her hair again and put a hand on my arm to steady herself.

"Whoa," she said, "head rush."

I put my hands on her shoulders to hold her up, and I felt my fingertips touch behind her shoulder blades. It always surprises me how thin and insubstantial some women's bodies are. Marjory opened her mouth slightly and leaned toward me, a tilted few centimeters that communicates a final invitation, but I held her back.

＊

I won't say that I'm the kind of guy that this kind of thing never happens to. Actually, over the years, it's happened more than I suspect is average. It's the shaggy bear thing again. Women feel safe and protected around me. Even Makiko does, though it would kill her to admit it—and did that first night in the diner when I'd put my coat around her. Women trust me, even after it is too late.

I could feel Makiko standing there in the hallway with us. But it wasn't faithfulness to my wife that made me brush my lips across the top of Marjory's forehead and push her gently away. You may think this is self-serving, but the hardest part about not making love to Marjory was not resisting desire.

I might have, in the last moment, yielded and bent her backwards over the dusty boxes filled with the medical records of the haunted, the dead, and the dammed. What stopped me was the realization that it would not be enough, that her hunger and loneliness could never be assuaged by one desperate fuck in the Lincoln school basement and that a lifetime of even my nurturing and care would never fix what was broken inside her.

"I better get back up to the office," she said, pretending to ignore what just hadn't happened.

"I know. I've kept you from your work."

"Not at all. Are you sure you've got everything you need?"

"I think so. I'll have to see how my photos turn out. I might be down again in the spring."

"If we're still here."

She smiled again and put her hands up, as if cradling a large beach ball inflated with all her sorrows and unmet desires. For a second, I thought she was going to throw herself into my arms. If she had, it would have been all over, but she shook her head like a boxer refusing to stay down, and I followed her back up the stairs.

Marjory walked me out to my car. While we had been in the basement, the weak December light had faded. Behind us, the proud tower

of Lincoln school became a dark monolith in an ominously quiet prairie
ocean. I thanked her again, and she gave me her card.

"If there's anything else you need, just call me. That's my home
number on the back."

"I'll do that," I said. Now that I'd managed to get us out of the basement with our virtue intact, I was anxious to be off.

"I'd like to see some of his work," she told me.

"I'll send you the catalogue from his show."

"He's had an exhibit of his work?"

"Oh yes, I told you—our Herman's become something of a sensation."

***

I drove down the circular drive and headed back toward town. It was
4:52. I'd been up now for over thirty-six hours. I hadn't eaten since grabbing a candy bar when I bought the film. I wondered if the pumpkin-
soup-and-quiche place was still open, but the thought of sitting down
and ordering a real meal alone depressed me.

Instead, I hit a Jack in the Box before the on-ramp. Negotiating
the drive-through window seemed too daunting a task with so many
choices. I knew whoever was at the other end of the microphone would
grow impatient waiting for me.

I parked my car, went in, and ordered, the only out-of-towner and
the only guy in the place over thirty. Nobody drank the coffee in here,
and the cup I got could have been sitting since the morning. Fast food
is a common-enough guilty pleasure, but now I only tasted its essential
blandness. The whole thing was a disaster, even the fries.

I should have stopped at the motel across the road. The only thing
that kept me headed out of town was the card in my pocket with Marjory's home phone number. I could see myself, restless and alone at two
in the morning. I thought I'd have the good sense not to call her, but I
didn't want to put it to the test. So I zoomed up the on-ramp and out
onto the road to nowhere.

Jack's coffee buzz didn't last fifteen minutes.

***

By the time the state patrol pulled me over, I was doing forty-five and straddling two lanes. I had both front windows open and some Rush Limbaugh clone was haranguing me about the dangerous liberal myth of global warming. I'd even slapped my face a few times, but it hadn't helped.

I maintain a sixties sensibility when it comes to anyone in uniform, so it's always a shock when the police are nice to me. The beefy kid in the uniform and Stetson didn't look old enough to be out of high school.

"Okay, Mr. Learner," he said after running my license, "this is what I'm going to do. There's a nice clean Motel 6 five clicks up the road. I'm going to let you drive up there, and I'll follow you. But I'm patrolling this stretch till oh-six hundred hours, and if I find you out here before then, I'm gonna put you in jail for your own good. Is that a deal?"

What could I say? I thanked him, and twenty minutes later, I sat alone in a sterile room without a minibar. I called Makiko but she wasn't home. I mumbled something into our answering machine, flipped a few channels, and fell into restless sleep.

The sound of someone pounding on the door woke me up, a businesslike rapping, without timidity, done by someone used to waking people in the middle of the night. For the first time in my life, I used one of those peepholes they have in motel doors. I saw my friend from the highway. His face looked extra large.

"Hey, Mr. Learner! Open up."

"What's going on? You decide to give me a ticket after all?"

"You'd better sit down," he said. I looked at his face. Standing in my doorway was the last place on earth he wanted to be.

"Is your wife named Makiko, Asian female, approximate age thirty-nine?"

I nodded as everything inside ran cold.

"I'm afraid I have some bad news," my trooper said. "She's been shot."

CHAPTER TWENTY-NINE

Officer Miller drove me back to Chicago. He said it wasn't any trouble, and he sure wasn't going to let me out on the road in the condition I was in. So I got my ride in a real cop car after all. I had to sit in back, of course. Even in my numb state, I imagined the thoughts of other motorists as we sped by them.

There goes public enemy number one.

Miller didn't have a whole lot of details. They'd taken her to Rush Memorial, which thanks to Chicago's long history of violence and mayhem had one of the best shock-trauma units in the country. She was listed as critical, but if anyone could pull her through, it was them, he told me reassuringly.

He seemed as relieved that she was alive as I. It must be the worst part of a highway patrolman's job, the late-night phone call, the knock on the door.

"I'm sorry, there's been an accident with fatalities—a thirty-nine-year-old female of Asian descent. We think it might be your wife … sister … daughter."

Mostly, we drove in silence. Occasionally, I looked at the dash. He had it dialed in at a steady 110. Every once in a while, he'd ask me how I was doing and tell me to "hang in there."

We were in the suburbs of Chicago in an hour and ten minutes. I felt as if we'd just demonstrated Einstein's theory of relativity. The closer we got to the hospital, the heavier I felt, and all the clocks were running slow.

"How did you find me?" I asked him.

"It came over the dispatch that you were somewhere downstate. Naturally, I remembered pulling you over."

"Nobody but Makiko knew where I was," I said.

"Well, she must have told them, then."

"That means she was able to talk."

"Yeah, I guess it does. You'll see, Mr. Learner. She's going to be okay."

***

The shock-trauma unit was on the eighth floor. I'd thought it would be downstairs near the ER, and I was expecting a scene from a TV show— blood, people screaming, junkies OD-ing, but at four in the morning, nothing much was going on. Just a janitor mopping between two yellow plastic sandwich boards—"caution."

A couple of nurses sat at the main desk, picking over the remains of a pizza. One of them offered to take me up.

We rode the elevator in silence, she avoiding eye contact, I trying not to think too far ahead. The doors opened out onto a small waiting room—a row of chairs, a potted plant, nondescript motel art on the walls.

It was déjà vu Miriam all over again. One end of the room sported a set of tomb-sized doors, admitting no one who wasn't "authorized." The waiting room was empty, except for one person: Adrian Holm.

He jumped up when I came off the elevator and put his good arm around me, the other supported in a sling. He had a bandage around his head too, but he looked so robust that he reminded me of a designated victim in a disaster drill.

"Thank God you're here," he said.

Even in this moment of agony and chaos, seeing Holm gave the whole thing another dizzying spin. For a mildly irrational second, I wondered if he'd been the one who'd shot her.

"She's still in surgery," he said. "They won't tell me anything."

"What the hell happened?" I screamed at him. He backed away from me and sat down in a chair. I sat down next to him. Up close, I could see that he was still shaking, and his eyes were red and moist. He'd been crying.

"I told you we should have put his stuff someplace safe."

"What stuff?"

Viereck's book—they tried to take it. They were going to ransack the whole apartment. You should have seen her, Nate. She was a tiger. She was roaring at them, literally roaring."

"At whom? Just calm down and tell me what happened."

He nodded. "I was up at the apartment, reading the *Realms* and making some notes. Makiko must have seen that the lights were on because she came over. I guess we got into a bit of a row. I'd asked what her intentions were, was she planning to sell off the whole collection just to make a buck."

"Adrian, you didn't?"

"Me? Christ no. Jesus, Nate, how could you even for a moment think that I—"

"Whatever. Look, I'm sorry. Is she going to be all right? Isn't there anyone around I can talk to? What the hell happened?"

"They think she's going to be okay. I called 911. Those lads are amazing."

"Before you called 911."

"Well, we were up there having this discussion, and these blokes showed up."

"Blokes?"

"They had on balaclavas. At first I thought they were IRA. It's funny what goes through your head at a time like that. They wanted the *Realms* and all the drawings. They called them the work of Satan and said their existence carried the stain of blasphemy. But Makiko wouldn't let them through the door. She started screaming. She told them that Viereck had more love and appreciation of God in one of his sketches than they'd had in their whole lives. She called his work 'religious icons'—can you imagine? I never thought of them in that way, but she's right."

"Fuck Viereck," I screamed at him. "I don't give a fuck what they are. I've had it up to here with that demented little prick!"

"Hey, take it easy. Can't you see what I've been through?"

"I'm sorry."

"One of them pulled a gun. They told us to get out of their way. Makiko wouldn't budge. She told them that the pictures didn't belong to them, they belonged to everyone, and then one of them, I think a woman, said they were hers by birthright. What the hell did that mean?"

"Oh, fuck," I said, "Herman's purported niece. I should have known we hadn't heard the end of it. It's my own fault. I should have been there. They left us all these warnings, but we just blew it off."

"I don't think she meant to discharge her weapon. It was just one of those things, everyone was yelling, and then the gun went off. I got hit in the arm and something grazed my head, and then Makiko was lying on the floor. Jesus, Nate, it wasn't like you'd imagine it. Not like in the movies. Makiko's screaming her bloody head off. It was bloody awful. These guys took one look at what they had done, and I think it scared holy hell out of them. Anyway, they took off. Somebody must have already called 911 because the cops and the fire department showed up right away. They say another few minutes, and she would have bled to death."

I nodded my head at him stupidly, pretending I was taking it all in, as if dealing with gunshot wounds was part of my everyday experience. Right then, I felt like strangling the jerk. He hadn't even been the one to call the damn ambulance.

Instead, I sat in silence for a few minutes and then got up and went over to the double doors at the end of the waiting room. They stood, as solid and impenetrable as the gates of Mordor.

I pushed the button but nobody came, and after half a minute, all my fear and frustration turned into anger. I leaned on the buzzer for a good ten seconds, and then the door clicked open in my face as someone inside released a magnetic lock. A young woman in a raspberry colored scrub suit stood guard on the other side.

"I'm Nathaniel Learner. You have my wife."

"Ah, Mr. Learner. They found you."

"How's she doing?"

"We're bringing her out to recovery now. They tell me the surgery went very well. I'll see if I can find one of the surgeons to come talk to you."

She sounded polite in the way someone who had been lectured at about not being polite enough is when making a conscious effort to do better. I waited at the nursing station, and eventually, they corralled somebody from the back to come out and talk to me. He looked to be the same age as Trooper Miller. I was surrounded by children and totally dependent upon them.

Makiko's surgeon wore the same blood-splatter-hiding raspberry scrubs. He had flecks of her blood on his paper booties. His paper mask hung low on his neck like a gunslinger's bandana. Even though he'd been operating for the last five hours, he had a swagger to his walk that said there was no place else on earth that he'd rather be and that no one else on earth could do what he'd just done.

"It was touch and go there for a while," he told me casually, as if he'd just managed to salvage the fuel pump on my Volvo. "But I think she's going to pull through. There were a lot of organ systems involved, and we had to cross-clamp the aorta for almost fifteen minutes. We'll just have to see how she does, renal-function-wise."

Yeah, right—renal function. My mind rebelled. Once again, I was about to be plunged into a world of numbers that I didn't want to know anything about. With Miriam, it had been white-blood-cell and lymphocyte counts, fever, and hematocrits. What were they going to torture me with now?

"I'm calling in nephrology. We'll get a BUN first thing in the morning."

"Can I see her?" I asked.

He frowned slightly. "I'll get one of the nurses to take you back. We're going to keep her intubated for the next few hours."

I followed the nurse down a long tiled hallway. She didn't say much, but I was still way ahead of Dante. In the last thirty-six hours, I'd had Nurse Stark, Marjory, and now Raspberry Beret. Who'd he have, some bratty twelve-year-old? We got to another set of double doors. Nurse Raspberry gave me a concerned look.

"I want you to prepare yourself," she told me. "People come through these things looking pretty rough." I thought nothing could be worse than what I already imagined.

I was almost right.

It had been a quiet night in Chicago. There were at least ten bays in the recovery area, but only two of them were in use. My guide drew back the drapes. Two other medical people in uniforms hovered around the bed.

"This is Mr. Learner," she announced, warning them to be on their better behavior.

It took me a minute to find her among all the hardware. Never had I seen her looking so tiny. Everything else in the room loomed over her, trying to crowd her out, as if the pumps, IVACs, and respirators had their own *raison d'etre* and Makiko had been put there merely as an afterthought.

I thought I'd prepared myself, but when I finally saw her, my knees almost gave way. They'd taped her eyes shut, and they were recessed into her swollen face, as if she'd been under water for some time. A plastic breathing tube stood up on its own without the help from her lips. When the nurse who was taking care of her saw me, she went to the head of the bed and gently pulled the tape off Makiko's eyelids.

"Ms. Learner, your husband is here," she spoke loudly and close to Makiko's ear. Makiko opened her eyes, and the nurse motioned me to the head of the bed. I bent over and was blessed with a glimmer of recognition.

"Hey, sweetie, it's me." I thought I saw the edges of her mouth try to move into a faint smile.

"It's okay. You're going to be okay."

Makiko tried to move her hands up toward her mouth, and I noticed that they had them tied to the railings with a roll of gauze. Rationally, I knew they'd done it for her own protection, but after everything she'd been through, it seemed insulting, so unfair. There were so many things to be furious at that it was silly to focus on this small piece of recovery room expediency. Next to me, the nurse sensed my anxiety and frustration.

"I think we better go now," she said, gently tugging on my arm. "Give us a few more hours. We'll get the tube out of her throat. Then she can talk to you."

I reached out and took one of Makiko's hands and squeezed it softly. I imagined she squeezed back, and gratefully, I let them send me away.

"It's not as bad as it looks," the nurse reassured me once we were out in the waiting room. "It's going to be a few more hours before she's fully awake. Why don't you go home and try and get some rest."

***

Holm was still there. "How is she?" he asked, anxiously. I thought I detected a twinge of guilt in his voice.

"I guess she's doing okay," I told him. It made me feel a little better saying it, but I didn't really believe it. I sat down in one of the chairs. A small couch across from us was the only horizontal space available. It didn't look big enough to curl up on.

Holm sat down next to me. We were supposed to be friends. All should have been forgiven in this time of crisis, but he could sense that I wanted to throttle him. We sat there in silence, listening to each other breathe. Eventually, he got up and went over to the vending machines and got me a Coke. I thanked him.

"You going to be okay, chum?"

"Yeah, I'll be fine. Why don't you go on home?"

I had a lot to tell him, but it seemed beside the point. The discoveries I'd made in Lincoln, even the fact that Herman had died hours before, were unimportant.

"You okay to drive?" I asked him.

He held up his bandaged arm a few inches. "Sure," he said, "It's just a flesh wound."

I wanted to effing kill him! The son of a bitch had hidden behind the skirts of a woman who barely came up to his nipples. He'd let her take a bullet for him, and now he was John fucking Wayne. Flesh wound my ass! Definitely time for him to be on his way, and he knew it.

"Call me as soon as you hear anything," he said. I nodded. He patted me on the arm and headed for the elevator. I stared daggers until it collected him.

I felt as if they'd dredged *me* out of Lake Michigan, chilled to the bone. The few hours of sleep I'd had in the motel ran out like the last whiff of a dollar's worth of regular. I sat there, trying not to imagine the worst, a fool's task for someone with my emotional composition. Eventually, I pushed one of the chairs over to the little couch and fashioned a short bed. An industrial clock face stared down at me pitilessly. I would have gladly traded it for the portrait of our Savior. Despite everything, it was only four thirty, hours from daylight.

By six, I gave up and banged on the palace gates one more time. The nurse who opened up seemed surprised to see me.

"You still here?" she asked. I couldn't tell if it was a question or an accusation. Apparently they had a back way out of the place because Makiko had been moved to a different floor. They directed me to surgical ICU.

"This is just the OR," she told me.

When I found her, they already had her in a recliner. They'd taken out her breathing tube, and she smiled weakly when I came in. She held out a hand to me, but I could see that even that amount of movement was painful. Naturally, I started to apologize, but she cut me off with a shrug.

"Please, Nate, not now," she told me.

"We should have done something, called the police, gotten a restraining order. You never know what people like that are capable of. They're barbarians."

But Makiko didn't seem to care.

"What's done is done. They say I'm going to be all right. Maybe it's for the best."

I couldn't believe what she was saying, but there's nothing like a brush with death to bring out the saintliness in us. While I sat there holding her hand, she drifted back off to sleep. In a little while, the nurses came in and got her back into bed.

"You should go home, Mr. Learner. You need to get some rest, maybe a shower? She's gonna need all your strength."

That showed what they knew.

"That's okay," I told her, but she insisted.

"Really, you look pretty bad. Go home, take a nap, and put on some clean clothes. You'll feel better. If anything changes, we'll call you, but she's doing great."

CHAPTER THIRTY

I couldn't remember if this was the second or third morning that found me standing on my street watching the sun coming up.

Everything that had happened before Nurse Stark's phone call felt remote, lost in dreamtime. When my cab had started down the block, a squad car still blocked the street, its inexhaustible lights strobing away in the weak winter light.

Herman's old apartment had yellow crime scene tape around the steps. *Hey*, I thought, *just like TV*.

It pleased me that the CPD took Makiko's assault so seriously. What I didn't know was that the cops were more or less waiting for me to show up.

While I stood there a uniform approached me.

"You Learner?" he asked.

I nodded.

"Detective Reynolds has been waiting for you. Stay right here."

It wasn't a request. I stood on the sidewalk while the cop went to round Reynolds up. He popped out of a squad car and double-timed it over. He wore a CPD black windbreaker. He looked as if it had taken him a long time to work his way up to detective and that part of him would still be happier breaking heads in the Loop.

"Mr. Learner?"

I nodded again. It was still me, though I suppose someone could have convinced me otherwise with a little effort.

"I'm investigating the assault with deadly force that occurred here. I believe you know the victims."

"She's my wife."

"I understand that she's in critical condition."

"I'm just coming from the hospital. They think she's going to be okay."

Reynolds looked a little disappointed. "I understand you weren't home at the time of the shooting."

"That's right."

"Can I ask as to your whereabouts?"

This was the point where I was supposed to say, "Surely you don't think I had anything to do with this," and Reynolds says, "Don't call me Shirley."

"I was downstate."

"Is there anyone who can verify that?"

I sighed. I wasn't really worried. The Illinois State Police could provide a pretty ironclad alibi, but realizing how long this plodder was going to take to get around to identifying the real suspects made me want to yank his chain. Of course, I could have saved him a lot of time, but I didn't want to cooperate. I'd had enough, and Inspector Clouseau here provided the last straw.

"Do you know a Detective O'Malley?" I asked him.

"Mike O'Malley? Sure, everybody knows Father Mike. He's a legend."

"You think we could get him down here?"

"He a friend of yours?"

"He contacted me about another case. He thought I might have a lead."

"Not one of his famous cold cases?"

"Yeah, I guess so."

"Mike's with homicide, so unless your wife doesn't make it …" He paused. He'd put his foot in it, but he didn't pretend to be that upset. It must happen to him all the time.

"Look, detective, I didn't shoot my wife. We both know that, but I'd really like to speak to Mr. O'Malley about it. You think you could help me out here?"

"Sure, Mr. Learner, but let me tell you. There's only about a three-day window for a case like this. If we don't make an arrest in the first seventy-two hours, our chances of solving the case go to zero pretty quick. So if there's anything you want to tell us, you should do it now."

"It'll wait a few hours," I said.

"I could bring you down to the station," he advised me.

"Look Detective, I've been through a lot. I'd like to change and get a few hours' sleep before I go back to the hospital. You think you could help me out here? I'm sure you're an excellent detective, it's just that I'd feel better talking to someone I know."

Reynolds looked pissed. Like everyone else I'd met that night, he wasn't used to dealing with the educated middle class. I was making him almost as uncomfortable as he was making me.

"All right, Mr. Learner. Everybody wants Father Mike to hear their confession. There's just one more thing."

"What's that?"

"Don't leave town."

I couldn't believe he'd said it, but he had.

***

Once Reynolds cut me loose, I took off across the street. I wanted to get up to my apartment where it would be quiet, warm, and safe. Only, when I opened the door, the emptiness hit me at the deepest, most visceral level. I roamed around the vacant rooms like an abandoned puppy.

It didn't matter that I knew she was in hospital. My desire to be with her overwhelmed reason. It was only when I stuck my head into the bedroom and almost called her name that the image of my own folly caught up with me.

"Get a grip," I said. Then I did what any sane person would do in this situation. I got the emergency bottle of Stoli out of the freezer, found some grapefruit juice, and made up a tumbler-sized Greyhound.

Despite myself, I became reflexively hungry, but there was nothing in the house but a can of Nalley's Chili. After that and the vodka, I went looking for some Pepto, settled for a handful of Tylenol and a dollop of soda bicarb from a half-empty box of Arm & Hammer that I found abandoned in the back of the fridge.

After the burp of relief, I lay down fully clothed on our empty bed, my body vibrating like a tuning fork, exhausted. But I couldn't get my eyes to stay closed for more than a few seconds.

Outside, the street came alive with morning traffic. Even with the shades down, I could sense Chicago going about its business. After a half-hour, I gave up and sat on the bedside, thinking the unthinkable. I saw the whole hospital experience with Makiko through the lens of what I'd gone through with Miriam.

Why should this time be different? The nurses and doctors would pump me up and then deflate me, and my hopes would gyrate up and down like share prices on a third-world stock market. Makiko's numbers, whatever they were supposed to represent, would look good, then there would be a complication. Some test would need to be repeated, and I'd wait for the results at her bedside. A day later, no one would remember that the test had even been done. And then one day would come that slowly blossoming realization that it wasn't going to end well.

"It's not the same," I told myself. "This is trauma. If they can get her through the first few hours, or days, she'll be fine."

But I was primed by generations of skilled pessimists. It was in my blood. Don't taunt Gd. Don't tempt Him by getting your hopes too high. He likes to play tricks. He has a flare for irony. Only, who is it that stands outside of Gd's infinite universe and gets his little jokes?

Knowing what you know about me by now, would it be believable if I told you that I sat at the side of the bed and prayed? That I offered up bargains, presented legal briefs on my behalf? Hadn't I behaved nobly in the Lincoln school basement with Marjory? Wasn't my faithfulness worth anything?

Naturally, I didn't do anything that transparent. It would only have reinforced the hypocrisy that was going through my head. But underneath, the prayer was there. It's the one cliché about Gd I've never been able to escape: "There are no atheists in foxholes."

I wandered down the hall to the spare bedroom I used as my office. Halfway, I passed the closed door to Miriam's bedroom. It had been months since I'd gone in there. When forced, I'd enter it with tunnel vision, doing whatever minor chore I needed to do without looking to the right or the left.

Since Makiko had moved in, I'd been feeling increasingly guilty about leaving it untouched. I knew she could use the space. She was tired of having to practice in our bedroom, always half-terrified that I would trip over her cello in the middle of the night. But she'd never said anything to me about the Museum of Miriam, never implied that it was time for me to move on.

I stopped at the door. What if the worst happened? There wasn't enough room in the apartment for that many ghosts. Where would I sleep? I considered a raft of options, but in the end, it boiled down to a simple transaction in the karmic marketplace.

Poor Miriam had to go.

I had to clean out her room, replace the child's linoleum with a muted oriental, cover the walls with acoustic tile, and move in a piano so Makiko could work with her accompanist. She deserved no less, and it would all be done by the time she came home.

Starting now!

I looked down at my hand gripping the doorknob. As clear as a photograph, I flashed to the day I'd opened the door to Herman's apartment.

Would I be here now if it hadn't been for what had happened then?

"It's all about opening doors," I said aloud. The approval of some faceless therapist rang in my ears.

I turned the knob.

CHAPTER THIRTY-ONE

Since Miriam's death, hearing the word "closure" sets my teeth on edge.

Naturally, once I began listening for it, every other story on the news used it somewhere. People were always looking for "closure," "finding closure," or "needing closure." The bereaved families of murder victims standing on the courthouse steps after years of delays and setbacks, imperfect justice finally done. The aging relatives of airmen from the Second World War waiting on the identification of remains found in the melting snowpack in the Sierra Nevada. The gaunt faces of the bereaved staring into the camera after an errant molar had established the identity of some scattered fragments of bone as a missing ten-year-old. "Well," they'd say, "at last we have closure."

It made me want to shout obscenities at the screen. Did anyone who has suffered the loss of a child ever have closure? Were they able to put their grief in a little walled-off place, trotting it out on holidays and special occasions, like a special Christmas ornament or an heirloom menorah?

But that morning, overcome with fear and loneliness, as soon as I walked into Miriam's abandoned room, I saw my grief for what it *really* was: obstinate, spiteful anger. Against my will, I felt the soft hand of closure stroking my cheek.

I remembered riding in O'Malley's car, driving silently back from our meeting with Herman. I felt a deep convulsive sob of sadness and compassion for the parents of poor lost Annie. At least I knew where my Miriam was.

Would I trade her grave for the uncertainty, the slim imbecilic hope that must still visit them in the middle of the night, that someday the phone might ring, the door might receive a knock, and Annie, dream-boat Annie, would appear, spinning a tale of abduction and servitude too fanciful to imagine?

Something *had* changed in me since Herman's dying in my arms. In the last two days, I had shot my first roll of film in years, and I'd faced a new loss that I couldn't even begin to contemplate. Now closure stared me in the face, and I blinked.

***

Entering Miriam's room was the reverse of my experience that first day I'd gone up to Herman's apartment. Both were tombs. But in here, there was no shock of discovery. Miriam's room looked unchanged from the day we'd taken her back to the hospital for what turned out to be the last time.

In the week after the funeral, Tamar had been in once or twice and minimally straightened things. At least there were no cups or breakfast plates at the bedside. Miriam's pajamas had been picked up off the floor. The bed had been made. Even the chess-set-worth of amber medicine vials had been swept off the top of the nightstand.

Later, when we divided our things up for the divorce, we'd talked about clearing out the room. I'd offered Tamar our apartment, of course, but by then she was done with me and our real-estate fiefdom on Webster Avenue. She'd had it with stopped-up toilets, blown fuses, and all the paperwork: the rental agreements, the tax assessments, the fee-simple, and the party of the first part.

"You've made your life too complicated," she'd told me as she took a last look around and gave me the pro forma, no-contact kiss on the cheek.

"I've got to get some simplicity back in my life," she'd said. "I need to be able to hear myself think."

Two weeks later, she moved in with a thirty-four-year-old public defender and her two kids. Since then, Miriam's room was all mine.

You've seen this scene played out over and over on those "disease of the week" TV dramas—the hollow-eyed mother sitting on the bed clutching a teddy bear while the husband (who hasn't gotten laid since the kid croaked) ineffectually tells her it's time to "let her go."

You have your own idea of how to dress the set—lots of pink, rows of stuffed animals on the bed, an ornate blue ribbon from some sporting event (preferably equestrian) hanging from the bedpost. In one corner, put a dollhouse, seldom played with, but cherished, made by some doddering, devoted relative. On the far wall, a bookcase filled with middle-of-the-road children's classics: *Black Beauty*, *A Wind in the Willows*, *Alice's Adventures Underground*. Add a poster of some magically virginal pop diva whore. Make everything sunny and bright, hinting at the promise of a fulfilled life as mother, lover, and confidant, now cut short by Gd's capricious will.

You realize by now that, even allowing for a parent's understandable penchant for hyperbole, Miriam was no ordinary child. Her room wasn't like that, not with her penchant for melancholia, nurtured by the dark forces of her parents' sensibilities. On the wall over her bed, in a baroque frame (one of Tamar's amazing Goodwill finds), hung a really good reproduction of Dali's *Persistence of Memory*.

Facing it from across the room, she'd put up a poster from that famous trip to the Modern where we'd fallen in love with the Rousseau that had set Herman's party in motion: *The Sleeping Gypsy*.

Then there was a precociously good still-life she'd done at some summer arts program, one of those poems or works of art that kids sometimes do, where you just shake your head and wonder, "Where did that come from? Who were they channeling?" In this case, Van Gogh.

Oh there were a few girlie things—a row of Breyer collectible horses. I think they were the form of an early bribe. She got one each time she went to the hospital for a test or a procedure. Eventually, she lost interest.

Miriam didn't need bribes. She didn't need us to make her illness into some sort of game. She was too much the stoic.

I sat down on her bed and took inventory. The space revealed more about her character than I remembered. Even before she got ill, the room possessed a dark energy, portending a future filled with unsuitable lovers, questionable career choices, and the odd bottle of Prozac.

***

Out in the hall, I'd thought I could complete the cleanout in an hour or two. Wasn't it a simple matter of cramming her stuff into a few cardboard boxes and hauling them down to the basement?

Now my plans ran up against the hard reality of sleep deprivation and emotional exhaustion. I wasn't sure I could do this alone. I needed someone in here with me, someone to hold things up, someone to help me sort her stuff into the inevitable piles—someone to help me cry and make me laugh.

There were only two people in the world that could do that. One of them lay suspended between life and death in a surgical ICU. The other I hadn't talked to in over a year. I had thoughts I'd long defended myself against. After all this time, I wanted to call Tamar. I needed someone to take care of me. Anyone.

She should be here, I thought. We should be doing this together. Divorced couples get together for the weddings of their children, their graduations, all life's big events. Why not this? I was overcome with nostalgia and longing for a woman I once thought I knew, followed by a countercurrent of resentment. How could she leave me to face this alone?

***

The stages of grief are not laid as out neatly as you would think from reading all those helpful books about the subject. They describe an orderly progression of stages, an up-escalator moving from denial to acceptance.

It's not that simple. The stages of grief are jumbled. Emotions that you think you've finished with forever recur. One day's acceptance is replaced by anger the next. Even primitive denial resurfaces.

So now, sitting in Miriam's room, surrounded by precocious trappings of a life she never got to outgrow, I was furious with her all over again. Why had she left me such a damn mess? Why was it my job to clean it up? And why wasn't Tamar, the one person who should be here, to help me? Why did she look at me as if I were responsible for a twenty-year prison sentence she'd served for a crime she hadn't committed?

I tried to tap into some of the techniques that Dr. Holm had given me to use at times like this. He'd done so apologetically, a tacit agreement between us that these psychological coping tricks, borrowed from pundits on afternoon TV shows, were beneath a man of my insights and sensitivity. Just "reprogram it," I told myself.

I got up, went back out into the kitchen, and grabbed the same unused box of Hefty bags I'd taken to clean out Herman's apartment.

I'll start with her clothes, I thought. *I'll bring them down to the homeless shelter. Miriam would like that.*

***

It didn't start badly. The stuff in her dresser didn't carry much of an emotional impact. Her socks and underwear, all so generic, bought in semi-wholesale lots from places like Costco or Penny's. They could have belonged to anyone. Then a faint odor coming from the long-closed drawer blindsided me, a faint ghost of Miriam's unique smell, a combination of the way her shampoo interacted with her hair, the disinfectant we'd used to try to minimalize her risk of infections, and under it, almost below my olfactory radar, the smell of her prepubescent girlishness, of periods that were about to start, of discoveries that would never be made.

Did I hold her underpants up to my nose? I'm afraid to ask that question of myself. I could see it as a tabloid headline:

"Perv Dad Sneaks into Dead Daughter's Room to Sniff Her Panties."

I did. I held the pink tricot up to my face, and I breathed in. I had visions of myself staring down at an infant's disproportionately large, puffy genitalia. I remembered changing diapers, wiping away human-looking stool, actions that today would bring me to the point of gagging but done then without fanfare or psychic impact. I sniffed. Then I put my hands in my lap, the underwear as limp in my fingers as a dead bird.

Superficial, maudlin thoughts washed over me. I thought about all that she would miss, had already missed. Then I relived my own adolescence, the sweatings and the gropings. The girls I had used and had been used by, in turn.

"Maybe you're better off to be well out of it," I told Miriam's faint odoriferous ghost.

I thought of O'Malley again, the pride in his voice when he told me his daughter was studying to be a nun. It seemed so medieval at the time, so unfair of him to want to deprive his daughter of all life had to offer. But now I saw his point, his desire to spare his daughter all the sloppiness and pain of sex and family, passion, fury, and rejection. And sight unseen, compared to O'Malley's daughter, I knew Miriam would have had enough sloppiness and pain for both of them.

Thinking about nuns pushed me back to pragmatic sanity. I'd gotten too close to the edge of the imponderables that as adults we learn to avoid. There was no point in going there. Mechanically, I stuffed her clothes into the sacks.

Once done with her clothes, I turned to Miriam's books. I thought I might hold onto them for a while. We had plenty of room in the cellar, and there were still boxes of Tamar's and my old college stuff down there. *No Exit, Howl, Being and Nothingness, Story of O, Practical Anatomy and Physiology.*

Books are hard to throw away, especially if you haven't read them. Now Miriam's collection could join ours, creating an unbroken generational string of abandoned intellectual pursuits.

I tried not to read the titles as I pulled them off the shelves. She had all the appropriate classics—*Alice, Pooh, Toad and Mole, Huck* and *Tom*, an oversize, hardcover copy of *Watership Down*. When she'd gotten sick, one of Tamar's friends had bought it for her, hoping that she would be engrossed enough to tolerate the long waits in doctor's offices and the hours in the hospital while they dripped various poisons into

her veins. We'd had a discussion about whether or not it was "appropriate" for a twelve-year-old. I'd thought it might be too much for her, but
she'd devoured it in what seemed like a single sitting. I'd meant to read
it along with her but never got the chance.

Maybe now, something to keep my mind from going where it wanted
to go. It might even put me to sleep, but as soon as I pulled *Watership* off the shelf, I noticed that it didn't feel right. The weight was too
light for its size, and the pages didn't rustle in my hand. Right away, I
knew what it was.

I'd found Miriam's stash box, a simple but effective piece of kid spy
craft. She'd glued the pages together and then cut out the center with an
X-Acto knife making a box. At one point, Tamar had talked about getting her some pot to help with the nausea of chemo, but Miriam hadn't
needed it. Maybe because she'd had her own supply?

I looked inside. There were no baggies, pipes, or vials, just a bunch
of folded papers: letters. I picked up the top one and looked at the hand-
writing. Even before the words formed before my eyes, I knew whose it
was—legible as a fifth grader's, the same childlike cursive that he'd used
to label all his drawings.

Herman Vicreck had been writing to my daughter.

Dear Miriam:

Thank you again for the box of paints. You are right: the
colors are deeper than the ones from Woolworths. I must say it
makes me sad that you don't want to use them for yourself. I'm
sure Mr. Nathan is a very good artist, being a professor of art and
everything, but you should still be able to paint what you want to
and not worry about how good it is. I know you are worried that
you don't have enough time to do all the things you would like, but
for real artists like us that will always be true, even if you work at
it night and day. You can't worry about time running out. We are
all part of eternity. Anyway, I don't think you are going to die. I'm
sure your parents love you very much and they have found the best

doctors in the world to take care of you. I know now that God must have made some deal with YOU KNOW WHO so that my baby sister and poor little Annie Proturick, whose picture was taken from me in the middle of a vicious snowstorm, had to go away so that YOU could be here to grow up. I know that makes you very angry and you say mean things about HIM, but that's just the way Mr. Nathan has raised you, and even he doesn't know deep inside himself how he really feels. Get plenty of rest, the weather is due for a big change, and I know you will feel better soon.

Your friend — Herman.

Dear Miriam-

I'm sorry to hear that you were back in the hospital. And I'm glad that you are doing better. Mr. Nathan told me that you had a high fever and that you were talking out of your head. I worked at the hospital for many years, and it always made me very nervous to hear people crying out in pain and confusion. I think that when people are very sick their minds are open to powerful outside influences and that OUR LORD AND SAVIOR often comes into their hearts, but I also know that SATAN can try and bend a sick person's soul to his will and that the DEVIL can take many forms and disguises. Nothing is as innocent and free from evil as it sometimes seems ...

There were maybe four or five of them in all, undated, but I got the feeling they spanned the last year of her life.

Dear Friend Miriam:

Today I read in the newspaper about a huge tornado in
Oklahoma. Tornados come from changes in air temperature and
pressure between the highest layer of clouds and the weather on
the ground. When the warm air is sucked up into the atmosphere,
it creates a GIGANTIC SWIRLING VORTEX of immense force.
It has been a long time since I've seen a tornado, but the memory
of the time I was in one in Muscatine, Illinois, is very much with
me at all times. Sometimes I think it would not be so bad to be
sucked up by a tornado like that little girl Dorothy and her poor
dog, like the one you gave me a few years ago that disappeared,
even though I told you that it was not my fault that he ran away.
    I know that the thought of dying makes you very sad, but you
shouldn't worry about what is waiting for you on the other side. I
think that the weather, tornados, and hurricanes are what happen
when God's finger reaches down through the clouds and touches
the earth, so being sucked up into a tornado wouldn't really be so
terrible. I know that in my story tornados often chase innocent
children, but this is just me telling stories ...

    I could barely finish. His letters were like his paintings, a combina-
tion of innocence and creepiness, magnified by knowing that Miriam
had been keeping them a secret. Then, at the bottom of the pile, I found
a yellow folded piece of newsprint. Most likely, I saw the general outline
of her features through the back of the page, but even before I unfolded
it, I knew what I'd found.
    I held up the lost photograph of Annie Proturick.
    With everything that had happened in the last two—no, now three—
days, I didn't think I had enough neurotransmitters left to register more
shock. But the hair on the back of my neck stood straight up. I sat on the
floor, my back resting against the side of Miriam's bed, and my thoughts

circled randomly, like a ball in a roulette wheel. The odds that it would land on anything cogent were not great.

Herman's portrait of her only did Annie crude justice. With this picture plastered across the front page, I could see why her disappearance had captured the imagination of the city. She looked adorable. The photo the papers had gotten their hands on had originally been taken at Sears or at one of the class photo days that they had at the school. I could tell in a glance that it was the work of some assembly-line hack, but even so, he'd captured something precious and unique, an irrepressible love of life, an effortless ability to spread joy and wonder to anyone she met.

The obvious things about Annie, Viereck had captured: her braids, her slightly buck teeth, the unself-conscious smile that made you want to gather her up into protective arms. *How could anyone have wanted to harm her?* I thought, just like a million Chicagoans had as they had sipped their breakfast coffee all those years ago.

But then that was the whole point, wasn't it? The compelling desire of the murderer to do the unthinkable? Did he want to strike back at Gd or to emulate him? What did the loss of Annie amount to, compared to the fury of a tornado and a schoolhouse blown to bits? What was Annie Proturick compared to Anne Frank? It wasn't Herman, I had to remind myself, but that horrible friend of his.

It seemed a moot distinction, though, Herman getting off on a technicality.

Well … I had forever to ponder what evil lurks in the hearts of men. My real concern, the question desperately begging for an immediate answer? How had Annie's picture gotten into Miriam's possession?

There were only two possibilities—three if you count the intervention of some divine sneak thief. Either Herman had given Miriam the picture and then, lost in some Freudian labyrinth of repressed memory, had forgotten that he'd done so.

Or—and this seemed the inevitable truth—my daughter had taken it and, despite being aware of Herman's anguish, had not given it back.

How could she have been so cruel, especially after establishing this secret friendship that I, and I assume Tamar, knew nothing about, and surely would have gone to any length to discourage if we had? Was it some inner streak of adolescent rebelliousness, the only way she could keep control over some small part of her world while the rest deconstructed in front of her eyes?

But Miriam, a girl who would sweep a spider up onto the edge of a magazine and carry it downstairs to be released? Why would she punish him like this?

Bleary eyed, I stuffed the letters and Annie's picture back in its secret box.

Miriam, Herman, that horrible Larry, even most assuredly poor Annie: they were all dead I reminded myself. Did any of it matter, anymore? Wasn't there some way I could rid myself from this obnoxious little man and his malignant obsessions that worked their way in and around everything I held dear?

He'd corrupted me, covered up a horrible crime, almost gotten my wife killed, and now he had turned my sainted daughter into a petty, vengeful sneak. I wanted to throw the hollowed-out novel into the box with the other books and let the letters and the picture stay hidden. But there was no way.

I got up off her floor and took the book into my study. Maybe Makiko could help me make sense of it when she got home. But what would I do if that never happened? Who would help me then? I put the book on my work table and fought back a wave of panic.

"It's going to be all right," I told myself out loud.

Then the phone rang on my desk, as if it knew I was standing there. I was sure it was the hospital. I didn't dare not answer it.

"Hello?" My voice was a soft tentative question.

"Is this Nathan Learner?"

"Speaking," I said.

"This is Ms. Arronson from Scully-McMann Funeral Directors. We were wondering if you had any chance to look over the brochures we sent you. We need to make arrangements in the next day or two."

"What?" I yelled into the phone. "She's still in the intensive care unit. They said everything was going to be okay."

"I'm sorry Mr. Learner—am I calling at a bad time?"

"A bad time, what the hell is this? Who are you?"

"I'm calling about Mr. Viereck. I understand that you will be handling the details of his interment."

"Oh, I thought you were calling about my wife. She's at Rush Memorial. Naturally, I expected the worst."

"Oh, no! I'm so sorry if you misunderstood. This is about Mr. Herman Viereck. We need to discuss his funeral. Scully-McMann has a very attractive package that we've put together for the families of clients who come to us from the Little Sisters. It's simple but very respectful. It's only $1,298. Of course the casket *is* pretty bare bones."

She said the last with a totally flat affect. The pun was so minimal I couldn't bring myself to point it out to her. My thinking she'd called about Makiko put my sleep-deprived brain into a mood of reckless euphoria. Thank Gd for some comic relief.

"I think Mr. Viereck deserves better than that," I told her.

"Perhaps you'd care to come in, and we can discuss it in greater detail."

"I'm sort of busy today. I have to get back to the hospital."

"Oh yes, did you say it's your wife? Nothing serious I hope."

"They say she'll be fine."

"I'm glad to hear that. We can discuss this at a later date. There is a holding fee, however."

"Doesn't he have to be, you know, interred by sundown?"

"Oh no, that's only the Heebrayish and Muslemic tradition. It's not part of the Catholic faith. We've waited for as long as six months, provided that the remains are in an appropriate condition. Go ahead and take your time, Mr. Learner. Take your time."

CHAPTER THIRTY-TWO

Perhaps, remembering your own episodes of fatigue and exhaustion, you're waiting for me to tell you that after Arronson's surreal phone call, I finally fell into a deep, restorative sleep. It didn't happen. Instead, I got into the shower, shaved, and trying to look presentable and trustworthy, headed back to Rush Memorial.

Over the next few weeks, as Makiko progressed through the hospital's arcane hierarchy of ICUs, SCUs, and PCUs, I reclaimed my sleep-deprived hours in short increments, a restless nap here, two or three hours there. Even today, twenty years later, there are days when I feel a residual fog of fatigue and confusion that has never lifted.

Anyway, I'll spare you the suspense of cheap literary construct. Makiko survived with her organs intact. Days after she was out of danger, one of her nurses casually told me that she had gone into cardiac arrest on the operating table, but she (the nurse) didn't feel that Makiko had suffered what the medical profession euphemistically calls a "cognitive deficit." But even before the nurse mentioned it, I think both Makiko and I were aware that the trauma had caused psychic changes, some perhaps, for the better.

From that very first day when I returned to the hospital after trying to empty Miriam's room, I could already tell Makiko's personality had undergone a subtle change. Her refusal to blame Herman's niece was my first clue. Even now, she doesn't take the same delight in righteous indignation that I'd encountered that first day at the Starlight diner. She has a certain willingness to let things slide, to not take life so seriously.

***

When I got back to Makiko's room, things felt less tense. She remained surrounded by hardware, but no one hovered at her bedside.

"Hi," I said.

She opened her eyes and looked up at me, her face puffy and her lips cracked and bruised. I thought those bastards might have beaten her up before they shot her, but it was just the assault of surgery.

"Hey, Nate. How was your trip? You get any decent pictures?"

I grabbed her hand and began apologizing. I had this enormous backlog of things to be sorry for. First, I apologized for Herman Viereck's very existence. Then for not being there with her in his apartment. Then for letting her take the bullet that assuredly should have been for me. I apologized for my years of low-grade depression, my self-absorption, my passivity in not dealing with things the way I should have. For letting my grief over Miriam turn to sludge.

I felt a shudder of guilty relief that at least I didn't have to apologize for making love to poor Marjory mere hours before, but I felt like apologizing for almost doing it.

It didn't matter. Makiko wasn't in any state to be holding grudges. She, too, had withdrawn into her own shell of self-recrimination.

"It was stupid," she said, her voice harsh and barely above a whisper. "I should have just let them have the damn things. I don't really care that much about them. It was just the idea of those bastards telling other people what to think. What gives them the right?"

"I know," I told her. "But we need to get his stuff out of there. His works need to be some place safe where people can study them."

"You really think anybody cares about that crazy old man?"

"They do," I said. "People just can't help themselves."

"And look where it's gotten me. Shot to shit."

"We could transfer the whole lot to Dave's gallery. I'm sure he could sell off a lot of it."

"No," she said, "that wouldn't be any different from letting those fundamentalist assholes get their hands on them."

She moved in the bed, struggling to sit up. I told her we didn't need to discuss it right then, but she was insistent.

"Don't you see? That's the significance about the apartment. His art was his life. Some artists we know would be just as happy selling life insurance. They're trapped in a safe routine, turning out the same piece over and over. Everything in Herman's rooms is part of what he was all about. The collections of string, the Madonnas, the syrup containers, even the chair he sat in—they're all the same as the work he put on paper. It's the conceptualized whole that we need to keep together."

I agreed with her. The conceptualized whole. All I wanted to conceptualize whole was her kidneys.

"We'll talk about this later," I told her.

CHAPTER THIRTY-THREE

"What do you think?" O'Malley asked me. "Should I get a couple of uniforms down here and have them dig the place up?"

"Mike, from what I know about you, they'd do it with their fingernails if you asked them."

O'Malley smiled. I wondered how calling him Mike would go over, but he didn't seem to mind. After all, I'd virtually solved the case for him. We were a crime-busting duo.

The two of us were standing in the cellar of a small bungalow just south of Oz Park. There were thousands of these modest brick houses in Chicago, all built after the fire. They'd been ignored for years, but now they were getting facelifts. So far, this one had yet to catch the eye of any yuppies, flippers, or small-time developers. Its cellar was still in its half damped-earth, hand-dug, original condition, Larry Cerinzki's last known address.

A few days after Makiko's brush with mortality, O'Malley called me to apologize for Detective Reynolds's high-pressure tactics. But he wasn't above a little arm twisting of his own. By then, Reynolds had been up to the hospital to interview Makiko, but he had complained to O'Malley that she had been less than helpful. I could tell that no matter how strong my alibi, his cop worldview wanted me as the prime suspect.

"These people who allegedly assaulted her, these three so-called masked gunmen, is there any reason why she would want to protect their identity?" O'Malley asked me.

Of course there was, but how could I explain that, in our own way, we felt what had happened was our own fault? We were dealing with a karmic ledger in which a simple "an eye for an eye" would not balance the books. We had Herman's work, and somehow it had to be paid for.

Anyway, what would arresting Herman's alleged niece prove? A trial would only give her a forum, a chance to hold Herman's art up to the harsh light of public scrutiny. I had no doubts that by most people's standards his work was obscene. She and her church would doubtlessly be seen as martyrs. Someone would take up their cause and set up a legal defense fund. They'd ask for DNA testing to prove that the woman and Herman were related. There would be a civil suit. Even if she eventually went to jail, Herman's work would be subjected to the court of public opinion. I didn't think they'd be as kind as the professional art critics.

Naturally, I wasn't the one to explore all these ramifications, but Adrian Holm worked the whole thing out in his head in a matter of hours.

"It'll be a total disaster," he told me. "All it will do is give these lunatics a forum from which to rant and rave. People will call him a freak and a monster. These "fundi" bastards will come off looking like low-rent saints. You and Makiko won't be able to walk out of your apartment without some mob howling at you. She might even get shot again."

So I—the three of us—played dumb. It surprised me how casual the police were about the shooting. By the time I left for the hospital that first morning, they'd rolled up all their tape and had left.

Where was the CSI team? Why weren't they measuring the blood splatters on the wall and dusting the stairwell for shoeprints? CPD was on the clock and on a budget. Once Reynolds realized that he couldn't make me the assailant in some art-scene lover's triangle, he lost interest. So he'd asked O'Malley to talk to me and gently shifted Makiko's file to the bottom of the stack.

When O'Malley started in on me about the shooting, I brushed him aside. He knew I was hiding something, but before he could get cagey, I hit him with Herman's deathbed confession, and he forgot all about my nearly murdered wife. I told him how I'd actually met this Larry at Herman's birthday party and how he had given me the willies even then. " I think he worked for the city as some kind of file clerk."

O'Malley asked me a few questions about what he looked like, his height and weight, that sort of thing. It turned out I could do better than that. In one of the boxes in the apartment, I'd found a picture of him and Herman. It had been taken at an amusement park, one of those booths where people stand behind a cutout and stick their heads through. This one had a western theme. Herman and Larry wore Stetsons: "Bound for California" in block letters along the bottom.

O'Malley studied the picture. "I knew he was hiding something," O'Malley said.

***

"To my surprise there were ten Larry Cerinzkis working for the city of Chicago. That was before they started including ID photos and name badges," he told me without a trace of professional pride. It hadn't been hard for O'Malley to narrow it down to five possibles. Then he went house to house till he'd found someone who remembered him.

"This woman next door made him right away. She was only eleven years old at the time, but she's still living at the same address. That's Chicago for you," he said, spreading his fingers over the top of the wheel, "stable neighborhoods and families. She said all the kids on the block were afraid of him."

***

My head scraped the tops of the joists. Only half of the cellar had a cement floor—a washer-dryer, a furnace, and a hot-water heater, an ill-used assortment of tools, old coffee cans filled with nails, all stuff I knew from a hundred estate sales. The far end of the basement had never been completely excavated, just packed dirt, barely more than a crawl space. As far back as we could see with O'Malley's flashlight, a dynasty of owners had crammed it full of old bicycles and rusted lawn chairs. I tried to imagine Larry, so neat and fastidious in his out-of-date Homburg, with his sleeves rolled up, bent double and digging a shallow grave.

I didn't want it to be true. As much as I was pulling with all my heart for O'Malley to go out a winner, I didn't want him finding Annie down here. Despite all the violence and weirdness of the last weeks, I still wanted to think of myself as a slightly eccentric but basically ordinary guy living a slightly eccentric but ordinary life.

Ordinary guy's wives don't get shot. They don't invite child murderers to birthday parties. But then and there, I knew there was no way we were going to walk out of this basement and not come back with picks and shovels.

Where was Carter's rag-headed Egyptian crew when we needed them?

"Don't we need some kind of court order?" I asked him. I'd watched as many crime shows as anybody. "What if the judge thinks there's insufficient evidence?"

Out of courtesy, O'Malley considered my question. In the half-light of the basement, I could see that he smiled slightly.

"I know a few people," he said. "It shouldn't be a problem."

CHAPTER THIRTY-FOUR

More people showed up for Herman's funeral than I'd expected. Even with the identity of Makiko's assailants officially unknown, rumors of her martyrdom on the altar of free expression had spread through the Chicago art world. That someone with Makiko's reputation had risked her life to protect his work only added to Herman's growing reputation as a persecuted and misunderstood genius. The high romance of the untaught naïf was too good of a story to let die.

Not that the chapel was packed with Chicago's glitterati. But I recognized a smattering of faces I hadn't expected. Of course, Adrian Holm and Dave Crandall were there. Dave brought his tattooed sidekick. Hackett from the *Trib* was there, as were people who had worked with Herman at the hospital and people from the neighborhood, and even some of the parishioners from St. Barts, where Herman had attended mass, sometimes three times a day.

For a wacko recluse, he'd touched a lot of lives.

With Makiko still in the hospital, it left me to handle the secular end of the service. The idea of trying to summarize Herman's life seemed daunting at first, but once I realized that I'd been giving his eulogy, in one form or another, for months, it all fell into place.

For visuals, I developed the pictures I'd taken at the Lincoln school. They'd come out exactly as I'd envisioned. I still had the touch. I also had the snapshot of Herman, Ron had taken years ago. I enlarged it, and with Herman's chronically pissed-off scowl, the little portrait captured essentially everything about him people remembered.

Makiko and I discussed whether or not to bring any of his art to the chapel, but we'd vetoed the idea. It seemed too much a sales promotion. There was going to be enough of that in the months and years to come.

After I'd let Ms. Arronson up the ante by selling me a respectable casket, she didn't have to work too hard to get me to spring for an open viewing. Even as she worked me, I couldn't help but admire her technique. She knew right away she had to pitch with a two-strike count. A Jewish intellectual at war with death? People like us didn't want to give the dead their due. Bury 'em fast in a plain pine box, that's our credo, or scatter the ashes, and shut the door on memory. Plus, as everyone knew, even though you could no longer say it out loud, we Jews were cheap.

"An open casket is in keeping with the Catholic tradition," she reminded me gently. What could I say to that? I was an anthropologist on an isolated atoll. My supply ship wouldn't be back for months. I didn't want to get off on the wrong foot and queer my relationship with the natives. I'd never get my thesis done. Plus they might eat me.

"I know you may think it's old-fashioned," she told me, "but you'll see. It gives people comfort. Seeing the deceased at rest helps provide a sense of *closure*."

Maybe it was the way she said it, but for the first time, the word didn't bother me. I nodded in slight agreement, and Arronson knew she had me.

"We won't overdo it," she reassured me, the way she had about everything I was paying for. "He'll look quite natural."

So I signed off on the package.

"Then there's the matter of the headstone," she added, while I was in the mood to be cutting checks. We settled on Indiana granite, a generously sized four-by-three on a raw cut base.

"It includes up to twenty letters, not counting dates of birth and death," she reminded me. I thought for a moment.

"Patronus Innocentium," I told her.

She looked a little lost.

"It's Latin—protector of the innocent," I said.

Arronson assured me she could bring the whole thing in for around ten grand. It seemed fair. Since Herman's death, Crandall had already tacked another zero onto his prices, and dealers and interior designers were calling him from around the globe.

"They want a large piece for their permanent collection at the Collection des Arts Brut in Lausanne," he sang over the phone. "They see him as a bookend to their Wölflis, a spanning-the-century sort of thing."

"It's not the same genre," I protested, but I was starting to sound like a broken record to my own ears. People had been calling poor Herman "crazy" ever since he was six years old.

So I splurged on the funeral. Maybe it was to make up for the limited attention we'd paid to Miriam. But as you'll see, I had my own reasons for accepting the open casket idea.

They'd scheduled the service to begin at ten, but I got there early. Scully-McMann did business in another recycled *fin de siécle* mansion. This one sat back on its own corner lot and was a little less grand than the one renovated by the Sisters of the Poor, but still humbling when you walked up to the front door. Their parking lot was large enough to accommodate two or three funerals at once, but right now, it was virtually empty. When I walked into the entrance, a small reader board announced that Herman was the only thing on today's menu.

Nobody else had arrived yet. A harried-looking guy who was trying to remember that he was no longer selling tires tried being polite, but he didn't quite know what to do with me. I got the feeling that this might be his first funeral.

"I guess you can wait in there," he told me, and he pulled back a fire-resistant faux velvet curtain. I wandered in to one of the smaller side chapels.

The rows of set-up folding chairs reminded me of one of the small theaters Makiko's quartet sometimes performed in. I guess that shouldn't have surprised me. A funeral is just another form of show business. It's all sizzle and a very small steak—just like the art world, Gd knows.

Herman and I were alone for the last time. Better than I could have planned. The coffin lay open. Even from the far end of the room, I could see his distinctive profile jutting above the casket's rim. Even with a shave, the heavy-handed makeup, and dressed in the same brown suit he'd worn that first day I'd visited him at the Sisters, it looked enough like him that there was no doubt.

Here lay Herman in the pickled flesh.

**

Slightly squeamish but emotionally on guard, Nathan Learner stands over the coffin and pays his last respects. Much as he would like to feel something deep about the passing of a fellow soul into the unknown void, he finds it hard to associate the rubbery mannequin in front of him with the frightened child he'd held in his arms a short eternity ago.

Instead he feels a familiar form of dissociation. He has become the chronicler of his own life, as if he is standing on a chair next to himself, camera prefocused and now held high over his own head to get a bird's-eye view of Nathan Learner looking down on Herman Viereck.

Is that really Herman? Is it really himself looking down at him? He doesn't know.

**

I looked around furtively. Not that I thought what I was about to do was illegal, just a little peculiar. I took out the scrap of newsprint. I opened it and looked at Annie's bucktoothed smile one last time. I planned to tuck it down one side of the casket, but that didn't seem intimate enough.

Finally, the poignancy of what I was about to do hit me. A welcome tear forced itself from my eye, relieved at my ability to mourn him.

If only he had lived one or two more days, I could have given him the picture. Only if I had cleaned out Miriam's room a few days before I had. But of course, if Makiko hadn't been shot, I wouldn't have, and if Herman hadn't died, I never would have been out of town.

A butterfly flaps its wings in the Caucasus, and the Boston Red Sox get rained out. Everything's a long chain of causes and effects. No use trying to rearrange the past. Miriam's letters, Annie's picture, Tut's busted chariot; it's too fucking late for Herman.

It's too late for all of us.

Herman's hands lay folded across his chest. I recreased the picture a couple of times. Gingerly taking his arm by the sleeve, I lifted it against his embalmed resistance. Then I placed the folded picture on his breast and let his hand drop. The picture stuck out a little at the edges, but I didn't think anyone would notice.

When we're up against it, all our intellectualization goes out the window. It didn't matter at all what I thought I knew. The here and now felt as elemental as a Neanderthal burial site. I forgot my defiant atheism. I forgot the trendy platitudes of the new agers and their whining attempt to have it both ways.

I don't know if I believe in God, I mean not some old guy in white robe and flowing beard, but there's got to be something out there, don't you think? I mean, it can't just all be this random colliding of atoms … can it?

Well, hell if I know.

I put the picture under his dead hand. He felt like a rubber chicken you'd buy in a novelty store. Instinctively, I put my hand to my nose and sniffed my fingers. A faint, sweet industrial deodorant odor lingered. Viereck smelled just like the floor of the hospital he'd spent his whole life cleaning.

"There you go, pally," I whispered and turned away from him for the last time.

I sat down on one of the chairs and waited, anxious for a good crowd, like the day we'd given him the birthday party.

For the first time, I understood why the ancient Greeks hired professional mourners and wailers. I felt like going out and grabbing a few extra people off the street, maybe a few of those guys who stood holding signs on the freeway on-ramps—"Will work for food."

First Adrian Holm came in. I hadn't seen him since the night at the hospital. He still had his arm in a sling. I felt sure that by now he wore it solely for theatrical effect. He went up and stared down at Viereck for a second or two.

"I guess all his secrets have died with him," he told me.

I nodded. Screw the bastard. I still had the folder from the Lincoln school on my desk, but since the night of what I'd taken to calling "the accident," I wasn't sure that I wanted him to have it. I felt that he hadn't spilled enough blood to be entitled to the solution of Herman's final conundrum.

We were supposed to start at ten, but the priest was late, and everything dragged. When I finally got up to give my own little summation, my back hurt, and my stomach growled. My talk came as comic relief. I told about Herman grinding me on the rent, about his claiming to have been born in Brazil, and the time he sang to us in Portuguese. I gave witness to the indomitable power of the artist that lives in all of us, able to overcome any obstacle of birth once it is touched by the spirit, by duende.

While I gave my eulogy, I looked up and saw Tamar pull back the curtains and take a seat in the back. I smiled at her, and she put up her hand and waved. She'd called me, of course, when she heard about Makiko. She said nothing truly personal or especially heartfelt, just condolences. It would have been pretty cold not to, but I appreciated the gesture anyway.

"I don't know what to say," she'd said.

I agreed. It was one of those events that were beyond words.

"It's just not fair. You shouldn't have to go through this, Nathaniel."

What she meant, of course, was that I shouldn't have to go through this "again."

I hadn't expected her to show up. When we divided our property, all the tenants became mine. She hadn't even come to the opening of Herman's show, but Dave told me that she'd stopped in with her new friend in the middle of the week.

"Your old lady looks good as a dyke," he'd told me.

After I sat down, Dave said a few words about Herman's growing legacy. After that, Adrian got up and said a few too many words. He had the last ones.

At the end of the service, people milled around. I'd sprung for a few plates of cheese and crackers, and the same cheap Chard we'd served at his opening. I made my way through the crowd to where Tamar stood.

"Thanks for coming," I told her. She nodded. The least she could do.

"The whole thing is pretty fantastic, isn't it?" she said. "All those years, and we never knew what he was up to. And now he's gone. There are a lot of questions I'd like to ask him."

"You and me both," I said.

I was having a hard time looking her in the face: an unlikely combination of nostalgia and guilt-tinged relief. Tamar looked—well, old. She seemed to be going down without a fight, as if moving in with another woman had taken the last of her rebellious energy, or maybe she didn't feel the need to impress me anymore.

"So, how are you doing?" I asked her, using that intimate tone we used to share. Only now it sounded false and slightly unctuous in my ears.

"I'm doing okay," she was quick to assure me. "It's been a real trip trying to parent a couple of teenagers, but they've been great about the situation. We certainly wouldn't have been that understanding when we were their age."

"Everything's different now. I guess it's just not that big a deal, anymore," I said.

"What isn't?" She was enjoying pushing my face in it a little

"You know. The two of you … Carrol."

"Cheryl."

"It's just, all those years we were together. I just never would have guessed that you were gay."

"It's not what you think," she reassured me.

"What is it that I think?"

"You know, that it's a reaction to you personally. That somehow you failed as a man. That our life together was a sham."

"I don't know, Tamar. It's only the fundamentalist Christians who still insist that being gay is a conscious choice. I mean, I used to think we were pretty good together. Now I can't help but wonder what was going through your head while we were … you know?"

"I told you, it's not that simple. The whole thing with men and women, starting over again at my age; it just seemed too complicated. Men are so demanding. You have to keep pretending to be something you're not. Cheryl understands me. She gets me. You know what I mean?"

Well, I did get it, sort of. Except for the anatomy. Of what gets put where.

Here was Herman adding them to his little girls. They were so ridiculous, hanging there. Who could blame Tamar for wanting to get away from the whole messy business? Maybe I'd give it up myself.

"I cleaned out Miriam's room," I said.

Let's see if Cheryl got that.

Tamar looked pained. "We probably should have done it years ago."

We? I thought to myself, but I decided to let it go. "I put all her books and artwork in the basement. There's that still life she did, the one that looks like a Van Gogh. I wonder if you want it."

"No, that's okay; you keep it. She got all her talent from you."

"I'm going to take her clothes down to the homeless shelter on Sprague. I think she'd like that."

"Yes, she's probably pissed at us for waiting this long."

So it was our own private double funeral, triple if you count Annie's picture, but more about that in a moment. Between Tamar and me, I don't know which of us looked more pitiful. I moved a step closer and held my arms out, not exactly inviting an embrace, but close enough. Tamar leaned in and I put my arms around her. After hugging Makiko, it was something of a shock.

Catharsis? Tears? Not quite. There's only so much the human psyche is capable of in real life. I held onto her a scant two seconds, and then with a little shudder of mutual relief, we gently pushed each other away.

There was only one thing left. Miriam's secret box, but I didn't tell. In the final analysis, Tamar was right. Miriam was my daughter, my kindred spirit. She had my anger, my mule-headed, egotistical grandiosity, the will to will. What would Tamar's knowing about the purloined picture add to the mystery? There was too much to explain, too much backstory that Tamar wasn't a part of anymore.

I looked over her shoulder. The ex-tire-salesman had closed Herman's lid and began wheeling the gurney out the back of the room.

Miriam's secret was safe with me.

CHAPTER THIRTY-FIVE

I was home taking care of my wife when he called.

They'd sent Makiko home with a colostomy, but they'd assured us it wasn't permanent. Once all the other holes, made by, or necessitated by, the damage seven grams of metal ricocheting around inside her abdomen succeeded in healing over, everything could be more or less reconnected.

It felt odd, the two of us at home in the middle of the day, like playing hooky. We'd adjusted our lives to the rhythms of the sick room, the pills to take, the sponge baths and swabbings, the measured recuperative walks down our hallway.

I started to feel as if I were recovering myself. A melancholy but not totally unpleasant feeling of being wounded affected us both. We ate sparingly of bland foods. We took naps and went to bed early. I bought her *Cosmopolitan* and *People* magazines.

The weather, paying Herman some sort of backhanded compliment, turned unseasonably warm and benign. And then the phone rang.

It was hard to tell from the sound of his voice what O'Malley was feeling.

"Professor Learner?" he asked, his tone unchanged from that day he'd first called me.

"Yes, Detective?"

"I'm calling you from the Dillon residence, over here on Thirty-fourth. We've finished our investigation."

He paused. I thought he was going to tell me they'd come up bust, another empty tomb in the Valley of the Kings. But O'Malley was enjoying his little theatrical performance. Gd knows he'd earned it.

"We found human remains, a juvenile. There're a few pieces of clothing, but they're in pretty rough shape. Forensics is looking at them, and the coroner has her old dental records—but I'm pretty sure it's Annie."

"Wow, Detective," I said, but the whole thing remained unreal. Despite all the newspapers, movies, and TV shows, we live untouched by crime. Maybe in a lifetime of urban living, someone will break into your car or snatch your purse on the El, but rarely anything more than that.

Now, in the space of two weeks, mayhem had turned my life upside down.

As soon as the reality of what he'd found sank in, I felt the last, deep-down queasy horror that I had so far avoided facing. Herman had known about Annie. He might even have known about her location in the basement, and he'd kept it secret. Was that why he'd kept her picture, as a guilty reminder of his own complacency? Is that why Gd snatched it away from him, using my poor Miriam as His cat's paw and then letting a sneaky aberrant white blood cell get rid of the evidence?

O'Malley was the detective, but I couldn't ask him.

Instead, I asked for sordid details. The owner of the house had been pissed as hell, but a court order was a court order. O'Malley came back with all the hi-tech equipment they hadn't trotted out for Makiko's lowball crime-scene investigation—the mobile forensic lab, coroner's vehicles, and a squadron of squad cars to cordon off the streets. The locals sensed something big was up, and they needed crowd control.

They were going to take an archeological approach and divide the cellar into a grid with crisscrossed twine and dig test holes in all four quadrants, but O'Malley explained that, working on a hunch, he'd crawled over the packed earth on his hands and knees. I wondered if he'd taken steps to protect his suit.

Six-foot-four Larry would have to have dug virtually lying on his stomach. O'Malley's first notion was to dig near the finished part of the basement, where Larry could have stood for at least part of it, but then he thought, no. He didn't think Larry was a typical serial killer. Instead, he saw a man whose impulses had simply spiraled out of control, and after the fact, he was filled with guilt and self-loathing, not enough to turn himself in, but enough that burying Annie would be an act of atonement.

So intrepid O'Malley crawled into the darkest corner of the basement and stabbed his pocketknife into the dirt. He found a spot that didn't feel right.

"She was laid out a few feet from the far wall. Her arms looked like they'd been crossed over her chest," he told me over the phone, and I could hear his voice crack. "She had a rosary with her. It looks like he put it in her hand."

"That must have been pretty rough," I told him. I had to say something.

"After all my years in this business, you still wonder what kind of guy could do something like that. And Viereck, he knew all the time, playing the imbecile with us up at the Sisters that day. Protecting him all those years. I don't know, Professor, maybe he was some kind of genius like you say, but I think he's almost as responsible as his friend."

"Maybe so," I told him. I'd been thinking the same thing ever since the night Herman had died in my arms.

"I'd like to think that what kept him from doing something like that himself was his art," I said. "It gave him another outlet, some way to process his impulses. There's something you should know about Herman," I added.

"Yeah? What's that?"

I told him about the operating room at the Home for Feeble-Minded Children and how they'd fixed Herman's impulses for him.

"I mean, it has to be some kind of sexual thing, doesn't it? When these guys do something like this? Would Herman still have had those kinds of impulses?"

"I don't know, Professor." It grew quiet on his end of the phone. O'Malley didn't want a lot of medical explanations. He just caught the bad guys.

"Well, it's going to be quite a story," he said at last. "I hope you're ready. I bet Channel Five will be showing up at your door any minute."

"You don't think you could keep Viereck's name out of it, say you were acting on an anonymous tip?"

"After twenty years, somebody just drops a dime?"

"Why not? Look at all those stories about people paying library fines fifty years late."

"It'll never work. Those guys are like vultures. Remember, Annie's picture was hanging in your gallery."

"I guess you're right."

"Hey," he told me, "it will only add to the mystique. His stuff will be worth a fortune."

"Why, Mike, where did you learn so much about the art world?"

He chuckled. It was the first time I'd heard him laugh. I guess he deserved it.

"You're a lucky guy, Mike," I told him.

"I am?"

"It's not everybody who can wrap up his career like this, leave on such a high note."

"I've still got a few others I'd like to work on. Maybe they'll let me keep a desk."

"Take care of yourself, Mike," I told him. "It's a dangerous thing to find what you're looking for."

CHAPTER THIRTY-SIX

O'Malley was right, of course. Finding Annie pulled the thumb out of the dike. If we'd been waiting for something to push our complex financial, legal, and moral involvement with the *Realms of the Unreal* over the edge, she did it.

As soon as I got off the phone with O'Malley, the flood began. The art critic from the *Trib* called first. After years of berating herself for not moving to New York when she had had the chance, something was happening on her beat that made these years in exile worth it.

"We've got a slew of crime reporters out at the house now," she told me. "Every media outlet in the city is tripping all over themselves, but I want you to give me the exclusive."

"The exclusive on what?" I tried halfheartedly, but I knew there'd be no escape.

The next day, the picture I'd so carefully placed in Herman's embalmed hand was available on any street corner for twenty-five cents. The *Trib* reran the photo they had in their archives. All Herman would have had to do is give them a call, and he could have gotten fifty copies. Annie's pigtails, her buckteeth, and shy, Mona Lisa-ish grin smiled out at everyone from the front page.

TWENTY-YEAR MYSTERY SOLVED

In a bizarre and poetic ending to a case that held Chicago in its thrall over twenty years ago, the skeletal remains of ten-year-old Annie Proturick were discovered in the basement of a private residence on Shattuck Street. Long-time Chicago residents will remember that Annie's mysterious disappearance terrified parents in the Chicago area when it occurred in 1954. Despite a massive search and the following of hundreds of leads by the Chicago PD, no clues to her whereabouts were ever found, and no suspects were ever identified.

Detective Michael O'Malley, a thirty-year veteran with homicide, was initially assigned to the case and was present when the child's skeletal remains were unearthed in the far corner of a deserted basement. The residence is believed to be the last Chicago address of Larry Cerinzki, a clerk for the Chicago Department of Roads and Construction.

Over the years, Detective O'Malley had devoted countless hours of his own time in trying to resolve the mystery, and he told the press that the case would have gone unsolved if it weren't for a series of unusual events that have rocked the normally staid Chicago art world …

Herman's and my name did not appear till I turned to the inside to finish the article. But that was enough. People I didn't think I owed the time of day to began calling, asking if they could come up and have a look at the apartment. They sounded sincere enough about wanting to know more about Viereck and his work, but I had to keep reminding them that they weren't going to a crime scene—at least not the one they had in mind.

Dave Crandall quickly made plans to have another show. He kept getting calls, bumping up the prices, and hassling me to let go of more material. In the month after the discovery of Annie's remains, Makiko and I made more than we would in two years of my salary.

It added up to too much money. We burned through all possible excuses: back rent, front rent, finder's fees, estate executer's fees, even taking-a-bullet-in-the-gut fees. I began to feel like a grave robber myself. When was the Chicago Board of Antiquities going to step in and take away my permit?

Of course, Holm sued us. We should have seen that coming. There were a couple of nasty letters in the *Chicago Arts Weekly* about how a once well-respected professor of photography and design had let greed endanger his reputation and good standing. Makiko, who was trying to get back into performing, had some frosty reactions at auditions. She and I took to having bickering arguments in the middle of the night, and I began to jump every time the phone rang.

Lumping this all together explained why Makiko, the director of the *Chicago Institute for Intuitive Art*, and I now stood in the narrow defile running down the middle of Herman's overstuffed apartment. I'd sat Kip Stone in the usual place of honor on Herman's busted desk chair and propped the *Realms* open in front of him. Wisely or not, we'd sliced out some of the longer foldouts, but there was still plenty to look at. We waited for him to finish. It usually took under ten minutes, but I finally had to pull the book gently out of his hand. He looked up at me, and there were tears in his eyes.

"It's just so sad, the poor crazy bastard. All these outsiders, they're the last of the true romantics. Of course, it's the formalism and structure that makes him so unique. At first, you think he's just sticking to classical convention, but he really invokes something a lot deeper." He paused but couldn't help himself. Art-speak oozed out of him.

"It's just so damn real," he said at last, and then we offered him the collection.

"It needs to be kept together," I told him, "someplace where people can come and study it, learn from it."

Kip closed the *Realms*. Pages were already starting to pull loose from its primitive binding. He got up, and we let him wander around the room. Now that he'd seen the holy of holies, he took in the clutter with a fresh eye—the box of Pepto bottles, the Madonna collection, the balls of string, the boxes of broken eyeglass frames, all of it.

"The whole room is his work of art," he announced. "It wouldn't work to just take the writing and the pictures. There's a powerful subtext here."

"The Lausanne Institute in Switzerland has expressed an interest in obtaining some of his work. Maybe they'd want what's in the apartment," I told him. They hadn't really said so, but it was a logical salesman's move. Ms. Arronson would be proud of me.

"I just think that, as a Chicago artist, his stuff should stay here," Makiko added.

Stone nodded. I could tell he'd covered that ground in his own mind already. After a minute or two, he turned to me.

"What if we took it all?" he asked.

"What do you mean?"

"The whole apartment. What if we moved everything to the institute and reassembled it all in one place? You know, like one of those rooms at the Cloisters they brought over and reassembled. I mean, these pictures are fantastic, but it's the whole environment that conveys what's so powerful about him. This room is the real work of art."

There's a natural animosity we artists feel toward gallery owners, museum curators, and even our patrons. They have all the power, but it's hard to find a curator who's actually produced a body of work. They've never gone through the creative mill, never scraped six months' worth of blood and sweat off a canvas, or intentionally run a sheaf of negatives through a shredder.

No matter how much they may say they love your work, there's always an undercurrent of resentment and jealousy. I can appreciate their situation. After all, who daydreams at thirteen about being a cataloguer of other people's creations? Despite my prejudices, I had to admire Kip. He was totally right about the apartment.

Standing next to me, Makiko didn't pause to give his suggestion a moment's thought. Opportunity was knocking, and we might not get another chance to open the door.

"That's a fabulous idea, Kip." Then she paused and looked over the stacks of boxes and piles of papers as if seeing them again for the first time. "So where would you put it all?" she asked.

It didn't take the institute long to make their move. Kip got back to us in a week. The CIIA didn't have the space at the moment, but they were planning on moving into a resurrected brick warehouse on Addison Street in the next year or two. They'd be happy to store Herman's belongings in a safe, climate-controlled storage locker until then, except for the actual art and his writings, which they hoped to make available for study. The Museum of Folk Art in New York had already expressed an interest in showing Viereck's work.

We jumped on it. I expected the institute might take years to arrange for the actual transfer. Funds would have to be cobbled together or stolen from other worthy projects. Committees needed to be formed, egos massaged, axes of every size and shape had to be ground. After thirty years of university life, I knew what Kip was up against. You couldn't organize his board of directors to go eat a free lunch.

I steeled myself to waiting, but somehow, he pulled it off. I suspect Makiko's friend Jeff might have had a hand in cutting the miles of red tape. Outside of us, he had slowly become the owner of more Herman Vierecks than anyone.

***

A few months later, I stood in the center of the apartment staring at bare walls. It took Carter five years to sort through the boy king's stuff, photograph it, and box it up for shipment to Cairo. They tell me that even after almost eighty years and several worldwide tours, some of his original crates are still unpacked. It took us only a couple of hours to empty Herman's tomb.

Jeff's lawyer made Makiko and me legal executors of the estate, allowing for periodic sales of Herman's works as well as all reproduction rights with the two of us receiving a percentage. All of which continued to infuriate Adrian Holm and other purists who appeared out of the woodwork.

***

Not that I thought about the financial details at the time. I just wanted to be free of the *Realms* once and for all. Kip got together a work party of art students and volunteers, including an emeritus professor of archeology. He helped us lay out a grid for the floor plan of Herman's apartment. Then we numbered each box and stack of papers, each ball of twine and broken table as to where in the grid they needed to be placed.

I took pictures of everything, and we got the whole shebang into a twenty-four-foot U-Haul. We even rolled up the paint-spattered linoleum, pried the window frames loose and took enough plaster off the walls so that we'd be able to match the color and texture. I thought the last was overkill, but I didn't appreciate the obsessive power of the curatorial mind.

I followed the truck to the storage facility and helped them unload. Then we all shook hands, and I turned down their offer to go for pizza.

When I drove home, Makiko had gone back to our apartment to take a nap. She still claimed to be "recovering," but I could feel the shadow of a permanent change slipping across her normally cynical but basically cheerful countenance. Much as we hated to come to grips with it, I knew she'd been shot with a magic bullet.

I found a parking spot in front of my house and got out. Looking over at Herman's windows, you could tell by the dark lack of reflection that the rooms were empty. Instead of going home, I went back.

Up the dark stairs to the second floor, Herman's door gaped wide open. I stood alone in the middle of his empty room. His spirit hadn't yet left, but his presence felt faint.

"Hey, Mr. Nathan."

"What is it, Herman?"

"I like those pictures you took, the ones from the school. They were very realistic. I mean they really captured the mood."

"I did the best I could. The place shouldn't be forgotten."

"It's okay, but it never helps. You can't teach people anything they don't want to learn. You'll see. When they open it up again, it will be the same as ever. It's better to make your own place, your own world where you can control the weather. You gonna take any more photographs?"

"*I don't know, Herman. I'm feeling real old right now. The world is full of pictures. Does anybody need more?*"

"*You don't do it for the world, Mr. Nathan. You've got to do it for you. They won't let you alone, otherwise. You can't sleep because they'll come for you in the night and make you do horrible things. You have to keep writing. You have to watch the weather. Too many mistakes are being made.*"

"*I'll remember that,*" I said. "*You take care now, you hear?*"

***

The day had turned warm, and a fresh spring light came in through the dusty windows. But a shadow fell across the floor. Had his spirit departed?

For a rational man, I had a surplus of magical thinking, lately. *It'll be a relief when we finally gut this place,* I thought.

I took one last look around, and then I heard a faint humming. I could have ignored it as an auditory hallucination, but listening to it made it sound louder—a droning, mechanical thrumming.

At the far end of the little room that had been the apartment's kitchen, Kip and his crew had left the stove and the refrigerator. All the time that Herman had been in the Sisters and now, months after his death, the apartment's vintage Norge had soldiered on, turning on and off at the whim of a mechanical brain older than my own, a brain that did only one thing and it did it well: sensed temperature.

Over the years, the damn thing had cost us a fortune in electricity, and I'd never had the sense to upgrade it. Now, annoyed with myself, I went over to the old reefer and, with a grunt, shoved it away from the wall. Its power cord appeared frayed and cracked. A black smudge of carbon stained the wall where a short had almost set the place on fire. It would have saved us all from this perilous adventure.

Half-expecting to be jolted across the room, I grabbed the cord a foot away from the plug and yanked. The compressor came to a stumbling halt. Did it, too, have a small machine soul linked to Herman's?

It occurred to me that I should check the fridge. In all the time Herman had lived there, I'd never seen him carry in a bag of groceries.

There wasn't even a teakettle on the stove. Still, the reefer had been left running. I stood in front of the machine, my hand on the deco handle. I felt an icy, clairvoyant tingle.

If I'd thought about it for another second, I would have run out of the apartment, but instead I jerked the door open.

The shelves were empty, but right below eye level sat the freezer compartment: a shoebox-sized space now coalesced into a pellucid block of ice. But deep in the ice I saw something dark.

I looked around for a tool. The small stove supported three-cast iron spiders. I grabbed one and started smashing at the freezer compartment. Chunks of ice sheared off and broke into smaller pieces that slithered across the floor.

I had found the tomb's sarcophagus.

After a few horrid minutes, the black lump in the center of the ice began to show fur and ears, a mummified mouth with wasted lips, and large canine teeth. It was the little dog we'd given Herman for his birthday.

There was a thick twine noose pulled tight around its neck.

***

Their limo arrives with the promptness you expect of the Swiss, but instead of their main location downtown, we pull up in front of a four story townhouse in an up-scale residential section. I enter a small foyer and ring a little bell on a Louis XIV side table. I hear rustling in the back, but the woman from Sotheby's with the seductive voice has stood me up. Instead a dapper child in concrete gray Armani, sporting, not one but two earrings, comes out to greet me. Yes, I assure him, the flight was smooth and uneventful, ditto the room at the *Baur au Lac*, "A coffee would be lovely, thank you." But it's a bit of a strain taking the conversation much further. I'm a headliner without an opening act. There's little for us to do here but to go look at his painting and get me the hell out of Dodge.

On the small elevator going up to the studios, he's effusive about their up-coming auction and throws in enough obscure buzz words about outsider art that I'm not sure what he's talking about. Naturally, the Viereck is the star of their show, but I get the feeling that next week when the house is pushing a Lot of Greek amphora he'll sound just as knowledgeable and just as enthusiastic. No wonder Makiko chose to stay home.

When we get off, Mr. Two Earrings is joined by a small gaggle of suits and one guy in a dun-colored lab coat with a vest pocket full of tiny brushes; but still no Julie Christie. I shake a lot of hands, modestly downplay the usual compliments. Two Earrings's boss fills me in. It's the usual story a broken line of provenance. Their Viereck came out of the estate of a New York trial lawyer. His children said he'd bought it at the annual outsider art expo held in the Puck Building in SOHO. They produced a bill of sale, but the dealer who sold it had a terrible reputation and had actually done fifteen months for fraud. The prior owner couldn't be identified, and neither the Chicago Institute for Intuitive Art nor the Museum of American Folk Art in New York had the picture documented in their catalogue of Herman's work.

I tried to reassure them. We'd sold and even given away lots of Herman's stuff in the early days, and even though part of Viereck's appeal is its primitive, childlike quality, it would be harder to fake than most people imagine. His style was so iconic.

Everyone nods their heads. They're liking what I have to say, but it ain't money in the bank. Would the work have to go on the block with the dreaded asterisk next to it?

They lead me through a few galleries overflowing with high-end garage sale detritus. I could spend days rummaging back here, but I'll never be able to find my way back out without them. At last we enter an almost empty room, sunlit by a bank of windows overlooking an inner courtyard. The Viereck is waiting for us on an easel, sandwiched between two protective layers of Plexiglas.

As I said in the beginning, it has been a while since I paid serious attention to the actual work, and I get a pleasant shock. There's nothing as powerful as a first impression, and the scroll screams Viereck. Looking at the work with refreshed eyes, I feel vindicated. It *is* a work of tremendous emotional power and artistic originality. I was right about him from that first day when I popped open his battered trunk;

me—Nathan Learner, a low-rent Pandora, letting loose Herman's world of woes. Had I slammed the lid too late?

It's only when I start to examine the work, trying to give Sotheby's their money's worth, that tiny fingers of doubt tug at the base of my spine. First off, even though the work is quintessential Herman Veireck, I can't for the life of me remember seeing it. Of course there were probably thirty or forty of his large fold-outs tucked into the body of his text, and I'd never actually done a systematic inventory. Who knew what had walked out of his studio in those first days. Could Holm have taken it? Even Makiko might have let it go out the back when I wasn't looking.

The painting is typical of his themes and motifs, so much so that it starts to backfire. Every iconic image he is known for is in the piece: the lowering sky with its dirty grays and blacks, a phalanx of Glandelinian solders goose-stepping across a field of exploding red poppies, the seven Vivian Girls, running for their lives, their extra equipment penciled in and flapping in the breeze. There's even a butterfly angel hovering in the upper right hand corner, lit in a single ray of celestial light. If someone were going to fake a Veireck, there's not a cliché that he'd left out.

Behind me, I can feel the pressure mounting. Six pairs of eyes boring into my back are waiting for an answer. I murmur something encouraging. I've brought with me the slides I'd made for Crandall's first show, but I know this one isn't in there. Maybe I'd gotten tired or bored or had run out of film. I can tell them the colors are right, the cheap paper, starting to deteriorate is just what he used, but anybody could find a *Big Chief* pad of old sketch paper up in an attic somewhere. Am I to be reduced to art-speak and hand-waving?

And then I see her. She's down in the left-hand corner, drawn free hand and seemingly disconnected from the chaos that surrounds her. He's added another little girl. The girl has a dog on a leash, and it is pulling her along with the violence of a tornado. I peer in again, bad as his draftsmanship is, Veireck had managed to capture enough of Miriam to make her recognizable as my daughter. The dog matched the one we'd given him too, only its mouth is open and blood drips from its fangs. The eyes are yellow, dead and evil.

I stand up and back away from the painting. It's like the night he died. *"Is there anything you want me to tell Miriam when I see her?"* How could he? How could he reach out like this, twenty years later and squeeze my heart?

"Well?" Two Earrings's boss asks.

"You don't need to worry," tell him. "It's the real deal."

"Tell me, do you remember when you let it go and who you sold it to?"

"No, I've never seen this one before." Viereck stealing my daughter has made me vindictive. Let them sweat a little.

"But you're sure, the painting is authentic?"

"Oh yes, quite sure."

"But how do you know?"

"You see this little girl?' I tell him, pointing to Miriam. "That's my daughter, and she's been dead for over twenty years."

***

But it's only once I'm safely alone, in the back seat of the limo, heading to the airport that it comes to me. Miriam knew. She knew about Viereck hanging the poor stupid little dog and stuffing him into the icebox.

> *SATAN can try and bend a sick person's soul to his will and … the DEVIL can take many forms and disguises, Nothing is as innocent and free from evil as it sometimes seems.*

It was the kind of thing she could not, would not forgive. She might have been mature beyond her years, but in the simple equations of good and evil of a twelve-year-old, nothing could explain away what Herman had done. She would never understand about his tortured soul and its murderous hallucinations. She knew how Viereck felt about the portrait of Annie he'd cut from the newspaper. Knew it could never be substituted, and she'd taken it to punish him.

It wasn't all that much, but I thought I could live with it.

THE END